JASON DONALD

Choke Chain

VINTAGE

1 3 5 7 9 10 8 6 4 2

Vintage
20 Vauxhall Bridge Road,
London SW1V 2SA

Vintage is part of the Penguin Random House group of companies
whose addresses can be found at global.penguinrandomhouse.com.

Copyright © Jason Donald 2009

Jason Donald has asserted his right to be identified as the author of this
Work in accordance with the Copyright, Designs and Patents Act 1988

First published by Vintage in 2018
First published by Jonathan Cape in 2009

penguin.co.uk/vintage

A CIP catalogue record for this book is available from the British Library

ISBN 9780099527060

Printed and bound by Clays Ltd, St Ives plc

Penguin Random House is committed to a sustainable future
for our business, our readers and our planet. This book is
made from Forest Stewardship Council® certified paper.

For

Liz, Ayron, Marijke and Clinton

The major changes in history have resulted less from revolutions displacing kings, than from individuals ignoring kings and giving their allegiance to spiritual values instead.

Theodore Zeldin, *An Intimate History of Humanity*

There can be no keener revelation of a society's soul than the way in which it treats its children.

Nelson Mandela

Hail

It dared us to move closer. The cloudbank piled up ahead of us like a huge serving of grey cauliflower, squat and heavy, waiting. Kevin paid no attention. He kicked a stone and watched it skip down the centre of the empty street. I went barefoot. My shoes dangled by their laces from my school bag, bumping against my bum. These clouds were dark and heavy on top but flat and septic yellow underneath. Hail clouds. In the distance the first flash of lightning lit the underside of the storm. I immediately started counting.

'One one-thousand, two one-thousand, three . . .'

The thunder grumbled past us. It was two kilometres away. But moving towards us. There was still time. Kevin looked up and then checked to see my reaction. I began walking faster. He ignored the stone he had been kicking all the way from the school gates and we concentrated on getting home. Our steps were synchronised at first, but Kevin's legs were too short to hold the rhythm. He jogged a little to keep up, then marched in step again taking long awkward strides.

'Alex, should we start running?' said Kevin, glancing up at me.

Mom once said that she had seen a hailstone the size of an onion smash through the windscreen of a car. She also said that if we ever saw a hailstorm we had to start looking for shelter straight away. Running home was not safe. We had to go straight to the nearest house and wait on their stoop till the storm passed. But we weren't supposed to hide under a tree. Never, never under a tree.

'Let's just keep going,' I said.

At the end of the road we turned left up the hill.

Only four blocks to go.

The tar was still warm under my soles and the atmosphere felt humid like being inside a tent. There was no wind, no breeze. I imagined Mom standing at the back door watching the storm get closer, worrying about the plants in the front garden. She believed that each type of storm has its own smell. But the air smelled like air to me.

At the top of our street I stopped for a second. Behind me was a clear blue sky yet above us the clouds were as thick as smoke. It was getting colder too. I folded my arms and rubbed away the goose bumps. Everything had breathed in. Not a single leaf twitched in the trees. The nearest house had high walls and an electric gate. The one next to it had a sign saying, BEWARE OF DOGS.

Our entire neighbourhood flashed silver as thunder exploded and shook the ground.

Kevin screamed and ran towards our house.

'Kevin, wait! Don't . . .'

The downpour came so thick he vanished.

Tiny ball bearings of ice stung my calves and neck as I dashed forward. Seconds later it was like running on marbles. Pain jolted up my legs every time my bare heels landed on a solid ball of ice. Little ice pellets jammed between my toes. I caught up with Kevin who was running under his bag for shelter. They were now the size of apricots crashing onto my head and shoulders. The force of it bent me double and I stumbled, almost tripping over. Through the deluge I could see Mom waiting by the front door, arms folded tightly across her chest.

'Quickly, quickly get inside!' she shouted.

'Mommy!' screamed Kevin. Even through the rush of rain I could tell he was crying.

Mom ran out and tried to protect Kevin as he came charging through the front gate. I was right behind them. The three of us got inside at the same time.

'It's OK. You're OK, son, you just got a fright,' said Mom as she knelt down and held Kevin close to her. Using the flat of her hand she rubbed away his tears.

Hail smacked off the roof. The noise became deafening as the hailstones got bigger and bigger. It sounded like a waterfall crashing onto our house.

'What on earth were you thinking, Alex?' shouted Mom.

'I told him not to run,' I shouted back.

'That's not good enough. You could have been killed!'

Mom clutched Kevin close to her, checking the back of his neck for bruises. Shivering in my wet shirt, I took my bag off and dropped it on the floor. My shoes were full of little white globes. I poured them into my hand trying to think what I could have done differently. If we had left school ten seconds later we might not have made it. Mom was right. It was stupid to keep going. I should have made a plan as soon as I saw the clouds. I should have forced Kevin to listen to me.

Large wet patches formed on Mom's blouse as she held onto Kevin.

'I'll get some towels,' I shouted.

Mom grabbed the back of my shirt and pulled me to the ground. 'No! Stay with me!'

The sitting-room window suddenly exploded. The curtains reached in toward us as a freezing gust of air blew in through the burglar bars. Among the shards of glass on the carpet lay a chunk of ice the size of my fist. Another window smashed in the kitchen. Kevin clung to Mom's neck. From down the passage I heard glass shatter in the bathroom. Mom grabbed my wrist and pulled me to the floor. Together we crawled to the centre of the living room and huddled together behind the coffee table while our home disintegrated around us.

Choke Chain

Gutters

The storm moved on. The hailstones hammering the roof relaxed into a rattle of pebbles. For a few minutes heavy rain soaked the ground. Then, with an inbreath, it all stopped.

Nothing moved.

The three of us stayed huddled together. Mom's arm wrapped around my chest. Her warmth seeped through my wet clothes. Droplets dripped from the window and a slow rumble of thunder moved down the shallow valley of our neighbourhood. The electricity cut out, leaving the living room gloomy. Both Kevin and Mom tilted their heads back, looking at the ceiling, their mouths open and breathless.

We waited, listened.

The thunder grumbled again. Further away this time. I touched the back of my head and found a soft lump forming. There was no blood on my fingertips.

Mom slightly relaxed her grip and said, 'You know, thunder is the sound of God rearranging his furniture.'

She always said the weirdest stuff. I shifted onto my knees and rolled my eyes, hoping Kevin would see me, but he kept staring at the ceiling. The chilly breeze moving through the house made me shudder. I had to get out of my wet school shirt.

7

'Watch your feet, Alex,' said Mom, holding me back, 'there's glass everywhere.' I slid away from her, stepping carefully across the green living-room tiles. Kevin followed, crunching across the broken shards in his school shoes then disappearing into his bedroom.

As I trod carefully past the bathroom I noticed the curtain above the toilet was hanging to one side. There was glass in the bathtub.

'Mom,' shouted Kevin, 'my bedroom window's smashed.'

'And the one in the bathroom's gone too,' I added.

'Just . . .' Mom hesitated, deciding what to do first. 'Just don't touch anything,' she shouted from the living room.

She came up behind me and peeked into the bathroom.

'Alex,' she said, 'get changed and help me clean this up.' She made it sound like a punishment, as if all this was somehow my fault.

I went to my room and shoved the door closed. It was warmer in here. My window wasn't broken and the carpet felt soft under my toes. I peeled off my wet clothes, dumped them in the corner. In the mirror I noticed red blotches on my shoulders where the hail had stung me. These pink leopard spots were down the backs of my legs too.

I stepped into a pair of shorts and pulled a T-shirt over my head. Then put on my thickest socks and takkies, tying the laces tight. Through the window I noticed the roof of our garage was covered in ice, like a cottage from a Christmas card. I opened my bottom drawer and pulled out a red jersey with a yellow stripe across the chest, the one Mom knitted for my birthday.

Mom was in Kevin's room wearing gardening gloves. Leaning over his desk she worked free the jagged bits of window stuck in the frame and gently placed each fragment into a plastic bin. The bed was covered in deadly-sharp splinters and Kevin stood with his back to the wall, watching her. The muscles in her calves flexed as she stood on tiptoes reaching for stalactites of glass hanging from the window frame.

'Should I take Kevin outside?' I said, hoping she'd want us to keep clear of the glass.

'No,' she said. 'Go get the hoover.'

In the kitchen cupboard, next to the mop and broom, was an octopus of untidy tubes, loose attachments and half-wound electric cable. I lifted it out and carried it across the living room, careful not to slip on the wet tiles.

Mom had collected up all the big pieces on the carpet and the small bits which had landed on Kevin's bed. I plugged in the hoover.

'Get right in under his desk,' said Mom above the machine's whine.

I moved the wide head over the carpet again and again. Kevin watched with his hands in his pockets. 'Mom, can I go outside?' he said.

'No, Kettle, you're still in your school clothes,' said Mom.

He began unbuttoning his shirt and kicking off his shoes.

I changed the attachment to a narrow nozzle and continued cleaning into the corners, around the desk legs and under the bed. I even hoovered the bed. Once the whole room was thoroughly done I switched it off and helped Mom take the duvet cover off Kevin's bed to be shaken outside and then washed.

'I'm dressed,' said Kevin, holding up his hands. 'Can we go now? Please. Everything's done.'

Mom sighed. 'Go on. Get out of my hair. Go play.'

We didn't need to be told twice. I was dying to get out there and see what had happened. Kevin raced towards the front door but I walked.

'But don't eat the ice,' Mom's voice dwindled as we left.

Every centimetre of lawn, every rooftop and every potted plant was covered in white. The air was crisp and clear of smells. Each step was a slippery fight for balance. Sunshine glinted off every surface. It was exactly how I imagined snow to look, except these snowflakes were all different sizes. Some were shaped like golf balls, some were like marbles but mostly there were tiny grains of ice, billions of them, as though a truck had spilled polystyrene stuffing the length of our street.

It was already beginning to melt. Dripping sounds splattered through the stillness. A slow sludge-river formed along the edge of the pavement and disappeared down the concrete storm drain. Somewhere in the neighbourhood a dog barked, wanting to be let in.

The garden had been obliterated. Mom's vegetable patch was buried. A few brave leaves still clung to the branches here and there, but most of the blossoms lay amongst the ice. An entire branch from the apricot tree had broken off and lay propped up against the back of the house.

'Look at this one,' shouted Kevin, obviously delighted.

I turned to see him holding a hailstone shaped like a figure-of-eight.

'These two are stuck together,' he said.

'What have you got in your mouth, Kev?' I said.

Kevin spat out a ball of ice. 'Nothing.'

'You're not supposed to eat the ice.'

'Why?' he asked.

'I dunno. 'Cause Mom said so.'

The dog continued to bark, bark, bark, every few seconds.

Kevin hurled the odd-shaped hailstone at the wall of the house. I expected it to smash like a clod of earth but it bounced off the brick, without even chipping, and rattled across on the ground. He bent down and found another piece the size of a peppermint and popped it into his mouth.

'What does it taste like?' I asked.

'Cold,' he said, crunching it between his teeth.

I chose a small one, brushed a fleck of mud off it, and placed it on my tongue. It was rougher than I expected and tasted like ice. Wild ice. Not from around here.

'Hey, Kev. Watch this,' I said. Tilting my head back as far as it would go, I spat the ball straight up into the air. It hovered above me for a millisecond and dropped back down into my open mouth.

Kevin giggled, looking left and right, trying quickly to think up a trick to top mine. He picked up a large hailstone. 'OK. Watch this!' he said and hurled it as hard as he could. It landed on the roof of the servants' quarters at the bottom of the yard. Five or six hailstones rolled down the roof and clattered to the ground.

Rebecca appeared in the doorway of the quarters shaking her head.

'Are you OK, Rebecca?' I said, carefully picking my way over to her.

'*Ja, baas*. OK.' She stood with her hand on her cheek.

She hated thunderstorms. Most blacks I knew were terrified of big storms, which was stupid, but some of them would scream as soon as the thunder clapped.

'Did your room get wet?' I said. 'Did the water come through the roof again?' I mimed water sprinkling down with my fingers.

'Little bit, *baas*,' said Rebecca. 'I close my eyes. I pray to God. "Please God, save me," I say.'

'Did your window smash?'

'No. Window is OK.'

'Some of the windows in the house are broken. Mom's clearing up the glass.'

'I help the Missus with the glass,' said Rebecca.

I wasn't sure if she meant it as a question or a statement, but she turned in to her room and seconds later came out with her shoes on. Wrapping a scarf around her head, she carefully made her way across the slippery, uneven ground up to the house.

A grinding, revving noise came from down the street. It sounded like Dad's car. Kevin heard it too and ran towards the front gate. He slipped, got straight up and scrambled on.

'Dad! Dad. Look. It hailed when you were away,' he said, holding the gate open. 'And guess what? The windows got smashed and . . . and we had to run all the way home.'

The tyres on Dad's Datsun spun as they fought for traction. The wheels mashed the ice into our driveway and snaked to a stop. Kevin closed the gate and ran over to Dad.

'Hey, Dad, look how big this one is,' he said, holding up a beauty between his thumb and forefinger.

Dad got out, pushed Kevin aside and stood staring at the

bonnet. He slowly lifted both hands and interlaced his fingers behind his head.

'No, no, no, no,' he whispered to himself.

The entire car was covered in dimples where hailstones had pounded into the bodywork.

'Fuck,' he suddenly shouted, kicking a new dent above the front wheel. He slammed the car door shut and marched past Kevin, who was still holding out his prized hailstone. Kevin dropped it and we quietly followed Dad into the house.

Mom looked up from the hoovering as Dad threw his denim jacket on the sofa. She switched it off and brushed her hair away from her forehead with the back of her wrist.

'Bruce,' she said, tilting her head to one side, 'you're back late.' She sounded pleasant enough but something else was buried in her tone. Something she was trying to let only Dad see.

Dad glanced at his watch but caught himself and changed his movement into folding his arms, as if that was his intention all along.

'Have you looked outside?' he said. 'What do you expect?'

Across our open-plan living room and kitchen I could see Rebecca silently move out of sight towards the back door. Mom said nothing. I could tell she wanted to ask something else but she kept her mouth shut. She let the question hang in the air, unasked.

'If you must know,' said Dad, 'there's a new foreman at work, the friendly type. He wanted to buy some of us a drink. I couldn't say no, could I? Which is why I'm late.' The more Dad explained the louder he got. 'Which is why I got caught in the middle of a bloody hailstorm. Which is why my car is now totally fucked. Are you happy now, Grace? Huh? Any more questions?'

Mom watched blankly as Dad flopped into his favourite chair. She took in a slow deep breath and began wrapping the electric cable around the hoover.

She stood to her full height and said, 'Bruce, the gutters need clearing.'

Dad looked away and slowly drummed his fingers across the padding of the armchair.

12

'You'd better clear them before they fall off the side of the house. And I'll look out the car's insurance papers,' said Mom in a clear steady tone.

'We're not covered for storm damage, you're wasting your time.'

But Mom went into their bedroom anyway.

He turned his eyes on me.

'Alex,' he barked, making my heart jump, 'you're helping me. Go fetch the broom and the garden trowel and meet me outside.'

Right away, I went to the kitchen. Rebecca was still there, in the far corner. She handed me the broom without making eye contact. Behind me I heard Kevin ask, 'Dad, can I help?'

'No,' said Dad.

Dad leaned the ladder against the side of the house and climbed to the top.

'Broom,' he yelled.

I handed him the broom.

Holding the very tip of the broom handle, he reached as far up the roof as he could and brushed the melting hailstones just left of the ladder. The hail splattered to the ground and I jumped two steps back to avoid being drenched. Dad reached for the trowel in his back pocket and began scooping out the ice which had gathered in the gutter along the edge of the roof. I ducked between the ladder and the house to make sure I was behind him.

Once one section was cleared, we moved the ladder a few metres to the left and started the next bit, making our way round the entire house. The neighbours across the street were doing the same thing. I'd never spoken to them. The dad of that house had a big belly. He was wearing long green rubber gloves and clearing his gutters with his hand. When he saw Dad clearing our roof he stopped and waved. I waved back. Dad didn't bother.

Rebecca swept the path from the gate to the front door with a thick grass broom. Kevin helped Mom cut out cardboard patches to seal up the broken windows till they could be properly fixed. As we moved the ladder in front of Kevin's bedroom window

Mom was sealing the final rectangle of cardboard to the window frame with masking tape while Kevin held it in place. She pulled a long stretch of tape and bit the end off. Dad swept the roof quickly. Neither one looked at the other.

After about an hour and a half Dad and I were finished. We folded up the ladder and carried it back to the garage. Inside was Mom's white Passat station wagon taking up most of the space. It was safe and dry. I helped Dad balance the ladder across the rafters, being extra careful not to knock anything over. Dad rubbed his hands on the back of his jeans, then we went outside to take another look at his car.

Apart from being covered in thousands of tiny dents, the roof was caved in, the bonnet didn't close properly, a side window was cracked, a rear brake light was smashed and the wing mirror was broken. We stood in silence, both of us with our hands in our pockets.

'Maybe your mother's right,' he said. 'She nagged and nagged for us to get insurance, so eventually we did. Maybe that wasn't such a bad idea.'

Dad smiled and rubbed his chin.

'What are you going to do, Dad?' I asked, nudging him deeper into his new good mood.

'Dunno yet. But I'm working on a plan.'

Dr Strange

Kevin was nineteen short and he'd been talking about it all week. It was Friday, pocket-money day. So straight after school we changed out of our uniforms and headed to the shop.

'Look what I've got,' said Kevin.

In his hand was a big round lump of ice.

'Where did you get that?' I said.

'From the freezer. It's a hailstone, from the storm.'

'And you've kept it for over a week?'

'*Ja,*' said Kevin, watching a droplet run down to his elbow and drip to the ground.

'So what are you gonna do with it?'

'Lick it.'

It was weird to think that during the middle of last week everything was covered in ice. Now the gutters, the pavement, the roads, everything was blanketed in jacaranda petals.

A car drove past leaving two tracks in the purple, the flowers gently popping under the weight. Kevin picked one up and twirled it between his forefinger and thumb. 'Why do they pop like that?'

'Because of the shape,' I said. 'Look.'

I picked up a fresh one that hadn't been trampled.

'If you hold the petals closed with your fingers, like this, then open your other hand flat and . . .' I squashed the flower against my palm and it burst with a happy little popping sound.

Kevin tried but he was too eager, too violent, all you could hear was the clap of his hands.

'You have to be gentle. See,' I showed him again.

Kevin dropped his half-melted hailstone, which wrapped itself in lavender petals as it rolled into the drain. He bent down and chose a freshly fallen flower, then carefully closed the petals and popped it against his palm. His grin was automatic. He picked up another and tried again. By the time we got to the shop our hands looked bruised.

Kevin went straight inside and said to Mr Cupido, 'Can I have three packets of Marvel Super-Hero Trading Cards.'

Mr Cupido kept the box behind the counter, high up next to the cigarettes. He leaned back on his stool and stretched his arm up to the box. His hairy belly button peeped out from under his

T-shirt like a big eye lazily opening then going back to sleep. Without saying anything he tossed the packets on the counter.

'Can I choose them myself?' Kevin asked. He asked this every week. Every week he got the same answer.

'If I let you little lighties choose I'd be here all day waiting for you to make up your minds.'

'You're here all day anyway,' I said.

Mr Cupido glared at me. I pretended not to notice and fiddled with some lollipops sprouting out of a jar.

'Do you want the cards or not, you little buggers?'

'We want the cards,' said Kevin. He put two rand on the counter. Mr Cupido gave him forty cents change, eyeing me all the time.

Kevin opened the packets immediately. He got,

two Spidermans

two Magnetos

two Lokis

one Daredevil

one Professor X

one Lizard

one Hulk

one Juggernaut

one Flash

one Mr Fantastic

one Dr Doom

one Storm.

But no Dr Strange. Never Dr Strange. Nobody had him. Kenneth Beukman said he had him but he never brought him to school.

The strange thing about Dr Strange was that the collector's book had him under 'Hero' instead of 'Villain'. Dad said that's what made him so powerful. You never knew if you could trust him, so everyone wanted him on their side, just in case.

Still, Kevin was happy with his loot. His album was mostly full of villains and today he got three more, Lizard, Loki and Dr Doom, but he also got Flash and Storm.

'Even though Storm's a girl,' said Kevin, closely studying her picture, 'she's still a hero. Now I only have . . .' he paused and, using his fingers, silently subtracted his new cards from the ones he still needed, 'I have fourteen more to get.'

He put the cards in his pocket and placed his last forty cents in front of Mr Cupido.

'Can I get some change for TV games?'

Kevin always spent his pocket money as soon as he got it, then he would nag me all week for cans of juice or sweets.

Mr Cupido picked at something in his teeth for a minute, then opened the till and sprinkled ten-cent pieces across the counter.

We went to the back of the shop and each put in a credit to play Double Dragon. Once, we completed the whole game with only three lives. We had figured it out. It was always better to play Two Player so you could cover each other. If you kept to the bottom of the screen and fought back-to-back you had a chance of clocking the game.

We started off strong. I picked up a barrel and threw it at the Gangsters. We ran over and I stole one of their baseball bats but Kevin only got a knife. He hit the wrong button and threw it instead of stabbed, so he was left fighting two Gangsters with lead pipes while I held off the others. The Gangsters beat a life out of him.

On the second life he was more focused. We easily made it through the next two levels. But we both lost lives getting past the Bikers. At the Jump I forgot to press Run and Jump together to clear the gap so I just walked off the cliff, which was a stupid, stupid, stupid thing to do.

That was my last life. I was out. Kevin did well to get to the next level but it was impossible to complete it on your own. He was fighting the End of the Level Boss who we nicknamed Mr Stupido. Kevin tapped the Attack button as fast as he could but as he tried to collect a Power Up, Mr Stupido threw an oil barrel and that was it for him. Game Over.

We went outside and sat down on the step next to an old black man fixing the tyre on his bike. He leaned back on his elbow and picked up his can of Coke, curling back the ring pull as he opened it. He flicked it away and it landed with a tinkle on the tar. Thousands of these silver hoops lay embedded in the road like flat bubbles.

Vim came speeding up on his BMX and smiled as soon as he saw us.

'*Haai, wat maak julle?*' he said. (Hey, what are you guys doing?)

He stopped right in front of the sun. I had to shade my eyes to see him.

'Nothing much,' I said, 'Kev was just buying some trading cards.'

Vim let his bike drop as he hopped across the hot tar in his bare feet and squatted down in the shade next to us. 'Can I see what yous got?'

Kevin flicked through his cards, showing each one to Vim but not letting him touch them. Before he got to the end Vim asked, '*Het jy Dr Strange gekry?*' (Did you get Dr Strange?)

'*Nee,*' said Kevin. (No.)

'Does anyone at your school have him, Vim?' I said.

Vim shook his head. 'Nobody's got him. I heard some boys at school was talking. They said maybe the company didn't print that card. So everyone keeps buying packets of cards to finish the collection but you can never make it finished.'

He struggled with English so I corrected the sentence for him. '. . . but it's impossible.'

'*Ja,*' said Vim.

I had never thought of this and by the expression on Kevin's face, he refused to accept it.

'*Waar is jou fiets?*' said Vim. (Where's your bike?)

'*Dis by die huis. Ons het geloop,*' I said. (It's at home. We walked.)

Vim stood up and said, '*Ek moet na my tannie se huis toe gaan.*' (I have to go to my auntie's house.)

'OK. See you later,' I said.

He hopped on his bike and pedalled on down the street.

Kevin shuffled his new cards, sorting out the 'keeps' from the 'swaps'. I knew he was chewing over the idea of Dr Strange not existing.

'Kev.'

'What?'

'Do you want a drink before we go home?'

'*Ja.*'

I stood up and checked how much change I had in my pocket.

'What do you want?' I asked.

'Fanta Lemon,' he said. 'No, wait. Fanta Orange. I'll have Fanta Orange.'

Business

Dad put his breakfast bowl in the sink and poured himself another coffee. He added milk and two sugars and tasted it. Frowning, he put the mug in the microwave for a full minute. After the ping, he sat down at the table and stretched his arms above his head. Steam curled out of the coffee mug, sparkling in the morning sunshine.

'Alex, I've got some business to do today,' said Dad. His breath threw the coffee vapours into violent spirals. 'I could use some help if you want to tag along.'

'OK,' I said. We went into town most weekends. It was always fun.

'You never let me come,' started Kevin.

'We'll only be gone for an hour,' said Dad. 'You stay here with Mom.'

'But I don't wanna stay!'

'Bruce, maybe you should *include* Kevin on your little trip this morning. It might be fun to have a boys' day out.' Mom looked over her shoulder as she spoke while her hands kept washing the dishes.

19

Dad leaned back in his chair and gave his why-the-hell-are-you-doing-this-to-me sigh, which he always used on Kevin.

'OK, fine,' said Dad. 'Come if you want, but you're just going to get dragged around town. I have appointments and things. I don't want you moaning 'cause you're bored.'

Kevin tried not to smile. 'I'll just quickly put my shoes on,' he said.

'Hurry up,' said Dad. 'We don't have all day.'

Kevin dumped his bowl in the sink and ran to his bedroom.

Even by mid-morning the car was hot and airless. The backs of my thighs burned when I first sat down on the front seat. It was even too hot to sit on my hands so I tried pressing down with my arms and hovering my butt a few centimetres above the scorching fake leather but I couldn't hold it for long.

Dad took his sunglasses from his shirt pocket, flicked open the arms, and slipped them on. He rolled down his window and hung his elbow out. As we drove into the city the buildings grew taller and closer together.

There was a specific odour to Dad. Working under cars all day made him smell like the inside of a toolbox. Even after a bath, his hands had a whiff of wiped-clean spanners. But because we were going out this morning he must have slapped on some Brut. The mix of smells reminded me of the time Kevin and I had sprayed our names on the garage floor using a can of deodorant. We lit a match to our names and watched the blue flames race across the oil stains on the concrete floor.

'Alex, take the wheel for a second, will you,' said Dad.

I grabbed the steering wheel with my right hand and gently kept the car from drifting into the other lane. Being half in charge of a car made me feel bigger, more grown up. Dad lifted his hips and struggled to get something out of the pocket of his jeans.

'Got it,' said Dad, holding up a packet of chewing gum. 'You want some?'

I kept my eyes on the road and nodded. He fiddled with the

wrapper then popped two sticks of gum in his mouth. A waft of peppermint breathed over the top of Dad's aftershave.

'Here, open your mouth,' he said, holding the gum in front of my face.

I opened up and the gum went straight in. For a split second his finger touched the tip of my tongue and my whole mouth turned to metal. I let go of the steering wheel and chewed fast to get rid of the taste.

'Can I have some?' said Kevin, from the back seat.

Dad tossed a bit over his shoulder and Kevin scrambled onto the floor of the car to find it. He crawled back up onto the seat and sat cross-legged, chewing.

'What business have you got to do today, Dad?' asked Kevin.

'Well, a lot of things,' said Dad. 'I want to drive out to a car dealer later this afternoon, and I need some new shoes and maybe pick up the latest copy of *Car Magazine*. Oh, and I need to make an appointment to get my eyes tested.'

I thought back to what we did last Saturday. Last week's business included,

looking through car magazines

walking around furniture showrooms

comparing the prices of video machines in four different shops

buying socks

trying on suits

getting Dad's eyes tested

talking to a sales assistant about portable video cameras.

We parked in the furthest-away corner of a supermarket car park, our usual spot. As Dad had explained many times before, it was perfect because it was free and near the centre of town. We locked up and went to the hole in the fence. I held back the wire as Dad and Kevin slipped through, then Dad held the wire up for me. Once we were all on the pavement Dad adjusted his sunglasses, tucked his thumbs into his belt and swaggered across the street. Kevin and I marched behind, ready for a day of business.

'Where are we going first, Dad?' said Kevin.

'The optician,' said Dad.

'Where's that?'

Dad stopped and turned to Kevin. 'Are you going to bug me with questions all day long?'

'No.' Kevin lowered his head.

'Good. 'Cause if you're going to pester me, you can wait in the car. You understand?'

'Yes, Dad.'

'OK, now you two stand guard. I have to take a piss.'

Dad faced into a doorway and unzipped. I turned my back and watched the people walking up and down doing their shopping. A trickle of pee ran between my feet, seeping into the cracks of the pavement and I quickly jumped aside in case anyone thought I had wet myself.

'Done,' said Dad, wiping his finger on his jeans. 'Let's go.'

We passed a beggar with no legs and a few black women selling boxes of vegetables outside the post office. They were arguing and shouting with a group of black men who were standing across the street. The three of us completely ignored them as we went by.

After a few minutes Dad said, 'You know, if I had to, I could survive on the street.' His eyes narrowed and swept across the traffic. 'A man needs to learn how to survive out here on the streets, because you never know.'

Kevin squared his slim shoulders and slowly nodded. '*Ja*, me too.'

Turning to us, Dad said, 'For example, what would you do if some crazy drunk kaffir started causing shit? Out here on the street, no one's gonna help you. Seriously, what would you do?'

Kevin lifted his arms and let them flop down. 'I would tell him I haven't got any money, cause I'm just a boy.'

Before Dad could disapprove I chipped in, with my deepest voice.

'I would kick him full force in the nuts and run away.'

'That's more like it, Alex. But also, how would you give your-

22

self the upper hand? What about weapons? If you think about it, weapons are all around you. See!'

He pulled out a fistful of keys and held it in front of our faces. Each key poked out between his knuckles like bristles on an angry dog's back.

'This'll stop him! A punch in the eye and that's one less crazy fucker on the street.'

Dad began shadow boxing the invisible black man right there in the middle of the pavement. We watched, awestruck. A man in a suit walking towards us suddenly turned and crossed the street. I knew without a doubt, Dad could beat anyone in a fight. Nobody ever messed with him.

'Remember,' he said, 'there's only two people in a street fight, the winner and the loser.'

He tucked his thumbs into his belt. We walked over to the crossing and waited for the little green man.

'You have to do whatever it takes to be the winner.'

Once we got across the road Dad had more to say.

'Of course, as well as weapons you need wits. Smart people know how to get whatever they want, just like Face from the A-Team.'

'What?' I said.

Dad paused and gave me the only-an-idiot-would-need-me-to-explain-it-to-you sigh. This was his other special sigh, the one he usually used on me.

'Think about it,' explained Dad. 'Hannibal claims to be the leader but all he really does is find clients. Murdock is insane but he can fly planes. And the black guy . . . what's his name? Mr T? He's the muscle and drives the van. Face does every-thing else. The A-Team would be nothing without Face. He saves their butts every episode. If they're trapped in the desert, Face can find water, a radio and suncream. He doesn't need weapons. His special ability is to convince anyone to do what-ever he wants.'

I'd never thought about Face that way. To me, he was the one that the girls always fell in love with. And he was always

23

complaining. He was my least favourite member of the A-Team. But what Dad said made sense.

'I like Murdock the best,' said Kevin.

'That's 'cause you're an idiot just like he is. If you were any dumber you'd be Irish,' said Dad.

Instead of getting angry, Kevin twisted his finger against his temple, stuck out his tongue and made giggly crazy faces. Dad shook his head and walked on.

At the optician Dad made us wait outside while he made an appointment. Through the window I could see the receptionist with the dangly earrings. Dad was leaning against her desk chatting to her.

'What's he doing now?' asked Kevin.

'Nothing. He's still making his appointment,' I said.

'I'm bored,' said Kevin.

'Well, don't tell Dad, or you'll never be allowed to come with us again.'

Ten minutes later Dad came out and said, 'Right, let's go to CNA.'

CNA was one of my favourite shops. It was full of books and magazines and posters and pencils and tapes and it had air-conditioning. Dad went to his favourite spot and began flicking through car magazines. Kevin knelt on the floor, reading a Batman comic. But I wasn't sure what I wanted to read. I wandered through the aisles and eventually picked a copy of *National Geographic*. The cover showed hundreds of men and women all getting married at the same time. Inside, there were more photographs. Rows and rows of couples stood together in a huge hall, all saying their vows at the same time. All the women wore white wedding dresses. The men were all in black.

'I'm done,' said Dad, flicking my ear. 'C'mon, let's go.'

I dropped the magazine onto a pile of books and rubbed my ear on the way out.

We wandered round the streets and helped Dad do a little more shopping before eventually making our way back. Instead of going straight to the car Dad wanted to explore the supermarket and the little cluster of shops that surrounded it. We ambled past the entrance to the supermarket, then Dad stopped, turned and walked back past it again. I tried to see what he was looking at. There was a baggage check-in at the entrance and a small queue of shoppers waiting to hand in the items they had bought at the other shops before being allowed into the supermarket. Dad's jaw jutted out as he thought about something, then he joined the back of the queue.

Each bag checked in was exchanged for a green plastic disc with a number on it. Our bag contained one car magazine, one Batman comic, one box of razor blades, one pair of black socks and one pack of chewing gum – a good day's business. In return we got a plastic disc with the number 27 embossed on it. I assumed we were going into the supermarket but Dad took us out to the car park.

'I want you boys to get as many receipts out of that rubbish bin as you can. Meet me at the car in ten minutes.' Dad put on his sunglasses and sauntered off. Kevin and I looked at each other, then at the rubbish bin. We chose to accept our mission.

Ten minutes later Kevin and I returned to the car. Dad sat sideways behind the steering wheel, elbows on knees, chewing his nails. He balanced his sunglasses on top of his head and began carefully shuffling through the pile of till receipts I had given him.

'Too much . . . too much . . . too little . . . too much . . .' he mumbled to himself.

Sunshine burned the back of my neck but no matter how hot it got Dad always wore socks and shoes, jeans and a shirt into town. His neck was shiny with sweat, staining the collar of his shirt. As he concentrated, his heavy eyebrows lowered till it seemed as if each eye had been crossed out with a thick black marker pen.

'Aahhh . . . this one is perfect,' said Dad, holding up one till receipt and scrunching the others in his fist. He read it aloud. 'One pair of leather shoes and a shirt. Fifty-nine rand and ninety-eight cents. Do you know what this means, boys?'

'No,' said Kevin.

'It means a free lunch,' said Dad.

Kevin glanced up at me to see if I understood what Dad was talking about. I sensed Dad was planning another scam but I had no idea what it was.

'How does that give us a free lunch?' asked Kevin.

'We'll use this,' said Dad, tapping a finger against his head. 'Just like Face from the A-Team, we're going to apply the Bullshit Baffles Brains method.'

Dad stood up, folded the receipt and slipped it into his back pocket.

'Pay close attention, boys,' said Dad as we followed him across the car park. 'If you learn how to do this properly, you'll be set for life, you won't need anything else.'

We didn't discuss the plan but I knew what not to do.

'Listen, Kev,' I whispered, 'whatever happens don't say *anything* unless you're asked a question. Just agree with whatever Dad says, OK?'

Kevin nodded. He knew this was serious.

We went back to the baggage check-in. I handed over the plastic disc with the number 27 facing up. The fat black woman behind the counter gave us our bag.

'Where's the rest?' Dad started.

'Sorry, *baas*?' she said.

'The rest of my stuff, my other bags, the other bags I left with you?' His voice was already projecting across to the cashiers and the shoppers dutifully waiting in line at the checkouts.

'I dunno about rest, *baas*.'

'I demand to see the manager.' Dad slapped the counter as he spoke. His gold wedding band struck the surface with a threatening, mechanical sound.

Alec Roberts was the supermarket manager's name. But he introduced himself as Mr Robots. He blinked a lot when he spoke and his Adam's apple almost poked through his skin.

'What seems to be the trouble, sir?' he said.

Dad liked being called sir. He refused to shake the manager's hand and started his story.

'Well, this morning my sons and I were doing a little shopping. A boys' day out if you like. Only an hour ago I bought some new shoes and a shirt for an important business meeting on Monday morning.'

The manager kept smiling professionally as he listened to these details. Every now and then he looked at me and Kevin, then at the black woman who was standing with her hands on her hips, lips pursed.

'We left all our bags at the check-in,' Dad continued, holding up the plastic disc, 'and entered your supermarket looking for a birthday cake for the boy's elderly grandmother. When we came to reclaim our bags your employee, here, only gave us one bag. So I asked her where the other bags were and she pretended not to know what I was talking about.'

Mr Robots looked at the woman. 'What do you have to say, Lettie?'

'That one has only small bag, baas. I dunno about other bag. He say two bags, two bags. I give him bag. He say what about rest. I dunno about rest. Honest, baas.'

Dad jumped in quickly. 'What sort of establishment are you running here? I'm telling you my bag's missing. What am I going to do now? I need that shirt for Monday morning. I demand a refund!'

'Sir, please keep your voice down. Now, I can't actually provide you with compensation since our policy—'

'Your policy! Your policy what? Is it the policy of this store to rob its customers of their goods while entrusted to your baggage check-in?' Dad was in full flow, shouting and waving his arms. Mr Robots' smile was looking more and more like a grimace.

'Look,' Dad said, a little softer, 'what do I have to do to make you believe me?' He fumbled in his pockets. 'Look, see! I still have the receipt. Bought this morning, one shirt and a pair of shoes. See, it's all here. I'm not making this up.' Finally, he turned

27

to me and said, 'Tell him, son, what was in the bag, the one stolen from your father?'

Dad once said to me that the best way to lie was to raise your eyebrows, relax your cheeks and look straight ahead. This made your face look open, showing you had nothing to hide. I steadied my gaze on Mr Robots and delivered my line.

'Shoes and shirt.'

Kevin took hold of Dad's hand and nodded solemnly.

That settled it. Three white guys, with a genuine receipt, against the word of a fat black woman. We got R59.98 refunded to us, with plenty of grovelling from Mr Robots to encourage Dad to keep his voice down.

Kevin skipped as we left the building but Dad gently gripped the back of his neck. 'Try not to look so excited,' he said.

But by the time we got to the car it was Dad who was really excited.

'That was fantastic! Did you see the look on his face when I mentioned the cake for your poor, dear grandmother? Ha! You boys were great. We were better than the A-Team,' said Dad, touching each of us on the shoulder.

Kevin stood as tall as he could, grinning from ear to ear.

'It's like I was telling you boys earlier,' said Dad, as he unlocked the car. 'Winners and losers. Whatever it takes.'

Mulberries

Because I was the biggest I had to go first. Kevin took off his flip-flops, placed them next to the tree trunk and knelt on them. I positioned my bare foot on the base of his back above his hips and stepped up, grabbing the lowest branch and swinging my knee over. Turning onto my stomach, I reached down as he handed me both ropes. While I looped the top ends over a high branch, Kevin tied the bottom ends to the handles of each bucket, one for him and one for me. Finally, I grabbed my brother's wrist and pulled him up.

Kevin twisted and wriggled up through the branches. Because he was lighter he could get right to the top, to where the mulberries were ripest. He went so high up he swayed with the breeze. His bucket ascended into the leaves above me. Soon I could hear him dropping in handfuls at a time.

I hoisted up my bucket and started filling it. Mom wanted as many as possible for jam. Every year she would boil them in a huge pot, which grew a foaming pink scum. It stank of cabbage at first but when she added the sugar it began to smell syrupy.

Something jolted above my head, causing some overripe berries to tumble to the ground.

'Careful, Kev,' I said.

'What would you do if I fell?' I heard him say.

'I'd melt all your GI Joes and make a huge frisbee.'

'Well, you know what,' he said, trying to think of a quick reply, 'if . . . if you died I'd chop your bike into a million pieces.'

I found a purple-black mulberry and popped it into my mouth. They always tasted like the inside *and* the outside of a black grape. Instead of having a tangy skin and a sweet juicy centre, mulberries had both tastes mixed together. I always preferred mulberries.

'How many have you got, Kev?'

'Half a bucket.' He climbed across to another branch and said, 'Alex?'

'What?'

'What would you do if you had a million bucks?'

I thought for a bit. He had asked me this before. The object of the game was to give original answers.

'Hire scientists to train monkeys to do homework and cook breakfast. That way we could sleep late and play all afternoon.'

I heard giggling. 'I'd send my monkey to school as well,' he said, 'then I'd never have to go back there.'

My turn. 'What would you do if you were invisible?'

'I'd get into the back of the car and spy on Dad at work.'

I stopped picking and sat up. There was something really exciting about that idea. 'What do you think you'd see?' I said.

'I dunno. Maybe Dad would be late and then his boss would shout at him and say, "You're such a stupid-head."' Kevin laughed so happily I had to join in.

'What would you do if you could fly?' said Kevin, keeping the game going.

This had always been my favourite superpower. Actually it was hovering I fantasised about, not proper flying. At nights I would lie awake and imagine myself floating high up, watching the whole planet roll silently underneath me. While everything constantly moved I would be the only one staying still.

But my answer had to be original.

'I'd try flying underwater, you know, like a torpedo,' I answered.

'*Ja*, that would be cool,' said Kevin.

Holding my pickings with the rope between my teeth, I crawled over to another part where the mulberries looked blacker. I lay across a fork in the branches and looped the bucket handle over a broken stub. Lying still for a second, I let my focus switch from the green of the leaves to the red dust below and back again.

'Kev?'

'*Ja*.'

'What would you do if you knew the world was going to end? Say they announced it on TV and said we all had one hour to live before the earth was going to explode or something. What would you do?'

I could feel him thinking about it. A crease always formed between Kevin's eyebrows when he concentrated. We called it his 'thinking wrinkle'.

Then he answered, 'I would go to sleep.'

Videos

The video store was divided in two. Red shelves for Betamax tapes and the yellow shelves for VHS. Dad and I browsed the yellow shelves.

I wanted to see *Police Academy II* but Dad found an earlier Chuck Norris film he hadn't seen. The cover was black with Chuck Norris sitting cross-legged, meditating. His blond hair was glowing while his face was in shadow. Across the bottom of the box was the title, *A Force of One*.

'We're getting this,' said Dad, turning towards the counter.

I put *Police Academy II* back on the shelf.

The girl who worked in the video shop wore tons of make-up. She had a white painted face with red streaks across her cheeks and dark blue eye shadow. Her spiky blonde hair also had blue and red bits, either like Madonna or Cindi Lauper, I wasn't sure which.

'Now, we call you the "video girl",' said Dad, leaning an elbow on the counter, 'but surely that can't be your real name.'

She wrote the video code into the record book without looking up. While she wrote she chewed bubble gum with her mouth open.

'My name's Debbie,' she said, keeping her tone flat and neutral. The badge on her uniform read, *Elma van Niekerk*.

'We're closed Sundays, so this is due back on Monday by seven o'clock,' she said, holding out the video. She stared Dad right in the eye, her mouth still chewing round and round. Dad took his elbow off the counter and stood to his full height. He snatched the video and we left immediately.

The shock of leaving an air-conditioned shop and stepping into the mid-afternoon sunshine made my lungs feel airless for a second. Then warm air filled my mouth, my throat, my chest, and I felt normal again.

'What a bitch,' said Dad. 'There's no need to be rude, especially to a customer.'

He took long marching strides and I struggled to keep up.

'And did you see the way she kept chewing that gum? It's disgusting.'

I nodded and softly said, '*Ja*, what a bitch.'

We climbed into Dad's car and he reversed out of the parking space. In the late-afternoon light, each one of the million dents in the bonnet cupped its own tiny shadow.

'What gets me is the lack of respect,' said Dad, still annoyed with the video girl. 'You see, son, respect is what keeps society together. But people don't understand that.'

The lights turned from green to orange, and Dad sped up, slipping through as they turned red.

'Obviously, everyone should respect everyone else,' he continued, 'but also, you have to understand *where* you are. You know what I mean? 'Cause society's layered like a big cake. If you're the biscuit at the bottom, you have to respect that. Some people are an average layer of sponge from the middle. Others are the fruity spread of jam, which keep things together. Every now and again, you come across a tasty bit of chocolate chip. The lucky ones get to be the creamy white icing on top. And the most deserving are the cherries to top it all off. You understand what I'm saying?'

I nodded. But I wasn't really sure if I understood the world as well as Dad did.

We pulled in to a petrol station and a big Zulu man with muscles stretching his old T-shirt welcomed us towards the petrol pump with a wave of his hand. The sleeves of his overalls were tied at his waist.

'Hello, *baas*. Helloooo,' he said, showing us his gleaming white teeth.

Dad rolled down the window. 'Put five rand in the tank and five rand in the canister in the boot.'

'Yebo, chief,' said the Zulu, boogie dancing towards the back of the car.

'You see, Alex, that's what I'm talking about,' said Dad, nodding towards the Zulu. 'This guy understands the natural layers. He shows proper respect, he gets to be happy. Simple.'

Dad thumbed through a roll of money, picked out a ten-rand note. It was unusual for Dad to put so little petrol in the tank. We were nearly empty. He wrapped an elastic band around the wad and put it back in his pocket.

'Alex,' he said, leaning over and opening the glove compartment, 'take all these cassettes and put them in the plastic bag with the video.'

This was a command and not a suggestion. I grabbed a handful of cassettes and dropped them in the bag.

'Actually, wait. Stop.' Dad reached into the bag and pulled out the tapes. He shuffled through them, reading each label.

'I'll keep these three,' he said, handing me Michael Jackson's *Bad*, *The Power of Love* by Jennifer Rush and his favourite mix tape called *Bruce's Juices*. 'The rest I can afford to lose.'

I put these in with the video and stuffed the other cassettes back into the glove compartment.

The big Zulu put the filled canister back and gently closed the boot before coming back to the driver's side window.

'Ok, *baas*. Ten rand please, *baas*.'

Dad gave him the note without looking up. The big Zulu jogged over to the petrol-station office. He posted the money through a slot in the bulletproof glass to a squat blonde woman sitting at a till. She typed the amount into the register and tore off the receipt, slipping it back to the big Zulu with the tip of her fingers. As he came back to our car, he laughed and joked in his own language with another petrol attendant who was filling up a van behind us.

'Thank you, *baas*,' he said to Dad as he handed him the receipt.

Dad dropped a fifty-cents tip onto the Zulu's open hand and started the engine.

The Zulu flipped the coin. 'Thank you, *baas*,' he said, waving as we drove off. 'Nice day!'

* * *

We drove for about twenty minutes, listening to Springbok Radio and then switching to Radio 5. The shadows of tall trees flickered across the car. It felt like blinking your eyes very fast. I hung my arm out the open window and let the air ripple up my T-shirt. My hand surfed up and down through the wind as we sped along.

We overtook a truck that stank of diesel fumes and I realised that we weren't going home.

'Where are we going, Dad?'

'We won't know till we get there,' he said.

It looked as though we were on the outskirts of the city. We passed a woman selling watermelons on the side of the road. She sat on a rock, in the shade of her umbrella, waiting for customers. On the hillside ahead of us were the shambolic metal shacks of a black township.

'What are we doing out here?' I said.

'It's all part of the plan,' said Dad.

After about five minutes, Dad slowed down and turned right onto a dirt track. We followed it for a while, then stopped. Dad cut the engine. He got out and opened the boot.

'Open all the car doors and grab the bag with the video in it,' he said.

I stepped out into the sunshine. A breeze rustled across the top of the yellow veldt grass. We were alone. There were no buildings nearby, not even a wire fence, just silent, open scrubland.

'Dad, what are we doing here?'

He moved out from behind the car with the canister of petrol in his hand.

'You remember the hailstorm?' he said. 'You remember I said I was working on a plan?'

'Yeah, so?'

'Well, this is the plan. We're not covered for storm damage but we are covered for theft. And more importantly, we have fire insurance,' he said, splashing petrol across the back seat.

The petrol glugged out of the canister across the floor mats, the handbrake, the dashboard. The fumes overpowered every other smell. As Dad wet the bonnet the petrol gathered into tiny puddles filling each dimple left by the hail.

'The way I remember it, Alex, you and I were renting a video. We came out and discovered – *to our great shock* – that someone had stolen our car.'

He unscrewed the car's petrol cap.

'The thieves probably raced around for a while or maybe even used our car as a getaway for a bank robbery, who knows? But once these kaffirs were finished they decided to cover their tracks by dumping our car out here and burning it. Then they probably ran laughing into that township over there and got drunk, while you and I were stranded at the shops. An unfortunate case of bad things happening to good people when they least expect it.'

With the last dregs, he dribbled a muddy trail of petrol down the dusty track. This was the fuse. It ran about fifteen metres from the car.

'Alex, you'd better stand further back,' he said.

My mind flashed up every action movie I had ever seen, where the car explodes into an enormous mushroom of flames, and doors and wheels and glass fly in every direction. So I ran. I ran expecting to hear it blow up behind me. I looked over to see if Dad was running behind me but he wasn't. He was watching me run, so I stopped.

'OK,' I shouted, waving my arms.

He placed the empty canister back in the boot and sauntered over to the start of the fuse line, adjusting his dark glasses. From his hip pocket he pulled out a box of matches. He lit a match but it must have blown out because he threw it away. Turning his back to the breeze, he tried again. Again, it blew out. Then he knelt down over the trail of petrol and tried once more.

I expected the flames to sparkle slowly along the trail of petrol. But as soon as Dad touched the match to the ground, flames, a metre high, raced across the dirt and engulfed the car in fire. It sounded like a dog barking very slowly. Woooooff.

Dad held a hand across his face to shield himself from the heat. He staggered and tripped over backwards. Scrambling to his feet again, he picked up his sunglasses and came bounding towards me. He turned to take another look at the fire, still stepping backwards away from it. Suddenly he raised both arms up and howled.

'Owwwoooo! Makes you feel like the king of the world, hey, son,' he said, his eyes on the flames.

The inside was already a glowing orange furnace. Flames jumped two metres above the car but the smoke billowed thirty metres up in powerful flumes continually folding in on themselves. The heat from the car pressed against my face, pushing me back as sunshine scorched the back of my neck, forcing me forward. Breath came in short gasps. I kept my mouth shut tight but the stench of smouldering plastic had begun to coat my tongue.

'Burn in hell, you piece of shit,' Dad yelled at the car.

I wanted an explosion, a massive KABOOM. There was none. The fire snapped and flames licked across the seats and up over the headlights. A tyre burst and hissed. We watched for a few more minutes. Dad became expressionless, lost in unreadable thoughts. 'Bye-bye, little car,' he mumbled to himself.

He shoved his hands in his pockets. 'Let's get going, Alex, and don't look back. Pretend all of this smoke is none of your business.'

We made our way along the dirt track till we couldn't hear the flames any more. Ahead of us, over the tall grass, the roofs of cars became visible as they sped along the main road.

'How are we going to get home?' I said.

'I bet you think I hadn't thought of that,' he said.

Actually, I assumed he had thought of something. Dad always planned things out, even if it seemed as though he was making it up as he went along.

'You're going to get us home, son.'

'*Me?* How can I get us home?'

'Like this,' said Dad, holding out his thumb.

At the main road, we started walking towards the city.

'Hitchhiking is like fishing,' said Dad. 'You need the right bait for the right fish. In today's little exercise, you're the bait.'

'Why me?'

'No one in this country is stupid enough to pick up a single man walking alone down the side of the road. But a man with a child looks trustworthy, just a family man with a bit of bad luck. I'll bet you a buck that in ten minutes some woman – probably a mother – gives us a ride back to town.'

Sweat ran down into my eyebrows and my throat was dry from the smoke. I wanted to get home, to feel the cool living-room tiles under my feet. But I was also having fun. I liked the idea of it being up to me to get us home.

'Deal,' I said, shaking Dad's hand, 'and when we get back, you're buying me an ice-cold Sprite.'

Dad smiled and shook his head the way adults do when kids say something unexpected. 'You've got yourself a deal.'

I stuck my thumb out.

A truck roared up behind me and sped past in a cloud of dust. I pulled my arm in and covered my mouth as I coughed.

'You won't get a lift that way,' said Dad. 'If you've got your back to the traffic, you look like you're happy walking home. It's better to turn round and face the oncoming cars. Let the drivers see your face so they can judge what you're like before picking you up. But keep walking backwards. Good. Now you look desperate, like you've been stranded.'

'Why can't we stand in some shade and wait for a car?'

'Because it makes you look lazy. People think you can't be bothered walking and you expect a ride for free. No, trust me, walking backwards is the best way.'

I took small backward steps along the edge of the empty road. Dad walked a few metres down the dusty embankment, coaching me on my technique.

'That's good, son. Now, think of your thumb as a fishhook. Always keep it out so people can see it but as soon as you see a woman's car, wave your thumb up above your shoulder.'

I wondered what a 'woman's car' looked like. Maybe it was cleaner than other cars, perhaps they were pink. Mom had a white station wagon. The whole family could fit in it plus get shopping bags in the back. Maybe women had station wagons.

A brown bakkie was making its way up the road. I stepped back, checking over my shoulder that there were no rocks to trip over. As the bakkie got closer I waved my thumb above my head. Nothing happened. It didn't slow down. It whooshed past and kept going but thirty metres away the brake lights flashed and it pulled over.

My chest swelled with pride. 'I got one, Dad,' I shouted, but he was already jogging towards the car. I ran after him, the plastic bag full of tapes and a video bashing into my knees as I sprinted at full speed.

The passenger-side window opened only a few centimetres.

'Howzit, my friend? You need a lift?' said the driver. He wasn't wearing a shirt and had tattoos across his forearms. Next to him sat a woman with long, scraggly, grey hair. She was smoking a cigarette and didn't say anything.

'We got a flat tyre,' said Dad. 'We just need a lift to a tele-phone box and my wife will come and pick us up.'

'*Ja, lekker*, man, no problem,' said the driver. 'Hop on.'

Dad jumped onto the back and reached down to give me a hand up. I didn't take it. I didn't need it. With one foot on the back wheel, I swung my leg over and I was in.

The back of the bakkie was full of gardening equipment. There were rakes, spades, six bags of compost, stacks of empty ceramic plant pots and a collection of unpainted garden gnomes. I sat down in a whorl of old hosepipes and Dad sat on a box by the left rear wheel. He hung his arm over the side of the car and patted the panelling twice. We were off, bumping roughly back onto the tarmac. I pointed my face into the wind. The rush of moving cooled the sweat against my forehead.

I thought about phoning Mom and wondered what Dad was going to tell her. Then I pictured the flames. We were always told not to burn things in case we started a veldt fire. Maybe the fire from the car had spread and the whole veldt was burning right now. Also, wouldn't we have to tell the police?

'Alex,' said Dad. 'Don't bite your nails.' I immediately lowered my hand and tucked it under my leg.

When we got closer to home, Dad patted the side of the bakkie again and the driver slowed to a stop. We jumped off and the bakkie revved up and continued down the road. A tattooed arm hung out the window and waved goodbye.

The two of us now stood on the pavement of a busy road that ran alongside a rich neighbourhood. Across the road was a double-storey house. The light reflecting off the swimming pool danced across the windows on the upper floor. I had a rough idea where we were but I had never been on this street before. Dad seemed to know this area. He waited for a break in the traffic and crossed. I hesitated but followed, having to sprint the last few metres to avoid a lorry. Dad took long purposeful strides and every few steps I had to jog to keep up. In a few minutes we were approaching the shopping centre where we had hired the video. Without breaking rhythm we marched straight into the corner shop. Dad got two Sprites out of the fridge.

'You did well today, son,' he said, putting the bottles on the counter.

'How are we going to get home?' I asked.

'I'll phone your mother, she'll come and get us.' He smiled as if I was being silly.

He put three one-rand coins on the counter, and said to the shopkeeper, 'Can you open these bottles and also give me some change for the phone.'

I sat in the shade, on a low brick wall surrounding the base of a large jacaranda tree. Dad stood in the phone booth talking to Mom. I couldn't hear a word he said, but I sipped my Sprite and I watched his hands move. Each gesture was sharp and exaggerated, as if he was explaining the situation to her in person. He motioned towards the video shop with his palm turned up as though begging for coins. Then he turned towards the car park and appeared to brush away a fly trying to land on his face. I guessed he was describing the moment we came out of the shop and discovered the car was gone. He stood still and listened for a moment before quickly raising both shoulders as if to say, I don't know. Then he pointed sharply to where the car used to be and held up two fingers. At this stage I guessed he was explaining how two black men had been lurking around when we parked the car and he was sure they were the ones responsible. Dad made jabbing gestures at the ground in front of him to emphasise his point. Then he wiped the sweat from his forehead up into his hairline, looking stressed out and stranded and asking for Mom to come and fetch us.

Without hearing a word I knew the speech was good. He looked really upset and angry about his car being stolen. Every bit of the story had been delivered sincerely. It was as if he really believed what he was saying. When he came over to where I was sitting I thought of making a joke, something about Mom buying the scam. Instead, I put the Sprite bottle to my lips and emptied it.

Ten minutes later Mom arrived. She stopped without turning off the engine and the two of us got in.

'Are you all right?' she asked.

'I'm fine,' I said.

'I just had my car stolen. How the hell do you think I feel?' said Dad.

We drove home as a heavy mood hung in the car, the only sound being the hum of the engine and Dad sighing dramatically with his hand across his mouth.

That evening Mom and Dad spent a lot of time looking out papers and making phone calls. Dad always got stressed doing paperwork and it was best to avoid him. He drank one cup of coffee after the other. Mom didn't start making supper till seven o'clock. We ate yesterday's mince and boiled potatoes.

Kevin wanted to know what was going on. He kept asking questions and following Dad around the house, curious to learn what had happened. As Dad turned to reach for the telephone he bumped into Kevin again.

'MOVE, BOY, or I'll move you.'

The last bit sounded deadly. I knew Kevin was going to get it.

Kevin's bottom lip wobbled, then he started crying. I walked straight across the living room, grabbed his arm, and dragged him into my bedroom.

'Leave me alone. Let go of me!' he screamed, the tears running past his nose.

'Shhhh. Listen,' I said, trying to calm him down. 'Listen to me. Dad is very upset right now because his car was stolen. While we were at the shops someone drove away with his car, and when we came out it was gone.'

Kevin stopped crying, gripped by my story. I carried on.

'We think two black men – *robbers* – might have taken it, but we're not sure. So right now Dad has to call the insurance company and the police and report the crime. That's why he doesn't want you in the way. He's not angry with you, he just has very important business to do right now.'

Kevin's eyes grew wide as he thought over what I said. The story came out without any planning. I told it as though it was the truth and yet at the same time, if I really wanted to, I could see an image of our burning car in my mind. One felt as true as the other.

'Are the police coming to the house?' said Kevin.

I hadn't thought about it. But if Dad was calling them then they might have to come by and ask him some questions, maybe ask me some questions. My stomach jumped.

'No, I don't think so, why would they come here?' I said.

The crickets were chirping. Rebecca stood at the kitchen sink, washing the evening dishes. Mom was sitting at the kitchen table reading through piles of papers. Dad stood looking over her

41

shoulder. He had a cup of coffee in one hand and was picking his nose behind Mom's back. The doorbell rang and they both looked up together. Dad put down his coffee and opened the door. Two policemen stood in the moonlight.

'Are you Mr Thorne?' asked one of the officers.

'Yes, Bruce Thorne, that's me.'

'You reported earlier that your car was stolen. Is that correct, Mr Thorne?'

'Yes.'

'We need to ask you some questions to file a proper report.'

'Please come in, come in,' said Dad.

Both policemen were taller than Dad. One was young and, when he took off his hat, had very short black hair. The older one was heavy and had a moustache and glasses. They wore uniforms the colour of beach sand with black army boots and they both had guns. Black guns. With extra bullets in their belts next to the silver handcuffs. The older one had a walkie-talkie strapped to his belt that sometimes blurted out static and a voice speaking coded commands.

'Can I offer you gentlemen some coffee?' said Mom, very formal and polite.

'We don't want to keep you late,' said the older one.

'Not at all,' said Mom. 'Please sit down. My husband has all the information you need. I'll be back in a second.'

Mom slipped into the kitchen and before Dad said anything we all clearly heard Mom whisper to Rebecca, 'It's all right, don't be scared.'

Dad turned to me. 'Alex, go to your room. And take Kevin with you. I've got important things to talk over with the police.'

Kevin stubbornly slapped his feet across the living-room floor as he followed me to my bedroom. From behind the door we listened but couldn't really hear anything.

'Did you see their guns?' whispered Kevin.

'*Ja*, those are 9-mils, standard police issue,' I said confidently. I wasn't exactly sure if that was true but it sounded cool, like something you'd hear in a movie.

42

Kevin looked impressed. He nodded casually. '*Ja*, that's what I thought.'

'No, you didn't. You don't know anything about guns.'

'Yes, I do, those are 9-mils guns.'

'You're just saying that 'cause you heard me say that.'

'No, I amn't!'

The door opened and we both turned round. 'Alex,' said Mom, 'they need to speak to you, son.'

I had been expecting this. I would have to keep my face free of confusion. Raise my eyebrows so I looked open and willing to help. I didn't need to practise what I was going to say, the story had been told over and over all afternoon. I sat down on the settee next to Mom. Kevin stood next to the sofa, staring at the guns.

'Alex,' she said, looking into my eyes, 'these officers need to ask you a few questions about this afternoon. You don't need to be shy, just tell the truth.'

The truth.

Lying to the police would be easy. I didn't even know their names. They wanted to hear a story and I could tell it. I lied to Kevin so he knew what was going on and it kept him out of Dad's way. I didn't need to lie to Dad, and because he'd lied to Mom I didn't think I'd have to. But here she was asking me for the truth. And not to give her that felt terrible. It meant she wasn't on our side, she was left out. I wanted to have her with us, part of the plan, part of the fun. But that would mean telling the police. I tried to imagine what would happen if I sat here in the living room and told the police everything. What would they think of Dad? What would they do to him? What would Dad do to me?

'What did you see when you came out of the video shop?' said the older policeman.

The question had two possible answers, the truth or something else. Mom put her hand on my leg and squeezed my knee.

'Don't be afraid, Alex, tell them exactly what you saw,' she said.

I wanted to tell them. Maybe they all knew the truth already and this was a test, sort of, to see how I'd react. Dad looked directly at the younger policeman, offering me no clues about how to deal with this. But the way Mom smiled made me feel that maybe the truth would be OK.

'The car,' I said.

The words came out quietly and uncertain. Dad sat straighter, glaring at me as if I'd just sworn in front of guests. Mom too paused, she pulled back my shoulder and tried to look at my face. The policemen's eyes shifted from my face to Mom's to Dad's. I guess I'd said the one thing no one wanted to hear. And now, all these adults were staring at me, waiting for me to say something else, something believable.

I got this shaky feeling that I would be punished and not just the belt, something really, really bad. Dad could get in trouble too. Maybe the police would pull out their guns and point them at us, and it would all be my fault. This was the one moment my family depended on me and I was letting them down.

'The car . . . was gone,' I said, able to breathe again. Dad smiled for a second, then forced his face back into a serious frown. The younger policeman looked down at his notes and continued calmly with the questions. Mom relaxed back into the sofa, saying, 'Well done, Alex. See, that wasn't so bad.'

'Did you notice anyone hanging around the car when you went into the video shop?' continued the older policeman.

I glanced at the Chuck Norris video and Dad's three favourite cassettes lying on the coffee table, right in front of everyone.

'Yes,' I said confidently. 'I saw two black guys.'

'Can you remember what they looked like?' asked the younger policeman.

'No,' I said.

The answer came easier this time. It felt good to say the right thing.

Avocado

Mom sat at her desk, arms folded, looking out the window. She told us she was doing the bills. She said it was important. Kevin and I were not to disturb her.

Mom didn't believe in having closed doors in her house. At night she locked the front and back door but inside everything had to be open. The only time she ever closed a door was when she went to the bathroom. She tried to make Dad, Kevin and me shut the door if we took a quick pee but by the time she had finished shouting we were done.

Today her bedroom door was almost completely shut. Almost. There was just enough room for me to place my cheek against the wall and spy on her. I quietly watched her sitting. Her elbows rested heavily on the desk, her neck sunk into her shoulders. Now and again she would breathe in sharply and sit up a little straighter, then rest her chin on her hand.

When I came back an hour later she was in the same position.

Kevin wanted to look too.

'You can only look if you promise to be completely silent,' I whispered.

He promised.

Holding on to the door frame, he leaned forward and peeped inside. He stared at her for so long I began to get worried she might catch us spying on her. I tapped Kevin on the shoulder and signalled for him to move away.

'What's Mom doing?' whispered Kevin, showing me his thinking wrinkle.

I shrugged.

Kevin went to take another look but Mom was standing right behind the door. I froze, bracing myself for her to start screaming at us, but she said nothing. Her eyes were bloodshot as if she had been crying. Kevin blinked and tucked his hands behind his back. Mom made a gulping noise as if holding something down, then she stormed through the living room and out the back door. We raced over to the sliding doors and pressed our noses against the glass to see what she was going to do next. She marched along the slate path from the house and disappeared into the garage. We waited. My breath steamed up the glass, so I moved over a bit to see properly. Mom appeared, carrying the pick and spade. She paused, right in the middle of the lawn. Pressing down on the spade with her foot, she overturned a big clump of grass. I could see worms wriggling in the brick-red dirt. She scooped out a few more spadefuls of earth, then grabbed the pick and began hacking at the ground.

Mom usually spent a lot of time in the garden. It was her place. She kept the bushes neat and watered the flowers all by herself. But today it looked as though she was going to destroy everything.

Kevin flopped down on the couch. Dad came out of the bathroom with a towel round his waist and sat down on his favourite chair. He looked pink and drowsy from his hot bath. There were tiny dots of blood on his neck where he had cut himself shaving and he smelled of deodorant. He leaned forward till his belly squashed into three rolls of fat, then crossed his legs and began cutting his toenails. From where I was standing I could see right up his towel, so I went and sat next to Kevin.

'Dad, do you think Mom's OK?' I said.

The nail clippers snapped shut. Dad searched for the stray clipping and placed it onto the little pile he was gathering. He glanced out of the window and sniffed back some phlegm.

'You'll learn that women are full of awkwardness,' said Dad. 'Half the time they don't even know what they're all worked up about. It's best to leave Mom alone till she works it out of her system.' He switched feet and began trimming a rough bit of skin on his big toe.

After about two hours I went out to see her. The front stoop was so hot I had to run across it and cool my bare feet on the grass.

46

Mom hacked at the ground, loosening stones and grit so she could scoop it up with the spade. There were huge patches of sweat on the back of her dress and under her arms. When she leaned forward I noticed the dust between her breasts had turned into a thin layer of slimy mud.

'What you doing, Mom?'

'Planting an avo tree,' she said, tossing the soil to one side.

She didn't own an avocado tree. She hadn't even mentioned one before. The hole she stood in was big enough to bury Kevin up to his neck.

'Can I get you some juice?'

'Can't you see I'm busy right now?' She didn't look up.

I walked round to the back of the house and picked up my bike.

I cycled along the flat empty streets. Heat wavered and appeared as puddles in the distance. A plastic smell rose off the baking tar. Dogs lay under parked cars and didn't bother to bark as I passed. If I kept pedalling there was just enough breeze to make things bearable. I went out to the rugby fields. Flat, lush, open fields of nothing. This was my favourite place, my secret place. Out in the middle of the field, under a cloudless sky, the world divided into green and blue. I lay on my back and kept very still. I stayed like that till I could feel the earth rotating. It was a dizzy, falling-over-backwards kind of feeling, which meant I was spinning too. Then I tried to imagine floating high above the world but for some reason I couldn't picture it today. I kept thinking of Mom digging, sinking deeper and deeper into the orange mud of the garden.

The sun was setting when I got back and Mom was still digging. She stood waist-deep in the ground, scraping at the sides of the hole with the spade. The mounds of stony dirt next to the pit were almost as tall as Kevin. Male hoopoe birds, with their little brown Mohawk haircuts, hopped across the upturned ground looking for grubs.

'Hi, Sonny-o. Where have you been?' said Mom.

'I was just out on my bike for a while.'

Mom stood with hands on hips assessing the pit she was in. Her mood had changed.

'Give me a hand up, will you,' she said.

I squatted down and tried to grab her wrist but she crawled out of the ditch herself, which didn't make any sense. Why ask for my help if she didn't need it?

Mom followed me into the kitchen and drank some cold water from the fridge and washed her hands.

Dad was opening two huge family-size pizza boxes. He placed them on the table and put out a plate for each of us. Dad never ever did anything in the kitchen. I must have been staring because he said, 'Well, what are you waiting for? A golden invitation? Sit down. Tuck in.'

Kevin pushed past me and sat down. I sat next to him, watching Mom and Dad stand with their backs to each other. She washed her hands over the sink. He fiddled in the cutlery drawer.

Mom sat down at the table and showed us the blisters on her hands.

'Does it hurt?' asked Kevin.

'No, Kettle,' she said, touching his hair. 'It just shows I've been constructive. Next week, I'm going to buy a big avocado tree and plant it in that hole outside. We could do it together as a family.'

'I'll help,' said Kevin, through a mouthful of pizza.

'Thank you, Kettle, that's very kind. I've always been able to count on you.'

Dad stood up and grabbed Mom's keys off the hook. 'I'm going for a drive,' he said, marching to the front door. He hesitated, turned round, came back to the table and quickly snatched another slice of pizza.

'I'll be back late,' he said, shutting the door behind him.

The three of us sat in silence. My stomach sucked in. The mushrooms on my pizza appeared limp and slimy, making me nauseous.

'Why don't we finish these off in front of the TV,' said Mom.

We all stood up together as Mom closed the lids on the boxes. Kevin took his plate through and sat on the floor in front of the coffee table.

'Sonny-o, would you do me a favour and take some pizza to Rebecca for her dinner?' said Mom, placing three slices on a clean new plate.

I carried the plate out into the night and carefully walked round the edge of the pit as I made my way to the bottom of the garden.

'Rebecca. Can I come in?' I said, tapping on her door.

She opened the door only a bit and peeked out to see who it was.

'It's me. I've got your dinner.'

'Thank you, *baas*. Wait a minute, *baas*.'

She closed the door as I waited. When she opened it again I could see she was wearing her dressing gown, even though it was a hot night. She motioned for me to come in.

Her room smelled of boiling chicken. She was in the middle of watching *The Cosby Show* on her black-and-white TV. It was an older episode dubbed into Xhosa.

'Here you are,' I said, handing her the pizza slices.

The corners of her mouth dipped when she saw the food, but she politely said, 'Thank you, *baas*.'

The pizza went on the counter next to the electric hot plates.

'What are you cooking?' I said, pointing at the boiling pot.

'Is chicken.'

I nodded and looked about her room. The bed was up on bricks with boxes stored underneath. A thin net curtain was pulled in front of her clothes rail. Next to the TV was a picture of her son, Happy.

'If you want you can sit,' she said.

She only had one chair.

'Sit, sit,' she smiled.

Rebecca pulled out a plastic bottle crate from under her bed, turned it on its side, and sat next to me. We sat watching Bill Cosby trying to force his son to study harder at school. I liked the sound of Xhosa. It had lots of click-clock sounds, like trying to call a horse.

The adverts came on. Rebecca stood up and checked her boiling pot of food. She dished up for herself and put a little in a tin bowl for me.

'Eat,' she said, 'is good. Eat.'

The bowl was full of brown stew with chicken feet and potatoes. It tasted good, really good.

'Thanks, Rebecca,' I said. 'This is really nice.' I picked out a foot and sucked off the flesh round the ankle.

'You like tea?' she asked.

'No, thanks.'

The show came back on and Bill Cosby was showing his youngest daughter how to dance. Rebecca dunked her bread in the stew and giggled as she chewed.

When I finished my food Rebecca reached to take my plate from me.

'It's OK. I can get it,' I said, standing up and putting my bowl next to the cold pizza. When I sat down Rebecca said, 'Missus Grace worked very hard today. She is OK?'

'I don't know,' I said. 'I think so.'

Rebecca nodded without saying anything else.

At the end of the show Mrs Cosby came out of the bathroom wearing a slinky nightdress which made Bill Cosby sit up in bed. He rolled his eyes and said something that made Rebecca laugh. She rocked back and forward, covering her teeth with her hand. I laughed too, without knowing why.

Envelope

Kevin kicked stones into the storm drain while he waited. I locked the front gate and we began the fifteen-minute walk to school.

Monday morning.

I dragged my feet. Thinking about the double period of Afrikaans first thing in the morning made me want to throw up. Every class was the same. We had to read a chapter about the brave Boers ambushing Red Coats and fighting the Zulus. We read all about the speeches they made, and how they thanked God for protecting them. It was so boring. Usually we had to write ten sentences about the Boers. Then Mrs van Zyl checked our sentences while we worked through our grammar books. But the worst part was the spelling test. The test made me feel ill. Kevin must have noticed because he said, 'Did you learn your spellings?'

'*Ja*, but I'm still gonna get jacks,' I said.

Mrs van Zyl gave us one on the hand for every word we got wrong. That was the rule. By the end of the week I had usually forgotten about it, but at the start of each week I had to force myself to accept it all over again.

'How many do you think you'll get today?' asked Kevin. The leather straps on his school bag rapped in time with each short step.

'I dunno.'

'How many did you get last week?'

'Four.'

'And the week before?'

'Seven.'

'Did it hurt?'

'What do you think, genius?'

Kevin picked up a stick and whacked the leaves off a bush. Twirling it round like a sword he said, 'Some boys say if you rub raw onions on your hands then it doesn't hurt so much.'

'I tried it. It doesn't work.'

'What about gloves, have you tried that?'

Kevin did his very best to keep a straight face, but little sniggers forced their way through his nose. Even though I didn't want to, I smiled.

'Very funny, dork face,' I said, punching him on the shoulder.

'Ow!' He staggered sideways. 'I was being serious. When she calls you to the front of the class you could say, "Just a minute, Mrs van Satan," then you put on Mom's old gardening gloves. While she's giving you jacks and jacks and jacks you'll be standing there like this,' Kevin held out his hands, palms up, tilting his head side to side. 'La la la la la,' he sang.

I couldn't help smiling. '*Ja*, if only it could be like that.'

At the junction, we waited for a break in the traffic and crossed. A boy the same height as Kevin weaved in between the cars selling newspapers. The front of his shoes were cut open, letting his toes stretch out and touch the tarmac.

'Hey, chiefs,' he shouted, waving happily at us.

'Hey,' we waved back.

We said the same thing to each other every morning. Sometimes, one of us gave him an apple from our packed lunches, but not today. This paper boy was our marker. Waving meant we were halfway. It was now just as far to school as it was to turn back.

A little further on, Kevin swung his stick over his head and clipped a few leaves off a tree. 'Alex, why do they call it jacks?' he said.

'I dunno.' I thought about it a bit more and tried a proper answer. 'Maybe because of the sound it makes.'

'So why don't they call it "whacks"? 'Cause when you swing a stick it goes *whooo* through the air and when it hits you it goes *ack*.'

'It's called jacks, that's its name,' I said, but his argument was better than mine.

'Listen.' Kevin swung his stick through the air like a baseball player. It snapped as it hit a tree trunk. 'See? *Whack*.'

'*Ja*, OK, but what about Mr Murray? He's got a thin cane

52

that makes a *vip* sound, like it's cutting the air. So why don't they call it vips?'

Kevin thought about this and nodded. 'OK, who would you rather get jacks from, Mr Truman or Crazy Coetzee?' he said.

'I've already had jacks from Mr Truman,' I said.

'Really, when?'

'A few months ago. He's got a paddle with holes drilled in it. I think he made it himself. I had to bend over in front of the whole RE class. When that paddle hit, the noise gave me such a fright I jumped straight up. So I got another one for moving.'

Kevin stared at me. 'How many did you get?'

'Four.'

'For what?'

'I can't remember any more, probably talking in class,' I said, being casual.

'Did you cry?' said Kevin.

I had Kevin hooked. Telling the story afterwards was the only good thing about getting jacks. 'I tried not to but I couldn't help it,' I said. 'Mr Truman let me go to the toilet for five minutes to wash my face. I checked out my butt in the mirror and it was covered in little blue polka dots, from the paddle.'

We turned the corner. Dead ahead, at the end of the street, were the red iron gates of Highveld Crescent Primary School.

'What about you, Kev? Would you rather get Mrs Swart or Clarky?'

Without hesitation he said, 'Clarky.'

'Why?'

''Cause he's rubbish at giving jacks. He uses an old table-tennis bat and if you hold out your hand like this,' he held his palm up with the fingers bent right back, 'then it's not even sore.'

'I've never had Clarky,' I said.

'I've got him for maths,' said Kevin, 'and he's always sniffing his fingernails.'

'His fingernails?' I echoed.

Kevin shrugged.

At the school gates I nodded goodbye to Kevin and went to stand with my registry class. Everyone was talking and shuffling about, but the moment Principal de Kock appeared every class immediately sorted themselves into lines, smallest in front, biggest at the back. Every morning I stood between the same two people. Behind me was Andy Benson with his greasy ginger hair and in front of me, blocking my view of the rest of my class, were the pigtails of Charlene Bozman. Everyone agreed that she was the third prettiest girl in the whole school, but I liked her a bit more than everyone else.

The principal waited till we were all silent. Clarky was the vice head so he got to raise the flag while we sang the South African national anthem. After some announcements were read out, we all picked up our school bags and followed our teacher, in line, to the classroom.

Charlene's hand brushed against my thigh. At first I thought she wasn't concentrating and had bumped me by mistake. Then she started walking slower, her pigtails getting right in my face. She reached back and tapped my leg. What the hell did she think she was doing? I was about to prod her in the back, but my eye caught something. Her arm curled round behind her and she flapped an envelope like a bird wagging its tail feathers. She wasn't mucking about at all. Her closeness was a signal. She was trying to give me a note, probably to pass on to one of her friends further down the line. It might even be for me. Either way, she was doing it secretly. So secretly I almost didn't notice. I looked up to see if our teacher was watching. She wasn't. She was leading the march straight down the corridor. Keeping my eyes on the bobbles in Charlene's hair, I reached for the letter. My thumb rested on the paper and my fingertips touched tender indents between her knuckles. She had the softest skin. Instead of snatching the note I hesitated, my hand stayed where it was and, for a second, she didn't pull away.

When she let go, I had to stop myself ripping it open. I slipped the note into my back pocket, but took it out again and put it down the deep front pocket where it would be safer and unlikely to fall out or have someone steal it. Mrs van Satan hated people walking with their hands in their pockets but I didn't want to let go of the note. I had to relax. If I didn't, I'd lose the note. I forced my fingers to release. Bit by bit, I slid my hand out of my pocket.

The line stopped outside the classroom and waited for the teacher to open the door. A yawn was growing in my neck. It wasn't even a real yawn, just an urge to open my mouth as wide as possible and breathe. I swallowed it and stared at the back of Charlene's head. The hair parted down the centre. Follicles spread to the left and right, held tight by a pair of ladybird bobbles, leaving a thin white line of scalp. I zoomed right in on a single loose hair which was free and exploring the air around her head. I wasn't certain, but it appeared to be curious about me. It swayed and danced right in front of my nose, enjoying my attention. I raised my hand, wanting to let this cute, playful little hair rest on my finger. At the last second I caught myself and deliberately shoved my hands behind my back.

We marched into the classroom and stood behind our desks. Mrs van Zyl dumped her bag on her desk and stood in front of the class. I ran my thumb over my pocket to make sure the note was still there.

'*Goeiemore, klass*,' she said. (Good morning, class.)

We returned the greeting in our usual sing-song sort of way. '*Goei-e-mo-re, me-vrou van-Zyl.*'

We sat down, careful not to scrape our seats along the tiles, and started the lesson.

If I read it, if I took it out just to look at it, there would be trouble. Too many times I've seen pupils caught passing notes. You'd get jacks for sure. But worse, you'd have to read it out in front of the class. I'd rather get jacks every day than read out my note. I didn't even know what it said. It probably wasn't even for me. Maybe it was a joke.

No. It was for me.

The way Charlene gave it to me meant it was only for me.

And I didn't want to share that with anyone. I needed to wait. I could do that.

'Thorne. Alex Thorne?' said Mrs van Zyl.

I sat up straight. She was glaring at me over the rims of her glasses. Her white hair was pulled back so tight it was hard to tell if she was really smiling.

'What?' I said.

Giggles rippled across the class.

'Not *what*. The proper response is *Present*. Or else I mark you absent for the day.' She shook her head and scribbled in the register.

'Sorry, miss,' I said.

She took off her glasses and huffed angrily through her nose. Her mouth was as thin as a paper cut. 'You see this ring?' she said, pointing at her hand. 'I am a *Mrs*, not a *Miss*.'

'Sorry, Mrs van Zyl,' I said.

It was a bad start. Now she'd be watching me all day. I kept my head down and did my work.

When the spelling test came it was tough.

'*Koeksister*,' said Mrs van Zyl.

All heads bowed as we wrote down the word in our jotters. Spelling this word was easy, and as I formed the letters I pictured the sweet, sticky, plaited dough of a *Koeksister* dipped in syrup, till I had to swallow the saliva gathered under my tongue.

'*Versigtig*,' came the next word.

I knew it meant *careful*. But did it start with F or V? I took a chance and went with V.

'*Naartjie*.'

Dad still called them tangerines. I said the word to myself, *naar-chee*. The first bit was easy. I wrote it the way it sounded. But the second bit had a J in it somewhere. I wrote *jie*.

'*Vyfde*.'

Crap. This meant one jack for sure. It was the Afrikaans word for fifth, but I had no idea how to spell it. I tried sounding it out, *fayf-ta*. There was probably a D at the end, but did it start with V or F? I gambled again.

All the way through the test I kept getting mixed up, using Vs instead of Ws and forgetting that the letter Y in Afrikaans sounded like A in English. The whole thing was a mess.

Mrs van Zyl called the first student to her desk while the rest of us carried on with our grammar books. It was Andy. He stood in front of her desk as she marked his spelling test. Andy wasn't even born here. His family came from England. His spelling was worse than mine.

'Only six this week, Andy,' said Mrs van Zyl.

He held out both hands, palms up. Mrs van Satan lifted the thick wooden porridge spoon and hit him three times on each hand. Andy went back to his desk, rubbing his hands on his thighs and breathing hard. No one looked up from their books. The teacher called the next student, an Afrikaans girl who was at our school because her mother was Lebanese and only spoke English. Her book got marked and she went back to her desk without a word.

Next was Charlene. She stood at the teacher's desk with her hands behind her back. If she was nervous she didn't show it.

'Not bad, Charlene, only two this time,' said Mrs van Zyl.

On each hit Charlene twitched and sucked in air through her teeth. She picked up her jotter and went back to her seat, clenching her lips together to keep back the tears. When she sat down she looked at me for a tiny moment, then turned away.

I hated Mrs van Satan. What a bitch. If Dad was here he'd probably pick up that wooden spoon and smack her fat arse.

The next pupil was called and then the next. I had to wait till she got towards the end of the alphabet before she called my name. I looked over at Charlene, keeping my head low. She sat bent over her desk, pretending to work. When she thought no one was looking she licked her hand and blew on it. This was an old trick; it was supposed to cool your hand and take away the pain but it didn't work. Nothing worked. If I could, I would have taken her jacks for her. Perhaps I should tell her that at break time? But I wasn't sure if that would be a stupid thing to say to a girl.

'Alex,' said Mrs van Zyl.

I took my book to her desk and watched her mark each word. For the first time, I noticed that she didn't have eyebrows. There was no hair, just a black semicircle drawn above each eye.

'Your handwriting is so bad I can hardly read it,' she said. 'Is that supposed to be a V or a W?' Her little eyes pinched close together making her head look bigger. She wasn't giving me any clues. I'd guess wrong anyway.

I stood up straight. 'It's the letter W,' I said, hoping Charlene would see how confident I was.

'Well, if it's a W then it's obviously wrong, isn't it?' she said, arching her non-eyebrows. 'That's six this week.'

I clenched every muscle, making my body steel, and took my punishment without flinching. On my way back to my desk I glanced at Charlene but she kept her head huddled over her book.

At ten o'clock the bell rang.

'Quietly,' shouted Mrs van Zyl. 'Pack your bags.' She stood with her hand on the door handle till we were all standing at our desks, ready to leave.

'I will see you again on Thursday morning,' she said, pulling in her chin till the bun on the back of her head made her appear two inches taller. 'In the meantime I suggest you spend more time studying.' She opened the door.

There was five minutes before I had to be in maths. I zigzagged through the pupils who swarmed the corridor on their way to their next class. Running to the boys' toilet, I went into a cubicle and locked it. The note was still in my pocket. On the front of the envelope was my name written in a girl's handwriting and underlined four times, each line shorter than the one before.

The back had been licked closed. I carefully opened it, trying not to tear it too much, and pulled out a single sky-blue sheet of paper.

```
                              168 Bronkhorst St
                              Groenkloof
                              Pretoria
                              19 November 1987

    Dear   Alex Thorne

        I would be delighted if you could come to my
          Birthday Party

        on    Friday 24th of November 1987

        at    4 o'clock

    Special comments: We are having a braai and watching
    a video. Please don't tell everyone at school because I
    only invited 20 people. Thanx.

              Please RSVP (or just tell me at school)

    Yours truly,
                              Charlene Bozman XXX
```

I read it twice. What did RSVP stand for? It sounded very sophisticated and it meant I had to tell her something. Maybe Mom knew what it meant. The three Xs were the bit my eye stared at the longest. Did this mean she really liked me or was that just a fancy girlie way of signing her name? It didn't feel fancy. It felt like a code, a secret message to me. She had never even spoken to me before, she was just some girl in my class. But now this. I was one of the twenty people she most wanted at her party. Why? Was she in love with me?

Barefoot

Me, Vim and Kevin cycled the eight blocks from the shopping centre to our house. Along the main road we kept on the pavement, but once we turned into our neighbourhood the streets were quiet. Our rolling tyres whispered across the tar. We passed a thatched-roofed house with a huge open lawn. The sprinklers were on. A white cat stalked around the spray towards a huge grey cactus. At the next house, the security gate and garage door opened via remote and a silver car turned into the driveway. Two small children jumped off their wooden jungle gym and ran to greet their father.

Vim cycled out ahead. Behind me, Kevin pedalled hard to keep up. I let go of my handlebars, spread my arms out and enjoyed the breeze tickling through my fingers.

Vim popped the front wheel into the air and calmly cruised down the road on his back wheel. He was the best at wheelies I'd ever seen. I once saw him wheelie the entire length of his street, his front wheel tilting from side to side for balance. He could even go round corners on one wheel.

All afternoon we had been practising wheelies in the car park outside the Pick 'n' Pay. Vim showed us how, but every time I tried my front wheel hardly left the ground. I kept putting my foot out for balance. But I soon figured out the secret – don't stand up! Vim never did. He sat back in the saddle and pressed down hard on the pedals. The momentum whipped the front end up automatically. All you had to do then was keep going till you lost your balance. The first time I tried it, I set a personal best distance of five parking spaces.

Kevin struggled, however. His bike was too big for him. He jerked the handlebars as hard as he could but his front wheel never got more than a few centimetres off the ground.

As we turned onto our street, I raced out ahead of Vim and swung into our driveway. The Passat stood propped up on a jack in the garage. Both back wheels lay on their sides and tools were scattered all across the garage floor. Dad's legs poked out from underneath the car. I slammed the brakes, leaving a snaking black tyre skid on the concrete, and swerved onto the lawn to avoid Dad's shins.

Kevin arrived a few seconds later, jumping off his bike and letting it collapse to the ground.

A metal tool slipped and landed on the concrete under the car.

'Ow . . . son of bitch,' said Dad.

Vim didn't come into our yard. He sat on his bike looking back the way we had come.

'*Ek gaan kafee toe*,' he said, hoping not to disturb Dad. '*Kom julle saam?*' (I'm going to the corner shop. Are you coming?)

I glanced at my bedroom window, then over at Dad's legs. Would Dad be more irritated if we stayed and got in his way or if we were 'out gallivanting' all afternoon while he had to work? I climbed off my bike and gave Vim my answer.

'*Nie, ek dink nie so nie. Ek sal maar hier bly.*' (No, I don't think so. I'm going to stay here.)

Vim swung his bike around and cycled off down the street, waving a hand over his head. Leaning my bike against the garage, I waved goodbye.

'*Totsiens*, Vim,' shouted Kevin, walking towards the house. (Goodbye, Vim.)

Kevin pulled my T-shirt trying to get by. 'I've got first dibs on the water,' he said.

'No way,' I said. 'I was first home, I've got dibs.'

Kevin started running towards the back door, looking over his shoulder to see if I was chasing him.

'Kevin!' shouted Dad. 'Pick your bike up.'

Kevin slowed to a stroppy halt. His arms fell limp. He turned, rolled his eyes and sighed.

'I've told you not to leave your bike lying in the driveway!'

Dad studied Kevin's little tantrum for telltale signs of actual rebellion. Without making eye contact, Kevin stomped over, picked up his bike and shoved it next to mine.

Satisfied, Dad wiped the sweat from his forehead with the back of his wrist, aware that his hands were black with grease. He was wearing a white work T-shirt covered in black oil stains. The cut-off sleeves were used as rags. Dad turned his back on us and wiped his hands. We took our chance to get out of his sight and dashed towards the house and the ice-cold water in the fridge.

As we moved Dad said, 'Where are your shoes?'

We froze, standing at attention on the hot driveway.

Kevin's dirty toes curled up off the concrete. 'I left them in my room,' he said.

Dad sipped his can of beer and stepped out of the garage into the white-hot sunshine. His eyes narrowed into slits.

'Who's that kid you were with?'

This was a question for me. 'That's just Vim. He lives around the corner.'

I lifted one foot at a time, rubbing each burning sole up and down my shin.

'Vim? Sounds like toilet cleaner. Does he go to your school?'

'No,' said Kevin.

'But you're friends?'

'*Ja,*' I said.

'*Ja?*' Dad frowned, scrunching his beer can between his fists. 'Listen to yourself, boy. You're starting to sound like one of them.'

I kept quiet. Dad wasn't interested in an explanation. He turned back into the shade and flung the beer can into the bin. Kevin and I took the opportunity to jump onto the cool yellow lawn. Our movements were quick and precise as though having him see us move would make him angrier. I stood waiting, knowing Dad wasn't finished yet.

'I expected better from you, Alex. Your brother is a follower with nothing but shit between his ears. But you. You should know better.'

Sweat dribbled between my eyebrows and down the bridge of my nose. I couldn't figure out what I had done wrong. Dad only made us wear shoes into town, or to school. It was something more than just our bare feet.

'Listen to yourself,' said Dad, 'jabbering away in Afrikaans like you've forgotten how to speak properly.'

'But we have to learn Afrikaans at school.' The words came out without thinking. To disagree meant starting an argument.

'You're right,' he said, not mad at me, just thinking. 'Guess there's nothing I can do about the school system in this country. But that doesn't mean you have to *act* like some inbred Afrikaaner straight off the farm, walking around barefoot all day like an animal.'

He rubbed the stubble under his chin.

'It disappoints me, you know, to watch my own sons forget who they are, where they come from,' said Dad. 'Why can't you make English-speaking friends?'

'But what difference does it make?' The words popped out of my mouth as if someone else had said them.

Dad's head turned, trying to hear something he might have imagined. I stood rigid, expecting him to explode. Kevin's hands wrapped over his mouth but his eyes were delighted.

A sly grin worked into the corner of Dad's mouth. 'What difference does it make?' he said.

I blinked, surprised, not sure which way this was going.

'You're a chip off the old block, son, you know that?' said Dad, smiling and shaking his head. 'So, the young buck thinks he's tough enough to take on his old man, hey?'

He spread his arms like a wrestler and ran at me. He was just mucking about but it was better to get out of his way. I darted towards the house. I could hear his breath and his footsteps coming up fast behind me. An arm clamped around my legs in a rugby tackle. I crumpled to the lawn and tried crawling free from his sweaty, oily grip. His huge fingers dug into my ribs, tickling me, making me twist and squirm uncontrollably. We rolled around on the lawn with Kevin bouncing around hesitantly trying to join in. Somehow, I found myself on top of Dad and pinned his arms above his head.

'Ha ha! Beg for mercy,' I said, making a show of victory but knowing I could never actually win.

Dad just pushed. Even though I had him pinned and leaned on his arms with my whole weight, he just pushed. He lifted me right up and over. Within seconds our positions were reversed. He ripped out a handful of grass and tried to shove it in my mouth. I shook my head from side to side with my lips scrunched closed, refusing to let anything in. But Dad sat on my gut, knocking some wind out, my mouth opened and the grass went in.

'Victory!' he cheered, raising his arms above his head.

I spat out bits of grass and soil, struggling to breathe under his weight.

'And now, ladies and gentlemen,' said Dad, 'I will demonstrate the ancient art of grass torture on this puny, but deserving, little punk.'

Kevin – the traitor – kneeled next to my head, laughing at me.

'Nurse,' said Dad to Kevin, 'scalpel, please.'

'Right away, doctor,' chuckled Kevin. He plucked a long blade of grass and examined it, before handing it to Dad. I knew what was coming and twisted as violently as I could.

'No, no, no, no, no, no,' I said, but I couldn't help giggling.

Dad brought the blade of grass closer and closer like a dentist with a drill. He placed his palm over my forehead, and forced my head into position. Digging his right elbow into my ribs he held the single blade of grass, poised just above my nose.

'Now,' he said to me, 'if I remember correctly, you and I were having a discussion. But you decided to get cheeky.' His beery hot breath got right in my face.

'No, I wasn't being cheeky, I swear.'

'Wrong answer.'

The grass came closer and ever so delicately tickled my eyelid. It felt like a fly crawling over my face. I scrunched my eye closed and tried to break free.

'OK, OK, I was being cheeky,' I said, still full of the giggles. The lawn itched my back through my sweaty T-shirt.

'Good,' said Dad. 'Now we're getting somewhere. Next question. Who's the lord and master of the universe?'

I loved and hated this game. It all depended on who was holding the grass.

'Kevin's the master,' I said, determined not to give Dad anything for free.

'Wrong again.'

The grass went in my ear. It wriggled in deep, curling around in my brain and sending shivers down my spine.

I shrieked, scrunching my shoulder tight against my ear. 'I give in. Now get off me,' I said. 'I can't breathe, I can't breathe.'

'If you can talk, you can breathe,' he said. 'Now as I am your lord and master you have to do as I say. Will you continue to walk around barefoot and talk like an ignorant flat-head Afrikaaner?'

'What's wrong with bare feet?'

Dad grinned. 'You're not a fast learner, are you, boy?' he said, grabbing a fistful of my hair. 'I'll ask again. Do you promise to wear your shoes?' He forced my head to nod and spoke for me. 'Yeeesss, Daaaaad.'

'No, Dad,' I said.

His face, inches from mine, smiled. I was being difficult and for that I expected consequences. He headbutted me right between the eyes.

'Ow, what did you do that for?' I wasn't giggling any more.

'Say, "yes, Dad,"' he said, yanking my head forwards and back. The headbutt really hurt.

'Yes, Dad,' I said.

'Good. Next question. Am I going to catch you with that inbred lump of white trash? What's his name again?'

'Vim,' said Kevin.

'That's the one, Vim. What a stupid name.'

Dad peered into my face to see if I wanted another headbutt. I tried a diversion.

'But Vim's my friend, he's just—'

'Noooo, Daaaaad,' he said, speaking over me, forcing my head from side to side, 'I'll neeever seee Viiiim agaaaaaain.'

This wasn't funny any more.

'Ow, that hurts,' I said. But neither Dad nor Kevin seemed to hear me.

Kevin's face came into view over the top of my eyebrows. He looked at me with an odd expression that was hard to read with his features being all upside down.

'Dad,' he said, 'I think you should do the nose, now.'

'Good idea,' said Dad mischievously. 'He doesn't seem to be getting the message.'

'No, please. I'll be a good prisoner,' I said.

The blade of grass came closer. My toes twitched and contorted, then Dad shoved it straight up my nostril. Convulsions took over my whole body. Snorting hard to clear my nose, I covered my chin in snot. As I inhaled, I sniffed the grass all the way in till I could feel it stuck deep inside my head. Dad let go. Snorting, coughing and spitting, I shook my head trying to get it out. I clawed my finger up my nose but couldn't reach it. It caught the back of my throat, making my tongue poke out over my lower lip. Gagging, on the point of vomiting, I shuddered as the rubbery edges of the grass worked free and slipped to the floor in a puddle of gooey drool.

Kevin lay on his back and howled with laughter. 'That was so amazing!'

He tried to sit up but flopped back down, his body limp with hilarity.

'Ha ha ha! It went up your nose!' shrieked Kevin. 'And came out your mouth.'

'Shut up, dickhead!' I yelled as I wiped snot off my face.

'Hey! Watch your language,' said Dad, clipping the back of my head.

'Why can you swear and we can't?' I asked.

''Cause I'm big,' said Dad, 'that's why.'

Kevin laughed even louder, but it was forced. He was doing it because Dad backed him up. I wanted to scream at him but I locked up all those words inside me. Dad's manner was changing. He moved over towards the garage and checked the time on his watch. The game was over.

'OK, you two, go put some shoes on,' he said.

Still laughing, Kevin jumped up and ran into the house.

My legs itched from sweat and grass. Greeny-brown smudges stained my T-shirt. I got up and went inside.

From behind, Dad's voice called out, 'Alex. When you're done, bring me another beer.'

Knitting Machine

Monday, Wednesday and Friday nights meant English TV, proper TV. Shows from all over the world were broadcast exactly as they were meant to be, without being dubbed into Afrikaans. When shows like 'Buck Rogers' were dubbed, you could hear it was the same actor doing the voiceover for the goody and the baddie, which always annoyed me. But today was Monday and TV was worth the effort. I lay on the sofa watching the A-Team. Kevin sat on the floor making a fortress for his GI Joes out of a Kentucky Fried Chicken polystyrene bucket. In this episode the A-Team were trying to sneak onto a boat but to do that they needed scuba gear, so they turned to Faceman. Face put on a nice jacket, slicked back his hair and went to the nearest dive shop. Pouting and sad, he introduced himself to the pretty woman who owned the shop. He told her that he was a French magician. He looked deep into her eyes and said, 'Fantasy is my middle name.' But he told her that his emergency scuba gear had gone missing, making it impossible to do the final and most dangerous stunt of his magic show. The woman thought for a second, then said she felt lucky to have met him and offered him the gear for free. With a grin, Face walked out with two sets of scuba gear having not paid a penny.

All the way through the episode Kevin and I could hear the metallic breathing of Mom's knitting machine from her bedroom as she pulled the handle backward and forward and backward and forward.

Then a pause.

I imagined her threading a few needles or fiddling with a trapped strand of wool. While she stopped the TV sounded louder. Soon she started again, knitting another twenty rows, backward and forward.

The show ended with B. A. Baracus losing his temper and throwing Murdock into the water while everyone else laughed and shook their heads.

Next was the eight o'clock news. Some blacks had been arrested and a few shot because they were throwing stones at police vans, something about Mozambique, and Gary Player won at golf. It looked boring. Kevin leaned forward and turned it off.

'Alex, can I sleep in your room again tonight?'

'Why?'

'Just because,' he shrugged.

'I've got homework to do, so you can't pester me.'

I stood up and went through to Mom. I didn't bother to knock because I could hear her knitting. She swept the handle across hundreds of needles from left to right. Over and over, the hypnotic hum resonating off the walls. She hunched forward, the muscles in her back flexing with each sweep. Changing hands quickly without losing the rhythm, she kept working. From under the machine a long band of wool grew slowly to the ground. It looked like the front section of a jersey with blue and yellow stripes across the chest. Mom always did stripes, never plain. I had six jumpers in my wardrobe, all different colours, all stripes.

She stopped to unpick.

'Mom, we're going to bed now,' I said softly.

I could feel her smiling before she turned. 'OK, Sonny-o.'

'Kev's going to sleep in my room tonight.'

'Remind him to brush his teeth. I need to finish up here, then I'll come and say goodnight.'

68

I turned to go.

'Alex,' Mom said, turning in her chair, 'it's nice the way you look after your brother.'

I shrugged and waited at the door for a moment, trying to shape my question properly. 'Mom. Where's Dad?'

Her eyes jumped from her watch to the window to me.

'I don't . . . he's at work. He had to work late tonight. Late shift.' Glancing out towards the driveway, she tucked her fringe behind her ear. 'I'm sure he'll be back soon.' Her mouth smiled but her eyes didn't. She turned her back and carried on unpicking.

I closed the door behind me.

'Alex,' Mom shouted through the woodwork.

'*Ja?*' I called back.

'Make sure Kevin uses the good sleeping bag from the linen cupboard, it's quite cold tonight.'

'OK.'

Kevin sat in my room sellotaping super-hero cards into his catalogue. He was careful only to tape the top of each card onto the page; that way he could flip it up and read about each character on the reverse side. He had two new heroes, Wolverine and Ghost Rider. Mom said neither one of them looked like heroes to her.

'I had to swap eleven cards to get Wolverine,' he started, ''cause Wolverine is everyone's favourite. But now I've got him. I only need eight more heroes and—'

'Kev, you said you wouldn't bug me.'

He closed his mouth and I kept reading about the Dutch East India Trading Company. We had to read the whole chapter for history. As I read I could hear Kevin quietly counting his cards. He whispered each number to himself. I ignored him and focused on a paragraph about the first settlers. He started over, this time counting all the heroes. Then he started on the villains, piling them up as he counted.

'Kevin. I have to read this for tomorrow.'

'What?' he said. 'I was being quiet.'

I shook my head. 'Forget it. Go brush your teeth.'

While he was brushing I scanned the last two pages. No one planned to stay in Africa, they wanted to get to India. So they built a port in Cape Town as a halfway stop for the sailors. Simple. If I remembered that I would get through tomorrow's class.

Kevin turned off the light and crawled into the sleeping bag. After a few moments his voice broke the shadowy silence.

'Alex, why does everyone like Wolverine?'

'I dunno, because of his blades. He's just the coolest hero, I guess.'

'I like Mr Fantastic the best. He's like the dad of the Fantastic Four.'

'*Ja*,' I said, 'but his powers are stupid. He's bendy, that's it.'

'And he's clever. Don't forget. The card says he's even cleverer than Professor X. And his bending powers help him fly like a kite or he can suck in air and bounce. You can't even punch him 'cause he just goes soft.' Kevin thought for a moment. 'If I was a super-hero, I'd want to be Mr Fantastic, it would be so *lekker*.'

'I thought you liked Spider-Man,' I said.

'I do. I like Mr Fantastic first and Spider-Man second but they're both my equal favourites,' he explained. 'Who would you be if you were a hero?'

'I've always liked Iron Man.'

'Why?'

''Cause he doesn't have any powers. Think about it. He's an engineer who made this super armour-plated suit that can shoot lasers and has rocket boosters in the boots. That's it. And he once fought the Silver Surfer who has the power Cosmic.'

'But the Silver Surfer nearly killed him.'

'OK, but think about the courage he must have to fight immortal super villains wearing only a metal suit that he built in his own basement. He's the bravest hero of all. Once he puts on that suit you can't touch him, but most of the time he's just some guy.'

'I suppose so. He still has no powers.'

'You don't need any powers if you have that suit. And he's earned the respect of all the other heroes.'

In the dark, Kevin carefully thought over my views on Iron Man. After a while, he turned over on the floor. I could hear his breathing become heavier. On my back, I watched the shadows of the branches crawl along the wall. Sometimes it looked like faces, sometimes animals. Tonight I couldn't see anything, just dark shapes moving around my room. I rolled over and pulled the covers over my head. Kevin slept soundly, inhaling and exhaling deeply through his nose. I lay wide awake, wondering if Mom would come and say goodnight.

Jars

Kevin fetched the yellow bucket from the little stoop outside Rebecca's room and brought it up to the front yard where I was waiting for him. He squatted down and peered into the bucket.

'Will this do?' he said.

It was bigger than the margarine tub we had used before.

'This is perfect,' I said. 'There's no way they'll be able to climb out of this.'

We opened the garage door and stared at the glass jars. There were two rows of them, each one clouded with condensation from the heat and the lid screwed on tight. Mine were on the top shelf and Kevin's were on the middle shelf. We had been collecting for weeks. Any spider that Rebecca found crawling in the bathtub was carefully caught and kept in a jar. It wasn't only spiders. We had stink-bugs, wasps and fire ants, anything we could find. I had captured a green praying mantis and Kevin owned a scorpion that he found under a paving slab. He also had a red toad but it was disqualified for not being a bug.

After weeks of collecting, once all the jars were full, it was time for the Gogga Coliseum. We could have called it the Insect Coliseum but I liked the Afrikaans word. It sounded much more gruesome.

One by one we took each jar out of the garage, round the giant hole Mom had dug in the middle of the lawn, to a shaded spot of grass near the front door.

I arranged all my insects in order of size behind me. Kevin sat opposite me with his jars. Between us was the yellow bucket. Kevin liked to name his insects. His jars all had labels, like the *Mighty Razor Tooth* or *Blacky the Fearless*. He would whisper to them, giving them tips on how to handle the upcoming battle.

Kevin chose Conan the Incredible, a fat brown spider that had never before competed in the Coliseum. I went with a huge grasshopper. It wasn't an obvious choice but I was curious to see what happened. The grasshopper had a hard outer shell and sharp spikes along its powerful back legs. When you grabbed its head it would kick your fingers so hard you had to let go.

Kevin liked to do the commentary. 'That's Conan the Incredible about to crawl into the arena now, folks. He's looking mean and ready to rumble. His opponent today is . . .' Kevin stopped for a second and asked, 'What your *gogga*'s name?'

'He doesn't have one,' I said.

'Well, what do you want to call him?'

'I dunno.'

Kevin looked up to the left, twitching his thinking wrinkle. 'Today's contender is none other than Jiminy Cricket.'

'You can't call him that,' I said. 'He's a grasshopper.'

Kevin ignored me and went on with the commentary. 'That's right, folks, Jiminy Cricket wants to take a shot at the title.'

We threw both bugs into the bucket at the same time and waited to see what would happen. The grasshopper jumped right out of the bucket and hopped away. It was rubbish. What an embarrassment.

'And Jiminy Cricket has thrown in the towel! UN-BE-LIEVE-

ABLE. His manager had a lot riding on this fight and he's not going to be happy with the result.'

I knew what was coming to me. Even though Kevin was younger than me he could hit hard. Also, Kevin knew that when it came to my turn I was going to really thump him, so when he hit, he made sure.

A *lummie* was a punch on the arm. I could *lummie* Kevin's shoulder so hard his head jerked to one side. But worse than that was a *mousie*. If you aimed properly and got the sharpest part of your knuckle to hit the front of the shoulder, just where the arm joins the chest, then a little bump would form on the muscle like a tiny mouse under your skin. *Lummies* were bad but *mousies* killed you, you could barely lift your arm. Kevin always gave *mousies*.

I uncrossed my legs and knelt on the lawn. He stood up with a grin on his face. I didn't flinch or dodge or beg for mercy. I just had to take it. That was the rule. He gently put his fist against my shoulder taking aim, practising in slow motion exactly where he was going to land the punch. He wanted me to squirm, but I refused to look at him. Then he let me have it.

I scrunched one eye closed with the pain. I made it look worse than it was. I had rolled with it a little. He still got me, but not that good. And he knew it too. Next time though, he wouldn't be so eager. Kevin picked up the bucket and tossed the spider into the bushes.

I had to get him back, no more playing around. I had a daddy-long-legs, that's what we called it anyway. This spider had skinny spindly legs that arched out of its back, yet its whole body was no bigger than a guava pip. I had read in a spider book that it carried more venom than any other spider, but its jaws were too tiny to pierce through human skin. In the Gogga Coliseum it was unbeatable. I nearly went with him but decided to keep him back for a more crucial round. Instead, I picked up a jar and emptied a praying mantis into the bucket.

'You're sooooo dead,' I said.

'Ooooooh,' said Kevin, 'I'm sooooo scared.'

He turned around and selected a jar labelled *Stinger*. He opened the lid, careful not to get his fingers in the way. A small black scorpion slid out and plopped into the bucket.

'Round two in the Gogga Coliseum, and folks, I must say, this match-up is a real doozy.'

The scorpion crawled round the edge, dragging its tail along the ground. The praying mantis tilted her head like a wooden puppet, then cleaned her mouth with her long forearms.

'C'mon, Stinger! What do you think you're doing?' Kevin had switched from announcer to ringside manager. 'Don't be afraid of her, use your tail.'

He wiggled a twig in front of the scorpion, tapping it in the face. It grabbed the twig with one claw and the tail came up.

'That's it,' said Kevin. 'Now get her.'

He scooted the scorpion over to the other side of the arena. The praying mantis was ready. Her kung-fu fists attacked up and down like daggers. But the scorpion got in underneath her, jabbing her right in the chest.

'Yes!' screamed Kevin. He ran around, patting his mouth like an Indian chief.

The green mantis lay on her side, legs doing bicycle kicks in the air. And the scorpion went back to prowling around the edge of the yellow bucket.

I held my chin high, waiting for my punishment. Fair's fair. I didn't even try to call a foul. That scorpion was something else.

'I'm gonna get you good this time,' said Kevin, with an enormous smile on his face.

He went to hit the same shoulder as before.

'No. You have to hit the other shoulder,' I said.

'No way,' said Kevin. 'I want to get you on the same spot.'

'Yes way,' I said, standing up. 'You get to do the hitting, so I get to choose where.'

'That's not the rules.'

In the scuffle, Kevin bumped over the bucket.

'Oh, shit!' I shouted.

We jumped back and sprinted to the driveway, even though we had shoes on.

'Can you see it?' said Kevin.

'No.'

'If we don't find it we can never go on the grass again,' he said.

I scanned the grass from left to right.

'We'll have to tell Mom,' I said.

'Why?'

'Because what if she comes out here barefoot to water the garden?'

Kevin's eyes widened as he thought about it.

'We're not telling her anything,' he said. 'We'll find it. Keep looking.'

With hands on knees, the two of us stared at the lawn.

'I still can't see it,' said Kevin.

I thought I saw something move. 'What's that by your jars?'

We leaned closer. 'Nothing,' said Kevin.

Kevin looked at another spot, took a step forward and pointed. 'There it is.' He jumped on it with both heels, mashing it into the lawn. He stepped back and we examined the dent in the lawn. He got it. Half-buried it.

'Careful,' I said, 'the tail can still jab you after it's dead.'

'I'll just keep stomping it right into the ground,' said Kevin.

Knowing the scorpion was two inches under ground meant I could never sit on the grass again. I'd always imagine that segmented tail with its bulb full of venom poking up, waiting for my fleshy thigh.

'No. We should get rid of it properly, just in case,' I said. 'Keep your eye on it, Kev.'

I went into the garage and got one of Mom's gardening trowels. Outside, Kevin was standing still, staring at the ground. I bent down next to him and dug out the remains of Stinger, the champion gladiator.

'Let's bury him,' said Kevin.

I had a better idea. 'Let's burn him.'

'*Ja*! We could spray deodorant on him first and then set him on fire.'

'*Haai, wat maak julle?*' (What are you doing?)

I spun around. It was Vim. He had rested his bike against the fence and was about to open the gate. Vim loved burning stuff. I was about to tell him our plan when I remembered what Dad had said about him.

'None of your business,' I said.

I had promised Dad. He had made me promise, forced it out of me right here, right where I was standing. But it still counted. Dad would be furious if he found Vim in the yard with us.

Vim waited with his hand on the gate.

Sometimes friends just drifted apart. For a while you're best friends with someone and then you're not. For no reason. I hoped it could be like that with me and Vim. We wouldn't hate each other, but we would find new friends and do different things.

'You see, Vim, we have to do some stuff for our mom so . . . we'll see you later.' I tried to sound kind.

'Yous oaks don't look busy,' said Vim. He sounded so retarded when he spoke English, as though he had to think about each word.

I looked at the trowel in my hand, then at the jars all over the grass. I waited for a perfect excuse to unfold in my head.

'*Ons mag nie met jou praat nie,*' said Kevin. (We're not allowed to talk to you.)

Vim looked confused. '*Hoekom?*' (Why?)

'*Want jy's Afrikaans,*' said Kevin. (Because you're Afrikaans.)

That didn't seem to explain anything. Vim shrugged, waiting for the rest, the real reason. Kevin stuck out his chin and said, '*My pa het gese julle's mos almal platkop plaas apies.*' (My dad said you're all flat-headed farm monkeys.)

Vim let go of the gate. I couldn't believe Kevin said that. The veins in Vim's neck began to show. He flushed red. I expected him to scream at us, but he bit his lip. His eyes checked the living-room window to see if Dad was listening.

'*Ek sal jou moer!*' hissed Vim, his voice hoarse with aggression. (I'm going to fuck you up!)

Kevin stepped in behind me.

76

'Vim, it's not like that,' I began. 'Sometimes my dad says things . . .'

But he wasn't listening. He hocked up all the phlegm in his throat and spat a huge loogie at us. It was a beauty, all sticky gob with no excess spray. It came straight for us and landed in Mom's cactus, the one shaped like an octopus.

'*Blerrie rooinekke!*' yelled Vim, speeding away on his bike. (Bloody rednecks!)

I pointed the trowel at Kevin, holding the squashed scorpion up to his face.

'Why did you have to do that?'

'What? I only said what Dad said.'

I brought the scorpion right up to his mouth. 'I should shove this down your bloody throat.'

Kevin backed off and quickly batted the trowel out of my hand. For a second we both stepped back and watched it bounce, spotting exactly where the scorpion landed.

When he wasn't looking I lummied Kevin, hard.

'What was that for?'

I didn't answer.

'I'm telling Mom on you,' said Kevin.

I went into the house, into my bedroom, and locked my door.

Knuckles

We opened the front door. Dad glanced up from his ProNutro. His spoon hovered in front of his open mouth as he stared at Kevin's face.

'What the hell happened to you?' said Dad.

I paused. Dad was having breakfast in the afternoon. He must be back on night shift again.

'Where's Mom?' said Kevin.

'She's getting groceries. What happened to your eye?'

I chewed the rough skin under my thumbnail, waiting for Kevin. We'd shared a fragile silence walking home from school but here in front of Dad it was splintering. Kevin started snivelling. Sobs waited just under the surface, but he swallowed them, containing himself. He sucked air through his teeth and held it. He held it all together for one more breath.

Dad stood up. 'What's going on, Alex?'

I looked at my younger brother. Tears rolled down his cheeks as he stood rigid, defiant. Couldn't Dad see that now wasn't a good time? That he didn't want to talk about it? I answered so Kevin wouldn't have to, but the words felt like betrayal.

'Kevin was in a fight after school.'

The atmosphere in the living room held the strain for one more second, then it shattered.

'Just leave me alone!' screamed Kevin, shoving past me and running to his bedroom.

Dad's face showed nothing. He picked up his coffee, took a sip, and stared at the slammed-shut bedroom door.

'Is he OK?'

'I think so,' I said, knowing Kevin wasn't fine at all.

Dad gulped the rest of his coffee and went through to Kevin. Kicking off my school shoes, I followed, waiting outside Kevin's room, with my back against the wall, listening.

'Kevin, son,' said Dad, 'come on now, sit up.' I imagined Dad sitting on the bed rubbing Kevin's back. 'Let me see your face.'

Muffled broken sobs came from within a pillow.

'It's OK, boy,' came Dad's voice. 'You're fine. C'mon, be brave. Look at me.'

The sniffs became clearer as Kevin sat up.

'Yeah, that's a doozy! Looks like you'll have a nice black eye in the morning. I've had my share of shiners too, you know. Did they get you anywhere else?'

'They . . .' Kevin snorted back watery snot, 'they kicked me in the tummy.'

I stood silent in my socks, straining to hear.

'Let's see. Lift your shirt . . . does that hurt?'

'Uh-uh.'

'No? Then you haven't broken any ribs, so you're fine.'

The tears started again, relief mixed with anger.

'OK, son, it's all over. C'mon, be brave. Why don't you change out of your school uniform, wash your face, and I'll get some ice for that eye.'

Dad's shoes moved towards the door. I dashed into my bedroom, pulled off my socks, and began changing out of my school uniform. As I took my shirt off I had a quick flash of Kevin throwing his bag at Darrel.

Out the window, I saw that Mom's car was gone. Tiny weeds forced themselves up through our concrete driveway. The water ran in the bathroom sink and I heard splashing as Kevin washed his face. I listened carefully, trying to gauge if he was still upset. Another flash – boys standing in a circle, kicking. Kevin lying on his side, his elbows over his face. Blinking, I pulled up my shorts.

In the kitchen Kevin was eating ice cream while holding a half-full bag of frozen carrots over his eye. He looked calmer but closed up.

Dad stood between the fridge and the sink with his arms folded. 'Put on your shoes,' he announced. Then he became very serious. 'It's about time the three of us went to the park.'

The park's yellow grass was freckled with green thorn patches. Dad sat on the middle swing. Kevin and I sat on either side of him. We sat still, not swinging. Kevin leaned forward, head tilted to one side, hiding his black eye. His chains were knotted, making his seat higher so his toes dangled six centimetres above the ground. The trench under his feet was filled with fine orange dust.

Flat wispy clouds sailed under heavier ones higher up. Rain

was coming. Without sunshine the colours of the roundabout were less vibrant. Wind pushed by us forming little tornadoes, picking up crisp packets and dried leaves, twirling them around and dropping them a few metres away. Mom called these dust devils because they suddenly appeared, messed things up, and vanished.

Ignoring the wind, Dad inspected the border of black grease around his fingernails. He picked at each one in turn, working along his right hand, then his left. When he had finished, his curled fingers lined up for a final inspection. Satisfied, he interlaced his hands and looked over at Kevin.

'So tell me again what happened.'

Kevin's head sank lower. He mumbled something into his shirt.

'Son, look at me when I'm talking to you. What happened to you today?'

'They were calling me stupid,' said Kevin.

'Who were?'

'Boys at school. Bigger boys.'

'So what did you do?'

Kevin didn't answer. I had seen him like this before. Sometimes he just stopped talking. No matter how badly he got punished he wouldn't say a word. Somebody had to say something.

'He swore at them,' I said. 'Then he threw his school bag at them. So they all started calling him names.'

The way it came out was wrong. I made it sound as though Kevin started it. I had betrayed him twice this afternoon but it was easier to deal with than silence so I kept on talking.

'Kevin ran at Darrel and pushed him over. Everyone cheered, "Fight, fight, fight." Darrel got up and punched Kevin in the face. They all started kicking him in the stomach. Then they ran away laughing.' I stumbled over the last bit as my mind replayed shameful echoes of laughter.

A dust devil rounded the climbing frame. It sucked up some twigs and twisted in the middle, like a dancer wiggling her hips, then disappeared.

Dad looked at me. He stared right at me, his eyebrows pinching together as he worked something out. I quickly thought over what I had just said. He wanted to know what happened and that's what happened, exactly that.

'You were there?' he said.

My insides went hollow. 'I sort of saw it from . . .'

'You were there and did nothing?' His eyes looked right into me. I couldn't blink. This was all about me now. This was what I got for telling on Kevin.

'Answer me, boy.'

'Yes, I . . . I was there.'

'I don't believe what I'm hearing.'

Dad swivelled and faced me directly. The chains on his swing crossed over, forming a large X above his head. The full fury of his eyes scalded me. I gazed down at my white takkies. The laces on the right were coming undone.

'Alex, listen to me and listen good, because I'm only going to say this once. Blood is thicker than water. Friends come and go but families stick together. Kevin is your family, your blood. Next time he's in a fight you damn well better come home bloody too. Do you hear me?'

I wanted to look at him, to show that I got the message, but I couldn't. Not straight in the eyes. I glanced up and through the edge of Dad's sunglasses. I glimpsed Kevin's face, distorted by the lenses.

'I said, do you hear me, damn it?'

'Yes, Dad.'

I expected him to keep shouting but he didn't. The three of us sat quietly for a moment. Dad scuffed the front of his black shoe through the dust.

It didn't seem fair that I would have to fight for Kevin. I felt bad for him but every time someone called him stupid he would just explode, start screaming and swearing. This started fights. It was as though he wanted it. What could I do? After summer I was going to high school and Kevin wouldn't have me around. If he learned to calm down, control his temper, then he wouldn't come home bruised.

81

Dad watched the trees across the park. The wind in the leaves sounded like river water rushing over rocks.

'You know,' he said, 'this problem at school isn't going to disappear.'

He wrapped his hand around his fist and squeezed, crunching his knuckles. The snapping sounds reminded me of loose marbles in a pocket.

'You boys are going to have to take charge of this situation.'

He stood up, took a few steps towards the slide, swivelled on his heel and faced us.

'Let's see you fight,' he said, folding his arms across his T-shirt.

Dad's chains swung gently between us. Kevin still hadn't looked up.

'I mean it. Stand up. Show me how you fight.'

Did he mean act out the fight from school or fight each other? I checked Dad's face for clues. All I got was the waiting expression. If neither of us did anything he would get really furious. I would have to get up, set an example. I straightened my legs and took a few short steps.

Kevin stuck out his chin and shook his head, wrestling inside himself. He'd been fighting all day and now he had to go one last round. He took a deep breath and hopped down from the swing.

'That's right. Now face each other.'

Blue and yellow bruises were growing across Kevin's nose and under his left eye. His arms hung limp and heavy as he shuffled nearer.

'Go on.'

I raised my fists. Kevin, as always, copied what I did. His eyes were glassy with tears. I decided to let him get the first few punches in to make it look fair.

'Good. Now hold it right there.' Dad came over and stood between us. 'Alex, look how open you are. Your feet are too close together. Your hands are blocking your vision and not giving you much protection.'

With the back of his hand he slapped my fists away and I stumbled backward, clumsy and off balance. Dad turned to Kevin.

'Right, son, I'm going to show you some moves. I don't want to hurt you so stay absolutely still.'

Kevin tucked his fists in under his chin.

Dad rolled his shoulders and weaved his head from side to side like a boxer. He danced about in front of Kevin, then suddenly stopped, as if someone had paused the video.

'Notice my feet,' he said, without moving. 'The left foot is forward and both legs are bent. My body is side on towards my opponent, giving him a narrower target to hit. Also, the left arm can jab . . .' his fist shot out and stopped inches from Kevin's nose, '. . . or block. And the right hand is always ready, looking for an opening, and then POW.' In slow motion he rotated his body, delivering an uppercut to Kevin's jaw.

'OK, Alex, you come and take Kevin's place.'

I took up my position. Left leg forward, left arm up and my right pulled back under my chin. It felt easier facing Dad. This was like a game.

'Good,' he said, 'now look at my eyes. Never, ever, turn your back on your enemy. Always watch the eyes, they give away secrets, they tell you what's about to happen.'

Reflecting the sky, Dad's sunglasses became miniature TV screens showing cloudy chaos. I couldn't see his eyes, only bad weather getting worse.

Dad said, 'Are you ready? OK, hit me.'

This felt stupid. It wasn't a real fight. I tried a jab, but my whole body felt awkward, feeble. He blocked it away easily and kicked me sideways behind in the knee. Both legs slipped out from under me. In mid-air I twisted frantically for balance. My elbow landed first, then my face, then the rest of me. I lay on the ground with dust in my mouth.

'What did I tell you? Focus on the eyes. Remember, this isn't boxing. There are *no rules!* Always take your opponent by surprise.'

I turned over onto my hands and knees and spat out a throatful of gritty gob, which turned black as it hit the ground.

'You OK?' Dad said. 'You look winded. You OK, son?'

'I'm fine.'

Dad helped me up and brushed me off.

'If you're winded there's a way to deal with that,' he said. 'You know how in kung fu movies the fighters always make shouting noises when they fight. That's good breathing technique. When they scream "HUT" that's them emptying their lungs quickly so they don't get winded. Look, I'll show you.'

His left hand rested on my shoulder, his other hand curled into a fist five centimetres from my stomach.

'Now, I want you to take a deep breath and hold it. Clench your stomach.'

As I breathed in he punched quickly, up towards my ribs. Everything inside closed up. There was no pain and no breath. I staggered back a few steps. I felt my face puff out. Legs crumpled to the floor. Little paper thorns pierced my T-shirt and dug into my back. Still no breath. The sky above looked like thick poisonous smoke. I felt as though I was sinking to the bottom of a pool. Inside me something wound tighter and tighter. My chest heaved up and down trying to breathe but it was like forcing a bicycle pump with your thumb over the valve.

'And that wasn't even a hard punch,' said Dad. 'See, that's all it takes. If your breathing isn't right you can forget about it.'

I was sure I was dying.

'You're OK, son. You're fine.' He grabbed my ankles and started pumping my knees towards my chest. 'Just relax. And breeeeaathe.'

The first breath felt sucked through a straw. My chest and neck burned for more air. Water rolled out of my eyes, down into my ears. Not tears of crying, tears of . . . I don't know what. As my ankles raised my lungs filled a little. Dad pushed my knees towards my chest and I exhaled automatically. The next breath came easier, then the next. After a few moments I felt a bit better.

'OK, you're fine. C'mon, on your feet.'

Dad placed his hand on my shoulder again and pointed his fist at my stomach. I was still breathing heavily, sucking in air and slowly letting it out.

'This time I want you to shoot all the air out of your lungs as soon as I hit. Shout "HUT". OK? After three. One, two, three!'

There was no time to think. 'Hut!' I said quickly.

He got me in exactly the same place. I clenched my stomach muscles but he was far too strong. This time it really hurt. I stumbled around with a desperate airless feeling in my chest. I opened my mouth expecting panicked gasping. Instead, fresh warm air rushed in. Bent over with my hands on my knees, a sharp pain like a stitch lodged below my ribs. But I could breathe. After a few deep breaths I felt better. Dad looked over, his eyebrows raised into question marks. I forced myself to stand straight, hands on hips, and nodded like everything was OK. I exhaled through puffed-out cheeks, ignoring the burning in my chest.

'Right, Kevin, it's your turn.'

Kevin checked my eyes. He was reading me, figuring out how much pain to expect. I did my nonchalant face, like it was nothing. He walked over and took up the fighting stance in front of Dad, keeping his little fists close to his chin.

'Remember, son, watch the eyes.'

A dust devil started up behind the swings. It sucked up sand and bus tickets, swirling higher and higher, dancing and twirling away from us, through the bars of the climbing frame, like a ghost walking through a wall. A plastic bag spun round and round, stuck to the dancer's foot. Then the bag lifted and hovered in the middle, becoming the dust devil's head. It turned to look at us and made straight for Kevin, dancing round him, teasing him and flicking leaves in his face. Kevin narrowed his eyes but refused to move. Dad reached over to grab the plastic bag and Kevin kicked him, right on the ankle.

'Ow. Fuck!' Dad hopped about, rubbing his foot. 'What the hell did you do that for?'

He limped off toward the slide swearing under his breath. The dust devil followed him, did a little jig, and shrank into the ground. A smile nudged the edge of Kevin's mouth.

'Why did you do that?' I whispered.

'I don't know . . . I thought the fight had started. Do you think he'll be mad at us?'

'What you did was dumb,' I said.

Dad came back towards us, trying to hide his limp. If he wasn't angry before he would be now.

'Kevin.'

Kevin jumped when he heard his name.

'This is just pretend. Damn it, boy, I'm trying to help you.' Dad's mouth was a flat line. He sighed hard through his nose. 'But you did the right thing so I'm not angry. Just give those bastards at school the same medicine you gave me.'

That smile now took full control of Kevin's face.

'Right, boys, we're not done yet. I've shown you how to stand and how to breathe. Next is reading the fight. There are two types. First is the hit-and-run. Bullies fight like this. One sneaky punch and then they back off. Second is the wrestling match. Serious brawls always end up rolling around on the floor. In these types of fights you need small effective techniques to give yourself the advantage.'

Dad took off his sunglasses and lay down on his back on a patch of dried grass without thorns.

'Kevin, come here and sit on my chest.'

Kevin straddled him, his knees on Dad's shoulders.

Dad said, 'This is how most fights end up, with the bigger boy usually on top where he can punch your face or spit on you or whatever. There isn't really any way to defend yourself in this situation, but sometimes the best form of defence is attack.'

Dad shoved his thumb into Kevin's mouth, pinched the cheek and pulled him over to the side. A squawking sound came out of Kevin. He stood up and looked at Dad the way he looked at those boys in the playground. That thumb must have tasted disgusting. Kevin's tongue poked in and out like a lizard's.

'If you do this fast enough it will take your opponent by surprise and they won't have time to bite you.' Dad rolled over into a kneeling position. 'Right, I've got something else to show you. Alex, get over here.'

My chest still burned. I didn't want to learn any more fighting tips.

Cautiously, I stepped forwards. He stood up, moved behind me and wrapped his arm around my neck, his other arm locked behind my head, pushing it forward.

Dad spoke the way a teacher talks to the class. 'This headlock is called a sleeper. It doesn't choke you. Look, there's enough space between the Adam's apple and the elbow to allow for breath. It's designed to knock your opponent out. If I squeeze just a little, my bicep and forearm start to press against the jugulars on either side of the neck. This stops blood flow to the brain and the person faints.'

He squeezed. The skin on my neck squashed up into my cheeks. My eyes bulged, blood rushed through my ears into my temples. Dad pushed my head forward, forcing my chin into my chest. I felt huge reserves of strength in his arm. My head was about to burst like a pimple. There was so much pressure. I sucked air through clenched teeth. I couldn't take any more but he squeezed tighter. My legs scrambled around, struggling to hold me. The ground started to go blurry. Smudges of green and yellow and grey were crawling in around the edges closer and closer, till only a small circle of colour was left, and then came the black. My hands panic-slapped at his shoulders. He let go and the colours came rushing back. Drowsy, light-headed, I flopped to the ground. A dry heave forced its way up my throat. I was definitely going to throw up. I sat in the dirt waiting for it but nothing came out. Dad carried on talking.

'You can't really kill someone with this move but if you get the headlock on one of those dicks in the playground, then hold on for all you're worth. He'll start kicking and screaming but you just keep that lock on tight. When he passes out you can kick the shit out of him.'

Dad brushed dry leaves off his T-shirt. First off the back and then off the front between the lettering that read, **I'm OK. God doesn't make junk!**

He stared at us for a long time. I guess he was planning what to teach us next but the two of us must have looked pathetic, because he said, 'That's enough for now. Let's go home and get something to eat.'

After supper, Kevin and Mom watched TV while Rebecca washed the dishes. I went into the bathroom and locked the door. It still hurt when I straightened up and my neck felt funny.

What Dad had taught us made a lot of sense. I was sure he knew what he was doing. I just hoped that when the time came I could be as tough as he was.

I stood in front of the mirror and practised, block, then punch. My chest hurt as I moved. I lifted my T-shirt to see where Dad had punched me. Four pinkish blue marks spread across the base of my breastbone where his knuckles had connected. They would be black in the morning.

Blue

I knocked.

Three polite taps.

No answer.

I opened the door and peeped inside. Kevin's desk was pushed up against his bed. He had taken off the mattress and propped it up against the desk. Over the whole structure he'd draped two blankets. Kevin had built himself a den. A feeble shelter in the middle of his room, like a squatter's shack from a township. His bedside lamp was on inside, glowing orange through the blankets. I could hear him breathing, probably absorbed in his trading cards.

If I asked to come in he would say no. So I said, 'What you up to, Kev?'

'Nothing,' came his voice from inside the den.

I lifted the corner of the blanket and crawled inside. With the lamp on the air felt humid and close. Kevin sat cross-legged, playing with a lump of plasticine. He rolled it into a ball, then pulled it apart, slowly. The putty stretched, threadlike and fragile, till the tension became unbearable and the ends dropped like two limp tails. He rolled up the bits and started again.

I kneeled in front of him. We were like two Indians in a tepee, not talking, not looking at each other, just sitting. I picked at a scab on my knee.

Since yesterday something felt different between us and I didn't know how to fix it. I should have helped him fight Darrel. And he probably blamed me for telling Dad but I had no choice. Still, saying sorry wasn't enough.

'Kevin, I've got something to show you.'

'What?'

'Come, I'll show you.'

'I don't want to go outside,' he said, turning his swollen eye away from me.

'It's a secret place. Only I know about it.'

He looked at me, unsure. Between his hands a thread of plasticine hung delicately, about to break.

'I'll show you if you want.'

We didn't tell Mom where we were going, just grabbed our bikes and left. I doubt she even noticed us leaving. All she did lately was water the plants and sit at her desk, gazing out the window.

Our bikes rolled along the streets, under the shadows of tall trees and past dogs barking behind gates. Kevin wore my baseball cap pulled low to hide his eye. Now and again he tilted his head back a little to see where he was going but mostly he watched his feet go round and round.

* * *

89

The grass on the rugby fields was too lush to cycle across so we pushed our bikes out into the centre of the field.

'This better not be the secret,' said Kevin.

I kept pushing my bike, careful not to kick the pedal with my shin. 'We're almost there,' I said.

In the centre of the field, I laid my bike down and looked back at Kevin. He shoved his bike out ahead of him and for a moment it seemed to come alive and move of its own free will, then it collapsed onto its side, dead.

'This isn't secret,' said Kevin. 'Everyone can see us.'

'That's why it's perfect. I come here all the time. Because it's out in the open no one suspects it's a secret.'

Kevin wasn't sure.

'Look, try this,' I said.

I lay down with the sun behind me. As I rested my head back onto the freshly cut grass a spasm of pain shot through the bruises on my chest. But once I relaxed the pain disappeared. The back of my eyelids turned yellow. Kevin's shadow moved across my face and he lay down beside me.

'Now, take your cap off,' I said. 'Open your eyes wide and position your head so that you can't see the goalposts or anything in the edge of your vision. Look straight into the sky. You're only allowed to see blue.'

'This is crap,' said Kevin.

'That's because you're doing it wrong.'

'I'm just looking at the sky, like you said.'

'You have to do it quietly or it doesn't work.'

We lay in silence, sandwiched between the green and the blue. Everything was silent and simple. There was either up or down, earth or sky, green or blue. I lay there for a minute, my mind as empty as the sky, letting the blue seep into me. An insect crawled along my shin, but flew away when I twitched my leg. Kevin sighed loudly.

'What are we doing here?' he said.

'I come here to get away from . . . everything,' I said.

'You fall asleep on the grass?'

'No,' I said, 'I come here to think, dorkface.'

After a moment, he asked, 'What do you think about?'

'Just stuff,' I said.

Coming out here always made me feel better but explaining to Kevin how it worked was a little more difficult. I tried anyway.

'Sometimes I imagine I'm flying up and up till I can see the whole city. I look down on myself and I'm just a speck in the middle of a rugby field with my bike lying next to me. Then I fly even higher, till I can see the whole country. The bottom of Africa shaped like an ugly nose, far away from important countries. The only thing close to us is water and more Africa.'

A grasshopper landed on my arm and began folding away its wings using its back legs. I flicked it off and carried on talking.

'Eventually I land on the moon and the earth looks like a blue-and-white ball. I'm just a teeny-weeny germ lying on that ball looking up at the sky. In fact, I'm not even looking *up*. If the world is a ball floating in space then there's no such thing as up or down or left or right. You just are where you are.'

'*Ja*, that's amazing, Alex,' said Kevin. 'Wow. Gee. I feel better already.'

'C'mon, Kev, don't you think that's amazing?'

'No. It's stupid.'

'Don't you get it? You and I are stuck here, on this blue ball in space, and we can't jump off. Gravity glues us to the ground. And if everything seems upside down, well, it probably is. 'Cause we're stuck to the bottom of the world.'

I wasn't sure I was making sense any more. Kevin gazed into the sky. I could hear him rip out handfuls of grass as he thought about what I said. He sat up and looked at me.

'I know what you're doing,' he said.

Strong emotions wrestled around inside him. I thought he was about to cry but he looked away and swallowed hard.

'You think you can make things better just because we came out to this stupid place and looked at the sky. Big deal. Tomorrow dickface Darrel and his friends will probably beat me up again and there's nothing that you or the whole of space can do about it.'

Kevin stood up and straightened the baseball cap.

'Kevin, I wasn't trying to . . .'

He didn't wait. He picked up his bike and tried to cycle off, but the grass was too thick. Sinews in his skinny legs strained as he leaned his full weight over each pedal. The bike quivered as he tried to keep balance.

I sat watching him struggle towards the road. Dad had said families stick together, but I did nothing to help Kevin. He was brave and it cost him a black eye, I didn't get hurt because I was chicken. Dad knew it, Kevin knew it and now I knew it. I was a chickenshit and that was the truth.

I picked up my bike. Gripping the handlebars, I jogged it across the fields, faster than Kevin who was still wobbling on his bike about three hundred metres ahead of me. By the time he got to the road I was right behind him.

Kevin ignored me.

I didn't say a word. No need to. There was no reason to apologise and no need for chitchat. Kevin cycled off down the road. I don't think he had any idea where he was going. But I followed him, keeping my bike next to his so it looked as though we were going somewhere together. We went out to the new housing development. There were no houses yet, only streets and veldt. The blue-grey tar was so smooth our bikes glided along with a soft hush. Each street was trimmed with a fresh, neat kerb. Running parallel to the street was a white concrete pavement. Future residents of this neighbourhood would walk their dogs along these pavements and small children would one day draw on them with chalk, but for now they were blank and waiting to be useful. There were no cars on these roads, no one around at all. Still, the shiny new road signs seriously declared their instructions.

STOP.

YIELD.

And my favourite, the red and black T for DEAD END.

A few of the signs had been used for target practice. One

STOP sign had been potholed by a shotgun and someone had dotted the I in YIELD with a single bullet hole.

People said this was going to be a posh neighbourhood. Rich, young couples were on their way. Already, some of the plots of veldt, the ones on the corner with the most land or the ones with the biggest trees, had a SOLD sign posted for all to see.

On the corner of each junction stood a tall post with the street names printed in smart black letters.

Doberman Drive.

Corgi Crescent.

Pointer Street.

In our neighbourhood all the streets were named after trees. Close to school it was all famous mountains.

We cycled to the end of a cul-de-sac called Jack Russell Gardens and left the tar to continue along a dusty red footpath. It was one of our favourite routes. The path wound between umbrella trees casting great arcs of shadow. It zigged and zagged between shrubs and blackjack bushes, rolled up and down over the uneven contours of the rocky veldt. Eventually the path lost its charm and straightened out across a flat treeless bit of nothingness.

Kevin stopped, got off his bike and let it crash to the ground. He glanced at me, then turned and stared out across the veldt, his eyes hidden under the black shadow of my baseball cap. He picked up a stick and strolled off, whacking anything in his path.

I let my bike fall onto a bush and followed him. Walking was quieter than cycling and the veldt seemed even more alive. Little brown grasshoppers jumped from reed to reed, keeping perfect camouflage. Fat green locusts flew past on frantic purple wings. Ants marched in line, each carrying a white speck of something in their jaws. Cicada beetles chimed from hidden lookouts. Wearing flip-flops, I took care with each step. I didn't want to disturb snakes or scrunch a blue-black beetle. Twisting my hips between thorn bushes to avoid scratched legs, I heard hammering echo out across the flatness.

Kevin stood next to an ant nest as tall as his thigh. It looked like a massive mud egg, half-buried in the ground. The nest had probably taken a few years to build and in the heat the mud had baked into a hard crust. Kevin beat it, repeatedly, with his stick. He hit the mound so hard his stick snapped in half. So he used what was left in his hand to poke the nest, trying to bore a hole into the top. It was tough work. He jabbed and scraped but after a few minutes he'd only made a hole the size of a ten-cent piece. A few bewildered black ants crawled out of the hole and wandered about lost, before returning back down into their familiar tunnels. I wiped my arm across my forehead and waited for him to stop. He dropped the stick, out of breath. His socks were covered in blackjack seeds that Mom would make him pluck out one by one when we got home.

Kevin climbed onto the nest and began kicking at the hole with his shoe. Flecks of dirt sprayed in my direction and I ducked round to the far side, shaking the dust out of my hair. When I looked again, a piece the size of a plate broke loose and crumbled off the side of the nest. Kevin jumped down and we both stood back and watched. In the broken section there were holes and tunnels just like in a slice of bread if you look very closely. Millions and millions of ants crawled in and out of the holes. The bigger black ants ran about in a frenzy, their little feelers twitching, trying to make sense of the devastation, trying to comprehend what was happening to their home. A few minutes ago their friends had been working in this section and now, nothing. Even worse was the sun, scorching the nest. They would all have to burrow deeper down while the workers tried to repair the damage. You could see them panic as they scampered over each other. Some ants looked lost, while the little white grubs just got on with their day as if nothing had happened.

The nest became a small volcano oozing black lava as billions of ants crawled down the outside of their home and spilled onto the ground. Kevin opened his fly and began pissing into the seething black hole. The ants went from frantic to hysterical. Urine turned the crusty tunnels into a muddy pulp, crushing and drowning thousands of little worker ants. The rest fled, panic-stricken. Kevin swayed at the hips as he fired at them.

'Die, you black scum,' he said, making machine-gun sounds, '*ta ta ta ta ta ta ta ta*'.

Eventually, he ran out of ammunition.

'Why did you do that?' I said.

'Dunno. I felt like it.'

'You know the whole nest might die?'

'So. What are you gonna do? Run and tell Dad?'

He pulled up his zip and marched away.

'You're such a dickhead, Kevin.'

Butter

Mom discovered she didn't have enough butter so she sent me out to get some. I got to the shop at 5.58 p.m.

'Bugger off, we're closed,' mumbled Mr Cupido with a cigarette bobbing between his lips.

I went straight to the fridge at the back, got a large block of butter and held it up for him to see.

'*Jislaaik*, boy. Are you *blerrie* deaf? I said we're—'

I slapped the exact change on the counter and left before he could finish his sentence. From my back pocket I pulled out a scrunched-up plastic bag, put the butter in the bag and looped it over the right handle of my bike.

The sway of the bike caused the butter to thump against the front wheel. It would bump, swing out, and smack back into the fork, sometimes brushing against the spokes. I tried wrapping the plastic bag around the handle but this made it difficult to control the bike and the bag began working itself loose. I stopped and tried something different. What if I held the bag in one hand and steered with the other? Cycling on the flat was unstable but going downhill was scary. Using only one set of brakes, I nearly crashed into a parked car as I went round a corner. My shoulder began to take cramp as I held out the bag. I tried switching hands. The bike drifted off the road. I quickly grabbed the handlebars as my legs splayed for balance, and pulled up onto the pavement for a rethink.

Directly in front of me, the sun looked like a pink grapefruit segment slipping below the horizon. Streaks of yellow and orange yawned across the sky. Everything facing the sun shimmered in gold. Entire sides of houses were gold. My skin was the colour of polished bronze.

My mind went back to the butter. Maybe if I wrapped the bag around the butter and tucked it into the back of my shorts, the elastic in my shorts would keep it in place. I lifted my T-shirt and shoved the block down the back of my pants.

'Hey! Look! He's playing with his bum!' someone laughed. That voice, I knew that voice. The jagged shape, the threat, the way it cut into my head like a police siren. I scanned left and right.

Darrel came flying towards me on his bike. With the sun setting behind him the features of his face were darkened, but I knew it was him. His hair whipped in the breeze and appeared to be on fire. His three little demon sidekicks pedalled furiously behind him. Darrel's BMX was black with red pads on the crossbar. It was the coolest bike in school. He rammed his front wheel next to mine, leaned over and gripped my handlebars in both hands.

I was trapped.

The demons circled the two of us, chanting.

'Al-licks sucks dicks. Al-licks sucks dicks. Al-licks sucks dicks.'

'Shut the fuck up,' I said to the littlest, but he just smiled at me. As long as they had Darrel they weren't scared of me.

'Why do you have your finger up your arse, Al-licks?' said Darrel, in his whiny white-trash accent.

'What?'

Darrel slapped me, a stinger across the neck.

96

'What have you got in your pants?' he said.

I was breathing hard through my nose. Anger twitched in my jawbone. 'It's butter,' I swallowed back the lump in my throat, 'for my mom.'

'Aaah. Al-licks is going to the shops for his mommy.'

They burst out laughing. Hypocritical little shit eaters. They all had mothers. I'd seen them unwrap their packed lunches, with their girlie yoghurts, eating sandwiches with the crusts cut off.

One of them snatched the butter from behind me and handed it to Darrel.

'So. You were shoving butter up your butt, Al-licks. Is that *lekker* for you, huh?'

He tossed the packet over his head. It flew for a second like a comet, the plastic bag rustling through the air. It landed without bouncing.

Darrel's eyes never left me. 'You're a sick fuck, you know that? Acting like a pervert in the middle of the street.'

The chanting started again.

'Al-licks sucks dicks. Al-licks sucks dicks. Al-licks sucks dicks . . .'

They wanted me to start something. A reaction. Kevin would have gone berserk by now but I didn't give them anything. I glared straight at Darrel, my eyes squinting in the fading sun.

'Al-licks sucks dicks. Al-licks sucks dicks . . .'

One of the demons tapped the back of my head. I turned to grab him and Darrel punched me right in the mouth.

I saw it coming. The silver watch on his arm glinting as it flew towards my face. I flinched backwards slightly. His small fist squashed into my cheek as though sinking into putty, nudging in neatly between my cheekbone and jaw, with a force barely enough to push my head back.

'Hey,' I said.

They cheered and whooped.

'That'll teach you, *moffie*,' shouted one of them.

'*Ja*, kaffir lover.'

And then they were gone. Cycling down the road behind me.

'Al-licks sucks dicks,' came Darrel's final taunt, as the others laughed.

My breath was short. My fists tight. Darrel was such a fuckwit. I hoped he got hit by a fucking bus on the way home.

'Those fuckers are gonna get their lights kicked out one day,' I whispered, 'I swear to God.' I brushed away irritating tears with the back of my wrist.

'Bastards.'

I breathed in deep, held it, and exhaled through my nose. My heart pounded the front of my chest. As my fists relaxed the anger dissipated. When I opened and closed my mouth, my teeth felt numb, but only a bit. I tongued the inside of my lip but there were no cuts. I felt fine actually. I was fine. Nothing hurt. I was fine.

The plastic bag with the butter was still there in the middle of the street and the sun had set, leaving a bruised sky. A dog started barking, its snout snapping at me through the panels of a wooden fence. I walked over to the plastic bag and peered inside. The wax paper had torn and half the block of butter was mashed. Oily blobs of yellow clung to the inside of the bag. Luckily it hadn't ripped so there was no grit mixed into the butter. Mom could still use it.

What would I tell Mom? Not the truth, that's for sure. She'd ask me if I was OK about a million times. I'd have to tell the story over and over. She'd ask if I knew who did this to me and then she'd want to have a talk to my teacher or worse, she'd want to visit Darrel's parents and sort this out. And then, when Dad came home, I'd have to tell him everything and explain why I didn't fight back or run or do anything except get humiliated. No, I wasn't going tell anyone. What difference would it make? There's nothing they could do, not really. And it's not like I was bleeding. I put two fingers inside my lip to make sure. They came out clean. No blood. It wasn't even a proper fight. It could have been much worse. Besides, if Dad got punched in the face I bet he wouldn't tell.

I started cycling the last few blocks home. The streetlights were on, holding back the gloomy dusk, decorating the roads of my suburb in cones of white light. As I cycled under each street-light my shadow – an elongated upside-down version of me on my bike – swept by and projected out into the darkness.

The taunts echoed in my head. Little whispers.

Al-licks sucks dicks . . . Al-licks sucks dicks . . . Al-licks sucks dicks . . .

Over and over I saw the fist coming at me. And what did I do? I said, 'Hey.' I didn't shout or swear. I didn't block. Instead, I said, 'Hey.' What an idiot! Dad showed me how to block a punch but when the moment came I just stood there like a spaz, and took it straight in the face. Even Kevin fought back. But I said, 'Hey,' like, 'Hey, watch where you're going,' or, 'Hey, is that a new haircut?'

By the time I got home the whole world was dark. I locked the front gate and parked my bike in the garage next to Kevin's. Not wanting to talk to anyone, I stood in the coolness, listening to the crickets sing. The stars looked too far away to be real.

Before I went in, I reminded myself of the plan.

1st. Don't tell Mom what happened.

2nd. Act casual as if nothing happened.

3rd. Make sure the TV is on to deflect attention away from myself.

4th. When Mom asks about the butter tell prepared story.

5th. Go to my room for the rest of the evening.

Inside, Kevin was helping Mom bake. He was scraping the gooey leftovers from a mixing bowl with his fingers and licking them clean. Mom was leaning over the oven. I put the butter on the kitchen counter and went through to switch on the TV. I knew Mom enjoyed watching the news from the kitchen while she cooked. It was a news item about England voting for more sanctions against South Africa. Mom seemed interested. Maybe she'd be so engrossed she wouldn't ask questions about the butter. It didn't work.

'Alex, what happened to the butter?' came her voice.

I had my answer prepared.

'Nothing happened to it.'

'Then why is it mashed?'

'I dropped it.'

I could feel her waiting for a further explanation. I faced her and sighed theatrically.

'I was riding along when this dog ran out and chased me. I got a fright, dropped the butter and cycled away. Then this man came out and called his dog back. He locked it behind the gate and picked up the butter, saying he was really sorry. I said it was OK, took the butter and came home. No big deal.'

I tried to tell the story as though I was bored. And in a way I was, I couldn't be bothered talking to anyone.

'Are you OK?' said Mom.

'I'm fine,' I said, 'just fine. Why do you keep asking me all these questions?'

Kevin looked up from the bowl, all four fingers in his mouth.

The last bit came out wrong. Now Mom would suspect something for sure. I didn't wait for her to answer. I went straight to my room and closed the door behind me.

Frisbee

Charlene's party was starting in twenty minutes and I was ready. I had my good jeans on. It was thirty-two degrees outside but I had to wear them. These jeans were so cool they even made my old takkies look good. Mom wanted me to wear a shirt, but there was no way I was wearing a shirt, I'd look like I was going to church or something. Instead, I had on my favourite yellow T-shirt, the one with the surfer on the back. As soon as Dad got home from work he was going to take me to her house – to Charlene's.

I waited silently on the sofa reading a Spider-Man comic. It was one of those episodes where Peter Parker had to take more photos to pay for college, and because he was working so much – taking pictures of himself as Spider-Man – Aunt May was getting upset because he was never at home. And Mary Jane thought he didn't love her any more because he kept disappearing for no reason. And Peter was depressed because he couldn't tell them who he really was. It was crap. There weren't even any baddies.

Mom stood in the kitchen with scissors in her hand. Flowers from the garden lay on the counter in front of her. She picked one up, snipped a bit off the stem, and put it to one side. The ones with longer stems she arranged in a vase, but some of the shorter ones she put to one side. Occasionally, she sipped from a mug of steaming hot rooibos tea. The whole house smelled of sweet tea and flowers.

I peered over the comic at Kevin, who was sitting at the coffee table playing draughts against himself. He moved a red disc and then the exact opposite black disc. Leaning over his elbows, he stared straight down at the board, analysing it. After a moment he made another move and mirrored it. He studied the board again. I knew exactly what he was doing. He wasn't playing a game, he was testing out a theory. If you copy every move your opponent makes, even if you can see a better move, do you gain an advantage? I had tried it myself. It was a cunning tactic to frustrate your opponent, but you soon became vulnerable. The other side would always be one step ahead. It usually worked out better to be your own man, even if you didn't know what you were doing.

Dad tooted the horn four times, his signature, but something sounded different. Kevin jumped up and ran outside to open the gate for him. I stood up and touched the invitation in my back pocket. Looking at it one last time, I double-checked that my name was still on it. The mysterious three X's after Charlene's

101

name stared back at me. I picked up her present and tucked it under my arm. It had taken me ages to find it and I knew she would absolutely love it. It was a proper glow-in-the-dark Frisbee, wrapped in a square shoebox from a pair of Dad's boots, so it didn't look like a Frisbee.

Kevin came running back into the living room. 'Come see! Dad's got a cool new car,' he said, pointing outside.

Dad came through the front door with a huge grin on his face and dumped his bag on the floor. His clothes were still dirty from work. The stench of engine grease and petrol fumes overwhelmed any trace of tea and flowers. Through the window I saw a shiny red VW Golf parked in the driveway.

'How did you afford that?' said Mom.

'Don't worry. It's all taken care of. The insurance money came through,' answered Dad.

'But where did you get the extra money? The insurance was only enough to . . .'

'Dear God, woman! Don't you ever stop? I *said* it is all taken care of!'

'Fine,' said Mom, folding her arms. 'But where's my car?'

Dad sighed. 'I left it at work. I can't drive two cars at once, can I? So tomorrow you'll have to come with me to work, so you can drive your car back home. Are we done yet? Any more questions?'

'You remember you promised to take Alex to his party tonight?' said Mom, turning around and going back to her flowers.

'Yes. I remember,' said Dad, as he went to the bathroom and closed the door. For a second the three of us stood listening to his stream of piss splash into the centre of the toilet bowl. I decided to wait outside by the car.

'Alex,' said Mom.

'*Ja?*'

'Sonny-o, I know you've already bought a gift for Charlene, but I put these together for you to give to her.'

She handed me a small bunch of flowers, each one a different colour. The stems were wrapped together in tin foil and fastened with elastic bands. I held them at arm's distance, not sure how to tell Mom she shouldn't have bothered. I already had the perfect gift.

'Women love flowers,' she said. 'These will make all the difference, trust me.'

I politely sniffed them. No girl I knew liked flowers. What was the point in them? You put them in a vase and they're dead in two days.

Something secret was going on in Mom's head. She reached out and touched my cheek, then quickly sipped tea to hide her smile.

'What's so funny?' I said.

'Nothing,' she said. 'You're just growing up so fast.'

I wished she wouldn't say that, it always made me feel like a little boy.

'Are we ready to go?' said Dad, bouncing the car keys in his hand. He didn't wait for an answer. I followed him out to the car, carrying my present in one hand and Mom's flowers in the other.

'Have a wonderful time, son,' said Mom.

'Dad, can I come with you?' called Kevin.

'No.'

Dad had a packet of purple grapes on the dashboard. Steering with one hand, he grabbed a small bunch, plucked each grape off with his teeth and tossed away the stalk. Every now and then he spat the pips out the window.

His new car was spotless. It smelled of furniture wax and new carpets. A Popeye figurine dangled from the rear-view mirror and in the centre of the steering wheel was a shiny silver VW emblem.

'Do you like it?' said Dad, stroking the dashboard. 'It's a Gti.'

'What does that mean?'

'Means it goes faster. It's nippy too, see,' he said, swaying the car from side to side. 'It's designed for the city, so you can get in and out with no hassle. This car is perfect for me.' He revved the engine and changed into fourth. The top of the gear stick was designed to look like a black golf ball. The dimples reminded me of his old car.

We went by house after house and I wondered what Charlene's place looked like. Maybe they were rich and had a pool? Maybe they had big dogs? Would her parents be there? They would have to be. I bet her mom was very smiley and always offered you more cake, but trying to imagine her dad made me nervous. What if he was in the army and watched me all the time? Or maybe he liked to shout and drink and we'd have to have the party in another room while he watched rugby on TV. What would he say to Dad? I suddenly couldn't breathe. Dad would have to meet her parents. The adults would all shake hands and smile and then they would want to watch me give the flowers to Charlene and they'd all think it's cute, or worse, Charlene's dad would glare at me because some little lover boy is giving his daughter flowers and Dad would see this and glare back at him and then all hell would break loose!

'So, is this chick hot?' mumbled Dad, through a mouthful of grapes.

I realised I was scrunching the flowers in my fist.

'Huh?'

'This girl, what's her name again?'

'Charlene.'

'Charlene. So, is she your new girlfriend?'

'Uh, I think so.'

Dad spat out two pips, one bouncing off the wing-mirror. 'Does she know she's your new girlfriend?'

'I dunno. Maybe.'

'But she's a looker, she's a babe, right?'

When I thought about Charlene, I pictured her hair. It drooped over her shoulder like soft butterscotch toffee. Sometimes I imagined her running slowly towards me. To me she was the most beautiful girl in school but at the same time she was also just herself, just regular.

'I guess so,' I said, shrugging my shoulders.

'You *guess* so.' Dad giggled to himself. 'Yeah, well, I suppose no one looks at the mantelpiece when they're poking the fire, right?'

'What?'

'Nothing,' said Dad. 'Forget it.' He leaned his head out the window and spat out a mouthful of pips. Then he said, 'What's the house number again?'

'168,' I said. We passed by number 94 and I had to think of something quickly.

'Uh, Dad, why don't you just drop me at the four-way stop. I can find it from there.'

He turned and studied me for a long time without keeping his eyes on the road.

'What are you saying, Alex? Suddenly you're ashamed of your old man, is that it?'

I needed a back-up excuse. 'No. It's just that . . . you're still in your work clothes and I know how you like to get washed after your shift.'

He gazed down at his stained jeans and steel-toecapped boots. Then he smiled the same way Mom had before I left.

'OK, I get it,' he said, as his dirty fingers reached for more grapes. 'This is a solo mission, right?'

'Right,' I nodded.

I waited, but he seemed happy to leave it at that. He stopped the car at number 160 and I got out. Dad leaned out the window. 'Alex, what time does this party end?'

'Nine o'clock.'

'OK, I'll fetch you then.' He winked and said, 'Have a good time, son.'

The way he winked made me nervous. 'OK, Dad,' I said.

He did a U-turn, and sped off.

I was by myself.

Up the street, cars crowded around the driveway as other parents dropped off their children for the party. I could see a boy slamming a car door and going into the house. It looked like one of my classmates, Justin, but he seemed different without his school uniform, and the gift he was carrying was massive.

The shoebox I was carrying would never match up. And these stupid flowers! Not only did they cost nothing but I'd have to give them to Charlene in front of everyone. No, these flowers were a dumb idea. I threw them into a neighbour's bushes and marched up to Charlene's house.

There was no fence around their property. The house was brown brick and took up the whole plot, as if the house itself was a security wall. A grey brick driveway spilled out on the street. Her front door was solid green and next to it was a window behind security bars. I figured she must have a garden behind the house, but there was no way I could slip round the back. I had to go through. I pushed the doorbell.

A woman with a glass of wine in her hand opened the door.

'Halloooooo. I'm Pam, Charlene's mom.' Her Afrikaans accent was a lot stronger than Charlene's.

'Nice to meet you, Auntie Pam,' I said, adding the 'Auntie' to be extra polite. 'I'm Alex.'

Auntie Pam turned her head and shouted into the other room, 'Charleeene! Another one's arrived.'

As I stepped inside a barefoot girl came bouncing along the carpet towards me. It was Charlene but there was something new. She didn't have pigtails. Her hair was pinned back under an Alice-band and hung loose around her shoulders. She ran full speed and stopped still right in front of me.

Looking at each other, we both got a little shy.

'Hi, Alex,' she said, grinning.

'Hi, Charlene,' I said.

'Is that for me?' she said, blushing a little.

I looked down at the disguised frisbee in my hands.

'Umm. *Ja.* Happy birthday,' I said.

'Thanks.' She took it carefully in both hands and skipped through to the dining room, putting it on the dresser next to a pile of other presents.

'I'm going to open them all later, but right now everyone's out the back.' Charlene grabbed my hand and led me into the living room full of fat comfy sofas. Her skin was cool and I liked

106

the way she just took my hand and didn't mind holding it. She opened the sliding glass doors and we stepped out into the sunshine flickering off the pool. There were people everywhere. Boys and girls my age were running around in their bathing costumes. The boys dive-bombed and the girls tried to hold the boys' heads underwater.

On the far side of the pool, smoke billowed out of the braai. The smell of steak twisted up into the air. A few adults sat on the patio smoking and chatting, with half-empty wineglasses safely tucked under their chairs. Everyone was barefoot. And, apart from the adults, everyone was swimming.

My jeans felt tight and sweaty against my legs.

A man with a belly hanging over his shorts walked up to me. I quickly let go of Charlene's hand.

'Alex, this is my dad,' said Charlene.

He stuck out his hand and smiled warmly. 'Nice to meet you, young man. My name's Charlie.'

'Nice to meet you, Uncle Charlie,' I said, shaking his hand.

'Don't be shy, huh, feel free to jump in the pool,' he said. He turned to Charlene. 'Why don't you fetch Alex a drink?'

'OK, Pa,' and she skipped off to the other side of the pool.

I stood in front of Uncle Charlie while he sipped his beer and thought of something to say.

'So, uh, are you a rugby man?' he said. 'You like the Boks, huh?'

'Not really.'

'Cricket more your thing?'

'No.'

'Don't you do any sport at school?'

If I lied I could too easily get caught out, Charlene would know. 'Not really,' I said, scratching an itchy spot behind my ear.

Thankfully Charlene arrived with two tall glasses. 'Here you go.'

'Well, it was nice chatting to you, Alex,' said Uncle Charlie. 'Just make yourself at home. The food will be ready just now.'

107

Charlene and I sat down on a bench, and sipped our drinks.

'Thanks for the drink,' I said. 'That was ... you're very kind.'

'You're welcome,' she said, with a warm smile.

As she drank through the straw I noticed little bumps on her forehead. She had tiny pimples hidden by make-up the same colour as her skin. I thought about what Dad had asked, if she was pretty or not. I sipped once more and casually looked at her again, her chin, her mouth, her nose. *Ja*, she was pretty. Definitely. Even with the pimples, she was really pretty.

'Alex, are you sure you don't want to swim?' she said.

'No, I'm fine. I don't really feel like it.'

'Did you forget your trunks?'

I stared at her, amazed at how well she guessed.

'Ah, no, I didn't forget, it's just that, well, I had a cold a few days ago and my mom thinks it's best I don't swim, in case the cold comes back.'

'Oh.'

'What about you? Why aren't you swimming?'

Her first reaction was to blush deep red and become too shy to look at me. She was struggling for the words to form her answer. With new courage she tucked her hair behind her neck and looked right at me. 'No reason,' she said. 'I just don't feel like swimming today. Would you like some more Sprite?'

I had flat-out lied, but she was doing something else. For some reason she'd deflected the question away.

Auntie Pam came out of the living room, looking left and right. She saw us and called, 'Charlene, come quick. That's Granny on the phone for you, she's calling from Cape Town.'

Charlene jumped up and ran into the house, leaving me with her mother.

'Aren't you going to swim?' she said.

I decided there was no point in lying. 'I didn't bring my trunks.'

'*Ag*, don't worry about that, you can swim in your underpants,' she said, taking a sip from the wineglass.

There was no way I would ever, ever, EVER, strip down to my underpants in front of all these people. It was better to stick to the lie. 'I had a cold, you see, so I'm not allowed to swim,' I said, trying to sound as final as possible.

'Well, suit yourself. Maybe you could play football with those boys,' she raised one eyebrow, 'unless of course you're too sick to play.'

Football sounded better than watching everyone else swim. I stood up and joined some boys who were kicking a ball against the back wall. Some of them I recognised from school but there were others here too. I guessed they were either Charlene's cousins or friends from church or something. John, from my class, smiled at me and said, 'Hey, Alex, when did you get here?'

'I just arrived.'

'*Lekker* party, hey?'

'*Ja*, it's cool,' I said.

We kicked the ball around for a while. It was so hot my feet swelled up inside my takkies. I couldn't move properly in my jeans, everything was stuck and tight. I kicked off my shoes and rolled up my trouser legs. Stretching my toes in the fresh spongy lawn revived me. When I ran to get the ball each movement was looser, more comfortable.

Soon Uncle Charlie announced that the braai was ready. Young people got out of the pool while the adults stood up, brushing biscuit crumbs off their laps, and made their way towards the picnic table. It was laid out with carrot and pineapple salad, fruit juice, chicken drumsticks, steaks, *boerewors* and potatoes wrapped in tin foil and baked in the fire. A queue formed. Charlene's dog went from person to person wagging his tail, hoping for bones. From the patio I watched Auntie Pam shriek with laughter. She held onto her friend's shoulder and laughed and laughed till she wiped away tears with her finger. This really was a *lekker* party.

I filled my paper plate with food and stood looking for a place to sit down.

'Alex,' called Charlene, waving her hand to get my attention. 'Over here! Come. Sit.'

She and some of her friends were sitting along the edge of the pool with their ankles dangling in the water. I went over and joined the end of the row, dipping my toes into the lukewarm water.

'Alex, this is my friend Rina,' said Charlene, pointing to the girl next to me, 'and that's her brother Andre. They're from Jo'burg.'

'Hi,' I said, looking from one face to the other, wanting to say more.

With a mouth full of food, Andre said, 'Nice T-shirt.'

'Thanks.'

We ate and joked, as shadows grew long across the lawn.

For dessert each of us was given a bowl of litchis. A game formed where you had to spit the pip straight up into the air and catch it again in your mouth. Most of us stumbled around the lawn with our heads tilted back and mouths open like hungry chicks. People fell about laughing and bumped heads and some tripped over each other trying to catch the pips. But when someone finally caught one the whole party cheered.

Auntie Pam clapped her hands above her head to get our attention. 'OK, everyone. If you all want to come inside we're going to have some birthday cake, and then Charlene is going to open her presents.'

People picked up their paper plates and a few boys pulled T-shirts over their heads. I found my shoes, scoffed a cold bit of leftover steak and hurried into the living room.

All the birthday presents had been arranged on the living-room carpet. Charlene kneeled in front of them and everyone got comfortable on the sofas and floor. Just behind Auntie Pam, Dad was leaning against the door frame, casually nibbling at a handful of crisps, watching Charlene open the first present. I blinked my eyes tight shut and when I opened them he was still there . . . here, in Charlene's house. He seemed quite relaxed, as though he was supposed to be at the party. He had washed and shaved and was wearing his red T-shirt with the white lettering, which read, **I do all my own stunts**. What was he *doing* here? Was there a problem at home? I looked around for a clock, but couldn't see one. It couldn't be time to go already, could it? With a raise of his eyebrows he signalled that we needed to chat in private. Stepping over people, I picked my way through the crowd and we went into the kitchen.

'Why the hell are you barefoot?' said Dad. He wasn't angry. It was a serious question.

'I was . . . we were playing football,' I said, looking at the shoes in my hand. 'What are you doing here? Is everything OK?'

'I'm here to rescue you,' said Dad.

'What? Why?'

'When I dropped you off I could tell this party was a dud. Shit, son, look at these bloody people.'

'What's wrong with them?'

'Nothing, if you like that sort of thing. But you've shown your face, you've been polite, now let's split. C'mon, I've got a surprise for you.'

They started singing 'Happy Birthday' and I turned my head towards the sound, wanting to be through there with everyone else.

'C'mon, Alex, we have to go.'

'But I haven't said goodbye.'

'They won't even know you've gone. We'll just slip out quietly,' he said.

'But if I leave without saying goodbye then Charlene will think . . .'

Dad rubbed his chin. 'OK, I get it. You don't want the girl-friend to think you ditched her.' His eyes became narrow. 'I can handle this,' he said, 'and put your bloody shoes on.'

Dad put his hands in his pockets and walked through to the living room. I hopped behind him, pulling a sock up over my ankle. As soon as he appeared in the doorway Auntie Pam said, 'Oh, hallooo.' All heads turned to face us.

Dad held up his hand as though stopping traffic. 'Sorry to interrupt, everyone, but Alex has to say an early goodbye.'

Charlene stood up, leaving a gift half open on the floor.

'Oh, no. Are you sure?' said Auntie Pam.

Then Uncle Charlie said, 'Is everything OK?'

'Well, I don't want to get into all the details but Alex's mother has taken a turn for the worse,' said Dad.

The whole room breathed in.

'It's nothing too serious, but I think it's best that we go. Sorry to disturb you folks.'

'No, no, don't be silly, of course you must go,' said Auntie Pam, who was now the spokesperson for the whole room. Charlene tried to look past Dad to see if I was OK.

'Thanks for being so understanding. I won't disturb your evening any more.'

That was it, checkmate. I couldn't prove he was lying and I couldn't stay because everyone would think I didn't care about my mother. I shoved my hands in my pockets and shuffled behind Dad to the front door. Auntie Pam put her hand on my shoulder.

Before I knew it I was in the car waving goodbye and speeding down the street.

'That was easy. You know, for a moment there I thought that woman was going to burst into tears,' smiled Dad. He leaned over and turned on the radio, surfing through static for a good song. 'Listen, Alex, they might send you a card at school. I shouldn't have to say this, but, if they do, obviously, don't show it to Mom.' Dad found a song and turned up the volume. As soon as he let go of the dial, I leaned over and switched it off. Dad frowned at me, all confused.

'I wanted to stay,' I said, hoping to sound furious but instead sounding sad. 'She hadn't even opened my present yet.'

'Well, there's no point moping about it now. What's done is done. It's in the past. I just thought it might be good for us to spend some time together. We could go out.'

I turned away and looked out the window. There was no point in trying to answer back.

'You're not going to give me the silent treatment, are you, Alex?'

I didn't answer.

'Fine. If you'd rather spend your time with a bunch of strangers I can always turn this car around and dump you back there.'

I didn't answer.

'Do you want me to turn this car around? 'Cause I'll do it, you know I will.'

He paused, daring me not to answer.

'No,' I said.

'So it's decided. But if you're coming with me put a smile on your dial. I don't want you spoiling my night because you're tripping over your bottom lip.'

He switched on the radio and turned it up loud.

I had no idea where we were going and I didn't care. I kept thinking about Charlene, replaying the part where she grabbed my hand. But now everything felt smashed to pieces. She'd never speak to me again. Or worse, she'd feel sorry for me. I imagined her at school in a huddle of friends all excited and talking about the party. How could I go up and talk to them? They'd probably ask me about my mother and I'd have to keep making up stories to cover my tracks. But if I didn't talk to them then they'd think I was all upset about Mom dying or something. One thing was certain, I could never invite anyone to my home. If they saw Mom looking healthy, they'd ask too many difficult questions.

We pulled in behind a long queue of cars making their way up to the ticket office. The heads of two actors, thirty metres high, silently mouthed to each other on the massive drive-in screen. I recognised it as an advert for OMO washing powder. The main feature hadn't started yet.

'Tonight is a Chuck Norris double bill,' said Dad excitedly. 'Pretty cool surprise, huh?'

I was in the mood to see Chuck Norris break someone's neck.

'Yeah, it's cool,' I said.

'You sound overjoyed,' said Dad.

The poster up ahead showed a badly hand-drawn picture of Chuck Norris, with tonight's titles underneath. *Silent Rage* and *Code of Silence.*

'Listen, Alex,' said Dad, 'they're both rated eighteen so if the manager sees you he won't let us in.'

There were three cars between us and the ticket booth. I climbed over the back of my seat and huddled into a tight ball on the floor between the seats. Dad threw his jacket over me and I waited in the darkness listening to the hum of the engine.

Dad whispered excitedly. 'We're almost there, son. Keep quiet and don't move a muscle.'

Fluorescent light from the ticket booth scanned through the car like a searchlight. My breath under the jacket felt stuffy against my face. I heard Dad roll down his window and say, 'One, please.'

I wondered if the man in the ticket booth was trying to peer into the back of the car. I couldn't hear what was happening. It sounded as though change was being counted and then dropped into Dad's outstretched hand. The car moved forward and I pulled the jacket off.

'Get your head down, you fool,' shouted Dad.

I slunk down immediately but didn't understand what the danger was.

'I thought we were clear,' I said.

'You know what Thought did? He shat a brick and thought his arse was square. Don't think, son.'

I pulled the jacket back over my head. The car rolled up and down like a boat on the waves as he drove over the humps looking for a decent parking spot. We stopped and reversed slightly to get a good view of the screen. Dad cut the engine and pulled up the handbrake.

'Are you going to spend all night down there?' joked Dad.

He pulled the jacket off and I wriggled out from my hiding spot. I sat on the back seat with my arms folded, refusing to look at him. Dad sighed and swore something under his breath as he got out and slammed the door.

Faces moved on the screen but there was no sound. So I climbed over to the front seat, wound down the window and hooked the speaker over the edge of the car door. The sound quality wasn't great but the crackling stopped if you didn't touch it. I switched on the radio and found the station that was broadcasting this drive-in's soundtrack. Dad got in as the first film was starting. He stuffed handfuls of popcorn into his face and slurped from his can of Coke. His eyes never left the screen.

In *Code of Silence*, Chuck was a detective. While on a bust one of his old buddies shot an unarmed black man by mistake. To cover his tracks the old cop planted a gun into the dead man's hand, while Chuck looked on. Things looked bad for the old cop, a few months from retirement and his badge was on the line. But it was worse for Chuck. He was torn between doing the right thing by reporting what he saw or breaking the special code of silence that exists among cops.

Chuck reported it to the chief. The old cop lost his badge and Chuck lost the respect of the entire police force. Later in the film, Chuck followed a lead to a big drug bust in an old warehouse. He called for back-up, but because he broke the code every cop turned off their radio and refused to help. So Chuck stole an experimental robot policeman and headed off to face the bad guys alone.

At the break, enormous cartoons ran across the screen. Some cars left and others tooted their horns for the next film to start. I still wasn't talking to Dad.

'While you're in the huff, I'm going to take a shit,' he said.

He got out and closed the door, then stared at me through the open window. I kept looking straight ahead.

'We're supposed to be having a good time, Alex. Think about that,' he said. 'When I get back, I expect you to have grown up a bit.'

On the screen, the Coyote painted a tunnel on the side of the mountain. The Roadrunner ran right through and out the other side. Coyote stared at the painted tunnel in open-mouthed disbelief when a truck sped through and ran him over.

Egg Sandwiches

Our backs rested against the criss-cross wire fence while traffic swished behind us. From under this tree we watched the whole playground.

Today was Wednesday. My last Wednesday here. It must have felt like a Monday for Kevin because he had stayed at home for two days. He said his stomach hurt, but I think it had more to do with Darrel. Everyone knows the last week of school is always the worst for fighting because teachers can't give you detention over the summer.

My watch said 11.10 a.m. Twenty minutes till break-time was over. Two hours and five minutes before the final bell rang and we could go home.

Kevin opened his Tupperware lunchbox and said, 'Hey, Alex, look.'

Inside wasn't the usual cheap brown bread with the wholewheat seeds in it. It was expensive white loaf, pre-sliced, with a soft crust. Between the slices was juicy egg mayonnaise. And instead of the usual banana Kevin got a mint Aero. He peered over and saw that I had the same, except I got a Star Bar instead of an Aero.

'Can we swap 'cause I don't really like mint,' said Kevin.

I handed over my lunch and let him take whatever he wanted. It was weird that Mom had gone to all this effort. Maybe it was a bribe to make Kevin come back to school for the last few days of term.

Near the teacher's car park, a couple of Standard Three girls twirled a rope while their friends chanted and skipped. Sitting near to them was the older group – Charlene and her friends. They gossiped and laughed but never looked this way. I hadn't spoken to Charlene since the party and she hadn't spoken to me. No one had. Everyone felt too sorry for me because they thought my mom was dying. But I couldn't say anything. There was nothing really to tell them, and the more I kept quiet, the more they left me alone.

Kevin licked the inside of the wrapper, unaware of the chocolate smudges on his chin and fingers. I ate my sandwich and watched Charlene's pigtails waltz and whip around her neck.

If I could have one superpower, I'd choose to be invisible. Then without anyone seeing me I'd go over there and sit with them. Just sit. I don't know why. It would be nice, better than sitting back here as far away from everyone as possible.

But I was dreaming. I could never go over and chat with them and by the end of the week I'd never see Charlene again. She was going to Girl's High and that would be the end of it.

Little by little the urge to be with Charlene changed into an urge to walk out the school gates and never come back.

'I'm going to the toilet,' I said.

Kevin sat counting his trading cards. He nodded but kept counting under his breath.

'I'll meet you back here, and we'll try and get some swaps.'

He nodded again.

His black eye was now yellow and the swelling had gone down. I scanned the playground again. It didn't feel like trouble. Halfway to the school building I looked back and saw Kevin sitting with his legs pulled close to his chest. He rested his chin on his knees, still flicking through the cards.

Thankfully, the boys' toilets were empty. It was cooler in here, easier to breathe. Playground laughter echoed off the white tiles. I stood alone, resting against the big porcelain sink. Water from the cold tap was warm from lying stagnant in the pipes. I let it run till it cooled, then filled the sink and eased my hot puffy hands below the surface. My fingers swayed like seaweed. I lifted my head and stared into the half-open eyes of my reflection. The empty expression in front of me said nothing. I splashed my face and ran wet fingers over my scalp, turning my brown hair black. Droplets ran down the contours of my cheekbones. There was something about me that didn't look ordinary, the way I always looked. The area between my nose and eyebrows was becoming flatter and my jaw seemed to be growing too, as though my face was a thin rubber mask stretched across the square features of a grown man.

I just had to hang on for two more days. It would then be summer holidays and Christmas, and after New Year I'd go to high school. Things were tough enough with Darrel and his gang. But next year was going to be the hardest year of my life. I'd be forced to start all over again and I'd be the youngest. What could I do against boys who were eighteen, boys who drove their own cars to school? Trouble waited for me out there in the future. I could feel it. My throat tightened up. The boy in the mirror looked like he wanted to ask one last question.

Outside, Kevin wasn't where I left him. Our lunchboxes lay open under the tree. I scanned left. Smears of pale blue school uniforms quickly became little pockets of action. Standard One boys chased each other. Skinny girls' knees skipped. A football bounced three times before a boy kicked it against the bike shed.

The bike shed.

I rushed over and checked. Nothing. Nobody. I spun around. A clown face taped to the inside of a classroom window looked down at some boys huddled together making swaps. A teacher, with a pile of books gathered under her arm, carefully chose the correct key, then unlocked her car door. Back at our spot by the fence, a chocolate wrapper twitched in the hot breeze.

The traffic and squealing and laughter all felt like silence. Where was Kevin? I told him to wait. Where was he? If he's walked off I swear I'll . . . There! Over by the goalposts, Darrel held something above his head while Kevin jumped and snatched at it. I could see my brother's neck straining as he screamed but couldn't hear his voice. Darrel's buddies were circling, mocking. If I didn't get over there and drag Kevin away Dad would use the belt on me for sure.

I walked towards them, trying to come up with a plan.

Darrel had Kevin's cards. He took one from the pack. With his thumbs and forefingers he held it in front of Kevin and tore it down the middle. He ripped it into tiny bits and shoved the whole lot in his mouth, chewing slowly like a cow. Kevin lowered his head and charged but he got shoved back. As he lay on the ground Darrel spat the soggy bits of card at him.

My walking turned to marching.

Kevin scrambled up but didn't dust himself off. He set his feet the way Dad had taught us and raised his fists. Everyone burst out laughing. They hung on each other's shoulders, while one boy mimicked him, pretending to fight like an old-fashioned boxer. Kevin just glared at Darrel.

I started running.

Darrel threw up the cards and they sprinkled to the ground but Kevin didn't take his eyes off him for a second.

'So the little shit wants some more.' He swaggered over to Kevin with his chest puffed out.

'Get away from him, shithead!' The words burst out of me, angry and louder than I expected. I wedged my shoulder between him and Kevin and stood eye to eye with Darrel, not sure what was supposed to happen next. I expected a threat. The usual stuff: 'You're dead, Alex, blah, blah, blah.' Instead, Darrel's eyes widened and he unexpectedly grabbed my throat. I pulled at his wrist but couldn't break his grip. Was that it? He was just going to stand frozen and silent, holding my neck.

Actually, that was it. That was exactly it.

He looked stunned. He had no idea what he was doing. Darrel, the meanest bully in school, was scared.

I grabbed his throat.

We stood for a moment at arms' length, a stand-off. His waxy skin was lumpy with pimples. I felt his head tremble as fury welled up, giving him more and more strength. He gripped tighter, digging his thumbnail into the side of my neck. My shoulder hunched up in pain. It dawned on me that I was in the middle of a fight. A real fight. What was I supposed to do?

His free hand slapped me across the eye, the fingers connecting in a second of stinging darkness. Like electricity, white-hot rage blasted up through my chest and along my arm.

'Fuck you!' My voice sounded rasped and scratchy with his hand around my throat. I squeezed with all my might. My fingers

119

curled into a fist around his Adam's apple, making him change from red to purple. Our feet shuffled and kicked up dust. He took a few backward steps but his hand still clawed around my neck. I tried to think. What would Dad do?

The best form of defence is attack.

Kicking frantically, my shoe bashed into Darrel's knee. It buckled and we both went down, me landing on top of him. Air rushed into my lungs as he let go of my neck.

'I hate you. I hate you,' he kept shouting between choking and coughing.

We wrestled across the ground and I tried sitting on his chest but his movements were too quick, too energetic. He clutched at my school shirt and the top two buttons popped off. A flurry of fists and elbows thrashed between us. Hardly anything connected. I wanted to punch him in the face. I wanted to watch his head whip back as I smashed his nose flat against his cheeks. There had to be blood. I wanted everyone to look at his face and know what I had done to him.

Something smashed against my mouth. My head jerked back, everything flashed white. The metal taste of blood ran down my throat. The boys around me seemed to shriek from the far end of a tunnel.

There are only two people in a fight, the winner and the loser.

Darrel squirmed underneath me, trying to get out. He turned over onto his stomach and clawed at the dirt. I shook my head. A long drool of saliva and blood hung from my mouth. It dropped off and splattered in a gooey dollop on the back of Darrel's school shirt. He was trying to stand up. I lifted both hands and brought them down hard between his shoulder blades. His arms gave way and he flopped down onto his chest. Frantic wailing sounds came out of me as I punched and punched at his shoulders and neck. I grabbed handfuls of hair and forced his face into the dirt. Little puffs of dust exploded out the side of his mouth as he breathed. I tried bashing his face off the ground. His forehead butted the earth once but this only gave him more strength. He forced his arms under himself and tried doing an enormous push-up. But my weight was too much for him. I went back to punching his shoulder blades. I punched and punched and punched but no matter how hard I hit, it didn't feel like winning. He just lay flat and took it.

There are no rules.

I stood up. The circle of boys all backed away. I stomped on the base of his back. It still didn't feel like I'd done enough. I wanted to see his blood. I wanted to destroy everything he'd done to us. I wanted to make it all go away.

'Leave him alone,' shouted one of the boys.

I swung my fist wildly at him. Rage made my head crazy and my body numb.

'That's enough, Alex.' I knew that voice. It was Charlene. She stared at me with watery eyes. 'What are you doing?'

Somehow, I was winning and losing at the same time. Rasping noises came out of my mouth but it didn't sound like me. I had to keep fighting till I won.

My vision jumped from Darrel face down to Kevin crying to the angry boys to the forgotten football to the tree. I needed something to show itself to me, the one thing that would end this. The decider.

The tree. I ran up and grabbed a short log lying among the roots. Raising it above my head, I charged back into the fight. The tears were cold against my cheeks.

Darrel was on all fours, coughing and spitting out sand. When his friends saw me rushing towards them they scattered. The log swung down hard across Darrel's back, smacking his chest down to the ground.

There are no rules.

Darrel lay motionless. I lifted the branch up and aimed for the back of his head. I was going to stop it all. There had to be blood.

My whole body jerked to the side as someone tackled me from behind. The branch was ripped out of my hands. A huge arm wrapped around me and lifted me up. My screaming rage started up again as I kicked and wrestled in the air.

121

'Let go, I'll fucking kill you.' Little drops of red spraying out of my mouth as I screamed.

I collapsed to the ground as the heavier body behind me pulled me down.

'Calm down! Calm down, boy,' a deep booming voice shouted in my ear.

I struggled to get free but was trapped under someone.

'Calm down, Alex. Calm down, calm down.' The booming voice became gentler and gentler.

I eased off and gave in. Dozens of school shoes stood quietly around me. Behind them Darrel sat with brown dusty tear streaks on his face.

The man behind me let go and stood up. I sat up and looked into the glaring sunshine. Slowly, the face of Mr Peck the history teacher swam into focus. Next to him was the assistant head, his hand stretched out, offering to help me up.

Chairs

We waited, with our hands on our laps, outside the principal's office till our parents arrived. School had closed forty-five minutes ago. No one walked past and sniggered at us. No one ran and played outside. Through a classroom door, chairs lay upside down on the desks. An old black woman with a green cloth wrapped around her head mopped the tiled floor at the other end of the hall. As she bent over and dragged the bucket, grating metallic sounds echoed along the walls.

My lip throbbed. The nurse had strapped on a dressing that looked like a fat white moustache. I could hardly close my mouth and my tongue kept pressing the wound, testing the pain, immediately forgetting, then testing it again.

'Do you think they'll expel us?' whispered Kevin.

I raised my shoulders and let them drop. With most teachers I knew what to expect, but the new principal had only been here for a few months and everyone's stories were different. He wasn't like old Principal Maxwell who would lecture you for half an hour about responsibility and the importance of learning one's place, then give you three or four or five – you never knew how many – with a belt. This new principal was different. I had never been to his office but the stories about him were bizarre. Often, he gave students detention every afternoon for a whole week. Others said that he gave them jacks with a thick cane that was also a walking stick. There were even weirder stories. Some pupils weren't even punished. Instead, they were sent to see Mrs Koekemoer who worked in the library and she would ask them to draw pictures of their house and ask them lots of questions about their family.

'Do you think Dad will be angry?' asked Kevin.

'Who knows,' I said. My tongue deflected spit away from the bandage.

The cleaner woman sloshed her mop in the bucket and splashed the sopping grey threads onto the floor. She moved the mop backward and forward, slowly, without lifting her head.

All along the wall were pictures of children staring at me. The first one was a black-and-white photograph. The caption read, *Pretoria Inter Primary Soccer Champions, 1965*. The boys in the picture had slicked-back hair and wore vertically striped kits. In the photograph next to them were more soccer champions. Every year there were pictures of winners staring down at me, spelling champions, runners, swimmers and eisteddfod gold medallists. Suddenly in 1969 the photos changed to pastel colours, and as the years went on the colours got brighter but the students' faces looked the same. Everyone had a clear confident smile as if they had been told a grand secret. They were probably now doctors and astronauts and scientists, all grown up and important. Under the photographs was a long glass display cabinet full of trophies.

In the centre of the case was a large wooden shield with the school's badge and tiny silver shields all around the edge. Most had names engraved into them but some were blank, waiting for more winners. My name would never be engraved up there. My face wasn't in any of the photographs.

We heard shoes on the tiles at the other end of the hall. I could tell it was Dad from the sound of his walk. He came towards us with his thumbs in his denims as if he was wearing guns. Mom sped up to a trot when she saw me.

'What on earth happened to you?' she asked.

'I'm fine,' I said.

She knelt down in front of me and tried to peer into my mouth. 'Let me see, let me see.'

I allowed her to push my forehead back so she could see under my lip.

'Dear Lord, who did this to you? And what happened to your neck?' Pinching my chin, she twisted my head from side to side, examining the scratches around my throat.

'We got in a fight,' said Kevin.

'Did you win?' asked Dad.

'Bruce . . .' Mom turned and gave Dad the look.

Kevin kept talking, 'Alex was fighting this boy Darrel and he hit him with a massive branch, and then the teachers pulled Alex away. And the nurse had to put a bandage over Darrel's back and so we got taken to the principal's office.'

When Mom heard this she turned and looked at me as if she had never seen me before. Dad's smirk hovered above her head.

The door to the principal's office opened.

'Mr and Mrs Thorne?' said the principal, poking his bald head round the door.

Mom and Dad both said yes at the same time.

'I'm Principal de Kock.'

Dad's smirk grew to a full grin. The two men shook hands without saying anything. Dad tucked his thumb back under his belt. The principal turned and held the door open for us. 'Please come in.'

124

As soon as I stepped into the office I saw the canes. I went to nudge Kevin but he had already spotted them. I counted four, two walking sticks – one with an ivory duck's head for a handle – and two thin switches, probably branches from a weeping willow. They were all stacked in the corner in an umbrella holder.

Behind the big desk books covered the back wall from floor to ceiling. Principal de Kock seated Mom and Dad in the two chairs facing his desk, then he carefully sat down in his huge green leather chair. Kevin and I shared a small sofa near the door.

'I've asked Mrs Koekemoer, the school counsellor, to join us today,' said the principal. She stood up and shook hands with Mom and Dad. Mrs Koekemoer's chair, which was close to the window, was smaller than the principal's but more comfy looking than either Mom or Dad's. Mrs Koekemoer looked like a typical Afrikaaner *vrou*, the kind who had big hair, always wore dresses and baked a cake every Sunday afternoon. Dad folded his arms.

Principal de Kock leaned forward and got straight to the point. 'This morning there was an incident involving both your boys,' he began. 'It is my understanding that Kevin got into an argument with a group of boys over some trading cards. I was then told that Kevin attacked one of the boys and a scuffle started. At this point, Alex got involved and a fight broke out between himself and his classmate, Darrel.'

Dad tilted his head till the bones in his neck cricked. Mom didn't move a muscle.

'As they wrestled, Alex somehow received a split lip. Then, according to several eyewitnesses, your son lost his temper and began beating Darrel with a tree branch. If the staff members assigned to playground duty this morning hadn't intervened I fear that Darrel may have sustained even more severe injuries.' Principal de Kock leaned back in his grand chair and waited for a reaction.

Mom looked over her shoulder at me. 'Is this true, Alex?'

I knew she wanted me to say the whole story was a lie.

'Answer me, Sonny-o, please. Did you hit that boy with a stick?'

Her eyes were too much for me. I looked down at my chest and nodded.

'Principal,' she said softly, 'as you can imagine, I am shocked. Alex has always been a quiet, well-behaved boy. I don't know what got into him.'

'Well, Mrs Thorne, this is what concerns us too. If we felt this was an isolated incident, then we would deal out the appropriate punishment and that would be the end of it. However, many of the staff have noticed that both your sons have become distant.'

Mrs Koekemoer nodded seriously.

'According to his file,' said the principal, 'Alex's grades are excellent and we believe he could go on to do very well in high school. But this change in behaviour will not do him any favours.'

All the books behind his desk seemed to nod in agreement. I slouched low into my seat, trying to make myself as small as possible. Dad sat with his legs apart, rocking his chair onto its two back legs. He sighed through his nose like a bull.

Mrs Koekemoer shifted in her seat and spoke directly to Mom, in a smiley childish sort of way.

'Mrs Thorne, perhaps you could help us prevent a negative pattern of behaviour forming in your sons by giving us a clearer picture of their personal lives. Are they sleeping well? Do they eat regularly? Have you noticed any changes in your sons' habits? Perhaps there are some troubles at home?'

Whenever I open the freezer in our kitchen, a chilly white mist rolls down the shelves and creeps across the floor and clings to my ankles making me shudder, even in the baking January heat. The silence coming off Mom felt like this mist. The whole room fell quiet, waiting for her to answer. But she just sat there, thinking, realising deep secrets which she wasn't going to share with anyone.

Dad put his hand on Mom's thigh. 'Grace, I'll handle this.'

Dad rested an elbow on the desk and pointed right at the principal.

'Look, Mr Cock, I don't need you or anyone else telling me how to run my family.'

The principal stiffened. 'Believe me, Mr Thorne, we are not implying—'

'Just a minute,' said Dad, holding up his hand. 'You've had your say. Now it's my turn.'

Principal de Kock closed his mouth and levelled his eyes at Dad.

Once he got silence Dad continued. 'I agree with you, my boys are not fine. Not at all. Last week Kevin came home with a black eye. Did you know that? He's been bullied for months. It's about time someone put a stop to all the teasing and violence. So, I'm proud of Alex. He did the right thing protecting his brother, because obviously the school doesn't seem interested in dealing with its bullying problem.'

The principal's eyes grew wide. He shifted uncomfortably in his chair and glanced at Mrs Koekemoer for help. I loved it when Dad talked like this.

'Mr Thorne, no one's blaming you or your family. We are only concerned.' Principal de Kock gently patted his desk as he spoke. 'We simply feel this outburst of violence is the result of other underlying issues. However, Alex has finished Standard Five, essentially he is out from under our guidance. Since the term is about to end we felt it would be helpful to discuss these issues—'

'Yeah, I get it, Mr Cock,' interrupted Dad. 'You dragged me away from an important business appointment to tell me Kevin and Alex are being picked on. And yet my sons are somehow doing this to themselves because they have *family problems*. So of course it's not *your* problem, it's *their* problem. Right?'

'Bruce, that's not what he's saying,' said Mom.

'Stay out of this, Grace,' snapped Dad. 'You don't know what's really going on here.'

Mom froze. The mist coming off her chilled the whole room.

Dad turned back to the principal, about to restart his lecture when Mom suddenly stood up.

127

'Boys, we're leaving,' she said, hooking her handbag over her shoulder. 'Let's go.'

The principal stood up too. 'Mrs Thorne, there's no need . . .'

'Bloody hell, woman, calm down!' sighed Dad.

Mom's movements got quicker. 'No! I can't take this any more.' Tears were welling up. 'Alex. Kevin. Come!' she said, opening the office door.

Kevin and I got up to go.

Mrs Koekemoer was now on her feet too. 'I think it's best if we all take five minutes and continue this meeting once we've all calmed down.'

'I think it's best if you sit back down and shut up,' said Dad, pointing his finger at her. Then he turned on the principal. 'See what you've done?' he said, slapping the desk.

Mom was the first one out the door followed by Kevin, then me, then Dad. We shoved past the cleaner lady who was mopping right outside the office door. Our four sets of shoes clip-clopped down the hall as we marched straight to the car.

French Toast

I pulled back the curtain just as the orange sun began peeking over the next-door neighbours' roof. Stepping into a pair of shorts, I guessed I was the first one up. Our house felt whisper-still. I tiptoed toward the kitchen to get a glass of water.

In the sitting room I found Dad sleeping on the couch.

He had on linen pyjamas and no shirt. With one arm folded behind his head, he snuggled his nose into his armpit. He inhaled sharply through his nose and exhaled in grumbles. As he breathed the armpit hair was blown away and then sucked in towards him, like a storm in a tiny forest. His right hand slept down the front of his pants. A spare grey blanket from the cupboard lay crumpled on the floor next to him.

Suddenly both eyes opened.

'Uh . . . morning, Dad.'

He looked puzzled, unsure of where he was.

'Can I get you some coffee?' I said.

'What are you doing?' he groaned.

'Nothing,' I said, 'I'm just . . .'

Dad sat up, gathered up the blanket and pillow and went to his bedroom.

Mom and Dad said something to each other behind the closed door but I couldn't make out what it was. Seconds later, Mom came stumbling past me into the kitchen, rubbing the sleep out of one eye. She switched on the kettle and dug a teaspoon out of the drawer while she waited for the water to boil.

'What are you doing up so early, Alex?' She peered into her empty mug as she spoke.

'I couldn't sleep,' I said, but it didn't feel like a proper reason. So I cheerily added a bit more. 'I thought I'd cycle up the hill and have breakfast there,' I said.

Her neck turned slightly toward me. The sharp morning light backlit her head, darkening the features of her face. She considered me for a second, then sighed heavily and stooped to open the fridge. She stared at the cheese and leftovers. Through her nightdress I saw the silhouette of her drooping breasts and tummy. She looked tired, her whole body looked tired.

'So you'd rather sneak off at the crack of dawn than eat with us?' she said, closing the fridge.

I didn't know how to answer.

'Well, I don't blame you.'

I didn't know what she meant.

The kettle boiled. She spooned equal parts of coffee, sugar and creamer into her favourite blue mug and poured hot water over the mixture, filling it to the brim. She stirred and blinked. Watching her do this reminded me of her favourite joke.

Question: Why do Irishmen stir their tea clockwise, Scotsmen anti-clockwise and Englishmen whip the teaspoon from side to side?

Answer: To dissolve the sugar.

She loved that joke. And she would tell it again and again as though sharing some clever truth. I always laughed to cover for the fact that I didn't get it. Or maybe I did, but Mom just wasn't that funny.

'You can't go out this morning, Alex,' she said. 'I have an announcement to make. Go and wake up your brother. Tell him we're having French toast.'

I walked back down the hall with a head full of questions.

Half an hour later, Kevin and I sat at the table as Mom dished out hot eggy slices covered in cinnamon and sugar. Kevin had bed-head, his blond hair stuck up like the feathers on a duck's bum.

In the background I could hear Dad step out of the bath and pull out the plug. Water drained down through the pipes under the house.

'I have good news,' Mom said, sitting down in front of us. 'We are going on holiday. Isn't that exciting?' Her voice pitched higher as she faked being excited.

I was suspicious. Every summer we spent the first couple of weeks playing outside while Mom did some Christmas shopping. Sometimes we went to the municipal swimming pool in the city centre. On Christmas Day we always opened presents first thing in the morning, we went to church and had a braai in the evening. In January we did some back-to-school shopping before the term started again. It was the same every year. I couldn't understand this sudden change of routine.

Kevin was the first to speak. 'Where are we going?' he said, but it sounded more like, '*Why* are we going?'

'Well, boys, I thought we'd go to Durban.'

'But Mom, you always said it was too expensive and the beach is crowded and dirty.'

'Did I? I don't remember that. North Beach can be very busy but the other beaches are beautiful. And you might even see monkeys.'

Mom sipped her second cup of coffee. As she ran her hand through her hair the grey hairs close to her scalp became visible for a second, then disappeared.

'It's all arranged,' she said. 'We're leaving tomorrow morning at four o'clock, and staying with an old friend of mine from nursing college. You'll love her. You can see the ocean from her house.'

The bathroom door unlocked. We all stopped talking as Dad strode into the sitting room, shaved and dressed for work.

'Mom made French toast,' said Kevin.

'I'm already late,' said Dad, hooking his bag over his shoulder. 'Bye, boys.' He closed the front door and we listened to him start the car and drive off.

'Is Dad going to drive us there?' Kevin asked.

'No, Kettle. Your father has to work. It'll just be the three of us.'

Kevin looked over at me, his mouth full of food.

'That'll still be fun, won't it?' said Mom.

That night Kevin asked to sleep on the floor in my room, again. After we brushed our teeth, we heard Dad arrive back from work. He came straight into my room to say goodnight.

'Are you guys all set for your big day tomorrow?' he said.

'I can't find my swimming trunks,' said Kevin, pulling the shoes out of the bottom of my wardrobe.

'I told you, you can borrow a pair of my old shorts and swim in them,' I said.

'There, it's settled,' said Dad. 'You can use Alex's shorts.' He sat down on the end of my bed waiting for Kevin to get into his sleeping bag.

'But I want my *own* trunks,' said Kevin. He had been moaning like this all evening and I could tell he was about to start crying.

'I'm sure your mother will buy you some trunks when you get there.'

'But I want proper swimming trunks. I don't wanna swim in shorts.'

Dad glared at him. 'I said, your mother will get you some. Now lie down.'

'But what if we go to the beach first? What if she can't find the shop that sells swimming trunks?'

'She'll get you new trunks,' said Dad.

'But I want *my*—'

'Kevin, that's enough!' yelled Dad. He jumped up and grabbed a fistful of Kevin's T-shirt and shoved him onto my bed. 'Stop your bloody whining.'

Kevin's bottom lip began to quiver.

'And don't start crying now either,' said Dad, pointing his finger in Kevin's face. 'It's about time you grew up. I'm sick and tired of you acting like some snivelling baby.'

Kevin sat absolutely still. Not saying a word, not crying.

Nobody spoke.

Dad sat down on the end of my bed. As the three of us looked at each other the mood settled a bit.

'You know I'd come with you boys if I could,' said Dad.

'Why can't you come?' I said.

'Oh, it's complicated,' he said, rubbing his head with both hands. 'I've got lots to do. Maybe next time.'

Kevin picked up on this. 'Are we going on another holiday? With just you?'

'Would you like that?' said Dad.

'I want to go camping,' said Kevin, 'in a tent.'

'Camping, huh? Well, we'll see. Now lie down, Kevin.'

Dad picked at the dirt under his thumbnail. He shifted his weight and looked at me more seriously.

'Alex.'

'Yes?'

'You know how sometimes your mother and I leave you in charge of Kevin for the afternoon. And that means that you have to protect him and make sure he does his homework and stuff.'

'Uh-huh.'

132

'Well, since you're the eldest, I'm leaving you in charge, you understand? It will be up to you to look after your mother and brother, OK?'

'OK, Dad. No problem.'

Dad's eyes narrowed. 'This is serious business, Alex. They'll be depending on you, so you gotta be strong. While you're away you have to be the man.'

The way he said *man* pressed the air out of my chest.

Kevin shifted onto his knees. 'It's all right, Dad, we're coming back in two weeks.'

'I know, son, I know. It's just, the house is going to feel empty without you guys, that's all.'

He hugged us both tightly. My neck hurt as it squashed against his shoulder. Dad stood up quickly, turned off the light and closed the door behind him.

I lay awake in the darkness, listening to Kevin's breathing as I replayed my conversation with Dad over and over. Something very important had just happened, but my mind struggled to give it a proper shape. The shadows bent around my wardrobe and crept along the wall and gradually this horrible feeling began to overwhelm me, like I'd been given piles of homework, more than I could ever do. I buried my face deep into my pillow in case Kevin heard me crying.

Click

I felt myself waking up. Crackling piano music swam in between dreams of riding my bike through the veldt. I opened my eyes and found myself face to face with Kevin sleeping with his fist under his chin. As I stretched, my head pressed against the back of the driver's seat.

Mom switched off the car stereo. 'Morning, sleepy head.'

I blinked up at the tiny pinpricks in the station wagon's padded ceiling. The engine vibrated underneath me. Life became more and more lifelike. Vague memories of stumbling from my bed to the car in the middle of the night felt more like dreams. I sat up and stared at the back of Mom's head. Her eyes caught mine in the rear-view mirror.

'Did you sleep well, Sonny-O?'

'Uh-huh. What time is it?'

'It's just after seven.'

Outside, an early morning fog rolled between rocky crags. I rubbed goop out of my eye while a yawn climbed up the inside of my throat, forced my mouth open and escaped.

'Oooh, don't do that,' said Mom as my yawn jumped over to her.

Kevin sat straight up like a zombie refusing to die.

'What's happening?' he said.

'It's OK, Kettle,' said Mom, 'we're just going on holiday.'

I don't think Kevin heard her at all. He stared in disbelief at the countryside surrounding our car.

'Where are we?' said Kevin.

'We are just coming into the Drakensberg Mountains,' said Mom, 'about halfway to Durban.' She peered along the bridge of her nose trying to see Kevin in the rear-view mirror. 'Were you boys comfortable back there?'

'*Ja*,' said Kevin, still in a stupor. 'Mom, I have to go.'

'Me too,' I said.

Mom stopped the car and opened the back door for us. Kevin and I hopped out into a world that smelled of trees and moss. We hobbled across the gravel in our bare feet to a rock that stretched over the steep hillside.

'Don't go too close to the edge, boys,' said Mom.

Standing only in shorts and T-shirts, we shivered while we peed. Golden arcs of urine disappeared over the edge of the cliff with steam rising off and mixing into the misty morning. It became a game to see who could pee the furthest. Kevin waddled closer to the edge, tilting his hips as far forward as he could, but I still won.

Mom folded up the back seat, packed away the sleeping bags and put the suitcases in the boot, while we rubbed our bare arms to keep warm. I jumped into the front seat and Kevin sat in the back, leaning over between Mom and me so he didn't feel left out.

Mom got in and started the car. 'There's breakfast in that basket by your feet, Alex.'

I lifted it onto my knees, opened the Tupperware box, and handed a sandwich back to Kevin.

'What's on that one?' he said, pointing to a different sandwich.

'They're all the same, Kettle, peanut butter and jam,' answered Mom.

Happy with that, Kevin leaned back on the seat and tucked into his sandwich. I offered one to Mom too, but she shook her head.

I had never seen the Drakensberg Mountains before. At first they were just hills covered by low clouds but as we drove deeper into them they grew higher and steeper, till they loomed right over the road. They began to really feel like 'Dragon Mountains'.

Across a cliff face, different layers of rock showed how the mountains had formed over millions of years. They had been here, exactly as they were now, long before any white people came to Africa, before the time when black kings were in charge of everything, even before the dinosaurs. Each hillside and mountain peak breathed with a powerful silence as if they were sleeping giants who would crush us if they ever woke up.

None of us spoke. We left the radio off.

I took another bite of my sandwich and pressed my nose against the cold car window. Rocks burst straight up out of the ground, up, up, up, and out of sight. On the other side of the car, the

135

ground fell away sharply from the road, down into a hazy valley. If Mom took a wrong turn I pictured us plummeting, down through the clouds, with nothing to save us. But she didn't drive as fast as Dad. She kept both hands on the steering wheel and took each curve and twist in the road steadily. Her brown hair was pulled back into a tight clasp exposing grey streaks around her ears. The whites of her eyes were a little bloodshot from staying awake half the night, but she looked alert, almost as if she'd had a fright.

'Mom, would you like some coffee?' I said, holding up the flask.

'Not just now,' she said, without looking at me. 'I'll get some when we stop.'

We drove on without seeing any houses or power lines. There were no petrol stations, no cafés, no side roads. Except, ahead of us, two black boys were standing by the side of the road. One was as tall as me, the other one just shorter than Kevin. Neither of them wore shoes. The smallest one had a potbelly. Compared to the mountains, they seemed unbelievably tiny. At first I thought they might be walking home, but where did they live? And why were they out here this early in the morning? They stood close together and with blank faces watched our car approach. They didn't look sad or lost, just empty. Mom didn't stop. She didn't even slow down. As we passed I looked right into the oldest boy's eyes. He wasn't waiting for anyone and no one was coming to get him.

As we came over a ridge a new valley opened up in front of us. What we saw was so astonishing that Mom stopped the car. I knew immediately that this was the most incredible thing I'd ever seen. It was magical, like a drawing from an ancient storybook. Straight ahead, between all the sleeping giants, one mountain was floating in the clouds.

With blankets wrapped around our necks, we got out of the car to see it properly. It looked like a pyramid sailing down a river of mist.

The three of us stood silently, thinking about it. Little clouds of steam brushed against my face as I breathed.

'We should take a picture,' said Kevin.

Mom stroked Kevin's hair flat. 'We don't have a camera.'

'Why?' said Kevin sharply.

'I'm sorry, Kettle, we just don't have one.'

'But it's supposed to be a holiday!' His lip jutted out as though he was about to cry.

Mum kneeled down till her face was level with his. She reached out and rubbed his shoulders.

'There's no camera, sweetheart. But I could tell you a secret instead. Would you like that?'

Kevin sucked in his lip and shrugged.

'Did you know that God put a camera in your head?' she said.

We both blinked at her.

'It's true,' she continued. 'You see, when God made you he thought to himself, "Hhhmmmm . . . They look fine and well, but how will they remember all the incredible things I have created in the world? All the trees and the flowers and the sea and the mountains and the dogs . . ."'

'And the snakes?' said Kevin.

'". . . and the snakes and every beautiful thing ever made. Well," said God, "I'd better put a special camera in their heads to help them." So whenever you want to remember something that's very special, all you have to do is look at it, *really look hard*, then blink your eyes and say, "Click." Then you'll never forget.'

Mom smiled and gazed right into Kevin's face, as if it was a staring competition, but Kevin wasn't ready. A shy smile burst across his face.

'Click,' said Mum, blinking both eyes. 'Now I'll remember you just like that for ever and ever. I'll never be able to forget you.'

'Click,' said Kevin, looking at Mom. 'Now I'll remember you back!'

'Good,' said Mom. 'Now close your eyes and try to see the picture you just took.'

Kevin shut his eyes tight. He tilted his head slightly the way you do when playing blind man's bluff.

'I can still see you, Mom, you're still there,' he said.

She smiled at his closed eyes. 'Told you,' she said. 'Let's do Alex, shall we.'

They both turned and stared at me. My face flushed and I didn't know where to look.

'Over here, Sonny-o, give us a smile,' said Mom.

'*Ja*, smile, Alex, or I'll have to remember your ugly face for ever,' said Kevin.

I stuck my tongue out and pulled a silly face.

'Click! I got you, Alex,' laughed Kevin. 'You're gonna look funny for ever.'

Mom rubbed her hands together, cupped them over her mouth and breathed to keep them warm. 'Come huddle in closer, boys,' she said.

We snuggled in close, wrapping our blankets round each others' shoulders.

'Now take a good look at the floating mountain, so it will always be with you,' said Mom.

Together, the three of us said, 'Click.'

Ears

'Mom, my ears are sore,' said Kevin.

Mom glanced over her shoulder as she drove. 'Try swallowing.'

Kevin clenched his jaw. The muscles in his neck tightened and relaxed.

'They're still sore,' he said.

'OK, I want you to pinch your nose,' said Mom, 'keep your mouth closed, and blow as hard as you can.'

It sounded like a silly magic trick, but Kevin tried it, his cheeks puffing out as he blew.

'How are they now, Kettle?' said Mom.

'They're fine,' said Kevin, tilting his head from side to side. 'Why did they do that?'

'Because we're coming out of the mountains and travelling down to sea level.'

Mom seemed so sure about this, but I wasn't. I had never been to Durban but I had gone downhill in a car and on my bike and my ears had never ever hurt before.

But they began to hurt now. It felt like sinking in the deep end of the pool. Was this what Kevin had felt? Still, holding your nose was silly. How could that ever help your ears? I was old enough to know it was just one of Mom's little tricks to keep Kevin occupied.

The pressure built into a headache. I tried ignoring it but it got worse and worse by the minute. If I was going to blow into my nose I didn't want her to see me try it. I turned my head away and stared out the window. On the hillside trees with gnarled roots grew out of the rock face. Pretending to lean my hand on my chin, I quickly pinched my nostrils and blew. Popping noises came from inside my head, pushing from the centre out through my ears.

The headache vanished. Everything sounded clearer.

It was true.

Somehow Mom knew about making your ears pop and had never told us. What she said about 'clicking' had also been true. Closing my eyes, I could still see the floating mountain, exactly the same. I flicked through the memories and saw Mom kneeling in front of Kevin, just as she had done this morning. Even the tiny details were clear, the way Kevin's toes pointed inwards and Mom's visible breath disintegrating as it brushed against the grey blanket wrapped around Kevin's shoulders.

'When are we going to be there?' said Kevin.

'Not for a while,' said Mom.

The brake lights of the car in front came on and we slowed down round a sharp bend.

'Does anyone want another naartjie?' she said.

We both shook our heads. Kevin grabbed his nose, took a deep breath and popped his ears again.

Butterfly

My bum was numb. We'd been driving for hours but the signs for Durban said *8 km* and traffic was getting heavier.

'I see it!' squealed Kevin, squeezing himself between the two front seats.

I didn't see anything. 'No, you never.'

'I did. I saw the sea, right there.' He pointed at something through the front windscreen, something long gone.

We were still descending. The car twisted down bendy roads, through trees and past shops selling boogie boards and beach balls. The two of us sat up straight in our seats, trying to peer over the houses to get a better look. I knew it was right there, behind everything. I imagined it to be like the Hartbeespoort Dam only bigger and with waves.

For an instant, luminous turquoise flashed between the trees.

'Kevin, did you see that?' I said, twisting so quickly the seat-belt locked tight.

'I told you! I told you I saw it.'

'And did you see how big it was?' I said. 'It was ... it was *huge.*'

'That's the Indian Ocean, boys,' said Mom, 'and you know what? It's warm. You can swim in it all year round.'

140

'How do you know?' I said.

'Because I used to live here,' said Mom.

She had mentioned nursing college, but I never made the connection that she used to live by the sea.

'Did you swim in the sea every day?' asked Kevin.

Her expression became a little vacant. 'Yes,' she said. 'Every morning before class.'

I wasn't sure if I believed her. I couldn't imagine doing anything *before* class.

The car climbed a small hill, turned left and there it was, all silvery green under a hazy blue sky. The ocean. Vast. Flat. More water than I could look at.

'Wow,' said Kevin, rolling down the back window.

'Keep your arms inside the car, Kettle,' said Mom.

The air was richer and stickier here. It clung to my skin and smelled of rain evaporating off our street, only fishier.

'Quickly, Alex,' said Kevin, shouting from the seat behind me, 'say "click", say "click".'

'Click,' I whispered. And then it disappeared behind a petrol station. I closed my eyes to make sure it was still there. It was. All of it. Burned into my head. All that openness was part of my mind now. I could see it whenever I wanted.

Mom flicked on the indicator and we pulled into a small shopping centre and parked the car in the shade. I got out and stretched my arms above my head. My feet felt hot and puffy. Mom locked the car and said, 'I need to get some things from the supermarket before we go to Brandy's house. What do you boys want to do?'

She opened her purse and checked to see how much cash she had. Was she serious? Dad never let us do anything by ourselves.

'I want to explore that shop over there,' I said, pointing at the one called Camp and Climb.

'Can I go with Alex?' said Kevin.

Mom looked at the shop. There were knives and fishing rods displayed in the window. I knew she'd say no. There was no way she'd let us.

'Alex, are you wearing your watch?' she asked.

I took my hands out of my pockets and showed her my watch.

'OK, I'll meet you back at the car in fifteen minutes,' she said.

Kevin started running before she could change her mind. I couldn't believe it. 'Thanks, Mom,' I said.

She looked really tired but gave me a small smile and said, 'Fifteen minutes, I mean it. And make sure Kevin doesn't run off.'

'I will.'

I turned and ran to catch up with Kevin.

Fifteen minutes later, Kevin and I were sitting on the car bonnet, waiting. Mom came out of the shop with two grocery bags in one hand and a great big bunch of flowers in the other. Kevin slid off the bonnet and went to meet her.

'Here, take this,' she said, giving Kevin a bag to carry. I came over and helped with the other bag.

'Mom, Alex bought a penknife,' Kevin blurted out.

Only two minutes ago that little bastard promised never to tell. He had crossed his heart and hoped to die. I'd made him do it. Dad must have said it a million times: *That's your problem, Kevin, you never think!* I lummied him hard on the shoulder.

'Ow! What was that for?' whined Kevin.

'Alex! Stop that,' said Mom.

She frowned at me for a moment, then opened the car and put in the grocery bags on the back seat. Kevin hopped in, still rubbing his arm. Mom bent forward and handed him the flowers.

'Be very careful with these,' said Mom to Kevin. 'Hold them straight up so they don't get crushed.'

She closed the car door and turned to me. 'Show me the knife.'

I didn't want to. She would confiscate it and I'd never see it again.

'Show it to me, Alex,' she said.

I took it out of my pocket and let the knife lie in my open palm. The blade was tucked neatly into the dark wooden handle.

142

It was no longer than the width of my hand. Mom took it and opened out the blade till the copper lever locked. She checked the sharpness with her thumb.

'What do you plan to do with this?' she said.

I hadn't planned anything. I just wanted it. Holding it made me feel ready for anything. But I had to think of a proper reason. Something Mom would want to hear.

'I want to use it for peeling fruit,' I said.

'Peeling fruit?' She gave me one of her looks.

'And maybe some wood carving.'

Mom sighed and folded away the blade. 'Alex, I think you're old enough to have this.'

She handed back the knife. As I took hold she didn't let go.

'But there are conditions,' she said.

Our fingers touched as we held either end of the knife. Her skin was cooler than mine.

'If I ever hear about you doing anything irresponsible with this I'm taking it.'

I nodded.

'You won't get it back,' she said. 'Do I make myself clear?'

It was getting more difficult to look her in the eye. 'Yes, Mom,' I said.

'And the next time you decide to buy something like this, don't do it behind my back. I hate that.'

'OK.'

'And don't ever hit your brother again.'

'Sorry, Mom.' My eyes dropped to the ground.

She let go and I put the knife in my pocket.

We finally arrived at Brandy's house. There was no gate, no fence and no security. Her rockery garden stretched right up to the street. Mom pulled into her driveway and stopped right outside the front door.

A big Dalmatian came bounding round from behind the house, barking excitedly, he placed his front paws next to the wing mirror as I rolled up the window as fast as I could. A pink tongue slobbered up the window. His tail was wagging but it was hard to tell if he was happy or angry.

A woman with very short brown hair came up to the car.

'Down, boy!' she commanded the dog. But he went on yapping.

'Stripe! *Sit!* She pointed at the ground, waiting. The dog whined, licked his nose and sat down.

Mom opened her door and got out. As soon as the woman saw Mom she threw her arms around her neck. 'Grace, it's so lovely to see you,' she said.

Kevin leaned over from the back seat and whispered, 'Is that Auntie Brandy?'

'I guess so,' I said.

'Boys,' said Mom, 'come and say "hello".'

Kevin climbed out and I heard the woman say, 'My God, is that little baby Kevin? Look how tall you are.'

Kevin blushed as the woman bent down and reached out her arms. 'Come over here and give me a hug,' she said.

He stood rigid as the woman hugged him.

'Now, where's your brother Alex?'

The dog was still guarding my door. His tongue lolled to the side and I could swear he was smiling. Apart from his wet-black nose, he had one completely black ear. The rest of him was peppered in spots.

'Stripe,' called the woman, 'come here, boy.'

The dog sped to the other side of the car. I got out, closed the door, and stood with my hands in my pockets.

'Well, well,' said the woman, looking at me across the bonnet, 'haven't you grown into a handsome young man.'

I didn't expect that. I stood rubbing the penknife in my pocket.

'You don't remember me, do you, Alex?' she said.

'No,' I said, shaking my head.

She started coming round to my side of the car followed by Mom, Kevin and the dog. 'My dear boy,' she said, 'it's so wonderful to see you again.' Holding my neck in both hands she bent forward, waiting to be kissed. I pressed my mouth and nose against her velvety cheek, close to her mouth. Through one nostril I got a blended whiff of coffee and cigarettes, the other nostril picked up a perfume scent of roses from along her neck. It wasn't the same as kissing Mom. This was a real woman. As I pulled away I could feel a bit of moisture on my lips. My first impulse was to wipe my mouth. It took all my willpower to smile politely and keep my hands by my sides. I tried to say something nice.

'It's nice to meet you, Auntie Brandy.'

She looked right at me, taking me in. Her eyes were as brown as deep river water. 'Forget all that polite Auntie stuff. Just call me Brandy,' she said. 'Like the drink.'

'Auntie . . . Um. Brandy. What's your dog called?' said Kevin, as the dog licked his fingers.

'Stripe,' said Brandy.

'But he's full of spots,' said Kevin, a little confused.

Brandy lifted her index finger. 'That's because he's a Dalmatian.'

Mom ran her fingers through Kevin's hair as he patted the dog. Kevin's thinking wrinkle appeared on his forehead. He looked up at Mom then over at Brandy, knowing something funny had happened.

'Kevin,' said Mom quietly, like a secret, 'where are those flowers I asked you to hold?'

'In the car,' whispered Kevin.

Stripe quit licking and raised his ears.

'Go get them for me, Kettle,' she said.

Kevin ran round the back of the car with Stripe chasing after him.

Brandy took hold of Mom's elbow. 'How was your trip, Grace? You look tired,' she said.

'I am a bit,' said Mom. 'The traffic was quite heavy on the way down.'

Brandy studied Mom's face, waiting for Mom to say more. Kevin and Stripe came running back with the flowers. He was about to give them to Mom, but she signalled they were for Brandy. Kevin held them up for her to take.

'These are for you, Brandy,' he said.

Her reaction was extraordinary. Brandy loved flowers the way babies love peek-a-boo. Delight exploded across her face as she buried her nose into all those colours.

'Oh, these are gorgeous,' she said.

Kevin's chest puffed out with pride. 'Thank you, thank you, thank you. I'll put them in water straight away.'

It was much cooler inside her house. The three of us sat in the kitchen drinking iced tea, while Brandy clipped the stalks and arranged the flowers in a vase. As she cut, her bicep flexed under a silver bracelet high up on her arm. Her blouse looked Indian, with sparkling bits sewn into it. She had painted her toenails pale blue to match her flip-flops and above her ankle was a butterfly tattoo.

Kevin turned his chair away from the table and Stripe sat down in front of him, resting his head on Kevin's lap. As he stroked the ears back the dog's eyes bulged out a little. He bent over till their noses were almost touching and quietly said, 'Click.'

Mom and I both heard him say it. I grinned but she put her finger over her lips to keep it a secret between us.

'Can you boys swim?' said Brandy.

'Yes,' said Kevin, 'but I don't have any swimming trunks.'

'Well, that's not a problem, we'll get you some first thing tomorrow. And then you can swim with Stripe. He loves swimming. We go to the beach every day.'

'Can he really swim?' said Kevin, half speaking to the dog.

'Oh *ja*, he's a very good swimmer.'

'What else can he do?' said Kevin.

'I'll show you.' Brandy arranged the last flower, wiped her hands on a dishcloth and came over to where we were sitting. Stripe stood up and swiped his tail excitedly from side to side. She raised one finger to get the dog's full attention.

'Speak,' she said, and Stripe barked once. The three of us watching all smiled at the same time. Brandy and Stripe now had

146

an audience. They didn't take their eyes off each other, not for a second.

'Sit.'

Stripe sat down and folded back his ears.

Brandy held out her hand. 'Shake.'

Stripe placed his paw on her hand.

Then Brandy pointed two fingers at him, her hand shaped like a gun.

'Bang,' she said.

Stripe flopped over sideways onto his back.

The three of us gave a round of applause. Stripe snuffled and growled and came over to each of us to get his full payment of patting and congratulations.

'He also runs after sticks,' said Brandy, lighting a cigarette, 'but he never brings them back.'

Onion

'Alex,' said Brandy, washing her hands in the kitchen sink, 'in that cupboard by your knees are some onions. Get three out for me, would you, please.'

As I crouched down and peered into the cupboard, Kevin burst in through the back door, laughing and wrestling a rubber hoop from Stripe's mouth. The hoop dropped on the floor and bounced under the table. Stripe dashed after it, his claws scraping along the tiles.

'Fetch it, boy!' said Kevin.

Brandy got in between the two of them. 'Shhhh,' she said with her finger over her lips, 'your mother's still sleeping.' She herded Stripe back outside and closed the door. 'Go wash your hands,' she said to Kevin quietly, 'and then come through here and help us.'

Kevin turned and skipped towards the bathroom while Brandy put some water out for the dog.

I gathered the onions, put them on the counter and shoved my hands in my pockets.

'Now, choose a knife from the drawer,' she said.

All mixed together in the same drawer were wooden spoons, spatulas, chopsticks, bottle openers, can openers, knives and whisks. I chose the biggest knife I could find. The blade and handle together were longer than my forearm. It was almost a sword.

'Good,' she said, handing me a wooden chopping board, 'now peel those onions and chop them into tiny bits.'

I stared at the knife and then at the onions.

'Whatcha doing?' said Kevin, wiping his hands on his T-shirt.

Brandy handed him a peeler. 'You're just in time,' she said, placing a bunch of carrots on the counter.

'What's this for?' said Kevin.

But Brandy wasn't listening. She had turned her back and was leaning out the back door. She came back in with a bottle crate and put it on the floor for Kevin to stand on.

'You're in charge of the carrots and Alex is in charge of the onions,' said Brandy. The way she said it there was no debate.

Kevin stepped up onto the crate. He was now eight centimetres taller than me, which pleased him a lot. 'From up here I can see all the fleas crawling on your head,' he said to me.

'*Ja*, well, I can see all the boogers up your nose.'

'Now now, boys,' said Brandy, 'more chopping and less squabbling.'

Kevin scraped the peeler down the side of a carrot and held up the floppy length of orange peeling for inspection. I sliced an onion in half and began tearing off its paper skin with my fingers. I didn't want to do this. We were supposed to be on holiday and she was getting us to work harder than we did at home. Why did *we* have to make dinner?

'Don't you have a servant girl to do this?' I asked.

'No,' said Brandy, humming as she took some chicken wings from the fridge.

'Why not?'

'I live alone, so I don't need the help,' she said with a shrug. She poured oil into a pot and added one piece of chicken at a time. With her back turned she said, 'The real reason is, I don't believe in them.'

It was such a weird answer. I knew some people believed in Jesus and others believed in their ancestors. But servants? What was there to believe in?

'So who does your washing?' I asked her.

'I do. I make my own bed and I do all the cleaning. And I should warn you boys that after dinner, we are all going to do the dishes.'

'I don't like doing the dishes,' said Kevin.

'Neither do I,' said Brandy.

'So why don't you hire a servant?' I said. My logic was solid.

Brandy leaned against the counter and wiped her hands on a cloth. 'I did hire a woman once,' she said, 'but after a few weeks we'd become very close friends so it didn't work out. It was degrading for both of us. Only a child needs people to pick up their clothes and cook for them.'

'When I grow up,' said Kevin, 'I'm going to have lots of servants 'cause I hate making the bed and taking out the rubbish.'

Brandy laughed out loud. It wasn't a quiet giggle like Mom does. It was a big rounded 'HA!' so loud it made me duck.

She kissed Kevin on the head. 'Well, you'd better find a very good job. You'll need it to afford all your servants.'

Mom stumbled through looking sleepy and smiley. Her hair hung in scraggly tangles. She sat down at the kitchen table and rubbed her eye.

'You look like you slept well,' said Brandy. 'Would you like some coffee?'

Mom nodded.

Brandy flicked the switch behind the kettle and said, 'The boys and I will have dinner ready soon.'

'I see you're both helping,' said Mom. 'I'm very impressed.'

'I'm in charge of the carrots and Alex is in charge of the onions,' said Kevin.

'I can see that,' said Mom. 'What are you making?'

Only Brandy knew the answer. Kevin and I turned to see what she'd say next.

'Tonight I am making my special,' she lifted both hands and wiggled her fingers, adding flair, 'bottom-of-the-fridge surprise.'

'Fantastic,' said Mom, playing along with Brandy, 'that's what we have every night.'

After dinner, Mom washed, Kevin and I dried, and Brandy packed everything into the cupboards. There was no ice cream till after the dishes were done. Brandy sang along with her Aretha Franklin cassette as she carried knives and forks over to the drawer. Mom stood with her hands in the sink, bouncing her hips from side to side with the music. Every now and then, she flicked bubbles at us and pretended it wasn't her. I had never seen her like this. She was still being herself, only more awake.

By nine o'clock Mom said it was time for bed.

'Do we have to?' said Kevin.

'Yes, son, you've had a very long day. If you sleep now then you'll be ready for swimming in the sea tomorrow.'

This cheered him up. 'Are you going to bed too?' said Kevin.

'Oh, no,' Brandy chipped in, 'your mother and I are going to savour a bottle of Shiraz and gossip till things get silly.'

Mom gave Brandy a look. One of those hush-hush looks between adults.

'Can Stripe sleep with us tonight?' asked Kevin.

'You should ask him,' said Brandy.

Kevin bent over in front of the dog. 'Do you want to sleep with us, Stripe?'

The dog jumped up and walked in circles wagging his tail.

We brushed our teeth and went upstairs to the office. The light switch was hidden behind a bookshelf. On two sides the roof sloped to the ground, shaping the room like a tent. A small door opened onto a wooden deck and from there you could see the ocean. Brandy had pushed her desk and chair to one side and covered them with a sheet. Two mattresses lay side by side on the floor, all made up with sheets and blankets. Stripe stood on the mattresses, circled around twice and lay down right in the middle.

I switched off the light and got into bed. Stripe's body felt warm through the blanket. With the curtain drawn it was very dark.

'Do you like Brandy?' I said.

'No way!' said Kevin. 'She's old and gross.'

'I don't mean do you *like* her. I mean, what do you think of her?'

Kevin shifted under his blankets. 'You love her, don't you?' he said.

'No, I don't!'

'Alex and Brandy sitting in a tree—'

'Kevin, you'd better shut your mouth right now.' I tried to slap him but he hid behind Stripe, cuddling him tightly around the neck.

We stayed silent for a minute and then Kevin said, 'I think she's weird.'

Through the floor we heard Brandy laugh her big loud 'HA!' We lay still and listened to them drink and giggle. Mom never drank wine at home.

The waves outside grumbled and shushed themselves quiet, only to rumble again like a hungry stomach. The sound was so clear, so close, as though the waves were washing along Brandy's street and bashing against her front door.

'Can you hear that?' whispered Kevin.

'*Ja.*'

Stripe placed his paw on my shoulder and breathed hot doggy

breath into my face. I turned over onto my front, hugging the pillow underneath my shoulder.

My mind flipped through hundreds of moments from the past twenty-four hours. Glimpses of Mom. Moments where happy lines tweaked the corners of her eyes and her head tilted gently to one side. The closer I studied each little smile the sadder they felt.

Chocolates

I took my morning coffee white with two sugars, the same way Dad took it. But this was different to the stuff I drank at home. It was stronger, with real milk instead of powdered creamer, and Brandy only used brown sugar. I leaned up against the fridge and sipped. This must be how Dad felt in the mornings, the man of the house alone with his thoughts and his coffee, while Mom got breakfast ready. No one said much to me. They gave me space to wake up properly, which I liked. I stretched my arm out and yawned so everyone could see how tired I was.

'Mom, when am I gonna get swimming trunks?' said Kevin.

'As soon as we get to the beach, Kettle,' said Mom. 'Now, eat your breakfast.'

'But Alex has trunks and if we go to the beach and everyone's swimming and I can't then it's not fair.' Kevin's voice was getting higher and higher.

Dad would be reaching for his belt by now.

I sighed, long and slow. 'Kevin, please don't go on and on about your bloody trunks. No one cares, OK.'

Mom put down her coffee and Brandy paused halfway through

buttering her toast. Their faces showed the same expression, as if I had said something stupid.

Kevin went into overdrive. 'It's not fair! You promised. Everyone's going to be swimming but me. No one ever listens to me!'

I sipped my coffee and let Mom deal with this.

'Kevin,' said Mom, slapping the table, 'look at me.'

His mouth stayed open, mid-sentence.

'Listen to me very carefully.' Mom's voice was both soft and firm. 'After breakfast we are going to load up the car and drive to North Beach. As soon as we park, you and I are going straight to the shops to buy you a pair of trunks. I'll let you choose whatever colour you want. Then, we'll cross the street onto the beach and enjoy our day. OK?'

Kevin's eyes lowered to the cornflakes in front of him. 'OK.'

Mom wasn't finished either. She turned and spoke to me with the same no-nonsense tone. 'And as for you, *young man,* sit down and eat your breakfast.'

I poured the last few sips of coffee into the sink and sat down.

Driving to the beach, we stopped at the lights opposite a dusty parking lot with about twenty Kombis parked at odd angles to each other. Most of the vans were white. A few of the flashier ones had tinted windows and white-walled tyres.

Kaffir taxis.

A couple of taxi drivers whistled and waved for more people to get in their vans. I always wondered how the blacks knew which ones were taxis and which were regular vans, there were no markings to let you know. And another thing, how could ten people all be in the same taxi at once? Were they all going in the same direction? If not, how did they divide up the fare?

Stripe started barking at them through the open window. The ones that heard him very casually turned their backs and ignored us.

'What do you call ten blacks in a taxi?' said Kevin, announcing his joke to the whole car.

No one answered but I knew what was coming. Brandy turned around in the front seat and was about to open her mouth when Kevin delivered the punchline.

'A box of chocolates!'

He sat back, grinning, waiting for everyone to laugh. They didn't. Even Stripe stopped barking. Brandy raised her eyebrows and let the silence speak for itself. I must have heard that joke a million times and it was only funny the first time. But Kevin was just warming up. He'd memorised hundreds of jokes and could tell one after the other, for hours.

'OK,' said Kevin, 'why don't little black children play in sand-pits?' And with only a second's delay he went on, 'Because lions keep covering them up.'

'Kevin, I don't want to hear any more jokes,' said Brandy, pointing her finger.

'But that's Dad's favourite one,' said Kevin.

Brandy shook her head. 'Why am I not surprised?'

I rolled my eyes, expecting a speech about being nice to black people and not repeating jokes you hear at school even though everyone thought they were funny. And besides, she wasn't our mother, I didn't need to listen to her.

'What's the big deal?' I said. 'It's only a joke.'

I expected Brandy to explode, to get really angry and yell at me for being cheeky. She didn't. She shifted round in her seat till her knee wedged against the handbrake and put out her hand, expecting me to take it. Her eyes glinted like polished bits of tiger's-eye. I reached forward and put my hand on hers.

'Every joke, every condescending look, every sly remark, adds to the enormous weight that we force them to carry,' she said softly. 'Each joke assumes that one kind of person is more import-ant than the rest. It separates us from them, little by little, till we're so far apart we can't see them being crushed. That, Alex, is the big deal.'

Swallowing hard, I took back my hand and stared out the window at a very old man climbing into a taxi. A younger man gripped his elbow and helped him onto a seat. When he got comfortable

154

the taxi driver handed the old man his cane, which he balanced across his lap, and slid the door closed. Our car revved as the traffic began to move and Mom drove us towards the beach.

Grit

Mom parked at North Beach. We all got out and Brandy put Stripe on a leash so he wouldn't run into the road. She jerked the leash and told Stripe to sit.

'Grace, do you know where you're going?' said Brandy.

'I think so. If I go along Marine Parade and then up Sea View Road, we should find something along there, right?'

'Well, if I were you, I'd go to, um . . .' Brandy paused, and thought about suitable shops. Then she gave Mom a list of possible stores to visit. I let the women talk and wandered a few steps away from the car.

This place wasn't what I had imagined. A wide road separated the beach from the buildings. The city hid behind a wall of high-rise hotels that stood tall and proud, staring out across the sea. Between the beach and the hotels was a set of swimming pools and fountains and fairground rides that were slowly opening for business. It seemed weird to me that someone would build swimming pools so close to the beach.

Workers in blue overalls smoked and shuffled their feet as they swept the pavements and hotel entrances. Close to me a black woman with an orange cloth wrapped around her head wiped the tables of an outdoor café. A tall Indian man opened the ticket office to the House of Horror.

The ride closest to me looked like bumper cars but all the

shutters were down. On the roof was a neon sign, *Crazy Crash*. But with the lights switched off the letters were ashen and cheerless. Further down the street were Spinning Teacups wrapped in tarpaulin. In the distance the loops and arches of a rollercoaster were as lifeless as a sea-monster skeleton.

Mom and Kevin disappeared into the city while Brandy slipped on a big pair of sunglasses and pulled a floppy straw hat down over her ears. We crossed the road and stepped down onto the beach. Brandy took off her flip-flops and rolled up her trousers to just under her knees. I took off my sandals and sunk my feet into powdery soft sand. Everywhere tiny shells exposed their bellies and insects buzzed around dried-up twists of black seaweed. Closer to the water the sand was flat and damp. My feet no longer left potholes but thin impressions. The pressure of each step squashed moisture away from my foot, leaving a little dry halo around my toes. The ocean washed and dampened all other sounds. After a while, we settled into a rhythm of six steps to every wave.

Brandy let Stripe off the leash and he sprinted around in circles at full speed with his ears back and his tongue lagging out. She waved a stick above her head and threw it into the water. Stripe barked and splashed in after it. Biting down on the stick, he raced up the beach with it between his teeth, then lay down and began chewing at the wet bark.

Foamy surf splashed over my ankles. This was the first time I had touched the ocean. It was weird to think that I was standing on the very edge of Africa. There was nowhere else to go. Everything stopped right here. The beach was like a borderline. On this side was firm ground, but I could sense the sea daring me to step across the boundary and be swept out on its unsteady waves.

I stared out at the deep water, heavy cold surges of blue. But the more I looked the greener it became. The sea was definitely a murky green, I was sure of that. Yet, as soon as I changed my mind it began to look blue again.

'Your mother used to stand and watch the sea, exactly the way you are now,' said Brandy.

156

'Were you in the same class as Mom?' I said.

'No, I was a drama student, but we shared a flat together for two years. Your mother used to come swimming every morning before class.'

'And did she meet my dad here too?' I said, not sure if this was the exact question I was looking for.

'Sort of,' said Brandy. She placed a cigarette in her mouth and lit it, cupping the flame in her hands.

'You see, back when your grandparents were still alive, your mother went up to Pretoria to visit them over the Easter holidays. While she was there a few of her friends invited her to a dance. She told me that the dance hall was packed full and a young man asked her to dance by grabbing her from behind and forcing her onto the dance floor. It turned out to be Bruce, your father. At first she said she didn't like him at all, but apparently he was very funny and bought her lots of drinks. After the dance he drove her back to her parents' house.'

She exhaled and the smoke vanished in the breeze.

'The next day,' she continued, 'he showed up outside the house and they had coffee together. The following day he was outside the house again. And, according to your mom, he turned up every day waiting for her in his car. Eventually, her father, your *Oupa*, had to have a word with him. I don't know all the details, I can only tell you what I know. I'm sure if you ask your mother she'll add a whole different slant to the story. But a crucial detail is this, at some point she must have given him our address here in Durban, because a week after she got back, I remember she was all dolled up and about to go out on a date.'

That bit didn't sound right to me.

'Don't look at me like that,' laughed Brandy. 'Your mother used to go out on dates, believe me. So, anyway, we heard a knock at our door and I thought it was her date. When she opened the door there was Bruce. "Boo," he said and walked right in. I think your mom was very flattered that he had come all that way to see her. She introduced us and went through to the kitchen to make coffee. When her real date turned up Bruce answered the door. He took the flowers from the young man and said, "Sorry, pal, this one's taken," and closed the door. And that was that. Within three months they were married and soon after, you were born.'

I had never heard this story before, but it sounded like Dad. 'You don't like my dad, do you?' I said.

Brandy bent down and picked up a shell the size of a two-cent piece. She stubbed out her cigarette, all the while carefully shaping her answer. 'He's not all bad,' she said. 'If that man had half a brain he'd be an unstoppable politician.'

Kevin came skipping along the beach towards us and Stripe went bounding out to meet him. The two of them played and danced around each other. Kevin pointed his fingers and shouted, 'Bang!' Immediately, Stripe flopped to the ground.

'Good boy,' said Kevin, rubbing the dog's tummy. 'Good boy.'

Mom walked quietly up to meet us, smiling at Stripe wriggling on the ground.

'Did you find what you were looking for?' Brandy asked Kevin.

'*Ja*, I got really cool ones,' said Kevin, pulling down his trousers. Underneath were bright orange dayglo trunks, the kind you could see from miles away. My trunks were brown and boring. I knew I should try to say something nice to Kevin. As I opened my mouth Mom interrupted me.

'Alex, I got something for you too. But you have to promise to share it with your brother.'

She handed me a small black box. Inside were luminous, atomic shades of green, yellow, orange and pink. Futuristic colours.

'It's special suncream,' explained Mom, 'for your nose and lips.'

Surfers on TV wore this stuff and I'd always wanted to try it, but didn't want to act like an excited little boy. I was more grown up now. So I shrugged and said, 'Thanks,' and closed the box.

I could see from Mom's face I'd overdone it a bit. This wasn't the kind of 'thank you' she was hoping for. I didn't mean it that way. Whenever I tried to act like a man it always came out as boredom or anger. But taking it back and apologising was harder than promising myself to act better next time.

'Let's go. Let's go,' said Kevin, keen to get into the water. But Mom insisted on rubbing lotion on our backs.

The four of us found a quiet spot and laid out our towels to mark our territory. I opened the black box and said to Kevin, 'What colours do you want?'

'I know, make my nose pink and my lips orange,' he said.

I dipped my forefinger into the creamy lotion and carefully coloured in his nose.

'Go like this,' I said, jutting out my jaw with my bottom lip tight across my teeth. Kevin copied me. Using my middle finger, so the colours didn't mix, I painted his bottom lip orange.

'Now do stripes across my cheeks, like an Indian chief,' said Kevin.

'When you boys are finished doing your make-up, you should—'

'It's *not* make-up, Mom,' said Kevin, 'it's war paint.'

'Excuse me,' said Mom, smiling at Brandy.

After this comment I almost decided not to wear any myself. I gave Mom strict instructions: 'Only put some on my nose and lip, exactly like on TV.'

Her finger, covered in yellow paste, came closer and closer to my face. For a second I thought she might smudge it across my forehead as a joke. She didn't. She stroked the length of my nose, then rubbed some across my lips. If I crossed my eyes I could see a bright yellow blur on my nose. I turned round and let Mom rub suncream onto my back while Brandy rubbed lotion on Kevin.

'OK. You're done,' said Brandy. 'Now, do you see those two buoys out in the water?'

We both looked. There was no one in the water.

'What two boys?' said Kevin.

Brandy smiled to herself. 'The two orange balloons floating in the water. One's over there and the other one is right along the beach towards the pier. Do you see them?'

We nodded.

'Those are shark nets. Only swim between those two balloons.

It's not safe to swim anywhere else. If you do, the lifeguards will ask you to leave.'

I stared out across the water.

Sharks.

They expected me to go out there, with the sharks. Couldn't they bite through the nets?

'Don't look so worried,' said Brandy. 'Go on. Go have a good time.'

'C'mon, Alex,' said Kevin, jogging towards the waves. I caught up with him, trying not to look scared. Lots of people swam here every day, I reminded myself. This is what people did for fun. It had to be safe. Sharks probably didn't come here that much.

I jogged past a lifeguard who had a painted yellow nose just like mine. He winked like we were in a secret club. I winked back and suddenly felt braver.

A couple of toddlers splashed in the shallow surf. Kevin ran right by them and flopped forward into the water. He immediately stood up and shook his head as the next wave pushed him over backwards. It spat him out on the beach where he sat laughing.

'This is great fun, Alex. The water's warm. C'mon!'

He leaped back into the water as a wave rolled and frothed around his bright orange trunks. I lifted my chest and marched into the ocean. The water retreated, then rushed forwards and shoved me in the chest like a bully, trying to get me angry. My legs kicked for balance and by the time I stood up again there was nothing but foam around my ankles. Kevin's head and shoulders floated a few metres out among the swells. The waves seemed to rush right by without affecting him.

More determined than ever, I marched out towards Kevin. The sea slapped against me, pushing me back. I clenched my teeth, bracing myself for the next wave. It rose up and smacked me, full in the face, throwing me over backwards. There was anger in the water as it wrestled me head over heels. I fought back with all my strength, trying to keep upright. Somehow, I found myself at the surface and desperately gasped for air. But it was all a trick. An enormous wave thundered down on top of me. My body flopped about like a rag doll in a washing machine. Salty, grainy water burned its way down my throat, making me want to cough. Grabbing my mouth I panicked. Don't cough. Don't drown. Get out. Get out! My head bumped off the sandy bottom as I tumbled along the beach.

The water retreated. Crawling away, I spluttered and coughed up horrible salt water.

'Are you OK?' said a small girl standing next to me.

Before I could answer the sea kicked me from behind, throwing me forwards onto my chest and dragging me up the beach. Sand went down the front of my trunks and I swallowed more water.

The girl came up and patted my back with her tiny hand. 'Mommy says you mussn't drink the water 'cause it tastes bad.'

She was only about six years old, not even half as strong as me. How could she play happily in the water but I nearly drowned?

'Must I call my mommy?' she said, her blue eyes blinking at me.

'Leave me alone, you little brat.'

She stood straighter, her bottom lip quivering.

As I got up the water drained from my trunks, leaving a wad of sand to gather at my crotch. I scooped out handfuls of sloppy mud and flung it at the ground. But I couldn't get it all. A rough grit coated my trunks' built-in underpants. I waddled up the beach like a cowboy.

Mom saw me approaching and wiped her eyes with the back of her hand. Brandy checked to see what had startled Mom. As soon as she spotted me she quickly took off her sunglasses and gave them to Mom. They had obviously been talking. The atmosphere around them was thick with gossip and women's secrets.

'That was quick,' said Brandy, giving me a broad polite smile. 'Is everything OK?'

'I'm fine,' I said, 'just don't feel like swimming, that's all.'

Mom's face turned to look for Kevin. Even with her eyes hidden behind black lenses I could tell she had been crying.

'Where's Kevin?' she said.

'He's fine. He's still out there.'

Mom stood up. 'I'm going to check on him,' she said, leaving me to guess what she and Brandy had been talking about. Brandy offered no clues.

'Would you like a banana?' she said.

'No.'

I sat down with my back to her and dug my fists in the sand.

Toothpaste

I dried the last plate while Kevin pulled out the plug and drained the dirty soapy water from the sink. Our chores for the evening were done. For the last couple of nights we had all played either Monopoly or Cluedo. Tonight I felt like playing something else.

'Hey, Kev, do you want to play chess?' I said.

'Chess is boring,' he said, throwing the sodden sponge into the sink. 'I know, let's turn all the lights off and play Commandos with torches.'

I was too grown up for Commandos. 'I don't know, Kev. Brandy won't like us running around her house in the dark.'

'We could just play in our room,' he said. But we both knew that would be pointless.

The phone rang.

Mom put down her glass of wine and swapped tense looks with Brandy.

'Hello,' said Brandy into the receiver. There was a pause. 'Hang on just a moment, I'll get her for you.'

Brandy put her hand over the mouthpiece and whispered over to Mom, 'Grace. It's Bruce on the phone for you.'

Mom stood up and smoothed her blouse across her stomach. She breathed in and marched across the living room.

Brandy said, 'There's another phone in my room. It'll be more private in there.'

Glancing over her shoulder at us, Mom went into the bedroom. Brandy listened for a moment till she heard Mom pick up the other phone, then gently put down the receiver.

'Right, boys,' she said in a sparky voice, 'who wants to play Scrabble?'

I put the last cup into the cupboard and hung up the dishcloth.

'Is that Dad on the phone?' said Kevin.

'Yes, it is. He and your mother have a lot to talk about, so maybe we should give them some space.'

'Can I speak to Dad?' said Kevin.

Brandy came over and hugged Kevin. He rested his ear against her belly for a second and gazed up at her, waiting for an answer. She smoothed his hair down and said, 'He'll call back. You can speak to him then.' The moment Kevin turned his face away, she nodded to me, trying to get me on her side. 'Let's get the Scrabble out, so long.'

That phrase always annoyed me. So long . . . *as what?* But I knew the answer. We'll pretend like Mom isn't arguing with Dad, so long as I act like an adult and help Brandy distract Kevin for the next twenty minutes. Well, I wasn't interested. And I was fed up of being a grown-up only when it suited other people.

'Me and Kev are going to bed early tonight,' I said.

'Really?' said Brandy, trying to look at Kevin to see if what I said was true.

'Yes, we've got stuff to do upstairs. Don't we, Kev?'

Kevin blinked blankly as something powerful passed between us and he stepped away from Brandy. '*Ja*, we're playing chess,' he said, '. . . under the blankets.'

'Under the blankets?' said Brandy.

I looked her straight in the eye. 'Of course, that's how we always play.'

In the bathroom, I squeezed toothpaste along the bristles of my toothbrush. Kevin held out his brush and I squashed some out

163

for him. We brushed, staring at each other in the mirror, the lumps in our cheeks going round and round.

Kevin leaned forward and spat white foam in the sink. 'I saw Mom crying today,' he said. 'She was sitting outside on the swing chair by herself.' He put the toothbrush back in his mouth.

I carried on brushing round and round and round, pressing hard into the corners to get all the dirt out. The mint tingled on my tongue.

Kevin spat, rinsed his mouth and cleaned his toothbrush. He stared at my image in the mirror and said, 'Yesterday, I heard Brandy talking to Mom and she said, "Who will the boys live with?"'

With my mouth full of paste, I shrugged as if to say, 'So?'

'So . . .' said Kevin, 'do you think, maybe, Mom and Dad are getting divorced?'

I almost choked, spitting out the frothy white foam. I rinsed, turned from the mirror to look at him directly. 'This isn't like TV, Kev. They're not getting divorced, OK.'

He wasn't ready to take my word for it. 'Well, why isn't Dad here, with us, on holiday?'

'Didn't you hear what he said?' I said, raising my hands. 'He had to work. Do you think he can just leave his job because school closes for the summer? No. He can't. But that doesn't mean they're getting divorced.'

I liked the way it came out. Kevin felt the force of it, too. He turned his back, lifted the toilet seat and had a pee while I washed my face. I sensed him mulling it over. He needed time to let it settle in because he was younger and didn't understand things as clearly as I did.

As I climbed the stairs I heard Mom whispering loudly to Brandy in the other room. She was angry but trying to keep her voice down at the same time. I couldn't make out what she was saying and I didn't care. Let them have their little secrets. It would all blow over and be forgotten in a couple of days.

Kevin opened up the chessboard and started setting out the pieces.

'I thought you didn't like chess?' I said.

'There's nothing else to do.' He picked up two pawns, one of each colour, and hid them behind his back. 'Choose a hand,' he said.

I pointed to his right. He brought both hands forward and opened out his fingers. I was white and he was black.

After a few moves it was obvious that each of us was playing a very defensive game, waiting for our opponent to make his move. We both sat quietly in exactly the same position – arms and legs crossed – staring at the board. From underneath us the sound of Mom's sobs echoed up through the floor.

'Alex,' whispered Kevin.

'What?' I whispered back.

'Can I ask you something?'

'What?'

'Do you think Dad loves us?'

I sat straight. His eyes were glistening and filling up with tears.

'Don't be stupid. Of course he loves us, we're his sons.'

Kevin's lip trembled as he rubbed the back of his hand across his face. 'It's just that, sometimes, I think he only loves you, Alex, but not me and Mom.'

'That's not true, Kev,' I said, wanting to give him proof. 'You know that's not true.'

Jellyfish

Mango juice glowed bright and happy in the jug, but I couldn't stomach it. Coffee was the proper way to start the day. Each bitter sip made me more alert.

'C'mon, Sonny-o, sit down and eat your breakfast,' said Mom, moving all the time, pausing only for a second to place her palm across her forehead then finding something else to do. Puffy dark rings hung under her eyes. I sipped my coffee, watching her over the edge of my mug. She buttered each slice of bread as if it were a race, slapped on a slice of cheese and shoved them into a Tupperware tub, then packed up the picnic basket and took it out to the car.

I wondered if she'd slept at all. After all the crying last night, I guessed she lay silently on top of the bedcovers and waited for the sun to rise.

Kevin spooned cornflakes into his mouth and Brandy read the paper while waiting for her toast. Without looking up she said, 'You'd better eat some breakfast, Alex, before she loses her temper.'

'What's the big rush?' I sighed.

'She's just keen to get out and do things,' said Brandy, still not looking at me.

'What did my dad say to her last night?'

She lowered the newspaper. With a sharp metallic rattle, her toast popped up but she never took her eyes off me. 'Why don't you ask your mother about that?' After a moment's thought, she added, 'Maybe you should try talking to her while we're at the beach today.'

Kevin crunched on a fresh mouthful of cornflakes. I sat down opposite him and he kept crunching, his jaws going round and round. Before he swallowed he took another big spoonful and the crunching got louder, the chewing faster. Nobody needed to eat like that. I ignored him and put two slices of bread in the toaster, then stared out the window at the palm leaves and sky. Kevin stuffed his face with more cornflakes, crunching even louder.

Brandy looked at him. 'You seem very hungry this morning?' she said, with a curious smile.

Kevin smiled through hamster cheeks. His casual shrug made me wonder if he was playing some sort of game.

'Alex,' said Mom, coming back into the kitchen, 'have you still not had anything to eat yet?'

'Mom! I'm busy waiting for my toast. Stop nagging me all the time.'

'Don't get lippy with me, young man,' said Mom.

'I'm not getting lippy.'

'Yes, you are. Just because you're in a strange mood doesn't mean you've got to spoil this beautiful day for everyone else.'

'But I'm not in a bad mood,' I said, my voice suddenly pitching higher than I expected.

Mom put her hands on her hips and gave me a look as if I was being childish. 'Whatever you say, Mr Grumpy Head.'

Kevin crunched and crunched his cornflakes.

'When you boys are finished remember to quickly wash your plates. We're leaving in fifteen minutes,' said Mom. She turned and disappeared into her room. Brandy got up, rinsed her plate and mug in the sink, and went through to the bathroom where I could hear her brushing her teeth.

Kevin lifted the bowl to his lips and slurped the last mouthful of milk. He stood up and started putting all the breakfast dishes in the sink.

My toast popped up. I put the slices on my plate and reached for the butter and jam.

'I'll wash but you have to dry,' said Kevin, as he turned on the taps.

'No way. You washed last night,' I said.

'But you're still eating . . .'

'Just give me two seconds so I can finish my breakfast.'

Kevin put his hands in the water and started rinsing a mug.

'Kevin, stop doing that right now!' I said, careful not to shout.

'You're not the boss of me.'

I threw down my toast and stood up. 'I am the boss of you.'

'No, you're not.'

'Yes, I am! Dad said while we're on holiday I'm the man of the house, which means you have to do what I say. Now get away from that sink!'

I grabbed him by the shoulder and yanked him backwards, causing him to slip and graze his shoulder off a chair. It wasn't

167

sore but he started wailing like a big baby, just to get me in trouble.

'Get up. It wasn't that bad,' I said.

As I came closer he kicked me in the knee, so I kicked him back. Kevin jumped up and charged me. As we wrestled he managed to grip my hand and went to bite my thumb. I felt his wet lips and his teeth sinking in, so I slapped him, hard, across the face.

Now he really started screaming. Both Mom and Brandy came running into the kitchen. 'What the hell's going on?' said Mom.

'Alex hit me!' sobbed Kevin, holding his face.

Mom peeled his fingers away from his face and examined his pink cheek. She turned and stared at me. 'Is this true, Alex?'

I sighed and nodded.

Mom folded her arms. 'I'm surprised at you, Alex.'

'But he was going to bite me. What was I supposed to do?'

'If we were at home your father would give you the belt. You know that.'

I lowered my eyes and waited for Mom to dream up my punishment.

'But you're too old for that now,' she said. 'I'm not going to discipline you.'

I didn't expect that and she must have read the confusion on my face.

'How can you can solve your differences by hitting each other?' said Mom. 'You have to learn when to walk away, Alex. If you want to be treated like a grown-up, start being more mature.'

My heart sank. This was worse than getting the belt.

'Now, say sorry to your brother.'

They all stared at me, waiting. I had to apologise. 'Sorry, Kev.'

Mom turned to Kevin. 'You too, Kettle.'

Kevin threw up his hands. 'Me? But I didn't do anything.'

'Kevin . . .' said Mom, signalling with her eyes that she wasn't going to negotiate.

Kevin let out a long sigh and mumbled, 'Sorry, Alex.'

'Right,' said Brandy, clapping her hands together. 'Let's get moving.'

As soon as we arrived at the beach, Mom, Kevin and Brandy went straight into the water. But I didn't. The sea wasn't as fun as it looked and I wasn't in the mood to be around anyone. Being alone was better.

I walked up the beach by myself, rolling my new penknife in my pocket. The humidity was so intense it felt like breathing in steam but every now and then a fresh gust of sea air blew across my face, making the day bearable. A thick murky haze hung across the horizon and seemed to blend in with the ocean. Wave after wave washed across the beach till the sand lost its yellowness.

I missed my bike. What I really wanted to do was cycle out to the rugby fields and stare at the sky, to get that feeling of space. I missed the colours, the simple way in which everything was either pure green or pure blue.

I stepped over a massive lump of snot covered in sand, and after two more steps I saw another one. It was pink and slimy with long entrails stretched out towards the sea. A jellyfish. There were dozens of them washed up by the tide. I bent down for a closer look.

If Dad was here he'd probably pick it up and throw it at Brandy as a joke. Why wasn't Dad here? And what was he doing while we were away?

I opened my penknife and poked the jellyfish. It contracted a bit as I stabbed it, but only a bit. It was either dying or dead. You could see right through it to the sand underneath. Inside were bluish-white bits that must have been its brain. I sliced it quickly from one side to the other and watched it limply fold open.

It was obvious that Dad and Mom had had an argument. They had probably bickered late at night in their bedroom so Kevin and I wouldn't notice. Loads of parents fight. Mom probably decided to come on this holiday to take a break and let things calm down. There was definitely nothing to worry about.

Poking with the blade, I tried dissecting the brains from the heart but it all looked the same. There were no eyes or bones or anything. It was all a weird goo with no real centre.

But why did Mom have to cry all the time? Every time Dad phoned there were more tears. And I couldn't seem to help her. Every time I tried to act like the man of the house, somehow I made things worse.

It was pointless. I gave up the careful dissection and started hacking it to bits. Chopping and slicing till it was mush. I stood up and cleaned the knife on my shorts.

When I got back, I met Brandy walking up from the surf, picking her way through the little camps of families. She sat down on her towel next to me and put on her hat and shades. She didn't bother drying herself, preferring to let her wet skin dry slowly.

'Are you still in the huff, Alex?' she said.

'I'm not in the huff.'

'No? So what's going on? You seem . . . distant.'

I rested my chin on my knees and wiggled my toes under the sand, burying them deep down to where it was cooler. Brandy didn't seem to be waiting for an answer, which was good because I wasn't going to give her one. The two of us sat and listened to children shouting and playing and to the low thunder of waves. Seconds became minutes and still the two of us said nothing. After about five minutes, once I was sure Brandy wasn't going to talk to me, she leaned closer and said, 'Aquamarine.'

I looked at her not sure I'd heard her correctly.

'Whenever I look at the sea,' said Brandy, 'I think of the word aquamarine.'

I said the word quietly to myself.

'Did you know that aqua-marine literally means water-water?' said Brandy.

'*Ja*, I knew that.'

170

'I've always found that interesting,' she said. 'A word for water perfectly describing its colour.'

I heaped sand onto my feet, enjoying the feeling of the fine grains running through my fingers. We both became silent again but it felt friendlier than before.

'Well, it's too hot for me out here,' said Brandy, suddenly standing up. 'Shall we go for a swim?'

I shook my head.

'I didn't take you for a masochist,' said Brandy, standing up.

'What's a masochist?'

'Someone who enjoys hurting himself.'

'I don't enjoy it.'

'Then what? Are you afraid of the sea?'

I looked her straight in the eye and lied. 'No, of course not.'

'Then come with me,' she said. She reached out her hand, waiting for me to take it. 'Come on. Let's go.'

I took her hand and she helped me up.

We waded in together, up to our thighs, then up to our waists. A large swell began to curl at the top and rush towards us. Just before it hit, Brandy disappeared but I got hit in the chest, knocked over backwards and left on the beach with a mouth full of salty water. I was ready to leave.

'Are you OK?' said Brandy, rubbing my back.

I kept coughing and coughing but nodded that I was fine. She waited with me till I felt better.

'What happened?' she said.

'It just smacked me right in the face,' I said. 'It always does that. I don't think I'm a strong enough swimmer to be in the sea.'

'Nonsense, you're a great swimmer,' said Brandy, 'but don't fight it, you'll tire yourself out. C'mon, let's try again.'

She kept a tight hold of my hand as we waded back into the water. I looked around for Mom and Kevin but couldn't see them. It was better that way. I'd prefer they thought I figured this out for myself than have them watch Brandy hold my hand.

'Think of it as a game,' said Brandy, as the white surf rolled past our knees. 'When the waves are small you have to jump and when they're big you have to duck.'

We went in deeper, still holding hands. A wave curled, broke, and came rumbling towards us.

Brandy counted, 'One, two, *three*!' We jumped together. The wave lifted us up, held us for a moment, and lowered us down till our toes touched the sandy floor.

'Good,' said Brandy. 'Now let's go a little deeper.'

She must have seen my hesitation because she said, 'Don't worry. The ocean is like a big child, it only wants to play. You're never really in any danger.'

A big wave came tumbling angrily towards us. Brandy wasn't worried at all.

'Alex,' she shouted over the roar, 'as soon as it's close, hold your breath and dive underneath it.'

I nodded. It's not as scary as it looks, I told myself. It's only a game. The wall of water got closer. I filled my lungs and dived. Underwater I lost my grip of Brandy's hand and swam a few strokes. My knee rubbed against the sand on the bottom and I realised the water was quite shallow. So I stood up. It was only waist deep, and flat as a pool. Behind me the wave rushed up the beach.

Brandy grinned and splashed me. 'Well done,' she said, 'you made that look easy.'

I didn't want to make a big deal out of it. '*Ja*, it wasn't too bad.'

'Shall we go out a little deeper?' she said.

I shook the water out of my hair and said, '*Ja*, OK.'

Soda Float

For lunch Mom handed out cheese sandwiches from the Tupperware tub. The butter had entirely evaporated and the cheddar was sweating and rubbery. After swallowing one down I couldn't eat any more. Brandy only ate half of hers, but Kevin didn't seem to care how bad they tasted and asked for more.

Yellow, midday sun pressed down on the bodies splayed across the beach. The heat sucked the seawater off my skin leaving a salty white dust. When the breeze stopped, the air against my face felt like warm tea steam.

Brandy bit into a red apple and stared out across the sea. After a while she said, 'I need to go home quickly and get some more suncream, and I should check on Stripe too.' She turned to Kevin. 'Would you like to come with me?'

He looked surprised. '*Ja*, OK,' he said, stuffing the last piece of bread into his mouth. He wriggled his toes into his flip-flops and stood up, ready to go.

'Well then,' said Brandy, 'we'll be back in an hour.'

She stood up, wrapped a towel around her waist and looped her handbag over her shoulder. As she left she turned back as if she'd forgotten something.

'Grace,' she said, 'there are some nice shaded cafés if you go down towards the aquarium.' Brandy lowered her sunglasses. 'Perhaps you could take Alex for some ice cream . . . spend some quality time together . . . have a chat.'

Whatever private code had been passed between them, Mom didn't like it. She stared at Brandy for a full twenty seconds with her lips clenched shut. Finally Mom nodded and said, 'OK, thanks a lot, *Brandy*, for the suggestion. We might just do that.' Long after Mom stopped talking her head kept nodding.

Brandy straightened her hat, took Kevin by the hand, and disappeared between the parasols and sausage-pink bodies on the crowded beach.

* * *

We found a table in the corner. A waitress with dreadlocks and a yellow grin took our order. On her chest she wore two badges. The first was a little green badge with a silver star, the proof of her pass to work in the city. The second was a white name badge with the word *Hope* printed on it.

I ordered a soda float with Coke and banana ice cream. Mom wanted a glass of white wine, a large one. Instead of looking at each other we gazed around at the other diners. There was no music, just the clinking of knives and forks on plates and the low hum of private conversations. A large whirring fan slowly turned its head, as if carefully watching everyone. From the ceiling, red and gold Christmas decorations fluttered and spun every time the fan glanced at them.

The waitress returned with our drinks. She lowered her tray onto our table and put a little napkin down in front of each of us. Carefully, she placed our drinks on the napkins and grinned at us again. Her teeth were as thick as mielie pips and there were gaps between them. As if each tooth in her crowded mouth was shying away from the others.

Mom gently patted the table and said, 'Thank you.'

Using my straw, I poked at the dollop of ice cream floating in the tall glass. The Coke fizzed underneath. My little iceberg rolled on the surface. I jabbed it, trying to force it under but it kept bobbing up, still keeping its shape.

Mom took a gulp of wine. She put it down, then quickly changed her mind and took another sip. Eyeing me, she placed the glass in front of her and slid it to the centre of the table, still on her side but just out of reach. She leaned on her elbows and touched the tips of her fingers together, as if holding an invisible ball. The two of us stared into the ball for a few seconds. To me, the ball looked empty. To Mom, it contained all her thoughts, which she analysed one by one, deciding which to show me first. With a deep breath she interlaced her fingers and crushed the ball.

'Alex, I have something to tell you,' she said.

I sipped my drink. It wasn't the low hush – almost whisper – of her voice. It wasn't the tone either, or the way she forced herself to look me in the eye. It was all those things mashed together. This was going to be a prepared speech about her and Dad.

'Your father and I have been experiencing some difficulties.'

I knew it.

'There's nothing to worry about. We're not getting divorced or anything. It's just that . . .' she cleared her throat, 'everyone is different and it takes time to sort out those differences.' She lowered her eyes and I guessed she was inwardly glancing at the mental notes she had made because she quickly added, 'Kevin's too young to cope with this, so you have to promise not to tell him. But I thought you should know.'

That was it. Speech over. Now I would have to say something.

'What kind of differences?'

'It's complicated. Your father needs time alone to make some decisions. We both need to think things over.'

I didn't like the way she kept saying 'your father'. She usually said 'Dad' which is what we called him. The more she said 'your father' the more it sounded like he was only connected to me, as if he was standing outside the family looking in.

I sipped through the straw. 'Is that why we're on holiday? In case things get so bad that Dad walks out?'

'I told you, sweetheart, we're not getting divorced,' she said, shaking her head.

I kept staring at her till she told me more.

'But, yes, you're right,' she continued. 'We came here so I could get some space. It helps to get perspective, think clearly. I've had a good cry and it's been wonderful for me to see Brandy. Talking to her has helped get my thoughts straight.'

'What do you mean you had a *good* cry?' I said.

Mom gave me a little smile. 'I just needed to let it all out. I know it sounds silly, Sonny-o, but it helped.'

The waitress came back to our table and asked if everything was OK.

In a happy cheery voice Mom said, 'Everything's fine, thank you.'

We got another view of those yellow teeth as she turned and left. She wore no socks. Her red shoes were too small for her. So the backs of her shoes had been crushed flat, forcing her to shuffle about as if wearing slippers.

Mom reached for her wine.

'I've always wanted you to see Durban. I hope you're having a good holiday,' she said.

She was changing the subject. I stabbed the ice cream blob with the straw, holding it under, trying to drown it, but a small chunk broke off and it floated back to the surface.

'I know I've been a bit distant recently and I'm sorry,' said Mom. 'I really appreciate the good example you've been setting for Kevin. You've been a big help to me, son.'

I finally wedged the scoop of ice cream against the side of the glass and forced it under, right to the bottom, holding it there, watching it disintegrate in the black cola. I thought about what Kevin had said. Without looking up I said, 'Do you still love Dad?'

I expected her to say 'Of course I do!' but she didn't. For a moment she didn't do anything. She picked up her glass and drank the whole lot down, then sat back on her chair. Her eyes fixed on me.

'When I first met your father I fell madly in love with him. He was charming. There's always been something alluring about him that I can't quite put my finger on. He has a way of turning everything he does, even going to buy a newspaper, into an adventure. Being with him was always so much fun. I suppose I felt flattered that he even noticed me. But recently we haven't done anything together. And your father has done things behind my back. Some of which I know about, but I'm sure there's more.' She stopped herself. But my question still needed an answer. 'Honestly, son, I don't know. I'm confused and I don't know if I love him any more.'

Kevin was right and the force of it shot through me. I suddenly felt ten years older than the person I had been thirty seconds ago. I let go of the straw and the ice cream rose to the surface, shrunken but still alive.

'But listen, son, there's no need to worry. No marriage is perfect. At some point everybody has difficulties. The secret is to deal with them properly and move on.'

I couldn't tell if this was part of the scripted speech or not.

'It's like playing chess,' she said, although she'd never played a game in her life. 'If somebody bumps the board and all the pieces fall over then nobody's won and nobody's lost. The best thing to do is pick up the pieces and start over. That's what your father and I are doing. We're starting over.'

What she said sounded simple but there were hidden things to think over. Were she and Dad 'playing to win'? And who had spoiled the game by knocking over all the pieces?

Mom reached over and touched me. Her thumb rubbed the back of my hand. Even in the middle of summer her hands were cold.

'It's OK, Alex,' she said quietly, 'you'll see, when we get home everything will be back to normal.'

I shifted in my seat, folding my leg under me. Mom didn't let go of my hand. I wanted to believe her. I couldn't stand being the man of the house for ever.

'Are you sure?' I said, searching her eyes for something solid, something certain.

She leaned in closer, gripping both my hands in hers.

'No matter what happens, Alex, everything's going to be all right.' Her eyes began to fill, not because she didn't believe it but because she did.

Deep down I sensed this was a different kind of fight. There would be no winners. I finished the rest of my drink. Lifting the glass to my lips, I let the tortured dollop of ice cream slide down into my mouth.

By five o'clock most people had left the beach and gone home. The tide was coming in and the waves were growing bigger. Further up the beach, I glimpsed the silhouette of surfers standing straight up, chest out, as the white water thrashed around their ankles.

Kevin and I splashed in the waves. I loved the way the water hoisted me up like a father throwing a baby into the air, except the sea never let go.

Mom came down to the water's edge and waded in. She dived straight through the first wave and with her hair slicked back she kept swimming out towards the next. As I watched her, it dawned on me that I'd never seen her swim in the sea, not once this holiday had I been in the water with her.

She did the front crawl in a straight line, throwing one arm forward and then the other. As a wave came she ducked under it and when I caught sight of her again she was swimming steadily, even further out. Kevin doggy-paddled furiously behind her, his war-paint suncream glowing bright. He looked sketchy in the water but he was a steady swimmer, more determined than strong. Still, he couldn't catch Mom.

The first time he called out to her she didn't hear him. The roar of water drowned out the sound of his voice. The second time she stopped and looked around. When she spotted him he waved and paddled even more energetically towards her. With four long strokes she moved through the water and was by his side. Kevin wrapped his arms around her neck. Under his weight the water lapped around her mouth but she didn't mind. She ducked under the water out of his grip and came up smiling. Then she did the most amazing thing. She lay on her back, put her arms behind her head and appeared to go to sleep. Kevin rested one arm on her stomach and paddled with the other. They were out just beyond the breaking waves, but the swells were massive. The two of them dipped down out of sight only to be hoisted up higher and higher till they were almost vertical on a mountain of water and then they gently rolled over the top while the wave came crashing towards me. All the time Mom looked calm and unsinkable.

Kevin spotted me and waved.

'Hey, Alex,' he yelled, 'Mom floats.'

I waved back and shouted, 'I know.'

Litchi

On our last day of the holiday Mom took us to the beach with Stripe for a few hours while Brandy did some shopping. By the time we got back Brandy was already home, listening to Van Morrison and preparing a special meal for the evening.

Kevin went straight to the toilet and I flopped down on the sofa and began lazily flipping through one of Brandy's large picture books about the Kruger National Park. Stripe laid his chin on my knees, wanting to be stroked. I closed the book and rubbed the dog's black ear.

'Grace, would you like some coffee?' called Brandy from the kitchen.

'Tea, please,' said Mom, going through to the kitchen. 'Rooibos if you have any.'

'What about you, Alex?' called Brandy. 'Do you want anything to drink?'

'No, thanks.'

Stripe sniffed the floor by the corner of the sofa and his tail stopped wagging. He zigzagged down the hall with his nose hovering centimetres off the ground and stopped in front of Brandy's bedroom, tilting his head and wedging his snout into the tiny gap under the door.

The toilet flushed and Kevin appeared. He ran his hand along the dog's back but Stripe didn't raise his head or acknowledge him in any way. With his ears raised, he clawed the carpet trying to dig his way into Brandy's room.

'Come through and sit down, boys,' came Brandy's voice, 'I have a surprise for you.'

'We're just coming,' Kevin called back.

Stripe turned his head and started scratching with his other paw, stopping to sniff, before scratching again.

Brandy came into the living room holding a mug in one hand and a cigarette in the other. 'Stripe! No!' she shouted. But the dog paid no attention. She dropped her cigarette into the tea and it hissed to death as she marched right by me, dumped the mug on the coffee table and grabbed Stripe by the collar, yanking him away from the door. 'Bad dog!' she said, the thin muscles in her forearm tightening as she held him back.

Instead of bowing his head, Stripe began barking and growling. Something had him upset. Between barks, muffled yowling noises came from the other side of the door.

'What have you got in there?' asked Kevin.

Brandy blushed a little and she grappled with the dog.

'I was hoping to do this differently . . .' said Brandy, shrugging as if that was explanation enough. 'Grace, could you take Stripe outside for a minute.'

Mom dragged Stripe, who struggled the whole way, out the front door. Once he was outside it was easier to hear the strange yelping coming from behind the bedroom door. Brandy put her hand on the doorknob and paused.

'There's another two weeks till Christmas, however, since you're leaving tomorrow I thought I'd give you your presents this evening.' She smiled warmly at Kevin and said, 'This is for you, Kevin. Merry Christmas.'

As soon as the door opened a turbo-charged puppy sped through my legs into the living room.

'Cool!' shouted Kevin.

He chased it round the coffee table, calling, 'Here boy, here boy,' as the puppy whined in excitement. Kevin grabbed it with both hands, lifting it up so they could study each other face to face. It was mostly white with tan brown paws and a darker patch on one side. The pup's head and bum wriggled and swivelled in opposite directions. All paws pawed the air. Kevin brought it close to his chest and his face was immediately bathed in a million frantic licky-kisses.

'It's a Jack Russell,' said Brandy. 'She's only eight weeks old.'

Kevin looked up to make sure he had heard right and the pup began gnawing his ear.

'Ow!' he giggled.

He held it at arm's length, lifting it slightly to get a good view of the crotch. 'Are you sure he's a girl?'

Brandy sat down next to him. 'Trust me.'

Mom knelt on the carpet and said, 'Why don't you put her down, Kettle, so she can run around.'

We formed a circle as the puppy bounced from one to the other, getting to know her new family.

'What's his name? I mean . . . *her* name,' said Kevin.

'Well, I'm sure you know that all dogs have two names,' said Brandy, touching Kevin's hair. 'They have their *real* name, which they only tell other dogs, and the name given to them by their owner. Unfortunately, we'll never know her *real* name. But you can call her whatever you like. However,' said Brandy, holding up a finger, 'make sure you choose a name that fits.'

'What are you gonna call her, Kev?' I said.

Kevin's eyes rolled up to the right as if he was examining the front corner of his brain. 'I think, Speedy Gonzales.'

'You can't call her that,' said Mom. 'How about Patch? Because of that brown mark on her shoulder.'

Kevin didn't like it. Neither did I. It sounded like a dog from a storybook.

'What does the brown mark look like to you?' said Brandy.

Kevin picked up the pup and held it like a baby. He stared down at the brown spot on her side, tracing his finger across her short furry coat.

'It looks like a litchi.'

Mom grinned. 'That's perfect.'

'Litchi? Do you like that name?' he said.

The puppy lay in his arm, with her pink belly exposed, chewing his knuckle and making little growling noises. I stroked her ears, which were even softer than Stripe's.

Brandy got up and said, 'And this, Alex, is for you.'

I twisted round to see her holding a cube wrapped in red and green paper, bound together with a white bow. I had never seen such a well-wrapped present. It was perfect. Like the gifts you see in adverts. Brandy took a step forward and placed it on the ground in front of me.

'Thank you,' I said, feeling a little shy. I tugged at the bow with two fingers and let it flop loosely to the ground. Part of me wanted to rip the wrapping paper off but it felt wrong. I'd be destroying it. I took my time peeling off each bit of Sellotape till the wrapping paper opened itself like a flower.

Inside was a brand-new camera. Thin white arrows on the box pointed to each particular feature, flooding me with information about how special this camera was.

'I hope you like it,' said Brandy.

I stared open-mouthed at Mom and then at Brandy. I'd never had such an expensive gift before. It was too hi-tech and futuristic to be for me. This was more like an adult's gift.

'I do. I love it,' I managed to say.

'Good. I'm glad.' Brandy stood with her arms crossed and became a bit self-conscious. 'I just wanted to get something nice for the two of you,' she said.

Kevin jumped up and hugged her around the waist, with his ear pressed against her belly. 'Thank-you-thank-you-thank-you! This is the best present ever!'

I wanted to hug her too but it was trickier for me. I was taller. My face would get squashed against her boobs, which would be too weird.

'Thanks, Brandy,' I said. It didn't sound like enough but I wasn't sure what else to add.

She kneeled down next to me and kissed me on the forehead. 'It's my pleasure,' she said. 'Now, let me show you how it works.'

We opened the box while Litchi pounced onto the wrapping paper. Inside, the camera was packed with bubble wrap, which I let Kevin pop. The entire camera was sleek black and covered in tiny buttons and triggers. Brandy pulled out a second piece from the box covered in even more bubble wrap.

'This is the film cartridge, and it slides in here. Like this.'

She pushed it in till it clicked and went on explaining how

it worked. 'Now, you hold it like this and look through there. Then, when you're ready you push this silver button to take the photo. This is an Instamatic, so once you've taken your picture it will slide out the front and you have to be ready to catch it.'

It seemed simple enough, plus, I'd seen cameras like this in the movies so I kind of knew what I was doing.

'Would you like to take your first photo?' said Mom.

'OK. What should I take?'

'We'll pose for you here on the sofa.'

The three of them sat down. Kevin sat with Litchi on his lap. Brandy had her arm around him as if he was her own son. I took the camera, my camera, over to the window and looked through the viewer. Kevin sat up straight, extending his chin as high as possible to stop Litchi from licking it. I put my eye to the viewer and watched Mom fidget with her blouse, pulling it straight. Brandy crossed one knee over the other and straightened her shoulders.

'Whenever you're ready, Alex,' said Brandy. 'We're getting jaw ache from all this grinning.'

I pushed the button.

The camera whirred and vibrated ever so slightly in my hands and a square of paper slid out the front.

'Now don't flap the photo,' said Brandy, 'just hold it gently on the edge and wait for the picture to develop.'

I'd taken a pure white photograph, yet very slowly the things began to change. Outlines began to emerge. Figures came towards me through the fog, each one a different colour, each one distinct till three happy people and a dog were staring straight at me.

Meat

Floodlights the shape of UFOs bathed the freeway in golden light. All the shrubs and roadside trees were shades of orange. Ahead of us were the slow red brake lights of cars; across the barrier white headlights sped by in a flash.

At the exit we turned off into our neighbourhood. The streetlights were dimmer and spaced further apart. Our headlights created a ghostly grey arc that stretched only a few metres in front of the car before dissolving into the night. Kevin slept silently across the back seat. Litchi rested her chin across his shoulder. I felt numb from sitting in the car all day and being this close to home made me even more restless. I wanted to see my own room again, to ride my bike. Just be home.

When we got to our house the lights weren't on and the gate was open, which meant Dad was probably out and had been too lazy to close it when he left. Mom drove straight up the driveway. The white garage door loomed up in front of us, reflecting the glare of the headlights. We were back. The holiday was over. Mom switched off the lights. The engine rumbled and stopped. Silence rushed in from everywhere. In the stillness, my body sank into the seat. It was the opposite of pins and needles. It felt weird to stop.

Aware that we had arrived, Litchi started whimpering in the back. Kevin sat up, opened his door and let her out. I got out too, almost tripping over her in the dark, as she squatted next to the car and peed. I walked back up the driveway to the gate. The stars stared down silently. Crickets chirped their little high-pitched snores, over and over. The gate clinked shut the way it always did. We were home, locked in and safe.

I had imagined Dad would be leaning against the door frame with a coffee in his hand, waiting for us. He'd hug each of us, even Mom, and we'd all start talking over each other, telling our stories as fast as we could. But maybe it was better this way. Sometimes hellos are worse than goodbyes. Now I could go in, unpack and settle in, then when Dad came home I could say hello without being shy about it.

Mom fumbled with the keys at the front door as Kevin and I stood waiting behind her. The door opened and the light went on. I squinted round her shoulder into our bright glowing living room.

'Hello, anybody here?' shouted Kevin.

'I don't think your father's home, Kettle,' said Mom. She didn't say 'Dad' any more, always 'your father'.

'Is he working tonight?' asked Kevin.

Mom looked around nervously, then stroked the top of Kevin's head. 'I think he must be. I'm sure he said he'd be working late shift when we got back.'

Litchi ran into the living room barking and wagging her tail. Kevin chased after her. 'Yes. This is your new home,' he said in a baby voice. 'Do you like it? Huh? Do you like it?'

'Kevin,' said Mom, 'why don't you find a bowl and give her some food. She must be starving.' She turned and spoke to me more quietly. 'C'mon, Alex, help me unload the car.'

Under the bonnet the engine made ticking sounds as it cooled down. I grabbed an armful of sleeping bags and waddled to the front door. I dumped the whole lot on the sofa. The living room smelled weird. It felt different. I went back outside to get another suitcase. Mom was leaning across the back seat collecting sweet papers and naartjie peels when Kevin came running out.

'Mom! Mom. Come quick. The TV's gone!'

She uncurled from the car and frowned at Kevin as he grabbed her hand and dragged her inside. Looking over her shoulder she caught my eye for a second. Her expression told me not to let her face this alone.

'See? It's gone,' said Kevin, pointing at an empty corner of the living room.

Mom gazed at a dusty square on the tiles where the cabinet used to be.

'And Dad's chair's gone too,' said Kevin.

I spun around. Our chocolate-brown living-room suite still filled the room. The big sofa along the back wall, still there. The squat two-seater near the kitchen archway, still there. The single seat, Dad's chair, the one directly in front of the TV – or where the TV used to be – was gone.

'Are any windows broken?' said Mom, splaying her fingers. 'Is the back door locked?'

We spread out. The windows in the bedrooms were fine. None of the burglar bars were bent or cut through. Kevin's voice called through from the kitchen, 'The back door's still locked.' There was a pause. 'Mom!'

I met Mom in the hall as we rushed to the kitchen. Litchi barked and ran in between our legs, wagging her tail excitedly. Mom's fingernails dragged along the walls as she clambered over the pup. 'Move, damn it!' she roared.

Grabbing Litchi to keep her out of the way, I arrived in the kitchen seconds later. Kevin's arm pointed at nothing. Mom stared at the same nothing, one hand covering her mouth.

The microwave was gone.

'And look,' said Kevin, pointing at the dining table, 'they took one of the chairs too.' Our round table for four was now a table for three.

Mom put her palms together as though praying. 'OK . . . OK. Let's just calm down.'

I pushed Litchi's face away from mine to stop her from licking me. Kevin reached over and took the pup. He looked worried and hugged Litchi tightly against his neck. Mom stood motionless, wondering what to do next. I got the feeling we weren't about to get instructions any time soon.

'Mom,' I said softly, 'why don't I go down and check on Rebecca. Maybe she knows what happened?'

She blinked at me. 'Yes. That's . . . yes. You do that.'

'I'll go too,' said Kevin.

'No!' said Mom, a bit too loudly. 'No. You stay here with me.' She grabbed him by the shoulder and wrapped her arms across his chest, pinning him to her.

I buried my hands in my pockets and said, 'I'll be back in a minute.' They both nodded. I opened the front door and stepped out.

Beyond the dim light seeping through the living-room curtains was blackness. I sensed evil things waiting for me, watching me. My stomach clenched. I'm not afraid of the dark, I told myself, opening and closing my fists. Everything is where it usually is, I just can't see it.

Except tonight things weren't in their usual place.

It didn't matter. There was no one else to do this. I was the eldest, and until Dad got back, I was still the man of the house. And this is what men do, the dangerous stuff. I breathed in and took tiny steps across the lawn. Under my feet the texture changed from grass to mud. The pit. I remembered Mom had dug a huge hole in the lawn. Choosing my steps carefully, I picked my way round the edge of the ditch. As I moved further from the light of the living-room window, the darkness got thicker. It stuck to me like sweat. The only sound was the screech of crickets like tiny sirens. Steadily, I snuck to the servants' quarters at the bottom of the garden, till I reached the door to Rebecca's room.

'Rebecca! Rebecca, are you there?'

No reply.

I placed my hand against the door and the hinges creaked. I pushed it all the way open and leaned closer to peer inside. It was the darkest of dark in there. I forced my arm to reach round and pat the wall for the light switch. I flicked it on and light burst all over the room. Blinking for a second, letting my eyes adjust, I gave my brain time to understand what I was seeing.

A single light bulb dangled on its cord from the ceiling. Pale blue walls and a neatly swept concrete floor stared back at me. The bed was gone. Her black-and-white TV with the coat hanger aerial, also gone. The photos of her family, gone. It was completely empty. I stepped inside and peeked behind the door. Nothing.

I checked the outside toilet. Empty. A cardboard roll hung from the toilet-paper hook.

187

I switched off the light. In the sudden darkness a green imprint of her bare room stuck to the back of my eyelids as I sprinted back to the house.

Mom stood over the sink, shaking. From the back I couldn't tell if she was crying or strangling something. I moved closer and said, 'Rebecca's left. She must have gone back to Lesotho and taken some of our stuff.'

'Rebecca wouldn't do that,' said Mom without turning round.

'But her room is empty. She's gone. She must have—'

'It's NOT Rebecca,' said Mom, spinning round. Her fingers gripped chunks of raw meat. Glancing towards Kevin's bedroom she added in a low voice, 'It's your bloody father. I know it.'

Her eyes were red. A tear trickled down the edge of her nose. She turned away from me and continued rubbing the meat under water from the hot tap.

My first thought was, why would Dad rob us? But then I got it.

He'd moved out.

He'd left us.

He'd left us and taken the TV.

This couldn't be right. 'But you said you were working things out. You said you weren't getting divorced.'

'I know what I said, Alex. But all his clothes are gone. So what do you think that means? And he's taken the bed. Our bed! Can you believe that! So I guess muggins here will be spending the night on the *fucking* sofa!'

I'd never heard Mom swear before. No matter how angry she got she had never sworn. She peered at my blurry reflection in the darkened kitchen window.

'He's taken the coffee machine because, of course, none of *us* drink coffee. And he helped himself to knives and forks and, as you know, the microwave is gone, leaving me to defrost steak under the hot tap in order to put food on the fucking table!' She threw a handful of meat into the sink, splashing water all over the window. She swung around and stopped.

I stood rigid, not daring to say a word.

Her legs buckled. She slid down the counter till her knees were right up under her chin. Curled into the tiniest shape possible she began to quiver. Her whole body convulsed as huge sobs welled up inside her. Her fingers rubbed little bits of red meat across her face and into her hair. But she cried with the sound turned off. The loudest sound was tap-water dribbling into the sink.

'It's OK, Mom,' Kevin's voice called from his bedroom. 'They didn't take any of *my* stuff! All my GI Joes are still there.'

His voice got clearer, louder. He was coming down the hall.

Mom sucked in air and stood up, quickly wiping her face on her sleeve. Kevin couldn't see her like this. She turned her back on me and ran water over her hands, splashing her face a few times before burying it in a dishcloth.

'I checked the whole house and I can't find anything else missing,' said Kevin. He clutched his Marvel Super-Hero trading cards in his right hand as he came into the kitchen, then shoved them into his pocket for safekeeping.

'How do you think they got in?' he asked.

Mom wasn't ready to look at Kevin yet. Maybe she wanted to tell him, maybe not. I covered for her and stalled things for a bit.

'I checked Rebecca's room,' I said. 'She's gone. Moved out. Taken everything.'

'Are the police coming?' said Kevin.

At this Mom turned around. Her mouth smiled but her eyes were red and sad. She hugged Kevin round the neck and said, 'Now's not the time to worry about this. We'll deal with this when your father comes . . . when . . . later.'

With his head pressed against her stomach, Kevin couldn't see her face. But I could. She signalled with her eyes out towards the car. 'Why don't you help Alex unload the car? And make sure it's locked, OK?'

'Let's go, Kev,' I said.

We got everything out of the car, including all the bits of rubbish and empty juice tins. We locked the car and put the keys on the hook above the telephone. I folded the sleeping bags and put them in the cupboard while Kevin and Litchi played tug-of-war with a towel. We put Mom's suitcase in her room and closed the door. In my room we unpacked my suitcase, putting all the clean clothes back in the drawer and all the dirty ones in the laundry bin. For a moment I worried about how the laundry bin would empty itself now that Rebecca was gone. But I put it out of my mind and helped Kevin sort out his suitcase. Then it was time to feed Litchi.

We went into the kitchen and unlocked the back door. Mom kept her back to us while she cooked. We placed Litchi's food and water bowls on the concrete, then sat on the back doorstep and watched her eat. When she was done she sniffed the grass over by the washing line and did a poo.

'Good dog,' said Kevin.

'Boys. Dinner's ready.' Mom's head disappeared too quickly for me to tell if she was OK.

The table was set for three.

Mom always sat closest to the stove and Kevin sat down next to her. I had to sit in Dad's spot. It was the only place left.

Mom placed hot food in front of us. A pink bit of raw meat clung to the hairline just above her ear. She sat down and reached one hand out to me and the other to Kevin and bowed her head to say grace. I took hold of Kevin's hand to complete the circle. It was a long grace, thanking God for the wonderful holiday we had had together and the blessing she had in the two of us. She gripped my hand tightly as she talked to God and finished with a sincere Amen. Kevin and I said Amen, quietly.

Before I got the fork to my mouth Mom spoke.

'There is something I have to say.' Tears began to roll out the edges of her eyes but she shook her head, determined to press on. 'We weren't robbed. While we were away . . . your father moved out. I know it's hard for you to understand and it's a shock to me too, but . . .'

'Where did he go?' said Kevin.

'I don't know. He hasn't left a number or address . . .' Her hand lifted to her mouth. She fought back something that was pushing up from inside.

'I'm sorry. I'm so sorry.'

She stood up so quickly her chair fell over backwards, and ran to her bedroom.

We didn't move.

Kevin leaned back in his chair and gave me the I-told-you-so look.

'Eat your dinner,' I said.

He sat in front of his food and folded his arms. 'What's gonna happen now?'

I swallowed a mouthful of food and pointed my fork at him. 'Just shut up and eat your fucking dinner.'

Kevin glared at me as I shovelled food into my mouth. His breathing got heavier till his chin began to quiver.

'Why do you have to be like that?' he said suddenly, standing up. He waited for a second, before marching off down the hall.

I ate my dinner, watching steam rise off the other two plates.

Puncture

I opened my eyes. Sunshine sliced through a gap in the curtains like a laser beam, cutting my bedroom in half. Dust particles hung, perfectly still, waiting for the slightest disturbance to send them spiralling. I blinked the crust out of my eyes and wondered if Mom was up yet. I lay still, listening. Outside a bird sang *piet-my-vrou*, *piet-my-vrou*. Kevin couldn't be up yet either, I would have heard Litchi barking. I glanced over at my bedside clock. 10.31 a.m.

A car approached, moving up the street, getting closer to our house. The tyres rolled toward us with the sound of a long inbreath. My heart pounded faster and faster. Would it stop? But it kept going, passing by with a steady exhale.

I couldn't take it. A hundred blankets of heat squashed down on my chest. There was no air. Sweat on my back seeped through the sheet into the foam mattress. I had to get up. I kicked off the sheets and spread my limbs. All across my room dust particles hurried about in panic. Sitting up, I rubbed my head, then went over to the window and opened the curtains. Blinding-hot sunshine filled the room. I closed them again.

In the dim light I prodded at dark shapes on the carpet with my toe, searching for my shorts and T-shirt. I stepped into my shorts, fastening the button at the waist. At the end of my bed, under the pile of sheets, I found my T-shirt. It smelled OK. As I pulled it over my head the tag scratched against my throat. It was on back-to-front. Drawing my elbows back through the sleeve holes I wrestled it the right way round.

Dad is gone.

Like a slap to the back of my head, this thought hit me. It stopped me.

He'll never come back.

The T-shirt was twisted, tight and awkward, like a straitjacket.

I am on my own.

My arms paused, one over the other, wrapped around my body. The fingers settled in between the ribs and held on tight. I stared at my bedroom door. My head went empty. Everything slowed down. Gurgling sounds came from my stomach and my tongue gradually relaxed and peeled off my palate. The bedroom door was brown.

If I wanted to I could move. I just had to imagine my arms letting go and feel the muscles in my legs haul me forward. When the time came I knew I could do it.

A fly squiggled in front of my face, humming happily to itself. It landed on the doorknob. The two back legs rubbed together, cleaning each wing. It shifted, stared at me through massive eyes and flew off.

Gently, calmly, I untangled myself, freed my arms and opened my bedroom door.

Moving down the hall I swung open Kevin's door and Litchi burst through, ears back, tongue flashing in and out, tail wagging. I let her out the back door and went to make coffee. There was an empty space where the coffee machine used to be. I decided not to think about it and switched the kettle on. Waiting for it to boil, I opened all the curtains and the windows to let some air into the house. All the cushions from the sofa were gone. Mom must have taken them through to her room and made a bed on the floor. She couldn't have slept well but I made as much noise as I could so she would get up.

In the cupboards there was half a loaf of mouldy bread, which I threw out. An empty box of cornflakes also went in the bin. There was no fresh fruit or vegetables because neither Dad nor Rebecca had gone shopping before they left. I found a packet of porridge. I could make that. But it was too hot for porridge. The kettle switched itself off. I placed two tea bags in two cups, one for me and one for Mom, and poured in the boiling water. I reached for the milk in the fridge and poured lumps of cheese into the first cup. A sour stench came from the milk carton. That went in the bin too. The tea went down the sink.

Kevin stumbled into the kitchen. He sat down at the table for three.

'What's for breakfast?'

'Whatever you can find,' I said.

I peered inside the fridge hoping to see something I had missed the first time. In the door was an unopened carton of guava juice. Dad hated guava juice. It was the texture. But we loved it. I set out three glasses, one for me, one for Mom and one for Kevin, and filled each one to the brim. I placed Kevin's glass in front of him and he drank it down without saying thank you. I drank my juice, the whole glassful, without stopping. It tasted so *lekker* and gritty as it seeped down my throat and spread around my chest. I instantly felt better, stronger.

'Litchi is out the back,' I said. 'You have to feed her.'

Kevin didn't respond. I picked up Mom's glass and took it through.

Her curtains were drawn. They glowed a deep red as the sun tried hard to force its way through. The room was stuffy and smelled of sweat. As my eyes adjusted I said, 'Morning, Mom!' Somehow I sounded exactly like Mom when she woke us up for school, the same tone of voice. I tried again, this time deeper and more like a man. 'I brought you some juice.'

Mumbles came from inside the sleeping bag. The sofa cushions were arranged in the corner along the wall, far away from where her bed used to be. She looked like one of the homeless women who slept outside the train station, except Mom was white.

'What would you like for breakfast?' I said.

No answer.

Her sandals were on the floor by the door. A few centimetres closer to her bed lay her blouse, after that her bra, then her trousers and finally her panties. Her hair lay tangled across the pillow and across her face. I moved closer and she shrank a little deeper into the sleeping bag like a snail into its shell. A bare shoulder tightened up around her neck to protect herself. There was no strap. She wasn't wearing a nightdress. It was just her naked self in there.

I couldn't go any further. I stopped halfway across the room, next to her bra, and placed the juice on the floor.

'Mom,' I said, 'I'll just leave this here if you want it, OK?'

She didn't stir and she didn't answer. Taking three steps backwards, I turned to leave. On her desk I noticed some paper. Dad's handwriting was all over it.

> *This is for the best.*
> *Let the past stay in the past.*
> *Bruce*

I read it three times, examining the shape of each letter for clues.

'What are you doing, Alex?' Mom's dozy voice made me jump.

'Nothing . . . I'm just . . .' I slipped out and closed the door behind me.

In the kitchen Litchi sat on the floor looking up at Kevin, who was eating meatballs straight from the tin. He gave me a what-are-you-going-to-do-about-it look? I didn't care what he had for breakfast. I stood for a moment, wondering what I wanted to do next. Kevin watched me, then turned his head to see what I was staring at. I realised I was staring at where the fourth chair used to be. Kevin kept gazing at me as if I had something to say, as if I knew what to do next.

'Don't feed the dog at the table,' I said, then turned and went outside.

The heat was different here. In Durban the lush, moist air clung to you. When you went outside, you stepped into hot breath. You moved through it. But here, at home, the air was thin and dusty. Heat pressed down on the top of your head and shoulders. You had to walk with a stoop. I could feel it sapping my energy as I crossed the lawn to the garage. The grass hadn't been watered regularly and was turning yellow. Mom's crater seemed to take up the whole lawn. Mounds of orange sand surrounded the hole. It looked as if a bomb had fallen from the sky and landed in our garden.

I thought about Mom lying on the floor. It was strange to see her sleeping in this late. She must be really tired from all that driving yesterday. I could help by getting some groceries so she wouldn't have to go to the supermarket before she cooked supper. If I got bread and milk and a few vegetables then I could bring them back on my bike.

I opened the garage and saw two shelves crammed with jam jars, each one filled with a dead insect. Under the shelves, waiting like an old friend, was my bike, resting against the wall. My fingers gripped the solid handlebars. I was about to sit on it when I noticed the back tyre was flat.

No problem. I filled a basin with water and took it out to the garage. I removed the back wheel with my bike tool and, using three spoons, slipped off the tyre and whipped out the inner tube. I pumped it up a bit and submerged it in the water and waited for bubbles. I could hear hissing. A stream of bubbles came from the base of the valve. This was bad news, the worst kind of puncture. It couldn't be fixed. I'd have to get a whole new inner tube. I folded my arms and stared at the pieces of my bike lying all over the oily garage floor. It wasn't fair. Why did this have to happen to me? Why today? The bike was fine when I left and now it was fucked.

'It's totally fucked,' I said to myself.

It felt great to say. My anger found a shape when I said it. I clenched my fists and imagined throwing the whole bike against the wall. I'd smash up the lawnmower and start throwing Dad's tools all over the place. I could rip this whole bloody garage apart. I was on the edge of doing it, smashing everything up. I really was.

But I didn't.

'It's all fucking fucked,' I said, chewing my thumbnail to the nub.

I went inside and flopped down on the sofa. There was nothing I could do but wait. Dad would come or phone, but only when he was ready. And there was no way for us to contact him. Maybe Rebecca would show up but we'd have to wait for her too.

The rest of the day felt flat. I didn't read or tidy up or anything. I got up and wandered into the kitchen, then wandered back. Kevin lined up all his GI Joes, loaded a red plastic missile into the barrel on his toy tank, and fired, knocking them down one at a time. When everyone was dead he lined them all up again. Now and then he sat up straight and looked out the window towards the driveway.

Mom didn't get up. Not even to go to the toilet.

'What's wrong with Mom?' said Kevin.

This was the first time he had spoken to me without sounding angry.

'Nothing,' I said. 'She doesn't feel well, that's all.'

'I'm bored,' said Kevin, lying on his back, letting his arms flop by his sides.

So was I. 'Let's play a game,' I said, wanting to smooth things over between us. 'You choose.'

Kevin got up and went to his room. He came back with snakes and ladders – the dumbest game of all time. There were no tactics. You rolled the dice and waited to to see what happened. Sometimes you were far ahead and sure to win, then suddenly you were back at the start. But we played for hours because it was better than nothing.

I thought about the note Dad left. It was a note that said nothing. No reason, no address and no phone number. It didn't mention me or Kevin. It didn't say *Love Bruce*. It didn't even have *xxx* after his name.

Slowly, the sky turned orange. The sun set but it didn't get any cooler. The second hand swept around the clock again and again and again. The fan swung back and forward across the living room. There was no TV to watch and the emptiness of the day slowly became a creepy night-time silence.

I realised I could have gone to the supermarket on Kevin's bike. Why didn't I think of that before? But it was too late now.

We ate more tinned meatballs for supper.

At nine o'clock I went to bed. As I passed Mom's room I said, 'Goodnight, Mom. Sleep tight!' It was a stupid thing to say. Every time I tried to sound cheerful I just sounded dumb.

I took off my T-shirt and lay down on the mattress. In the dark I imagined the sea. It was still clear in my head from the first time I 'clicked' it. The water was everywhere. Aquamarine. Big and empty. The edge of the world. I heard the waves roll and hush.

I could definitely hear it. I sat up and strained to hear through the crickets. There it was again. I stood up and went to the window. The moonlight made my skin look dead. Holding my breath, I listened for waves. In the distance a set of lights rushed along to the sound of surf rolling up the beach. I crumpled back onto my bed. There was nothing out here. Nothing but traffic.

Ten Bucks

At 9.30 a.m the house was still silent. I stumbled through to the kitchen, switched on the kettle and nearly dropped the coffee jar when Mom said, 'Morning, Alex.'

She sat right in the corner, close to the window, holding a mug close to her chest.

'Um . . . Hi, Mom.'

'There was nothing for breakfast,' she said, 'so I went to the shop quickly. There's ProNutro if you want some.'

I opened the fridge and saw butter, milk, plums, cheese and two cartons of guava juice. She had also bought bread and rice and vegetables. I reached up and got a bowl out of the cupboard and filled it with ProNutro and milk. I sat down at the table.

'Did you sleep well?' I said, looking down into the bowl.

'*Ja*, fine.'

Which meant she didn't want to talk about it. I stirred milk through my cereal. Mom drank her tea, gazing out the window across the street.

The phone rang.

I put my spoon down and looked at Mom. At first she didn't move, she just stared at the phone as if it was simply another piece of furniture. She shuffled over, picked up the whole phone without answering and dragged it through to her room.

Kevin came through, rubbing his eye, and almost tripped over the telephone cable pulled tight across the living room. He opened the back door and let Litchi out.

'Who's on the phone?' said Kevin.

'Dunno,' I shrugged.

Kevin chewed his thumbnail as we strained to hear bits of conversation but all we got were mumbles. After about ten minutes Mom appeared, wrapping the cable around the phone. 'That was Brandy. She says she loves you both.'

Kevin looked at me and rolled his eyes.

The phone rang again, while Mom was holding it. It couldn't

be Brandy, not again. This time it had to be Dad. Mom un-ravelled the cable and disappeared back into her room. The ringing stopped.

Kevin stood up and moved towards Mom's room to hear what was going on.

'Fine!' said Mom, slamming down the receiver. She marched into the kitchen and announced, 'Boys, that was your father. He'll be here in ten minutes.'

A red VW Golf rolled into the driveway. Dad stepped out and swung the car door shut behind him. His hair had been cut. It was still the same style but tidier. Me and Kevin opened the sliding glass door and waited for him to see us. He had on a black T-shirt with the bold white letters *FBI* across his chest. The mirrored sunglasses made him look like a movie star. Tucking his thumbs into his belt, he grinned and came towards us.

'How's my boys?'

There was something sour in the way he said it. We were *his* boys. Not to be shared with Mom.

He put one hand on my shoulder and one hand on Kevin's. The sunglasses reflected the house behind us. It was our home in miniature, but warped and cartoony.

'I've got a surprise for you two. Wanna see it?'

Neither of us nodded. Kevin wriggled out from under Dad's hand.

'They were going to kill it,' said Dad, as he marched back to the car with his hand still firmly on my shoulder. Kevin followed a few steps behind.

'A couple of kaffirs at work had him tied to a telephone post out the back behind the warehouses.'

In the back of Dad's car was a skinny brown dog with one ear badly chewed off. It paced up and down the back seat. Its breath steamed up the window as it stopped and glared at us. Dad tapped the glass and it growled, showing us saliva and teeth.

'These kaffirs were going to sell him to a witch doctor. To be sacrificed,' said Dad.

'Why?' said Kevin.

'Come here. Look at this,' said Dad. 'Look. See? He's got one blue eye and one green, like David Bowie.'

'Who's David Bowie?' asked Kevin.

Dad was about to explain but said, 'Never mind. The point is the blacks believe it has two souls. When you sacrifice it one soul takes all your sins to hell and the other takes your prayers to heaven. Or something like that. It's all primitive ju-ju bullshit.'

Dad rested his elbow on the roof of the car. Under each bold letter across his chest were tiny words, only visible up close. *Female. Body. Inspector.*

He carried on with the story. 'I didn't like the idea of them just killing the poor mutt. The thought of it bothered me all afternoon. So I went up to the owners and asked how much they wanted for it. At first they weren't going to sell it but I convinced them to name a price. So they said fifty rand. Fifty rand! Can you believe that? I said ten bucks was a fair price. I gave them the cash and told them if they didn't like it they knew where to find me.'

Dad put his hand on the door latch. Kevin and I stepped back.

'I know it's a week early but I want to give him to you now. You two have always wanted a dog.'

He opened the door. The dog jumped out and began sniffing the grass.

'Merry Christmas, boys,' said Dad. He folded his arms. 'What? Don't I get a thank you?'

The two of us said thank you at the same time.

'I called him Ten Bucks ever since I got him,' said Dad. 'He seems to like it.'

'Here, Ten Bucks. Here, boy,' said Kevin, but the dog ignored him.

Dad bent down and snapped his fingers, trying to get the dog's attention. 'He isn't house trained yet, so you'll have to be firm with him but he's big enough to be a good guard dog.'

Litchi came bounding out, barking. Ten bucks immediately went over and sniffed her. The hairs on his back raised.

'What the hell is that?' said Dad.

200

'That's Litchi,' I explained. 'Brandy gave her to Kevin when we were on holiday.'

'Litchi!' said Dad, screwing up his face. 'That's the dumbest name I ever heard.'

The dogs circled around smelling each other, Ten Bucks trying to get his nose under Litchi's tail. She growled and nipped at him. With a snap, Ten Bucks bit Litchi. His fang pierced right through her ear. She howled and yelped, legs running in all directions at once.

'Get away from her!' screamed Kevin.

With one hand Dad grabbed Ten Bucks by the back of the neck and with his other hand he slapped the dog, hard, across the jowls.

'Bad dog,' growled Dad. He balled his fist and pointed his finger right at the dog's nose. 'Sit!'

The dog's good ear folded back and he sat. Litchi went on yelping and yelping. Kevin chased her round the garden, saying, 'Here, girl. It's OK, it's OK.'

'Nothing to worry about,' said Dad. 'They're just working out the pecking order. It's perfectly natural. Look. There isn't that much blood. Kev, why don't you run inside and get some plasters.'

Litchi ran back to the house, right into Mom's ankles. She picked her up and silently inspected the ear before handing the pup to Kevin. Mom folded her arms and glared directly at Dad.

Sighing heavily, he turned to me. 'Here, Alex, you hold Ten Bucks. I've got to exchange words with your mother.'

There was no collar. I put one hand under the dog's chin and the other on its back to keep him sitting. He stank of old rubbish bins and there were two blotches on his back covered in scabs. Kevin came out carrying Litchi and the first aid box and sat down in the shade with Litchi on his lap. Dad went inside and closed the glass door behind him. He looked like he was about to flop down into his favourite chair but he hesitated, it wasn't there. Mom and Dad stood facing each other, her arms folded, his hands on his hips.

Ten Bucks started growling and tried to move but I shoved his butt down and said, 'Sit,' as forcefully as I could. He squatted, almost sitting, but ready to pounce. As soon as I let him go he'd be after Litchi.

Kevin stuck a plaster over the hole in the pup's ear but it didn't stick properly; too much blood and fur. Litchi squirmed and whimpered on Kevin's lap. She was in real pain and wouldn't sit still long enough for him to help her.

I leaned towards him and said, 'Kev, take a dollop of Zam-Buk, rub it on some gauze and make a dressing, then use the tape to strap it to her ear.'

Using the tiny scissors he cut out a dressing that was a bit too big. He pulled out a section of tape and bit it off. Pinning Litchi to the floor, he wound the tape over the dressing and around her ear. He used far too much. Her whole ear was covered in white tape. All the while I held Ten Bucks back from doing any further damage.

From inside the house I heard shouting. It shocked me to see Dad holding his finger right in front of Mom's nose. I couldn't hear what they were saying through the glass doors, but I could tell Mom was furious and Dad was angry because she had no right to be furious. Or something like that.

'Do you think that's good enough?' said Kevin. Litchi's band-aged ear hung heavily to one side. She waddled with her head tilted, then sat down and tried to scratch it off.

'Maybe you should strap the ear flat against her head so she can't get at it,' I said.

Kevin wound more tape around her head and neck.

'Not too tight,' I warned him, 'or you'll strangle her.'

I looked up to see Mom pointing at the door, telling Dad to get out. Ten Bucks took his chance. I felt him move and I jumped back as his head twisted round and the jaws snapped centimetres from my hand. Instead of fear, I felt anger.

'Son of a bitch,' I yelled and went to kick him in the guts. But he was too quick for me. Kevin jumped to his feet and held Litchi high up, out of danger. Ten Bucks wasn't interested. He seemed happy enough to lope around the garden sniffing the walls of the house.

Dad opened the door so violently I thought it would bounce off its runners. He stormed across the lawn and placed both hands on the roof of his car. He bowed his head and composed himself. It seemed obvious to me he was going to leave. Dad quickly turned around and faced us.

'C'mon, boys, let's get out of here,' he said. 'Go get your shoes on.'

Kevin carried Litchi back towards the house. Mom touched his hair and said, 'On you go, Kettle. Your father needs to explain some things to you.' She took the pup from his arms. 'Don't worry. I'll take care of Litchi. She'll be fine.'

I went inside, slipped on my shoes, got my wallet and thought about what else I needed. The camera lay on my desk. It was too big to fit in my pocket. I'd have to carry it around all day. I grabbed it and ran to the car.

We reversed out the driveway in Dad's brand-new car. Mom didn't wave. From behind the glass she watched Ten Bucks prowl back and forward trying to get in.

Choke Chain

I assumed we were heading into the city centre. Dad loved the tall buildings, the gridlock, the energy. Whatever he had to say to us, he would say it downtown.

I rolled down the window and hung my arm out. The car door was so hot I instantly pulled it back in. Licking my finger, I rubbed spit on the burned skin near my elbow and blew cool air on it. It was a boiling-hot day again, easily thirty-eight degrees. I imagined cracking an egg onto the smooth red bonnet and watching it fry.

The traffic got heavier. Dad jumped from one lane to the other, trying to get through the gridlock, swearing at motorbikes weaving between the cars. We crawled by shops and restaurants and street hawkers selling fruit on the pavement. For a moment we came to a standstill near a black man dressed as Santa Claus. He stood with his back right up against a shop window, trying to keep in the shade. Hundreds of shoppers walked by, many of them carrying three or four plastic bags. The sweat ran down the black Santa's face into the white beard strapped under his chin. A brass bell dangled from his hand, which he didn't bother to ring. 'Kris-maas. Kris-maas,' he chanted, without ever saying 'Merry'. I lifted the camera to my eye, but I was too late. The car lurched forward and he was gone.

We found a free parking space across the street from a small shopping centre. Dad checked his eyebrows in the mirror, then got out, looked left and right, and started wrapping brown insulation tape around the parking meter in front of our car. He wound the tape round and around till the whole head was covered. It looked like a giant match poking out of the ground.

We were ready for business.

At the entrance the glass doors slid open and Kevin stepped through the metal detectors. Dad followed. I went through next. A single high-pitched bleep made the fat security guard fold his newspaper and stand up. He was wearing khaki shorts and black leather boots, with a 9-mil on his hip. He stepped in front of me and nodded, signalling me to hold out my arms to the side. The guard examined my camera before patting me down. I stared straight ahead. He was so hairy he had to shave all the way down his neck onto his chest and still some hairs curled out over his collar. Big hands paused on my bum and from my back pocket he pulled out my penknife. I swallowed hard. I had completely forgotten it was in my pocket. It rested in his massive palm, the blade hidden in the handle.

'It's a bit small, isn't it?' he said, watching to see how I'd react.

He had an Afrikaans accent, not too flat. I mimicked it and replied, '*Ja*. My Ma got it for me.' I shrugged and smiled as if to add, *Women? What can you do?*

He smirked and handed it back to me.

'*Ja*, well, we're only checking for bombs. But be careful with this, huh.'

He stepped aside and let me through. I joined Dad and Kevin and we walked off without looking back. My heart thumped against my ribs. I quietly inhaled as much air-conditioned oxygen as I could, trying to relax.

After a few seconds Dad said, 'I thought he was going to ask you out on a date.'

Kevin snorted out a giggle.

'Shut up, Kev,' I said, thumping him on the shoulder.

Enormous glittering snowflakes hung from the ceiling. Shop windows were decorated with spray-on frosting and plastic fir trees. Carol music floated above the clatter of shoppers' shoes. A squat woman dragged a toddler out of a shop. The little boy's eyes were pink from crying. 'I don't want that one, Mommy, I don't want it.' Ignoring him completely, she tugged his arm and they disappeared into the crowd.

Deeper in the mall Kevin saw a sign which read,

Santa's Grotto
Kids - Meet the REAL Santa!
Parents - Experience the old world charm
of a genuine European Grotto.
(R2.00 per person. Price includes free ice
lolly for under 12's.)

'I wanna go to that,' said Kevin.

Dad shook his head. 'No time, son. Get your mother to take you.'

Kevin stood, pointing. 'But you get a free ice cream.'

'C'mon, son,' said Dad, trying to reason with him. 'First, it's for kids. Second, it's a scam. There's no way I'm paying two bucks for an ice lolly. Third, we've got a lot to do today. And fourth,' Dad stopped trying to come up with reason number four, '. . . and fourth, we don't have time.'

Dad turned his back. The conversation was over. Kevin stuck out his bottom lip as we strolled past the winter castle and the unblinking mechanical elves.

We followed Dad into a store with silver cone-shaped Christmas trees by the entrance. Kevin refused to look at me because he was still in the huff. So, silently, we waited while Dad inspected waffle makers. He read every piece of information on the box and compared it with another toastie machine of the same price.

'This one here,' he explained, pointing at the picture on the box, 'is actually two machines rolled into one. It's the latest thing. You can make toasted sandwiches for lunch. Once it's cooled, you can turn over these metal plates and make waffles.'

I did my best to appear interested because it kept Dad in a good mood. Kevin rolled his head back and yawned as loud as he could. Dad decided to get it and we joined the back of a huge queue curling through a maze of ribbons. After about five minutes of waiting, Kevin sat on the floor with his head in his hands. Whenever the queue moved he shuffled along on his buttocks and slumped back into his own thoughts.

'Where did you get that?' said Dad, pointing with his chin at the camera looped around my neck.

'Brandy gave it to me. It's from Japan,' I said, holding it up.

'That figures. Buying you expensive things so you'd like her, is that it? Trying to get you on her side.'

'No,' I said. 'It was just a Christmas present.'

'Whatever you say,' he shrugged. 'But I know that woman from way back. I wouldn't believe a word she says. Trust me. She's a snake.'

I thought back to the time Brandy told the story of how Mom and Dad met. She made it sound like Dad was weird. I knew she didn't like him much but she wasn't a snake. Was she? I began to feel bad about the camera.

The woman in front of us glared at Kevin through her big gold-framed glasses, then lifted her nose and turned away.

'Get up, Kev,' I said, nudging him with my toe.

'Why?' he said, pushing my foot away.

'Because we're in the middle of a shop, you idiot.'

'Don't call me stupid.'

'I called you an idiot, you idiot!'

Kevin's face turned pink. 'Well, you're a . . . bloody *kak*-head!'

The woman with the glasses shook her head and said, 'Sis!'

Dad grabbed the back of Kevin's T-shirt, hoisted him up and slapped him across the top of his head. 'Watch your lip.'

'But he started it,' said Kevin, rubbing his head.

'I don't give a shit what he did. You behave yourself, you hear me?'

I was a bit shocked at how strongly Dad reacted. I didn't mean to get Kevin in so much trouble. If only I had kept my mouth shut. I sensed how desperate Dad was for us to have fun together. Which meant this whole day had been thought out, planned. And the one thing that got Dad angry was messing up his plans.

At the till Dad pulled out his roll of paper money. He pulled off the elastic band and unfolded a ten-rand note and a twenty-rand note and paid the full price without saying a word. Although he carefully folded the receipt and tucked it into his shirt pocket where it would be safe.

Dad gave me the toaster to carry. We left the shop, struggling against the stream of shoppers, and sat on the edge of a square water feature. A two-metre fountain shot out the middle surrounded by little sprinkling baby fountains. The water was chlorine clear. Coins twinkled under the surface and cigarette stubs floated in the corner.

Dad glanced at my camera again. 'Right, boys. This morning you only got part of your Christmas present,' he said, over the background babble and splashing. 'Now instead of wrapping up gifts the way we do every year I thought it would be great fun to give you each twenty rand and you could buy whatever you want.'

His eyes gleamed with excitement, trying to make it sound like all the money in the world. He thumbed through his wad of money and handed Kevin a curled-up twenty-rand note.

The plan worked, a bit. Kevin brightened at the sight of the cash. He examined it against the light, looking for the watermark the way we were taught, before shoving it in his pocket.

'Can we go to the toy shop?' asked Kevin.

'Of course! Anything you want.' Dad gave me my share with a solemn nod.

Kevin led the way to Games and Toys. The more he examined each toy the less grumpy he became. He knew exactly what he wanted. Almost exactly. It was either the GI Joe assault motorbike with sidecar and life-like rubber tyres or the GI Joe helicopter jetpack with actual spinning propellers. He read the back of each box while Dad priced remote-control cars. After a few minutes Kevin brought both boxes to me.

'What do you think, Alex?'

I was too old for that stuff, but I tried to be nice. I owed it to him after getting him in so much trouble in the other shop.

'I don't know, Kev,' I shrugged. 'I guess the motorbike and sidecar are cooler but you've already got a tank. Maybe you should get something that flies. But it's up to you, whatever you want.'

Kevin's eyebrows drew together as he considered my opinion. 'The jetpack *is* cheaper. I could almost get this and another GI Joe. Do you think Dad would lend me another two rand?'

I doubted it. However, Dad was obviously trying to make us happy so I said, '*Ja*, maybe. Ask him and see.'

Kevin put the motorbike back on the shelf and chose the GI Joe character he wanted. He took both toys to Dad to try and explain his case. I kept to my end of the aisle and watched Dad rub his mouth while Kevin asked him for more money. A boy's choir blared out across the shop's sound system. *Tis the season to be jolly fa la la la la la la la la la.* Dad shook his head and Kevin turned away, deflated.

'It was worth a shot,' I said. 'Why don't you get the jetpack and with the rest of the money you could buy super-hero cards.'

He liked this idea. The cards were laid out in special boxes near the till so the shop owner could keep an eye on them. Kevin could afford four packets. He picked up a packet and rubbed it between his fingers. Then hovered his hand over the packets and selected a second one. It looked exactly the same as the first. He turned it over and sniffed it. Something didn't feel right so he put it back. There was only one card he was after. It was all a matter of choosing carefully.

Dad put his hand on my shoulder and said, 'Listen, son, what were you thinking of buying with your money?'

'I dunno.' I thought for a second. Charlene's friends had all commented on my T-shirt at her party. 'Maybe a surfing T-shirt or something. Why?'

'Well, I was just thinking that your new dog doesn't have a collar.'

Kevin held a packet in both hands and closed his eyes, trying magically to feel if the one card he needed was inside. It must have felt good because he laid it to one side.

Dad kept talking. 'I don't want to persuade you one way or the other. It's your money. By all means feel free to buy whatever you want. I just thought I'd mention the collar thing. Think it over.'

There wasn't much thinking to be done. It was obvious he wasn't going to buy a collar and if the dog didn't have one we couldn't tie it up. Ten Bucks was dangerous. He'd bitten once and he'd do it again. Someone had to protect Litchi as well as Mom and Kevin. Besides, I'd probably never see Charlene again anyway, so the T-shirt was a waste of time. I had to get a collar.

Kevin had it narrowed down to six packets. An impatient queue was forming behind us.

'I don't know which ones to choose,' said Kevin.

'C'mon, son, they're all the same.' Dad grabbed two packets and tossed them back in the box. 'You've got to just try your luck, Kev. Now, let's pay for these.'

Kevin hesitated with the money in one hand and the packets in the other. He straightened his shoulders and handed over the cash. The woman behind the counter smiled the annoying way adults sometimes smile at little children, as if everything they do is cute. She handed him his change as the customers behind us pushed towards the counter.

Dad strolled with one thumb tucked into his belt and the other hand hanging loose. 'Don't drop your change in the plastic bag like that,' said Dad to Kevin. 'Let it jingle loose in your pocket, like I do. It makes you sound rich. People are attracted to the sound of money.'

We went into a DIY store, up the aisle past the hammers and vices and monkey wrenches, turning left towards pet supplies. 'Just for a look,' said Dad.

As we followed, Kevin held his bag up, letting it gape open. He dug around inside for a packet of cards and began ripping it open. Curly strips of paper flittered to the ground behind him while he quickly flicked through the cards searching for Dr Strange. It wasn't there. He dived back into the bag and tore open another set of cards. Again, nothing.

At one end of the shelf there were leads for small dogs, little chains as thin as a lady's necklace. At the other end were chains strong enough to tie up a dinosaur. Dad selected a fairly thick chain and held it up.

'This is what you want, Alex, a good choke chain,' said Dad, looping it through itself till it looked like a collar. 'You see, this goes over the dog's head and the lead clips into this bit here.'

Dad put his fist through the loop and let the chain droop loosely over his wrist.

'The dog is perfectly comfortable if it obeys the master. But as soon as he tries to go off on his own he'll choke himself.' To demonstrate, he moved his arm and the chain tightened automatically. 'And the more he resists the tighter the chain gets. No matter how angry the dog gets he'll soon learn who the master is. You'll have him trained in no time.'

Dad freed himself and handed me the chain. Reaching for a leash he added, 'You'll also need one of these. Oh, and you might as well get a cheap leather collar so it looks like someone owns him.'

I looked down at the twisted curly mass of leather and chains in my hands, then over at Kevin desperately examining the last few cards. His shoulder slumped and the bag with his new toys in it scuffed along the ground. Dr Strange wasn't there. He would never find that card. His collection would never be complete. It was more than bad luck. He looked hopeless. And for a second I was torn. Should I offer him my twenty rand to buy a whole pile of cards? Or should I buy a collar and leash to keep him safe from the scabby dog? The dilemma only lasted a second. I knew what I had to do. On my way to the till I picked up an inner tube for my bike. I dumped everything on the counter, including the crisp twenty-rand note. Dad rubbed his hands together and said, 'Who wants hamburgers?'

A tall waiter with blond hair cut into a flat-top smiled at us as we entered the restaurant. '*Dag se. Hoe gaan dit?*' (Hi. How are you?)

Dad walked straight up to him. 'Table for three.'

'No problem, sir. Follow me, please.'

The waiter showed us to a wooden table with a glass top and began handing out menus. Dad stopped him. 'We know what we want. Bring three cheeseburgers with chips. No salad. Tea for me. Iced water for the boys.'

The waiter nodded and left. Kevin opened the box and started assembling the rotor-blades on to the GI Joe jetpack.

'Not now, Kev. Put that away,' said Dad.

'But Dad . . .'

'I said, not now.'

He shoved his toy back into the box and rested his chin on the edge of the table, his mouth reflecting downwards in the glass. We waited for Dad to say something, to start the conversation we all knew was about to happen.

'When are you coming home?' asked Kevin.

My rattan seat creaked as I shifted forwards, curious to see Dad's reaction.

He took the sunglasses off the top of his head and placed them on the table. 'That's what I love about you, Kev,' he said. 'You just jump in with both feet. My sons aren't arse crawlers. I like that. You want to talk straight, man to man? Good. Suits me fine. What do you want to know?' he said, sweeping his arms wide.

Kevin hadn't taken his eyes off him for a second. He had his questions ready and aimed them right at Dad. 'Why did you take the TV? That was our stuff.'

'I took the TV because it's *mine*. Just like everything else in that house. I paid for every scrap of furniture. So when I moved out I took what I needed to cook and eat and keep myself entertained.' Dad raised a finger, indicating a lecture was coming. 'But did you stop to think about what I left behind? No. Of course you didn't. Let me spell it out. I left it *all* behind. You've got your cosy beds and a fridge and a stove and a garden to play in, everything you need. But it's still not good enough, is it? It's always me, me, me. You never stop to think about what other people need.'

Kevin hadn't expected this. His eyes narrowed. 'It's still NOT FAIR! You never even—'

'Excuse me, gentlemen,' said the waiter, suddenly laying a plate down in front of Kevin, then me, then Dad. Kevin huffed and pushed his plate away. Dad squeezed two chips together and shoved them into his mouth. The waiter talked non-stop. 'Here is some ketchup and mustard and peri-peri sauce. I'll just leave them here for you. And there's salt and pepper on the table.' He placed his arms behind his back and rocked on his heels. Fat red pimples dotted around his throat. 'Well. Enjoy your meal.'

'The tea,' said Dad, with his mouth full.

'Oh, *ja*! Sorry, sir.' The waiter took two steps sideways. 'I'll be back in a minute.'

I scooped a dollop of ketchup onto my plate. Kevin refused to eat. The mood at our table had changed, not much, but enough to allow me to ask my own question.

'So um . . . where are you staying now?'

Dad put more chips in his mouth. He swallowed and reached for the salt.

'This guy at work's got a granny flat. He said I could stay there for a while till I get things sorted.'

'Where is it?' I said.

'Just over the hill in Pretoria North. About five kilometres.'

The waiter appeared again. 'Here is your tea, sir, and some water for the boys. Sorry about the wait.'

Dad ignored him completely. The waiter smiled, hesitated, and went away.

'Did you and Mom have a fight? Is that why you left?' I said.

'No, not really.'

'It's because you don't love us any more, that's why,' said Kevin.

Dad sighed and sucked grease off his thumb. 'C'mon, don't be like that. You're my boys, right? Nothing in the whole world can change that. It's just . . . you know, it's hard to explain. Everything's been . . .'

He took a bite of his hamburger and chewed. We waited. We waited for a long time. I wasn't sure if he was going to say anything else.

'Sometimes,' he gulped down his mouthful, 'you just know it's time to move on.'

'But you're our dad,' pleaded Kevin.

'I'm still your dad and always will be, there's nothing you can do about that. Like I always say, blood is thicker than water. And we'll still have fun together. Hardly anything will change. I just won't be around as much. Besides, you guys are almost grown up now, you don't need me around all the time.'

The more he answered our questions the more confusing things became. If I could shape the perfect question, I could pin him down and find out exactly why he left. Yet, somehow, I knew it was hopeless. I'd seen him talk to a hundred different shop managers till they got so baffled they just gave up. We had done it together, as a team. It was a game. But now Dad was using Bullshit Baffles Brains Method against us! He was still playing games. Dad was on a team all of his own and I had never really been part of it.

213

I sank my teeth into the cheeseburger, ripped out a chunk and chewed. There was texture but no taste.

'When you moved out, what happened to Rebecca? Did she go back to Lesotho?' I asked.

'No.' Dad sipped his tea. 'I took her.'

This had never crossed my mind. 'Why?' I said.

'Why do you think? To cook and clean and iron my shirts. I can't do any of that stuff.'

'But who's going to clean our house?'

Dad pointed his fork at me, grinning. 'Believe it or not, there was a time when your mother was very good at stuff like that. You have plenty of time to find another servant girl, I'm sure you guys will be fine.'

Another dead end but I wanted to keep trying.

'How can her husband visit her if he doesn't know where she is?'

'That's not my problem. She's my employee. If she wants to get paid she has to go where the work is.' It was a simple point. Dad raised his eyebrows, showing how simple it was. But then he added, 'She's sharing servants' quarters with another girl so she's hardly going to be lonely.'

I had run dry again.

Dad leaned closer and whispered, 'OK, guys, stop eating.'

Kevin hadn't touched his food. But now he suddenly stuffed half his burger in his mouth and dropped the rest on his plate. Trails of lettuce hung from his lips as he chewed, glaring at Dad. I was still hungry, so I began stuffing chips into my mouth before it was too late. Dad opened his burger and dipped the half-eaten meat patty into his tea before slipping it back into the bread roll.

'Waiter!' Dad snapped his fingers above his head.

The blond teenager came striding up to our table. 'Yes, sir. Is everything all right?'

'Taste that and tell me what you think.' Dad pointed at the tea-soaked burger on his plate.

The waiter's eyes switched from Dad to the burger.

'Well, go on. Taste it!'

'Is there a problem with your meal, sir?'

Dad pushed the plate away. 'You tell me!'

The waiter eyeballed Kevin chewing, but before he could say anything Dad moved in for the kill.

'What kind of place are you running here? You can't expect us to eat this.'

'I'm so sorry, sir,' said the waiter, reaching over to collect our plates. 'I'll get the chef to make some new burgers.'

'No! Don't do that. I don't know what the hell you do to the food in this establishment but I can't stomach any more of it.'

'Well, sir . . . I . . .' He quickly gathered up the forks and knives. Dad winked at me before saying, 'Bring us two banana milk-shakes and I'll have a Castle lager – in a *sealed* bottle, if you don't mind.'

'Right away, sir.'

Lunch was over and done with. Our little chat with Dad was also done. I knew how things would go from here. We would drink our shakes while Dad argued with the manager. The more Dad raised his voice the more the manager would blush. Eventually we'd walk out of here without paying and the other customers would stare as we left.

I turned the salt cellar upside down over my glass of water and held it there till every white granule had vanished.

Squeaks

On the way out of the shopping centre, the security guard read Dad's T-shirt and gave him the thumbs-up. The glass doors magically slid open as if bowing to a king. Dad swaggered across the street and we followed close behind. The parking meter was still wrapped up and there was no ticket flapping under the windscreen wiper.

'Perfect Planning Provides Perfect Results,' said Dad to no one in particular.

He was in a fantastic mood. The restaurant manager had grovelled and called him sir and refused to allow him to pay for anything. We had even been given a coupon so our next meal would be free.

We got into the new car, turned the radio up loud and cruised through the city. Dad steered with his thumbs, bobbing his head and drumming his fingers along to Huey Lewis and the News. Even as his fingers tapped the steering wheel, I could make out the pale indent where his wedding ring used to be. Kevin rested his head out the open window and let wind whip through his hair.

'Hey!' Dad shouted over the noise. 'Do you guys want to see my new place?'

'I wanna go home,' said Kevin from the back seat.

'What?' yelled Dad, half turning round. 'I can't hear you!'

Like Kevin, I wanted to go home. All of us, together. But I was curious to see where he lived, to see what he left us for.

'I don't mind going,' I said.

'What!?' said Dad. 'You have to speak up!'

'YES,' I shouted, pointing straight ahead. 'Let's go!'

We drove into a neighbourhood I'd never been to before. The houses had rusty corrugated-iron roofs. In one front yard a man with long hair and oily hands was fixing three old cars at the same time. In the next dusty yard a barefoot toddler with ratty hair watched us pass. The head of a doll hung from her fingers.

We arrived at a house with an old caravan parked outside. The driveway was cracked concrete and the lawn was mostly dirt with blotches of dried weeds poking through. Dad's granny flat was actually a converted double garage. Where the big double doors used to be there were now two windows. Dad opened the side door with his key and stepped inside.

When Rebecca saw us she propped the electric iron on its end and shuffled over in her slippers to greet us. 'Hello, baas,' she said, too shy to look us in the eye.

'Rebecca!' cheered Kevin, wrapping his arms around her waist.

She stiffened and checked to see how Dad would react. He pretended not to notice and put his keys and sunglasses on top of the fridge. Rebecca blushed slightly and cradled Kevin's head in her hands.

'You are my favourite boy,' she smiled at Kevin.

I joined in and made it a three-way-hug. 'It's *really nice* to see you, Rebecca,' I said, loud enough for Dad to get the message. 'It's so sad that you're not with us any more. We miss you so much.'

'Thank you, baas. You are very kind. How is Missus Grace?'

'She's OK, but she's very sad just now.'

'She stays in bed all day,' said Kevin, 'and the whole house is a mess. When are you coming back?'

Dad interrupted. 'C'mon, guys, leave Rebecca alone. She's got work to do.'

Rebecca let go of us and moved behind the ironing board.

'Right, let me give you the guided tour,' said Dad. 'This is the living room . . .'

'Duh,' said Kevin, but Dad ignored him.

'. . . and over there is the kitchenette.' As he spoke a slight echo bounced off the bare walls. Dad's favourite chair and an orange plastic chair faced the TV. Our TV. There was a wooden box acting as a coffee table but nothing else in the room, not even curtains.

In the kitchen, only the microwave and the coffee machine had been used. The small stove wasn't even switched on. I noticed mugs that belonged in our house as well as plates and a dish-cloth. But there were some things I'd never seen before, used things, someone else's things.

'And this is the toilet and shower,' he said, opening the door so we could peek inside. 'Through here is the bedroom.'

We followed him into a large room, almost the size of the living room. The windows were closed and it smelled like old socks. He was still living out of suitcases. Some of the carpet tiles were peeling from the floor. In the centre of the room was an enormous bed with new covers. Above it hung a large poster of a tiger because, apparently, Dad had always loved tigers.

Kevin let his arms droop. He sighed to show how bored he was, went into the bathroom and closed the door.

'What do you think?' said Dad, pointing at the bed.

'It looks nice, I guess. What did you do with your old bed?'

'I sold it to a second-hand shop and used the cash to put a deposit on this one. Try it out,' said Dad, flopping across the mattress.

I sat down on the edge of the bed.

'Nice and firm, isn't it? But not too firm, and listen.' He bounced up and down. 'No squeaks!'

'That's great, Dad.'

'Yeah, it cost quite a bit and I plan to do up the rest of the place when I get some more cash. But I had to get a good bed first.'

He leaned forward onto his elbow. I could tell from his expression he was about to give important father-to-son advice. 'It's always important to invest in a good bed, son. There's no point cutting corners. Did you know you spend more than half your life in bed? The lucky ones even more time than that,' he said with a wink.

A sound at the door made Dad jump to his feet. He left the room so quickly I wondered what was going on.

'What the hell are you doing?' came his hushed voice from the other room.

'*Jislaaik*, Bruce! What's your problem?' came a woman's voice, louder and with a sharp city accent.

'My bloody kids are here! You said you'd be back at seven.'

'*Ja*, well . . . Becky and them wanted to go to the flicks. So I came home.' She sounded like she was chewing gum.

Kevin opened the bathroom door, put his hands in his pockets and went to see what was going on. I followed right behind him.

She was shorter than Mom but her big teased-up hair made her look taller. There were hundreds of bangles on each wrist and when she saw us her skinny legs teetered in red high heels, unsure where to go.

I lifted my camera and took her photo.

'Oh, Jesus,' said the woman. She lifted a hand with red fingernails to her forehead, trying to hide. 'Bruce, *do* something!'

'Er . . .' Dad showed us his happy face. 'Guys. This is . . .'

'I'm not calling her Mom,' said Kevin, folding his arms. 'You're not my mother, you know,' he told the woman.

'Thank God for that,' she mumbled.

Rebecca lowered her head and stepped aside, blending into the kitchenette.

'She's not your mother, you're right, Kev,' said Dad. 'This is Auntie . . . Auntie Poppy.'

'Auntie?' said the woman, slapping Dad on the shoulder. 'I'm not *that* old!'

'How old are you?' asked Kevin.

'Old enough,' said Dad, quickly answering before Poppy said anything.

Dad turned and stared at her with wide eyes for a full ten seconds and she stared back. After their silent debate the woman reached into her handbag and lit a cigarette. Dad turned to us. He was back in control.

'This is a friend of mine and you'll show her the same respect you show to every adult.'

The woman noticed Dad's sunglasses and quickly put them on, almost singeing her teased-up hair with the cigarette. She rested her elbow on her hip and flicked ash on the floor, then sighed, shifting her weight to the other leg, and took another drag.

'Now, why don't you shake hands and say hello properly,' said Dad.

Nobody moved.

She was the one who had taken our Dad. If it wasn't for this floozy, Dad might still be at home and everything would be fine. I'd been told a hundred times you should never hit girls, but I really wanted to punch this one.

'I hate you,' shouted Kevin. 'I *hate* you.' He ran outside. Dad just watched him go.

I didn't run. There was no point. The photograph developed in my hand, showing her blurred fingers fiddling with her fringe and an angry eye glancing at Dad. This woman was going to be part of my life whether I liked her or not. I walked towards her and she stiffened as I got close. Even in high heels she was only slightly taller than me. I put out my hand and smiled.

'Hi. I'm Alex.'

'I'm Pa . . . Poppy,' she said, quivering as she shook my hand.

'*Auntie* Poppy,' Dad corrected her.

She let go of my hand and adjusted the shoulder pad under her blouse. I kept smiling as wide as possible. 'You know, my Mom is a lot prettier than you.'

Her mouth fell open and I had time to notice that some of the glistening cherry-red lip gloss had smudged across her front teeth.

'Fuck you! You little brat!' she gasped. 'Bruce. Are you going to let him talk to me like that?'

Dad slapped the back of my head. 'Apologise to her, now.'

But I kept grinning. For the first time in a few days I felt great. Poppy threw her handbag into Dad's chair and stormed into the bedroom. Dad picked up the keys and shoved me out towards the car. I turned to wave goodbye to Rebecca but she wasn't looking. Her head was bowed low, and she was giggling into her fist.

Dad drove all the way home in silence, his lips tight, the muscles in his jaw flexing. As we got to the top of our street he stopped the car. 'I'm not going to bother coming in. I'll just drop you guys off here.'

Kevin opened his door and got out. He marched off towards our house without looking back. I got out and closed the door. Through the open window I asked, 'Will we see you again before Christmas?'

'Maybe,' said Dad, 'but I'm really busy right now so I can't make any promises.'

'Can we phone you if we want to talk?' I said.

'Um . . . actually, I don't have a phone in my new flat yet. But I'll try and call you from work,' said Dad. 'How's that?'

'Fine, I guess.'

'Don't forget these.' Dad handed me the collar and chains.

'Thanks. Bye, Dad.'

'Yeah. Goodbye.'

I followed Kevin down the road and as we got to the gate Ten Bucks ran up to the fence and barked at us. I supposed he would make a good guard dog if he only knew whose side he was on. Mom saw us and came up the driveway in her bare feet to open the gate.

'Shoosh!' she shouted at Ten Bucks. '. . . bloody mutt.'

Ten Bucks kept barking as she opened the gate. We slipped in behind her and Kevin dashed into the house. For a second the dog chased Kevin but quickly ran back to bark at us.

'Go on! Get! You horrible dog,' shouted Mom. She tried to chase it out the garden through the open gate but Ten Bucks held his ground, barking and showing his teeth.

'I got these,' I said, holding out the chains for Mom to see. 'We could tie him up behind the house.'

Mom thought for a second. 'I'll get him some food, then you gently slip the collar round his neck.'

She went inside. For thirty seconds it was just me and this angry dog. My dog. Strangely, I wasn't scared of him at all. I still felt good after talking back to Dad's stupid girlfriend. I felt bigger than usual. The barking stopped and Ten Bucks growled cautiously. Bending lower, I held out my hand but he didn't come any closer.

Mom returned with a bit of meat that she held out for the dog to see. She threw a bit on the grass and Ten Bucks swallowed it without chewing.

'There's a good dog,' said Mom, feeding it another bit. I reached out and stroked him behind his one good ear. His tail wagged slightly. Mom fed him another bit and stroked up and down his back. I rubbed under his chin, and Mom fed him another bit. Her fingernails were chewed right back and her wedding ring was wedged tight behind the knuckle. I massaged the dog's neck and gently looped the choke chain over his head. It was a bit tight but fitted nice and snug in the hollows behind his ears. Then I slipped the leather collar round his neck and buckled it tight, while Mom fed him another bit. Finally, Mom stood up and walked off showing Ten Bucks the last bit of meat. He followed eagerly.

Behind the house, I looped the leash around the steel drainpipe and clipped it onto the choke chain. The two of us backed off. Ten Bucks followed but suddenly stopped. Confused, he ran in circles trying to free himself. For a second I thought he might wiggle free but as the choke chain tightened it tugged against the leather collar making it impossible for him to reverse out. Then he lunged at us but the chain yanked him back. He lunged again and again, then gagged, coughing up phlegm, and lunged again.

Over the aggressive barking Mom calmly said, 'What did your father have to say?'

'Nothing much,' I said.

I stared into the dog's mouth as the teeth snapped shut and saliva sprayed through the air.

'I don't think he's coming back,' I said.

Mom watched a mosquito land on her forearm and bite. She waited till it drank its fill, then let it fly away.

'What are we gonna do, Mom?'

She turned away and walked back up the lawn. Ten Bucks lifted his head and barked even louder, not just at me, but at the sky.

Crackers

There were no clean glasses, no clean cups. I opened the fridge and drank cold water straight from the bottle. Dirty plates were wedged in the sink and dusty clumps of hair rolled across the tiles, gathering in the corner. We really needed Rebecca. Using a dirty knife, I cut a doorstep slice of bread and spread it with peanut butter. It was exactly the same breakfast I had had yesterday and the day before that.

Outside, Ten Bucks was barking. Always the same bark, *bow wow wow, bow wow wow*. He barked day and night. Any time now the neighbours would start complaining. I tried letting him loose two nights ago but it didn't help. He ran around the garden all night barking even more excitedly. So now we kept him tied up all the time. The plan was to tire him out but I could feel it backfiring.

Mom came into the kitchen and rinsed out a glass. Her hair was all tangled and she looked like she'd been crying again. She swallowed two pills with a gulp of water.

'I swear I'm going to kill that bloody dog.' She pinched the bridge of her nose, then looked at the mess all around her. 'Listen, Alex, it would be a big help if you and Kevin could tidy up because I can't . . .' Suddenly there were tears again. She held her breath and wiped each eye with her knuckle.

'It's OK, Mom,' I said, trying to sound strong. 'We'll clean everything up.'

'It's just, you know . . .' She clamped her lips shut, trying to keep herself together. 'There's so much . . .' she said, gesturing to all the scrambled thoughts above her head.

'It's fine, Mom. Really. Me and Kev will tidy, and get it looking the way it should.'

She touched my head and slid her hand down to my shoulder, slowly breathing out. 'I'm going to have a bath, then I'll come and help,' she said, leaving me alone with the mess.

I stared at the brown smudges on the plates from last night's mince and rice. I couldn't face cleaning them right now so I started with something else. While Mom filled the bath I went into her room and got the sofa cushions she had been sleeping on and brought them through to the living room. I collected all the cups from the coffee table, neatly piled Kevin's comics, then found the broom and swept the floor.

Next, I fetched the Christmas tree and decorations from on top of the wardrobe and began setting it up where the TV used to be. Litchi came running up to me wiggling her behind. The bandage was off her ear and I could barely see the puncture wound.

'What are you doing?' asked Kevin, only half awake.

'What does it look like, doofus?' I turned to face him. 'Listen, we have to clean this whole place up. Mom says so. It's already Christmas Eve and there's a lot of work to do. It's up to us to get everything ready.'

'I want to decorate the tree,' said Kevin.

It was the easiest and most fun job but at least he was doing something.

'Fine,' I said, 'I'll start in the kitchen.'

I wiped the counters, exactly the way I'd seen Rebecca do it, then scraped the plates into the bin, tied the bag closed and took it out to the street.

Round the back of the house I checked on Ten Bucks. His barking speeded up when he saw me but I wasn't frightened. He was getting used to me since I was the only one feeding him. I walked right up and stroked his head and for a few minutes the barking stopped. I picked up his food bowl and went into the garage. The big bag of dog food Mom had bought slumped against my bike. I dropped three handfuls of pellets into the bowl and brought Ten Bucks his breakfast. He wolfed it down while I used the hosepipe to fill up his water bucket.

Back inside, I found Kevin teasing Litchi with a string of tinsel. There were three baubles on the tree.

'C'mon, Kev, stop mucking about. You should have finished that tree by now.'

He rolled his eyes.

'I mean it, we've got lots to do today.'

He whipped the tinsel away from Litchi and stuffed it in the tree, grabbed the lights and looped them twice around, hooked the rest of the baubles on one branch and shoved the angel on top. 'There! All done. Are you happy now?'

I knew where this was going but refused to be pushed around. He didn't understand how important this was for Mom, for all of us.

'You're not done yet. We've got the dishes to do and then you have to tidy your room.'

'I hate the dishes.'

'*Ja*, so do I, but Rebecca's not here and Mom's not well. Now get in there and stop whining.' I grabbed his wrist and pulled him into the kitchen.

'Let go of me.' He wrestled his arm free and set his feet, ready to fight. 'I'm telling Mom on you,' he said.

'Go ahead. Tell her,' I said, pointing to her room. 'It's not gonna change anything. You can't eat Christmas lunch off a dirty plate, can you?'

'I don't care if everything is dirty. I don't even *want* to have Christmas!'

He marched outside still wearing his pyjama shorts with Litchi following close behind.

It took me an hour and a half to clean the kitchen. I washed every dish, scrubbed the pots, used the long brush to get to the bottom of each mug and wineglass. It took three dishcloths to properly dry it all. Then I put things in the cupboards and wiped away the bubbles by the sink. I scrubbed the stains around the hot plates on the stove and watered each one of Mom's pot plants. In Kevin's room I collected all the dirty clothes I could find. Through the window I watched Kevin line up a row of tin cans on the mounds of dirt from the hole Mom had dug in the garden. He grabbed a handful of stones, took ten steps back and began throwing them one at a time at the targets. I shook my head and got the dirty clothes from my room and shoved the whole lot in the washing machine. Then I knocked on Mom's door. It opened

225

slightly. She was sitting at her desk, leaning on her elbows, gazing out the window.

'Mom,' I said, but she didn't hear me. I tried again. 'Mom.'

Her head moved very slightly to the left. 'What is it, Alex?'

'I, uh . . . I need you to show me how the washing machine works,' I said.

She heaved herself out of her seat and followed me to the kitchen. I took small steps past the Christmas tree giving her plenty of time to notice it.

Mom scooped out a cup of washing powder from the box and poured it into a tiny tray that popped out the front of the washing machine. She turned the dial to *Main Wash* and the water began pumping in.

'That's all there is to it,' she said.

'OK. I can remember that.'

She took out a glass and poured herself some wine. 'The place looks nice, Alex.'

'It's no problem. Kevin helped. We wanted to get everything ready for Christmas.'

Mom nodded, drank half the glass down in one gulp.

'It's tomorrow, you know,' I said.

'What is?' said Mom.

I felt like screaming at her. It was so obvious! Instead, I kept pretending like we were having a normal conversation. 'Christmas,' I said calmly. 'It's tomorrow, the twenty-fifth.'

'Oh,' said Mom. She took another sip. The glass hovered by her mouth as she drifted into her thoughts. Something in the back of the fridge flicked on and a gentle whirring filled the kitchen.

'Mom . . . Mom!'

Her eyes came back to life.

'What are you thinking?'

'We need steaks,' she said.

She downed the rest of her wine and placed the glass upside down next to the sink. 'And firelighters,' she added, 'for the braai. And crackers . . . we have to get Christmas crackers.'

'*Ja*, we need all that stuff,' I said, holding my arms wide.

'Yes, we do,' she said to herself. Her eyes focused on me. 'Give me ten minutes, I need to change.'

Perfume

The hypermarket car park was so full we had to park in the far corner, miles away from the entrance. Weeds poked through the cracked tar because no one ever parked out here. Inside was chaos. Christmas music broken by announcements of special offers, long snaking queues at the tills, trolleys full of food and a woman dressed as Mrs Santa in a miniskirt with a tray of Kudu biltong for customers to sample.

Kevin disappeared into the toy aisle, the busiest aisle in the whole place. I followed, squeezing between two trolleys and stepping over a small child who was on all fours looking under the shelf.

'Kev, listen, have you got a present for Mom yet?'

'I'm not talking to you,' he said, turning his back on me.

I followed two steps behind. 'If you're still pissed off with me then, fine, be that way. I don't care. But I want you to listen for a second.' I put my hand on his shoulder.

He spun round. 'Don't touch me, Alex.'

'Wait. I need to talk to you for one second. OK? Just one second.' Kevin folded his arms. 'What?'

'Have you got Mom a Christmas present yet?'

'No.'

'Well, we need to try and get her one. It's important.'

'I don't have any money.'

227

'Neither do I,' I said, 'but we have to think of something.'

'Like what?'

'I don't know! Shampoo or candles. Something nice that will cheer her up.'

'But *how*? We don't have any money.'

I looked left and right to see if anyone might be listening but they were all too busy shopping. I could have shouted and no one would've noticed. 'That wouldn't stop Dad,' I said, 'so it shouldn't stop us. All we need is a plan.'

Kevin liked this. It was too exciting not to. He didn't say yes but I knew he was in.

We wandered around the make-up and hair curlers for a few minutes looking at possible gifts, watching the security guards and waiting for a plan to form itself. The difficulty wasn't in choosing the right gift, anything girlie would do. The real problem was finding something the right size to sneak out. Security at the tills was tight. They were very strict. No one was allowed to leave by wandering past the queues and slipping through the checkouts. If you weren't paying for groceries the security guards made you walk all the way round and out through the main entrance.

Beyond the tills were slim trees growing out of big stone pots. There were also little independent shops – key cutter, a biltong stall, a perfume outlet, an ice-cream shop and a suitcase seller. All of them existed outside the bounds of the hypermarket, past the security guards, but still under the same roof.

'I've got an idea, Kev,' I said, and whispered the plan in his ear.

We casually went up to the potted trees and leaned against them as if waiting for someone. The man next to us finished his cigarette and stubbed it out in the soil. I pretended to look over Kevin's head to see if I could spot Mom and at the same time I slipped a stone into my pocket. I nudged him with my shoulder and we moved on. The stone felt round and smooth and no bigger than my palm.

The lady at the perfume stall wore cartoon Santa earrings.

She was busy serving an old man in a pale blue safari suit and smiled as we approached. I grinned back, using my polite face. She placed three bottles in front of the old man, allowing him to decide which one he liked best, then she clasped her hands and looked down at us.

'Can I help you, boys?' Her accent was definitely Afrikaans, but in a city way. So I said, 'Merry Christmas, auntie,' trying my best to sound like her.

'*Ag, thank* you,' she said brightly. 'Merry Christmas to you!'

I switched to my Bambi face. 'Auntie, we need your help.'

As she raised her eyebrows her entire hairdo moved back five centimetres.

'*Ja*, you see, my brother and I have put our money together so we can buy something really *lekker* for our mom. It has to be really, really special because she's just had a baby and we want to take it to her in hospital.'

I thought I'd overdone it with the hospital bit. Obviously not.

'Ag, that is *so* sweet!' she cooed. 'Your mother's very lucky to have such nice boys.'

'Can we smell that one and that one?' said Kevin, pointing at the boxes behind the woman.

'Of course you can. There you go.' She turned to the old man and started gift-wrapping two bottles of perfume for him.

Kevin opened each box. He held up both bottles and shrugged. In the square bottle was liquid the colour of pee. The other bottle was oval and more flowery, more ladylike. I pointed at the round one. He took the lid off and sprayed the air.

'Yuck!' he said, sticking out his tongue.

The perfume lady glanced at us while she counted the old man's cash.

'Hey, let me smell,' I said, loud enough for her to hear.

I leaned forward and Kevin sprayed perfume right in my eyes. My left eye stung like it was wrapped in nettles. 'Aaaah! It's burning. It's burning!' I yelled. Tears blurred everything. I blinked and wiped and buried my knuckle deep into the socket. Nothing helped.

'Are you all right?' came the perfume lady's voice.

'I didn't mean to,' said Kevin to the lady. 'I wanted to spray my hand but it squirted out the wrong way.'

I stumbled around rubbing my eye furiously.

'Sorry, Alex. I didn't mean to,' said Kevin. 'Let me see.'

Kevin hooked his arm over my shoulder and huddled near me, and through the burning I managed to remember the plan. Bending over with my back to the woman, I slipped the perfume bottle under the waistband of my shorts and dropped the stone into the box. The switch was super slick. Dad would have been proud.

The perfume lady was getting more upset. She leaned over the counter and gently tried to pull my hand away from my eye. 'Don't rub it like that. You should rinse your eye under the tap. But don't rub it, that only makes it worse.'

'I'll take him to the toilet,' said Kevin.

Cupping my fingers over my eye, I gave her the perfume box with the stone in it. The weight was almost exactly the same and she took it without suspecting a thing.

'I'll be OK,' I said, moaning with pain. 'Can we pay for this?'

'First, go and wash your eye properly,' she said. 'I'll keep this here until you get back.'

Side by side we moved towards the toilets, with me limping for effect. The burning gradually died down and I said, 'You weren't *actually* supposed to spray me in the eyes, you moron!'

Kevin shrugged. 'It was an accident.'

'No, it wasn't! You did it on purpose.'

'So?'

I ignored him. He was too childish to talk to. Instead, I played the whole scam over in my head, the way Kevin covered for me, the switch, how easily we'd fooled that woman with her silly earrings. Everything had been perfect. Beautiful. My heart was pounding with excitement. Twenty-five metres in front of us stood the rectangular metal detectors and beyond them, the exit.

A hand rested on my shoulder. A big hand. An adult hand.

'Hello,' said a deep voice. I turned to see a black face with kind wrinkles around the eyes. He was smartly dressed in blue trousers and a white shirt. On the breast pocket were three badges.

His work pass, a security star, and his name, *Jackson*. He gave me a warm smile and said, 'What have you got, boy?'

I realised I was biting down on my lip. I exaggerated my mouth into ugly shapes. 'I've got a sore eye,' I said. 'I'm in terrible pain.'

His smile grew even bigger. I think he liked me. 'What's that? Under your belt.'

If I bolted right now I could make it. I could see myself nipping through the crowds like a rabbit. He'd never catch me. But when I glanced at Kevin I hesitated. Long black fingers drooped over his shoulder. Escape was impossible. In a situation like this Dad would go on the attack.

'I don't know what you're talking about,' I said, in a raised voice. 'I'm not even wearing a belt. I have to wash this eye before I go blind, blind *for ever*! You'd better call a doctor.'

Jackson stayed cool. He gazed over the tops of our heads and shifted his weight squarely in front of us, then his eyes settled back on me. 'No more games. Come. Let's go to the office.' He turned us around, guiding towards a green door.

I stopped. 'OK. Here. Take it.' I handed over the perfume. 'We were only fooling around. It was just a joke.'

Jackson examined the bottle without saying a word. His smile didn't move either.

'I've given it back, OK?' I said, nervously. 'We're sorry, but we have to go now. Our mom's waiting out by the car.'

I tried to walk away but his hand gripped tighter.

'This way, please,' said Jackson, nodding towards the door.

'C'mon,' I said, trying not to sound too angry. 'We were only playing, what's the big deal?'

'You did your job. Now I do my job.' The way he spoke was so relaxed, so controlled, I got the feeling he'd said that line every day. But I wasn't going to give up.

'Hey! Get your hands off me!' I grabbed Kevin's wrist and pulled him towards me. 'We are going home and you . . .'

Standing just behind Jackson was Charlene Bozman.

Charlene with her secret notes and gorgeous green eyes.

231

Charlene with the hair.

She was waving at me. She must have forgotten about the fight at school because she was waving at me.

Jackson grabbed the back of my neck, turning to see what I was looking at. Charlene lowered her hand and all the fight went out of me.

'Just come,' said Jackson, pushing us towards the green door. 'It will be easy if you just come quietly.'

Charlene looked at Jackson, confused. I wanted to explain, to tell her it was all a misunderstanding, that I was just trying to get something nice for my mom, that I wasn't like this, not really. I recognised Charlene's mother, Auntie Pam, standing at her side. The two of them had exactly the same expression on their faces, mouths slightly open, eyes blank, as though they were daydreaming. I looked over my shoulder to get a last glimpse of Charlene but her mother was already leading her away.

Jackson led us into a small white room with a table and two chairs. Another security guard closed the door behind us. He was also black. Kevin and I were told to sit down and the two men stood by the door. Jackson stared at us, scratching his grey sideburn with his pinkie.

We were too young to go to jail. I knew that. I hoped he wouldn't call the police. He'd probably just give us a warning, try to scare us, then let us go.

'What are your names?' he asked calmly.

I answered quickly before Kevin could say anything. 'I'm Neil and this is Derek.' I kept my eyebrows up and face open so it felt like the truth.

Jackson laughed out loud, shaking his head. 'You are an interesting boy!' he said, wagging his finger. He held up his hand with the pale palm facing me. 'Tell me,' he said. 'How many fingers do you see?'

I glanced at Kevin who was chewing his thumbnail, then back at the hand.

'Five?' I mumbled.

232

Jackson grinned at the other security guard and lowered his hand. 'That's good. For all the time we have known each other, that is the first truthful thing you have said.'

He turned to Kevin. 'But you, I think, you are not like your brother. So maybe, you and me, we can speak like equals. My name is Jackson Matlou. What is yours?'

'Kevin,' said Kevin, sitting up straight, shaking Jackson's hand. 'This is Alex.'

Jackson turned to me. 'Nice to meet you, Alex.' He wrote down our names on a hand-sized notepad. Behind Jackson's back Kevin stuck his tongue out at me. I must have moved or something because Jackson suddenly stopped and studied my face, then Kevin's, sensing something going on between us. His focus returned to Kevin.

'We need to speak to your mother. What is her name?'

'Grace,' said Kevin happily.

'Surname?'

'Thorne.'

'Thank you,' said Jackson, writing it down. He moved to the door. 'I'll be back in two minutes.' He said something in Zulu to the other security guard and left the room. For a moment it was silent. My knee bobbed up and down uncontrollably. Then we heard a polite woman's voice on the intercom.

'*This is a customer announcement. Could a Mrs Grace Thorne please come to the reception desk. Mrs Grace Thorne to the reception desk, please. Thank you.*'

I felt a bit sick. Charlene and her mom would have definitely heard that. Not only did I walk out of her party but she saw me fighting at school and now she had seen me getting busted for stealing. I bet she thought I was one of those bad boys they warn you about in RE class. She would never be allowed to speak to me again. It was over. Mom must have heard the announcement too. Instead of helping her, I was just another problem. How did this happen? What was I doing wrong? I'd planned everything properly. I said the right things at the right times. I copied everything Dad did, and yet, here I was trapped in the security office.

Kevin leaned back in his chair with his hands on his lap and sighed loudly.

The security guard at the door checked his watch.

There was a light tap at the door and we sat up straighter in our seats. Jackson came in with a cheery smile that showed all his teeth. 'Thank you for waiting,' he said.

Behind him was Mom. She stepped into the room holding her handbag in front of her with both hands. Her mouth was tight, her shoulders stiff. She rubbed the leather straps with her thumbs. Jackson stepped aside, allowing her to see that we were both OK.

And then the weirdest thing happened.

I burst into tears.

I couldn't help it. It all just erupted inside of me. I bent over forwards, hiding my face, and sobbed till my throat hurt. In my mind Charlene turned her face away and away. Mom rubbed and rubbed the straps of her handbag. I felt it all coming out in a way I'd never experienced before. Wave after wave of sadness. Real uncontrollable weeping.

'It's all right, son,' said Mom, rubbing my back. 'Whatever you've done, we can talk about it.'

That made it worse and I cried even more. Crouching down in front of me, Mom put one hand on my knee and searched in her bag for tissues. 'Shhh. It's OK, Alex. It's OK.'

Jackson cleared his throat and whispered something to the other security guard.

'Whatever the problem is . . .' said Mom.

Jackson clicked his tongue. 'This problem is very serious, Mrs Thorne,' he said. 'We caught your children stealing and this company takes shoplifting very seriously.'

'Stealing?'

'Yes. The oldest boy had this in his underpants.' Jackson held up the bottle of perfume for Mom to see.

I sniffed hard, wiping away tears that wouldn't stop.

'I'm terribly sorry about this,' said Mom. 'I'm happy to pay for the perfume.'

'This is very serious. Stealing is stealing,' said Jackson. 'If I let them go then they will come back, and steal again, and me, I will lose my job!'

'You're right,' said Mom, 'this is serious. I'll make sure they get properly punished when we get home. Believe me. They'll *never* do this again.'

Jackson rubbed his chin, deciding what to do next. The smile was gone. 'I have taken their names and we will keep it in our file.' He turned to us with his arms folded. 'If you ever steal again we will be forced to call the police and then it is out of our hands. Do you understand?'

'Yes,' I mumbled, feeling too low to look at anyone.

'Do you understand?!'

'Yes,' said Kevin.

'Now I want you both to apologise,' said Mom.

We both said sorry and Jackson opened the door. 'I don't want to see you again.'

I heaved myself out of the seat and we left quietly. Jackson escorted us past the checkouts, through the metal detectors and into the car park, where he crossed his arms and watched us drive away.

Door Frame

His eyes puffy with sleep, Kevin sat cross-legged on the floor watching Litchi chew one of Dad's forgotten socks. Last year Kev was the first one up, excitedly shaking the presents under the tree and trying to guess what was inside.

'Morning, Kev,' I said.

He shuffled round, turning his back on me.

I went outside and took Ten Bucks his breakfast. He had barked through the night, all the way into my dreams. When he saw me he yelped excitedly. I put his bowl down and he crunched the pellets while I topped up the water in his bucket. The sudden silence felt like a drink of cold water. Three bloated grey ticks nestled in the fur on his neck. While his head was bowed over his food I went and fetched more pellets. I brought back a massive tubful of dog-food, easily four times as much as I usually fed him. Ten Bucks greedily tucked into the extra food as I stood and watched, hoping he would gorge himself till his belly was so fat he couldn't move. Maybe then he would give us some peace.

I went back inside and closed the door behind me. 'Don't forget to feed Litchi, OK?' I said to Kevin.

'OK, *Dad*,' said Kevin, 'whatever you say, *Dad*.'

'Shut up, Kevin,' I said.

Mom came through with her hands behind her back. 'Merry Christmas, my beautiful boys,' she said.

Kevin rolled his eyes, not willing to play along.

'Merry Christmas, Mom,' I said, trying to help her salvage the day.

Mom held out stuffed socks, one for each of us. They were thin and hung like the knobbly legs of starving children.

'Oh wow, thanks, Mom,' I said. 'Thanks a lot.' But Kevin's deadpan stare told me I was overdoing it.

'Why don't you open your stockings while I make us a special breakfast,' said Mom.

We each took one and sat at the table. Mom busied herself by opening cupboards and trying to find something special to cook. Our stockings were almost identical. We each got fifty cents, a naartjie, a roll of peppermints and a tiny wire animal that I remember Mom buying from an African woman at the beach. I started peeling my naartjie, making a show of how much I was enjoying myself.

Our 'special' breakfast was porridge. Mom brought steaming bowls to the table, each one sprinkled with brown sugar and cinnamon to make it more 'Christmassy'. After a few spoonfuls Kevin stopped and pushed his plate away.

'I'm full,' he said. 'I can't eat any more.'

Mom reached out and touched his arm. Her tears were only seconds away but she kept strong.

I ate even faster. 'Mmmm. *Jis* this is *lekker*!' I said. 'How do you make it so tasty?'

Mom ignored me and spoke to Kevin. 'It's OK, Kettle. You don't have to finish it if you don't want to.'

Kevin left the table and flopped down on the sofa. When my bowl was empty I collected the dishes and put them in the sink before going through to the living room. Mom went into her room and five minutes later came back with two brown envelopes. She held them out for us, but changed her mind and placed them neatly on the tile floor under the Christmas tree.

'Those are for you two,' she said.

Kevin went over and picked them up. Each envelope was blank. He handed me one and we opened them together. Inside was a Christmas card with a picture of children in hats and gloves building a snowman. It simply said, *Love Mom*. There was also a twenty-rand note. Looking at the cash, I decided never ever to give money for Christmas. It was the most cheerless gift possible. Getting money felt sadder than getting nothing.

Mom sat on the sofa with one knee folded over the other, her toe nervously bouncing in mid-air, waiting for our reaction. 'I know it's not very much,' she said, 'but maybe we can go shopping soon and get something nice.'

'Thanks, Mom,' I said. 'Really. Thank you very much. This is great.'

She bowed her head slightly.

Kevin said nothing.

I had nothing to offer in return. She could have been surprised by a nice bottle of perfume, which would have really made her feel special. But I had screwed up. Badly. Now there would be no Christmas dinner, no crackers, and no proper presents for anyone, all because of me. Dad made a big mistake putting me in charge because I was useless at being the man of the house.

'You know what? I think I'll spend the money on some more camera film,' I said.

Mom moved forward in her seat. 'What a good idea.'

'Hey! We should take pictures,' I said, standing up.

I raced through to my room, grabbed my Instamatic. 'OK, who wants to go first?' I said. 'Kev, why don't you stand over by the Christmas tree so I can take a photo of you?'

He shook his head. 'Just take one of me and Litchi on the couch.'

He made silly goo-goo faces at the dog as I tried to get them both in the shot. The paper spat out the front of the camera and I gave it a few seconds to develop. The picture caught Kevin with his eyes scrunched tight and Litchi gnawing his nose.

'Your turn, Mom,' I said, quickly snapping a shot as she grinned at the camera. She must have moved because her whole head came out as a blur.

I tried again. 'Mom, why don't you stand by the tree, like this, so I can get a really good one this time.'

She stared stiffly into the camera. I took the photo and waited for it to develop. Out of the grey mist came an outline of Mom's head. At first it looked like an X-ray of her skull but as the image got clearer and I could see her eyes, sadness seeped out of her. She looked empty.

'You look great, Mom,' I said. 'See.'

She stared at the picture for a second. 'I look old,' she said.

'Not very old.' Somehow it didn't come across as a compliment. 'I like it. You look very nice. I'll keep this one.'

Mom clapped her hands together as a way of changing the subject. 'Well,' she said, 'I'd better start making lunch.'

She went into the kitchen and I heard the pop of a wine bottle being opened. I couldn't imagine what she'd find in there to make. There was no meat left in the house, only some rice and spaghetti, maybe a few vegetables, basically nothing. Usually we went to church for the Christmas service but I guessed this year we would skip it. If Mom was already drinking she'd be in no condition to drive us. We were stuck here for the rest of the day.

'Hey, Kev,' I said, 'should we mark the door?'

'I guess so,' he shrugged.

In Mom's room I got a pen and ruler from her desk before going to the door frame. Near the bottom was the earliest marking, from the year we first moved into this house. It read, *Kevin 1982*. The line underneath showed how tall he was back then. Above it, in the same colour ink, was my height marked, *Alex 1982*. It was strange to think I was so tiny back then. All the way up the door frame were similar markings where we had measured our height each year. It was a Christmas tradition and no matter how things had changed recently it felt wrong not to mark our growth.

'You go first,' I said to Kevin.

He stood up straight with his heels against the wall. Even though it wasn't a competition I always felt a little sorry for Kevin. No matter how much he grew during the year I was always ahead of him. So every year I balanced the ruler on his head and tilted it slightly upwards; that way he didn't appear too much shorter than me. I marked the frame and we changed places. Kevin reached up on his tiptoes to get the ruler flat along my head.

'Make sure you get it straight,' I said. 'Don't mark me shorter than I am.'

'It's straight, I promise,' said Kevin.

We stood back and examined our progress. We'd both grown a lot since last year but I had grown more, a lot more, and the gap between Kevin and me was bigger than it had ever been.

'Wow, you've really grown, Kev,' I said, as I scored our names into the wood.

Kevin didn't seem to care. He chased Litchi into his room and closed the door. After a few minutes I went into my room and sat on my bed. Ten Bucks started barking again. I laid out all the pictures I had taken so far. There was one of Brandy, Mom and Kevin all sharing the sofa in Brandy's house. I had a few photos of Kevin and in each one his dog was gnawing some part of his face. Then there was the one of Poppy. I hadn't shown this photo to Mom. Poppy's hand hid half her face except for one angry eye glaring at Dad. Next to this picture was the shot of Mom I had taken a few minutes ago. She did look old, older than I had ever noticed before. There was no photo of Dad and not one of me either. I picked up my camera and pointed it at myself, holding it out at arm's length, then pressed the button. But the photograph didn't come out very well. All it showed was my startled face trying to keep my eyes open for the flash.

Slugs

By the end of the summer holidays I was bored. I'd spent day after long empty day hiding from the heat and carrying a heavy boulder of thoughts around with me. Mom stayed in her room at her desk with a bottle of wine every day, occasionally coming out to shop for groceries or cook. The garden dried up and she didn't bother to knit on her machine. I kept the house clean, trying to force Kevin to help me but he rarely did. Like Mom, he mostly kept to himself and played with Litchi. For the first time in my life I looked forward to going back to school.

Sort of.

As I cycled to my first day of high school the butterflies in my stomach threatened to bring back breakfast. Everyone knew the stories of Standard Sixes being initiated by the seniors. I kept reminding myself it was just talk. If the stories were true then no one lived long enough to see Standard Seven. Still . . . I touched my trouser pocket and felt the iron of my penknife under the fabric. The best defence is offence.

Around the gates were hordes of brown and gold school uniforms. Parents dropped off their children and waved goodbye. Girls giggled in groups and teased up their fringes. Boys bounced balls. Everybody moved fast. All eyes darted about watching everyone else.

I got off my bike and stared down at my sky blue shirt and grey shorts. Blending in was going to be impossible. Mom had promised to buy me the proper uniform when she got some money. I pushed my bike through the gates trying to look as if I knew where I was going. I spotted the bike rack at the far end of the car park and headed towards it. Up ahead a car pulled into a space and a man got out, built like a rugby prop with shoulders growing straight out of the back of his head. For some odd reason, he was wearing a school uniform. Was this a senior? The boys in Matric were eighteen, some of them nineteen, but he looked like . . . like a grown-up.

'*Wat kyk jy?*' he growled. (What are you looking at?)

I flinched, ducking my head, and steered my bike away from him. My penknife tapped lightly against my thigh. I locked up my bike and waited for a moment, unsure what to do next. The bell screamed out telling everyone to hurry up. I strolled out towards the main building, battling against my nervy legs which felt sprung and ready to run.

'Hey, *domkop*,' shouted a tall boy. I looked around to see if he was talking to me.

'*Ja*, you, with the blue uniform,' he said. 'What you doing here?' The boy was wearing a silver prefect's badge pinned to his collar.

'Nothing. I'm . . . I'm looking for my class.'

'First you must to go to assembly. That way.' He pointed to a square building opposite the main gates.

'Thanks,' I said, but he just shook his head and walked away.

The noise inside the assembly hall swirled and echoed up into the iron rafters. Some students threw chocolate wrappers at each other, some hung over the backs of their seats, laughing. The older students sat near the back. I found an empty spot in the second row and sat down next to a boy with thick glasses. As soon as the headmaster walked onto the stage the noise died down. He placed both hands on the podium while the rest of the teachers took their seats behind him. With a nod from the headmaster a lady started playing the piano and the whole school stood up to sing the national anthem. We sang a few more hymns, then took our seats. The headmaster addressed the school in a serious, official tone. There were to be bomb drills and fire drills in the next week. They were going to be timed and we would continue practising them until the whole school could be evacuated in less than three minutes. The old intercom system had been replaced. All students wanting to sign up for after-school classes had to do so by next Friday at the latest. Mr Van der Walt was the new vice head but he would still be keeping his responsibilities as head of the maths department. However, as of this year, Mrs Rowen would be reducing her hours to three days a week and Mr Robertson would cover the rest of her music classes. The announcements went on for fifteen minutes and there was a long speech about the success of last year's senior boys rugby team and how the headmaster felt that if we applied ourselves and if the whole school focused on our motto, *Together We Thrive*, then this year we had the potential to represent the Northern Transvaal in the National Finals. At the end of assembly the whole school chanted the Lord's Prayer before being dismissed. Except for us, the Standard Sixes, we had to be assigned to a registry teacher.

We waited in silence, glancing nervously at each other, as the rest of the school exited the building. The students around me scratched their starchy new uniforms, many of which had been bought one size too big so they could grow into them. Through the crowd I spotted a colour other than brown or gold. Keeping my head low I kept watch. There it was again. Green! Thank God, I wasn't the only one still in his old primary school uniform.

The first group of names were called out and they left with

their registry teacher. The next teacher read out the names for her class. The boy in the green shirt picked up his bag and joined the group at the front.

'What is your name?' said the teacher, loud enough for everyone to hear.

'Andre Keeley, miss.'

She checked her class list and wrote something next to his name. 'I'm sure you're aware that *that* is not the appropriate school uniform.'

His head drooped onto his chest. 'Yes, miss.'

She tapped the top of her clipboard with her pen. 'Why is it that everyone else managed to dress themselves correctly except for you?'

'I don't know, miss,' he mumbled.

'Well, the school has strict regulations about dress code. If you are not wearing the correct uniform by Wednesday morning, you will be the first student this year to get detention. Do I make myself clear?'

'Yes, miss.'

She balanced her glasses on top of her head and tucked the clipboard under her arm. 'Follow me,' she ordered her class. They formed a single line behind her and left by the side door while the next teacher introduced himself. He wore a white shirt and the school tie and his beard was ginger apart from a grey streak on the chin.

'Good morning, everyone. My name is Mr Grant. I am the registry teacher for class 6C.' Without any more polite talk he began reading the names on his list.

Glancing down at my blue shirt I knew I was going to get a lecture for sure. The students around me knew it too. I sensed them leaning away as if I was radioactive. More than likely I'd get a two days' grace like that Andre kid, but what about after that? Mom didn't have a job. And even if she had the money, would she actually get out of bed and take me shopping? I needed more time. More than a few days.

'Alex Thorne.'

I stiffened when I heard my name. As soon as I stood up everyone held their breath. They knew what was coming. I joined my new class tucking my hands behind my back.

'Mr Thorne, I see you're not wearing our school colours. Why is that?'

'Um . . . sir,' I struggled to come up with an answer. I quickly worked up a story about visiting my sick grandmother but the moment I saw the expression on his face I knew lying would be pointless.

'It's a simple question, Mr Thorne, not a test.'

Giggles rippled through the pupils behind me. Mr Grant raised his eyebrows till he got silence.

I tried to answer softly so only he could hear. 'Sir, my mother's not been feeling very well, that's the truth.'

He smoothed the grey section of his beard and something in his eyes told me he understood my situation. 'Very well. You have until the end of the week.'

'Yes, sir.'

Mr Grant scribbled something on the register, before calling out the next name.

At break time I put my sandwiches in my pocket and walked along the hallway to the playgrounds outside. If I had dressed up as a clown I couldn't have stood out more. Everyone had something to say.

'Nice babygro.'

'*Ag moedertjie! Kyk die pratige babatjie.*' (Ah cute! Look at the beautiful baby.)

'Hey, homo, what happened to your uniform?'

A bread crust bounced off my head and one boy nudged me with his shoulder, told me to watch myself. I lowered my head and clutched the penknife tightly in my fist. As soon as I felt tears welling up I started running along the corridor, through the double doors and out into white sunshine. I wanted to keep going, grab my bike and pedal away as fast as I could, but I only made it to the far side of the playing field. I flopped down under some trees and wiped the tears off my cheeks, taking long deep breaths till I calmed down. This was worse than before. It wasn't just Darrel and his mates. It was everyone. High school was hell. And there was more to come. More fights, exams, jacks from teachers, detention, sports, mocking, bullying, teasing. How was I going to survive this place for *five whole years?* Leaning back against the tree trunk, I snapped a piece of bark into smaller and smaller bits.

Something smelled of cigarettes. Turning to my right, I watched a tail of smoke curl round the tree trunk and disappear into the branches.

I wasn't alone.

Slowly, silently, I moved onto my knees and peeked round the tree. About five metres away a group of three girls sat on their blazers eating crisps. Seniors. The girl with her back to me had big curly hair, which didn't move in the breeze. Next to her sat someone with her legs crossed, shins the colour of toffees, and a crisp packet nestled in the dip of her skirt. The third one had big breasts, bigger than most of the teachers'. The top two buttons of her school shirt were loose and a gold cross drooped down towards her cleavage. Her jaw moved from side to side, working over some chewing gum.

'Give me a drag,' said the one with the big boobs.

Her friend sighed out smoke and passed over the cigarette.

She took a quick taste and exhaled dramatically. 'I saw Paula smoking a cigarette before school.'

'So?' said the big head of hair.

'So,' she said, fiddling with the gold cross, 'someone *in her condition* shouldn't be smoking.'

Her friend breathed in sharply. 'No!' she said. 'I don't believe it! Are you sure?'

'Becky Schuster told me and she heard it from Christine de Villiers who was with Paula when she took the test. What I heard was that while Christine's parents were in Sun City for the weekend, Paula came over for the night and she took the test twice, just to be sure, and both times it was positive. I heard she's keeping it too.' She twisted the cigarette butt into the ground

245

and flicked it over her shoulder. I ducked behind my tree as the butt landed a metre away, all squashed and covered in lip gloss.

'Won't she get expelled for that?' I heard one of them say.

'Probably. She's not even legal yet. So the school's gonna phone her parents, maybe even the cops.'

'I heard she lives with her ouma who's got eighteen cats.'

'Whatever. The school will have to tell somebody, it's like, against the law if they don't.'

I moved my face along the bark, allowing one eye to peep round the edge. The girl on the right poured the last flakes from the bottom of the crisp packet into her mouth. She uncrossed her toffee legs and folded them to one side, leaning all her weight on one arm. 'Paula's such a slut, I mean, have you seen how ancient her boyfriend is? He's like, nearly *forty*.'

'I know! Eeeeewww!' said the one with big boobs. 'Can you imagine being with someone like that? It totally grosses me out!'

'I bet he's got flabby man-tits,' said the girl with big hair.

The other two began squirming. 'Sis! Don't say any more, you're giving me the *grils!*'

'I bet he's got a big sloppy dick and wiry grey hair on his balls!'

They all shrieked. Toffee legs laughed so hard she snorted.

Two other girls approached the group, one with a really short skirt and the other with her hair pulled back into a tight pony-tail. The girls sitting under the tree swapped secretive looks, trying hard to disguise their grins.

'Oh, hi, Paula,' said the one with big boobs, 'looks like you've put on some weight over the summer.' The three of them cracked up laughing. Paula went pale and stiffened, staring at each one of them until she figured out what was going on.

'Fuck you. Each of you!' said Paula.

'What's it like doing it with a pensioner?' said one of them.

Paula's eyelids lowered and she gave Toffee Legs the bitter evils. 'He's not *that* old.'

The girl with the short skirt sat down with the others. It was now four against one. But Paula only got tougher. She stretched

246

her chewing gum from between her teeth and twirled it around her finger. There was something familiar about her face.

'So what about school? You've still got two years left,' said the one with big hair. 'How do you expect to get a job if you don't finish Matric?'

Paula rolled her eyes and shoved the gum back in her mouth. '*Jissus!* You lot are so immature! Get this through your thick skulls, *school is bullshit*! I'm gonna move in with my boyfriend, who is a *real* man with a *real* job. I'll be watching videos all day while you pathetic losers are swatting for exams and learning your lines for the school play.'

Paula marched off but suddenly turned and spat her chewing gum at the girls. It landed right close to me and rolled in the dirt like a squashed maggot. I pressed my back flat against the tree, tucking my legs in so they wouldn't see my shoes.

'Hey! Who's there?' shouted one of the girls. My blue uniform wasn't the best camouflage. Immediately they were all around me, staring down at me.

'What do you think you're doing here?'

'Nothing,' I said, standing up. 'I'm just going.'

'You were spying on us, weren't you?' said the one with big boobs. She was the biggest, even taller than the one with big hair.

'No, I swear it, I was just having a sandwich,' I said.

'Don't try and bullshit me,' she said, grabbing my hair. 'You were spying, I saw you. How long were you there? What did you hear?' Four faces crowded round mine, each one sneering, disgusted. Their perfume was so strong I could taste chemicals at the back of my throat. Stories of heads in toilet bowls flashed through my mind. Whatever they were going to do to me would be bad.

'What's going on?' said Paula.

'This little pervert was spying on us. What's your name?'

'Alex. I'm new here.'

'*Ja*, we can see that.'

Paula pushed between them to get a look at me.

'Holyyyeeee GOD!' said Paula. She stared at me, eyes wide in shock. Her hands shot up to cover her open mouth.

'What is it?'

'What did he do?'

Paula was acting like she'd seen a ghost. 'This can't be happening. I don't believe it,' she mumbled.

Every face, including mine, was now frowning at Paula.

She turned away, hiding her face, her ponytail flicking over her shoulder. 'Just leave him alone,' she shouted. 'He's a stinking *gommie*. He's not worth it.'

'What? No way! This little brat heard everything we said.'

As they argued I made a break for it, wriggling out of their grip, and ran as fast as I could towards the school building. Halfway across the field the bell sounded and I kept running till I was back in my class.

After school I waited around in the boys' toilets for fifteen minutes till I was sure everyone had left the school grounds. I lugged my bag, loaded with new textbooks, across the teachers' car park and unlocked my bike.

There were still a few students lingering at the school gates, chatting in cliques till their lifts arrived. I put my head down and sneaked past them, turning right at the junction. Halfway up the road I spotted a red Golf, exactly like Dad's car. It was Dad's car. I could see him wearing his sunglasses, raking in the glove compartment for a new cassette. I felt such relief. He must have finished work early and come to pick me up. Once, in primary school, Dad had come to fetch me. When he saw me in the playground he hoisted me up onto his shoulders and I waved down at my friends as we walked out the gates together. Everyone laughed and tried to jump up and touch me. I felt like I'd won a race, like a champion. Thankfully, he had the good sense not to be waiting for me at the high school gates in front of everyone. It felt good to know he'd come for me. I hurried along the pavement wondering how I was going to get my bike in the back of the car.

Dad looked up and waved one finger at someone across the street. I checked to see who it was and there stood Paula, finishing off her cigarette and flicking it into the gutter. I instinctively ducked into the nearest garden and hid behind a bush, sneaking over till I could see Paula through the leaves. Dad hadn't spotted me. He was too busy staring at Paula. Once she was gone I planned to run over to Dad as if nothing had happened.

Paula stood alone on the pavement. She glanced up and down the street making sure she was alone. If she found me spying on her twice in one day I'd be a dead man. She didn't look pregnant to me. There was no bump yet. But I suspected that by Easter she'd have left school and I'd never see her again. She folded her arms and hurried across the street, heading straight for Dad's car. She opened the passenger side door and got in. Dad smiled and took off his glasses. He leaned over and kissed her on the mouth. I suddenly realised who she reminded me of.

Paula was Poppy.

Her hair was different and she wasn't wearing any make-up, but they were the same person. As they kissed Paula opened her mouth and their wet tongues rolled over and under each other like wrestling slugs.

Cracks

Dad put his sunglasses back on, revved the car and sped away from school. I stayed exactly where I was, staring at the empty parking space.

Leaves on the bush moved without rustling.

I could feel my skin from the inside. It clung to me as if I was standing in a collapsed tent. Colour drained from the world. The street looked like a washed-out old photograph, the sky was a misty cloud, the grass changed to ash.

The empty parking space got emptier.

Two school pupils walked along the pavement right in front of me and turned their heads to see what I was staring at. I squeezed my eyes shut. The image of Dad's tongue worming into Paula's mouth was still there. Short breaths clogged around my Adam's apple.

It was impossible to stay here. I picked up my bike and pushed it down the street, placing one foot in front of the other, in front of the other, in front of the other, avoiding all the cracks in case I broke my mother's back.

How could Paula be Poppy? One was only a few years older than me and the other looked like a grown woman. But she was her. Behind all the make-up and high heels, behind the school uniform, it was the same girl. The stupid way she flapped her cigarette around as if she was a movie star, it was definitely her. I saw her with my own eyes at Dad's flat. She lived there now, with Dad and his new bouncy bed. I imagined Dad lying on top of Poppy, their sloppy tongues going round and round.

Did she put on her school uniform while Dad watched?

Did Rebecca get their breakfast ready?

Did Dad drop her off at school in the morning? He never dropped us off.

And what about her parents? Did they know where she was?

Did they know about . . . everything else?

Deep in my head something turned. Something horrible I didn't want to think about. I felt I might be sick. If I admitted this to myself then everything would change. Things would never go back to the way they were. I tried to think about something else, but it just sat there in my head, soaking up everything else, growing darker, waiting for me to say it.

'Poppy is *pregnant* with *Dad's* baby.' I mouthed the words, making myself believe it. '*Poppy* is pregnant with Dad's *baby*.' Her baby would be my stepbrother, or maybe even stepsister. But she was only in Standard Eight! Not even in Matric yet. So how could she be pregnant? It felt wrong. Completely wrong.

This. Couldn't. Be. Happening.

Your stepmother couldn't be three classes above you. It just couldn't happen.

I was at a four-way stop. I waited for a break in the traffic. A black man in a dusty woollen hat moved from car to car, selling grey potatoes. I crossed over.

The pavement was old and uneven. Hundreds of cracks split the surface. My feet were hot and swollen in their socks and shoes. I thought about stopping and taking them off but I couldn't be bothered. It was too much hassle. This must be how Mom felt all the time.

Heavy.

Now I understood how getting up was too much effort. Eating was too tiring. I was sure she knew about Dad's girlfriend. She must know about the sex, too. But she couldn't know everything because Dad was trying to keep it a secret. I only found out by accident. Which meant . . . I'd have to tell Mom.

Pale slabs of concrete passed slowly under my black shoes. There were too many breaks in the pavement. One step after another, my broad feet came squashing down on four or five cracks at a time. Nowhere was safe to step.

By the end of the block, the concrete had disintegrated into grit. Chappies wrappers lay shredded in the stones and an empty Nick-Nacks packet blew against the spokes of my bike. The tread on the front tyre was almost worn through. Funny, I had walked all this way and never thought of using my bike. I looked up to see where I was and rushing towards me came Darrel and a group of boys.

Boys with toneless white faces, each one dressed in the same charcoal uniform. One boy's lips curled back exposing teeth and another one had nervous excited eyes. Darrel stood right in front of me. He still had the lumpy pimples all over his neck. His jaw jutted out, more like a cruel old man than a boy my age. This was his show.

251

While his mouth hurled swear words at me, I gently rolled my penknife around in my pocket. One flash of the blade and everyone would jump back. No one would touch me. I had beaten Darrel before and I could do it again, easily. But there would always be a rematch and next time they'd have knives. It would go on and on, like a silly primary school game, without any real winners or losers.

Darrel came closer, spit flying off his lips as he yelled, 'Answer me, you stupid fuckhead!'

I blinked at him, trying to think what his question might have been. He kicked my bike to the ground and grabbed my shirt collar. His pals got more excited. 'Do it, Darrel. *Bliksem that blerrie rooinek*!' (Batter that bloody redneck!)

My head felt droopy on my neck. I simply didn't have the energy to fight. I just wanted to get it over with. More than that, I wanted out. Out of this childish game. I wanted to get away from Darrel, away from Dad and Poppy, away from our messy house and away from the horrible heaviness in my stomach.

Losing was a way out.

'I'm gonna teach you a lesson,' said Darrel, leaning in close.

Losing would really piss Dad off.

I rested my forehead against his and whispered, 'Stop being such a baby and do what you have to do.'

He jerked his face back, as if I'd bitten him, glancing at the others for advice.

'Do it, man,' said one boy.

'*Ja*, just fucking *donner* him! He's a dick!' yelled another.

His fist pulled back, begging for an excuse to pound me. I closed my eyes, wanting him to do it.

But he couldn't.

I guess it's hard to fight someone who wants to be beaten. He lowered his fist. 'You're not fucking worth it, you fucking dumb piece of fucking shit!' he spat.

I shrugged and bent down to pick up my bike. From the corner of my vision I noticed a knee rushing towards me and I was suddenly flat on my back. Fists and feet hit every part of me as I tried to protect my head. There was lots of pounding but no

252

pain. I burrowed down away from the surface of myself. It felt like I was curled up inside a cardboard box while people slapped the sides. The sound reminded me of hail on the roof.

I felt nothing.

I felt safe.

When it stopped I opened my eyes. A brilliant green inch-worm pinched its way across the gravel. Its tiny yellow feet gripped tightly to the unsteady pebbles. In the distance black school shoes ran away round the back of the shops.

Cotton Wool

I sat on the kitchen counter while Mom prepared to dab Dettol on my knee.

'This is going to sting a bit, OK?' she said, pressing the cotton bud against the red exposed flesh. I sucked air through my teeth and my toes wriggled till the burning stopped.

Mom's voice was smooth and controlled. 'I know it hurts, son. You're being very brave,' she said. Something about the way she spoke helped me feel braver than I actually was.

'That's it, all clean,' she smiled and squeezed my shoulder. She cut a square dressing and rubbed Zam-Buk onto it. Her cool hand cupped my calf, lifting my leg. She pursed her lips and, for a second, I thought she might kiss the bloody scrape on my knee. Instead, she breathed cool air on the wound. It felt so good the tears welled up. I pulled my leg away in case I couldn't stop. If I started crying now, I would crumble. It would all come out, Dad, Paula, the whole story.

Mom pressed the dressing to my knee and taped it down.

Then she concentrated on the graze along my elbow. It didn't burn as much as my knee but she blew on it just as gently.

'Now,' she said, 'let's look at that eye.' She frowned a little before quickly forcing her face to smile. I knew it must look pretty bad.

Her soft hands rested on my cheeks, tilting my head to the side. 'Looks like you'll have a black eye for a few days,' said Mom, 'but it's not that bad. The best thing for it is ice.' She turned round and opened the freezer. With her back to me she asked, 'Are you ready to tell me who did this to you?'

This was Mom's way. When I staggered through the front door she put down her glass of wine and calmly said, 'Let's go to the kitchen and get you cleaned up.' It was the best thing she could have said. If she had panicked or cried or asked me too many questions, everything would have been worse. I knew she was desperate to know what happened. It must have been shocking to see me bruised and bloodied. But she waited till I was ready. She was strong that way.

I didn't answer her first question so she tried again. 'Did they bully you because of your uniform? Because if they did I'll get right on the phone to the headmaster and—'

'It wasn't that, Mom,' I said. 'It was Darrel and some other boys.'

'How many boys?' said Mom.

'I dunno, six or seven.'

Mom massaged a packet of frozen carrots to break up the bigger ice chunks and wrapped it in a clean dishcloth. 'Here,' she said, handing me the packet, 'press this against your eye and hold it there.'

I touched it gently to my eyebrow and felt an ice-cream headache start to build.

'Does Darrel go to the same high school as you?'

'No,' I said. 'I was walking home and they were at the shops. They wanted to get me back for the last time.'

Mom nodded thoughtfully. 'So Darrel did this to you?'

'Not exactly. I bent down to pick up my bike and someone kneed me in the head and then they all kicked me.'

Her eyes lowered to my school shirt. Some buttons were missing and the pocket was ripped. She undid the last few buttons and opened my shirt. The pink scratches didn't bother her. It was the bruise along my ribs that made her worry.

'Take a deep breath, son.'

As I inhaled, she asked, 'Does that hurt? Is it sore when you breathe?'

'No.'

She peeled the shirt off my shoulders and draped it over the chair. Her touch made me sit straighter, her fingers were cold from massaging the ice-pack. She prodded the area around the bruise and lifted my elbow to get a better look. For a few seconds Ten Bucks stopped barking outside. The silence felt impossibly good and I realised he must have been barking all this time. Then he started again, on and on.

'You're lucky, son, I don't think you've broken any ribs.'

I lowered my arm. Once she had checked me properly she sighed, rubbing her forehead. The two of us sat silent for a bit.

'There's something else bothering you, isn't there?' she said.

I nodded very slightly, hoping she wouldn't see.

'Do you want to talk about it?'

I thought about the tongues, about how Poppy was Paula, and she wasn't legal and she had to quit school because of the baby and Dad's new bed, the one that didn't squeak. It all came rushing into my head at the same time. The shame was so strong I couldn't look at Mom's face. I sat, gazing at my bandaged knee, wondering how I could possibly tell Mom all this.

She brushed my hair to one side, keeping me neat.

'When you were a tiny baby you never cried, even when you were hungry. You were always so good,' she said. 'You would sit up and look around you for hours, never making a sound. I would almost forget you were there.'

She bit down on her lip and studied the air above my head. 'I should never have let things get like this for you.'

'It's not your fault, Mom.'

'I don't know, sometimes I think I should have been more . . . attentive.'

The sound of Kevin heaving the garage door up broke the silence.

255

We listened to him put his bike away and drag the door back down.

'It sounds like your brother is back from the shops,' said Mom. Then in a lighter tone, 'I forgot to tell you. I have some good news.'

'What?'

'The hospital phoned today. There's a shortage of nurses and they liked my application. So they need me to come for an interview on Friday. Isn't that great?'

This was the first I'd heard of Mom applying for a job. I thought she just sulked in her room all day.

'So you're going to be a nurse?'

'Well, yes, I hope so. My qualification is a little dated and they mentioned the possibility of some extra training, but I'm in with a chance, a good chance. If I get this job, Alex, everything's going to be much better for us. We can get another servant girl, buy you a school uniform, pay the rent . . .' Mom pressed her hands together as if praying.

I tried to picture Mom in a white uniform with a tiny hat pinned to her head, walking from person to person, making things better, but no matter how I pictured it, it never felt right.

Tennis Ball

I lay in bed for two hours trying to enjoy the luxury of bunking off school, but black eyes are always more painful the next day. I got up and stared into the bathroom mirror at the puffy blue bruises on the side of my face. Overnight, the whole eye socket had swollen closed. If I opened my eye as wide as possible, it hurt. Scrunching it closed hurt more. Even so, I squeezed it closed again, reliving the moment the knee collided with my face.

Mom was in the kitchen, washing dishes. The pieces of cutlery made thin echoing sounds as she stacked them on the drying rack. Piano music squeezed through the tiny radio speaker that stood on the widow sill. I could hear her humming.

Squeezing toothpaste along the brush, I scrubbed my molars and spat loudly into the sink, adding my own sounds to the house. I ran the tap, washed my hands, splashed my face and dabbed my eyes gently with the towel.

As Mom moved about the kitchen, bursts of static interference scratched across the song. She stopped humming and turned off the radio.

Now there was only barking. Lifting my head, I stretched over and flushed the toilet. For a few seconds more the rush of water drowned out the barking.

Mom called from the kitchen. 'Alex.'

I leaned closer to the mirror. '*Ja?*' I answered, touching my cheekbone.

'Have you fed the dogs yet?'

'No.'

I went through to the kitchen where Mom was twisting the dishcloth into a mug. 'How's your eye this morning, son?' She put the cup down and lifted my chin, tilting my head to the side. Her fingers smelled of dishwater. 'It doesn't look too bad.' Her voice was cheery and over-acted. 'It takes a lot to kill a Thorne, right?'

'It's just a black eye,' I said, not letting on how painful it really was.

Sadness crept into Mom's expression. 'Well, you'd better feed those dogs before they tear the house apart.' She picked up another cup and wiped it dry.

Opening the back door, I paused with my toes hanging off the step. Morning sunshine warmed my legs. It was going to get hot again.

'Try feeding them together,' said Mom. 'We should be training them to get along.'

I shrugged. 'OK, if you think so.'

*   *   *

Round the back of the house Ten Bucks' leash snapped tight, tugging against the steel drainpipe as he strained to get near me, each bark demanding, food, food, food! A dusty arc the exact length of his leash surrounded him. Inside the arc was a kennel, which he never used, a few sun-bleached bones, tufts of fur and a punctured tennis ball stripped of its green fuzz.

Outside the arc was our garden.

Litchi ran in circles, stopping to lick my toes. I petted her for a second. The wound on her ear, where Ten Bucks had bitten her, had healed leaving a tiny lump.

I walked straight towards Ten Bucks and picked up his food bowl. He barked as loud as ever but his one ear folded back. I was the only one he allowed to get near him. He wasn't going to bite me. Litchi cowered just beyond the edge of the arc.

I took their bowls to the ten-kilo food packet we had stored in the garage. Litchi followed, bouncing beside my ankles. I scooped up handfuls of pellets and went back to the drainpipe behind the house.

Pausing at the edge of the arc I held their food at shoulder height.

'Sit!' I said.

Ten Bucks barked even louder. Litchi looked startled and confused.

I glared down at them, commanding respect, letting them know I was in charge. 'Sit! SIT!'

Litchi ducked her tail between her legs. Ten Bucks went on barking as before. It was no use. I put down one bowl in front of Ten Bucks who was guzzling before the dish touched the ground. The other bowl I placed a metre away for Litchi, who sniffed it and nibbled a single pellet.

Ten Bucks watched Litchi, more concerned with how much she was eating than with his own food. He suddenly growled and snapped at her but the choke chain whipped tight. Litchi scrambled off, too terrified to return to her bowl. I went over and picked her up, holding her close to my chest, her little body quivering in my hands.

'Bad dog!' I said, pointing at Ten Bucks. He ignored me completely and kept eating. I put the pup down next to her food and went back to playing policeman.

I moved closer to Ten Bucks, deep inside his arc, and this seemed to calm him down. He even let me stroke his back. I ran my hand down towards his tail across his greasy, coarse fur and over the bumps and scabs. Against my better judgement, I felt sorry for him. Someone had allowed him to get like this, he hadn't done this to himself. He finished the food in his bowl and slurped his wet nose while I tenderly patted the top of his head. 'There's a good boy. Did you like that?'

One green eye and one blue eye stared evenly back at me. They reminded me of the sea, yet not quite the vivid aquamarine that filled my holiday. In this dog the colours were just as intense, but segregated. Like Dad had said, half good and half bad. I studied one eye and then the other, testing myself to see if I could tell which side was good.

I massaged the back of his head but as my fingers brushed over the leathery remains of his chewed ear the calm left him. He growled, switching back to his angry, demanding self, showing his teeth, barking orders over and over.

I stood up and took his bowl to the garage to fill it up. He barked on and on, letting the world know he was the biggest dog in the yard. I brought back more food and found Litchi hiding on the other side of the garden. She knew the danger of being too close. Ten Bucks would sink his teeth into her, not because he was hungry but because he was stronger. Simple as that. Placing the food down for Ten Bucks, I bent down and called the pup to me. She trotted back and eventually began eating again.

The morning was getting hotter. I squinted into the sky. A pale haze covered the neighbourhood, more of a humid smog than a proper cloud, but the sun was harsh, it would be clear by the afternoon. Daylight made the throbbing in my eye feel worse. As I raised my hand to shade my eyes, the shadow of my arm moved across Litchi and she yelped, thinking I was going to hit her. My mind flipped back to yesterday at school when that older boy, with the rugby neck, had suddenly yelled at me. I had flinched in exactly the same way. She crawled back to her food with her head bowed and her tail between her legs. This was becoming the way she always acted, even when Ten Bucks wasn't around. Watching her irritated me, the whimpering, the cowering, always wanting to be cuddled and pampered. Litchi picked out a single pellet and dropped it in the dirt. She licked it once, got bored with her food and wandered off. I slid her food towards the big dog and let him eat the rest, knowing Kevin would probably give Litchi lots of little treats when he got back from school.

As I went back inside, I found Litchi sitting against the back door, whining.

'Litchi! Get away from there,' I said.

The whining got louder and she blinked her cute eyes, hoping I would open the door. I knew she would spend the rest of the day on the sofa, hiding. She hardly ever went outside and dug in the garden or barked at birds. Instead she shivered and hid under the coffee table, getting frightened at the slightest sound. It was pathetic. I bit my lip, trying not to get annoyed.

'You can't go in,' I said.

She pretended not to understand. The whining changed to barking. Muscles tightened between my shoulder blades. Who the hell did she think she was, barking orders at me?

'You can't go in,' I said, as the anger twitched into my fists. 'Bad dog!'

Litchi stooped low and wagged her tail uncertainly. I tried to move her with my foot but she wouldn't take the hint.

'Damn it, Litchi, stop being such a fucking little brat. Go play! *Voertsek!*' I said through my teeth, kicking her much harder than I meant to.

She ran off, yelping and cowering from me. The edginess that had filled me a second ago vanished. I went to pick her up but she bolted, thinking I was going to beat her even more. It was too late to say sorry.

When Kevin got back from school he took a long drink of water from the fridge and sat down in front of the TV. Except, there was no TV. Without saying a word, he got up and went to his room. Mom and I looked at each other for a second.

'Why don't you try talking to him,' she said.

'Why me?'

'Because you two are close.'

I studied her expression to see if she was joking. She wasn't. He was just my little brother. I had never really thought of us as being 'close'.

His bedroom door wasn't properly shut so I nudged it open and saw him lying on his bed.

'You can't come in,' he said.

I moved closer, saying, 'Are you OK? You look pissed off?'

'I said you can't come in. Get out of my room!'

I stepped backwards off the bedroom carpet onto the tiles in the hall. 'There. I'm out. Are you happy now?'

Kevin lifted his head to see if my toes were touching the carpet. Satisfied, he rested his head back on the pillow. I waited for a second before asking, 'Do you want a sandwich or something?'

'I'm not hungry,' said Kevin.

I rocked onto my heels, trying to think of another question. 'So, what's it like being in Standard Four now?'

'I hate it.'

'Why?'

'No one believes you.'

'What do you mean?' I said.

'Nothing,' said Kevin. 'I don't want to talk about it.' He picked up an Avengers comic and pretended to read.

I waited. I stood there for a full minute listening to Ten Bucks bark and was about to leave when Kevin closed the comic and said, 'Do you remember the floating mountain?'

'Of course,' I said. 'Why?'

He started to say something but stopped himself. 'It doesn't matter.'

'No, tell me. What's this got to do with school?'

Kevin sighed. 'Today in Mrs van Zyl's class we had to write about what we did for the summer and draw a picture. So I drew the floating mountain, but she said it didn't look real. She said I had to draw what we *actually* did for the summer, not some made-up story.'

I folded my arms. 'So what did you do, Kev?'

'I said it *was* real. We really saw a floating mountain, just like in the drawing.'

'And then what happened?'

'She told me not to be stupid and everyone laughed,' he said, lowering his eyes.

I knew there was more. 'And then?'

'And then . . . I ripped up my drawing and called the teacher a stupid sock puppet.'

I couldn't help giggling. 'A *sock puppet*? Why did you call her that?'

A big grin grew across Kevin's face. 'I don't know. I was doing my best not to swear.'

'So did you get jacks?'

His smile disappeared. '*Ja*, obviously.'

'How many did you get?'

'Only three.'

Kevin sat up and kicked off his school shoes. I reached in to close the door so he could change out of his uniform.

'Alex,' he said.

I paused with my hand on the doorknob.

'What do you remember about the floating mountain?'

'Um . . .' I let go of the door and thought for a second. 'I remember it was really early and there were clouds under us in the valley. As we came round the corner it was right in front of us, just this one peak floating by itself. We stopped the car and watched it hovering in the mist for about twenty minutes. Then we clicked it. The three of us all clicked it together.'

'So you saw it. It was really real, right?' said Kevin.

'*Ja*, it was real.'

Kevin nodded to himself.

'So, do you want a sandwich or not?' I said.

'*Ja*. Is there any cheese left?'

'Dunno . . . I think so.'

262

He looked at my face, at the bruising. 'How's your eye?'

'It hurts,' I said, lightly touching my fingers to the swelling. 'Mom's given me some painkillers.'

'It looks cool,' said Kevin. 'You look like a boxer.'

'You think so?'

'*Ja*. You look just like Rocky.'

Smiling hurt, but I couldn't help it. 'Thanks, Kev.'

Mirrors

I dragged the slicer across the block of cheddar and placed the shavings of cheese on Kevin's sandwich. Through the sliding glass doors I watched Mom fill in the pit that she had dug months earlier. She worked hard, not like the weary road diggers who held up traffic for weeks while they scratched away at the ground. No, Mom was putting her back into it, shovelling as much as the spade could hold into the ditch, then twisting round, scooping up more earth and tossing it into the hole. She must have given up on planting an avocado tree. Ten Bucks quietened down to catch his breath and I thought I heard Dad's car pull up in front of the house. The engine stopped and the front gate creaked open and was left to slam shut. It was definitely Dad. I closed the sandwich and cut it in half. Mom sank her spade into the dirt and leaned on the handle.

'What are you doing here, Bruce?' said Mom, wiping away the sweat around her throat.

'Nice to see you too, Grace,' said Dad, taking off his sunglasses. 'Am I not allowed to pop by and see my family?'

Mom tucked a fist onto her hip. 'We can't just be your family whenever it suits you,' she said. It was weird to see her like this, only a few weeks ago she spent whole days in bed. Now, the anger steaming off her was so strong I could feel its heat in the living room. Something had changed. I wondered how much she knew about Dad and Poppy.

'What do you want?' she said.

Dad put his hand up. 'Calm down, Grace. I just dropped by to see my boys.' He was being polite, avoiding the argument head on, which meant he was up to something. 'And I brought you this,' he said, holding up a grocery bag. A wet, pink mass pressed against the plastic.

'What is it?' said Mom.

'It's a hindquarter,' said Dad, moving towards the house. 'C'mon, I'll show you.'

I didn't want to see him. If I faced Dad right now he'd stare at my swollen black eye and I'd stare at his mouth thinking about tongues rolling and licking each other. It would be too weird. Grabbing the sandwich, I darted through to Kevin's room.

'Dad's here,' I whispered to Kevin. He took the sandwich from my hand and the two of us peered along the passage at our parents.

Dad thumped the meat down on the counter and unwrapped it, exposing the wet flesh. The smell of blood slipped into every corner of the house.

'This guy at work went hunting over the weekend and came back with stacks of meat. I think it's impala,' said Dad.

Mom wasn't impressed.

'Don't give me that look, Grace,' said Dad. 'I'm providing for my family. The least you could do is show a little gratitude.'

Mom's reaction was to try and say five different things at the same time. Her mouth moved but only confused bursts of air shot out. She took a deep breath, and folded her arms. 'Fine. Great. You want to spend time with the boys. You want to *provide* for them. Good. Alex needs a new school uniform and Kevin has outgrown his.'

Mom sat down on the edge of the sofa, grabbed a pen and notepad from the coffee table and started scribbling. 'Here,' she said, handing Dad a note, 'that's the address. You'll get every-thing they need from this shop.'

He took it and stuffed it into his back pocket. 'OK, I'll look into it,' he said. 'Maybe we'll go at the weekend.'

'Now, Bruce!' said Mom. 'Before the shops close.'

'What?'

'He needs the uniform for tomorrow. So you're taking them *right now*.' She turned her head and called, 'Boys. Come through here. Your father's here to see you.'

Kevin went first and I followed. He held Litchi under one arm, using his other hand to eat his sandwich. Dad noticed my black eye but I avoided him by staring at the meat.

'You want to provide for your sons? You want to stop this from happening?' Mom pointed at my black eye. 'Then make yourself useful.'

I didn't like the way Mom told him about my eye. She was using me like a chess piece to put Dad into check. Dad chewed his thumb and spat away a tiny fleck of fingernail. There was only one move he could make.

'OK, Alex, let's go,' he said. 'I need to have a little chat with you anyway.' He took the car keys from his pocket and twirled them round his finger.

'You have *two* sons, remember?' said Mom, pushing Kevin towards him. 'Take Kevin too and make sure he gets school shoes.'

'But I don't wanna go!' said Kevin.

Mom wasn't in the mood to argue. 'You're going.'

Dad rolled his eyes and sighed, 'C'mon, shit for brains, move it.'

Kevin put Litchi on the floor and fed her the rest of his sandwich.

I didn't want to be near Dad so I got in the back of the Golf with Kevin.

'Alex, get in the front,' said Dad. 'We need to talk.'

I crawled over onto the front seat and fastened the seatbelt. This was exactly where Paula sat. Her legs touched the seat exactly where my legs were touching. This was where she had leaned over and opened her mouth. I glanced at Dad's face. The bristles on his chin were as rough as sandpaper. That's what Paula felt when her cheek rubbed against his. I gazed at his lips and imagined them opening, his wet tongue slowly coming towards me, wanting to be inside me, to suck me in.

'Alex, are you deaf?' said Dad. 'Answer me, boy. Who hit you?'

'I . . . I don't know.'

'What do you mean, you don't *know?* Was it some guy at school? Because all you've got to do is point him out and I'll catch up with him. No problem.'

'It wasn't anyone at school,' I said. 'It was Darrel and his buddies.'

Dad took his eyes off the road and stared at me. 'I thought you got beat up at school because of your uniform.'

The moment Mom mentioned my eye I knew this would happen, I'd get cornered and be forced to doublecross her. It would go back to being the three of us against her.

'It wasn't anyone at school,' I said.

Dad gripped the steering wheel till the veins in his neck stuck out like earthworms. 'That lying bitch!' he said, punching the steering wheel. 'I swear she makes me want to . . . Everything she says is a lie, everything she says. I'll bet you don't even need uniforms, do you?'

I fixed my eyes straight ahead at the road.

'Anyway, fuck it,' said Dad. 'I shouldn't have expected anything else from her sort.' He switched on the radio and rubbed his forehead.

Kevin sat directly behind me. In the wing mirror I watched him open his mouth like a fish and breathe against the window. On the misted glass he drew a skull that slowly vanished as the steam disappeared.

Driving fast, Dad said, 'Did you get a punch in?'

'What?'

'What did the other guy look like? You must have got a few hits in.'

I lifted my chin. 'I didn't fight back.'

'What!?' said Dad, swerving the car as he threw me a look. 'You mean you didn't throw a single punch?'

'No.'

'Why not?'

'I didn't feel like it. Fighting's pointless.'

That thumped air out of his chest. 'Well . . . shit. What can I say?' Dad shook his head. 'I'll bet your mother's proud. But I'll tell you this free of charge, you're in high school now, if you don't start throwing punches from day one, you're going to get a lot worse than a black eye. Trust me.'

'But I don't want to fight all the time.'

'It doesn't matter what you want. If you don't make people think you're tougher than you are, you'll get trampled on for the rest of your life. Not everyone gets to be Gandhi.'

After a moment Kevin asked, 'What's a gan-dee?'

'Shut up, Kevin!' said Dad.

We arrived at a squat flat-roofed building with square pillars at the entrance. Painted across the front of the shop was a massive red sign. **SCHOOL UNIFORMS.** Something about the over-sized, block shape of the letters, made this place feel like a school. Since there were no markings in the gravel car park, Dad pulled up as close as he could to the entrance and skidded to a halt. Dust settled around us as we walked in.

The shop had an empty-Tupperware-lunch-box smell and the patterns on the linoleum floor reminded me of school corridors. The place was busy. One mother carried a huge bundle of trousers and shirts draped over her arm, while her three children followed her to the checkout. Another woman held up a shirt to her daughter's chin, measuring the size. There were stacks of uniforms everywhere, some maroon, some blue, some khaki, different colours for each school across the city. A shop assistant in her sixties smiled as soon as she saw Dad. 'Mr Thorne, how nice to see you again. How is that lovely daughter of yours?'

Dad cleared his throat. 'Fine, fine,' he said very quickly. 'Look, I don't have a lot of time . . .'

'And these must be your other children,' smiled the woman, touching Kevin's blond hair. 'Such good-looking boys. And . . .

oh, dear! What happened to your eye? Have we been in the wars, young man?'

'I got beat up,' I said proudly, throwing a glance at Dad. The way I said it puzzled the woman. She stared at me with her head tilted. 'Well,' she said, 'we can't always win, can we?'

'We're just going to look around,' said Dad to the shop assistant.

'OK. Just call if you need me,' she said.

Her friendliness felt out of place. It was always Mom who took us uniform shopping. So how did this shop assistant know Dad? The answer stalked through the veldt of my mind, hidden but creeping closer. Then it pounced.

He'd brought her here.

That's why this woman recognised him. Dad had been here, recently, with Paula, to buy her a school uniform. I bet they pretended to be father and daughter. They probably made a game of it, winking at each other behind the shop assistant's back.

Dad moved off but quickly noticed we weren't right behind him. 'Wakey, wakey, boys,' he said, snapping his fingers.

We followed him to the shoe section.

'OK, let's get this done,' said Dad. 'You need shoes, right?' he said to Kevin.

'*Ja.*'

Dad leaned in close to Kevin, their faces almost touching. 'What? Sorry? I can't understand you.'

'Yes.'

'Ah, that's better. Now you don't sound like a bloody retard.' Dad shoved his hands in his pockets and pointed with his nose. 'Since we're finally speaking the same language let me explain what's going to happen. Kevin, you're going to stay here and try on shoes till you find a pair that fits. Alex, you're coming with me.' He turned and walked to the other side of the shop, leaving Kevin to examine the underside of a shoe.

'Choose a good pair. One that'll last all year,' I said to Kevin.

'There's no size on this one,' he said, holding it up.

Dad started snapping his fingers again.

I took the shoe from him. 'The size is on the inside, Kev. Look . . . here.'

'Alex. Are you deaf?' yelled Dad from the other side of the shop

'Just give us a minute, Kev, OK?' I said.

I quickly walked over to Dad, who was staring at his watch. 'So what do you need?'

I glanced at the piles of brown and gold uniforms. He had gone straight to my school colours without asking for any advice. He must have been here with Paula.

'Everything,' I said, 'I need the whole uniform.'

We started with the long trousers. 'Well, there's no point getting you these because it's summer,' said Dad. 'We'll get shorts for now. What size are you?'

'Dunno,' I shrugged.

He picked out three different sizes. 'Try these on, see which fits you best.'

We also picked out three different sizes of shirts, a blazer, a brown-and-gold striped tie and a pair of socks. While Dad was looking for the right sizes a woman holding a baby on her hip stared at me across the piles of clothes. She studied the swelling around my eye, glancing at Dad, watching his movements. I knew she thought Dad had done this to me. Secretly, I hoped she would say something, just to see what Dad would do. Would he deny it? Or would he just say it serves me right? She grinned politely and lowered her eyes. I watched the back of her head as she walked down the aisle.

'There's a free fitting room,' said Dad. 'Let's go.'

Taking the clothes into the cubicle, I closed the black curtain behind me. Full-length mirrors hung on three walls. Straight ahead of me, was me, and to the left and right were a million copies of me stretching out to infinity. When I raised my hand, they raised their hands. When I leaned to the side, I saw the back of my head in the mirror behind me, and the backs of a million other heads exactly like mine.

'It's hard to believe you're already in high school,' came Dad's voice through the curtain. His tone was chatty, as if we were pals again. 'So how is it?'

'It's horrible,' I said, taking off my T-shirt. As I raised my hands above my head a jolt of pain ran through the bruising in my ribs.

'What did you say?' said Dad.

I held my breath for a second and let it out bit by bit. 'I didn't say anything.'

'Have you met any girls at your new school?'

'No,' I said. 'I've only been there for one day.'

'Listen to the voice of experience, son. High school is a great place to meet girls. Trust me. Get in there while you still can. One day you'll understand.'

A completely empty face stared back at me as I buttoned up the school shirt.

Dad's voice carried on. 'Man! What would I give to be in high school again! They say it's the best years of your life . . . then again, they also say youth is wasted on the young.'

I didn't want to hear this, not today. I shook my head, wishing he would shut up. To the left and right, a million versions of me shook their heads too. The first shirt was too tight so I tried on another.

I heard Kevin move on the other side of the curtain. 'Dad, I can't find any shoes that fit me,' he whined.

'Think, boy,' said Dad. 'Use what little brains God gave you. Do I work here? Huh? No, of course not. So how the hell would I be able to help you? Go over there and tell that lady what you're looking for and stop annoying me every five minutes with your little *problems*.'

Kevin's feet clomped off.

Reflected in the mirror, in the gap under the curtain, Dad's shoes paced up and down.

'Honest to God, Alex, things need to change. It'll be better once the divorce goes through. You don't know your mother like I do. She's poisoned my own sons against me, twists everything I do. It's taken me a long time to build up a good name for myself but she

270

won't stop till she drags it through the mud. All she's interested in is money, *my* money. It's unbelievable.'

'She hasn't said anything bad about you,' I said.

'Ha! Yeah, I'd like to believe that,' said Dad. 'I'm telling you, I can only take so much shit from people. That woman is a frigid old money grabber and she'd better watch herself. I'm not all bark and no play, you know?'

I'd never heard the word *frigid* before. It sounded like *fridge* and *rigid* rammed together, meaning Mom was cold and stiff, or maybe square and strict. Whatever it meant it I couldn't bear listening to him any more. I rested my forehead against the mirror, praying for silence.

'Anyway, it doesn't matter,' continued Dad. 'I've got other things in the pipeline right now, other options, business ideas. And I'm really glad you got the chance to meet Auntie Poppy. She really likes you.' His voice lowered, almost whispering into the curtain. 'You know, she told me she saw you on the way to school the other day. Did you . . .' He paused, taking great care choosing his words. 'Did you happen to see her, Alex?'

I remembered her getting into Dad's car. I saw their mouths open, watched their tongues mating.

'Alex? Alex, are you listening to me?'

'She's not my auntie, Dad. She can't be. She goes to the same school as me.' I whipped open the curtain. 'And I know she's pregnant.'

Dad narrowed his eyes. 'Have you told your mother about us?'

'Not yet. But when I do you'll be in big trouble.'

He clutched my neck with such force I heard my teeth snap against each other.

Dad forced me backwards into the cubicle, closing the curtain behind him. His other hand covered my mouth and shoved my head back against the mirror.

'Don't you *ever* speak to me like that again,' hissed Dad.

I got such a fright I began to wet myself. I clenched my stomach tight but a trickle still came out and dampened my underpants.

His face came right up to mine. 'Who the fuck do you think

271

you're talking to?' Bits of spit hit me in the face. Every muscle in his chest was like steel. I couldn't move. To the left and right a million copies of Dad pressed in against me.

'You don't know anything about Paula, and if you talk to anyone it will be the biggest mistake of your short little life, believe me.' Fury distorted his face so much he stopped looking like Dad. 'I started you and I will fucking end you! Do you understand?'

I couldn't move.

'Do you understand?' he growled

My whole body was shaking and I started to cry.

He let go of my mouth and I sank to the floor. 'Blubbering like a baby won't help you.' Dad pulled his shirt straight and picked up his watch. The strap had snapped when he grabbed me.

'OK, enough of that, you're embarrassing yourself,' he said. 'Get up.'

Dad looked at the two piles of uniforms on the floor. 'Is this the stuff that fitted you?'

I wiped my eyes, my hands quivering uncontrollably.

'Look at me when I'm talking to you! Is this the stuff?'

It was hard to tell which sizes he was holding up. 'Yes,' I said.

'Good. Let's pay for these and get out of here.' He gathered up the clothes and left.

My heart hammered against the walls of my chest. I sat still, fighting hard against the urge to give in and sob. I was sitting too low to see my reflection, but the mirrors looked like a gloomy corridor stretching out for ever.

I met Kevin and Dad at the checkout. The sales assistant who had recognised Dad was folding the clothes and carefully placing them in a plastic bag.

'Are you sure you only want one of each?' she said.

'I'm sure,' said Dad.

'You know, I always recommend that parents buy at least three shirts, three trousers and three pairs of socks. That way you'll always have one on the child, one in the wash and one in the drawer.'

Dad put both hands on the counter. 'Just pack the damn clothes, lady.'

Her smile vanished. She lowered her eyelids and straightened up to her full height. 'Fine,' she said, shoving the blazer into a separate bag.

Kevin tugged Dad's arm. 'I couldn't find any shoes.'

'That's 'cause you were mucking about, weren't you?'

'No. I was looking, but I couldn't find any.'

The woman pretended not to listen and typed the prices into the till.

'Well, it's too late now. You had your chance and you blew it. Next time you'll do as I say, when I say.' Dad unrolled some twenties from his wad and tossed a hundred rand on the counter. One of the notes slid off and dropped on the ground at the woman's feet but she didn't even look at it. She glared right through Dad, her lips pressed tight together.

Dad noted the challenge. He snatched the bags and said, 'Let's go.'

'But what about my shoes?' said Kevin.

'Talk to your mother about that.'

But Kevin wouldn't let it go. All the way to the car he whined and argued till eventually Dad said, 'Shut up, Kevin! Get in the car and shut up. I don't want to hear another word out of you.'

Kevin crawled onto the back seat. Dad swung in behind the steering wheel, put on his sunglasses, wound down the window and we spun off into the traffic. Driving really fast, he overtook a lorry and cut through a petrol station to avoid the red lights. Kevin held on to the back of my seat to stop himself being thrown from one side of the car to the other.

'Move your head, Kevin. I can't see out the back,' said Dad, into the rear-view mirror.

Kevin flopped backwards. 'It's not fair.'

'Don't start, boy.'

'But what am I going to wear to school?'

'Wear the shoes you wore this morning,' said Dad.

'But they don't fit properly.'

273

'Then get your mother to buy you a new pair.'

'But she said *you* have to buy me shoes.'

Dad changed gear as we sped past a row of townhouses. 'Read my lips, Kevin. I don't give a shit what your Mom said. Now, I'm warning you, shut your mouth or you're going to really piss me off.'

But Kevin was more stubborn than that. 'Why does Alex always get stuff but I don't? It's not fair!' he shouted, kicking the back of Dad's seat.

Dad slammed on the brakes and Kevin was thrown forward as the car screeched to a stop. The car behind us swerved into the other lane, nearly smashing into us.

'*Haai! Wat maak jy?*' yelled the man, thumping the horn. (What are you doing?)

The smell of burnt rubber came up through the floor. Dad twisted round and faced Kevin, who was rubbing his chest.

'Get out,' said Dad.

Kevin looked confused. He glanced at me to see if he had heard Dad correctly.

'But I don't know where I am,' he said.

Dad exploded. 'GET OUT OF THE FUCKING CAR!'

Kevin opened the door and stepped onto the pavement. Dad pulled away so quickly the door slammed shut by itself. I rolled down my window and stuck my head out. Kevin sat down on the kerb, picked up a stone and threw it across the street. We turned the corner and he was gone. Dad wouldn't go back for him. He would just leave Kevin all alone even though it was about four or five kilometres back to the house and Kevin didn't know his way home. Someone had to go back.

I had to go.

We would be safer together and maybe if I phoned from a café or someplace then Mom would come and pick us up. I had to get out of the car but Dad was driving too fast. If I waited till we passed someone's lawn maybe I could jump out and hope for the best. Could I tuck and roll like in the movies? We were getting further and further away from Kevin. I had to go now. I could do this.

Moving casually so Dad wouldn't notice, I laid my hand on the door latch and hooked my forefinger over the lever. I slowly pulled till I felt resistance. The car slowed down and stopped at a red light. This was my chance. I pulled the lever tight. The mechanism began releasing the latch. Just a little more and the door would pop open. A single twitch of my finger would be enough. Dad shifted his hand on the steering wheel and I drew back just a fraction. He was close enough to grab me. I let all my breath out, hoping to stop my hand from shaking. I had to go, but I couldn't move.

The time on my watch was 4.29 and thirty-five seconds. If the lights were still red by exactly 4.30 I'd jump out. I promised myself, and hoped to die.

Fifteen more seconds. All I had to do was tug the lever a few more centimetres.

Ten more seconds. I imagined flinging the door open and stepping out with my left leg first.

Five more seconds. Would I be quick enough? What if Dad grabbed me? What would he do?

Three more seconds. If I got out it would be over. I would never be his son again.

4.30. How had this happened?

4.30 and one second. The green light flicked on.

4.30 and two seconds. Dad revved the car. I had promised. This was it. I hoped to die.

The door clicked open almost by itself and I scrambled out, stumbling onto the pavement. I heard the car jolt and the engine cut out but I kept running, heading back the way we had come, back to Kevin. I ran holding my bruised ribs, expecting a red Golf to pull up beside me and for Dad to force me to get in. I kept looking over my shoulder but nothing was chasing me. Dad wouldn't go back for Kevin and he wasn't going to come back for me either. I ran even faster, feeling new freedom with every step.

At the corner I spotted Kevin, sitting in exactly the same position as before. When he saw me, he stood up, wiped his eyes and put his hands in his pockets. His blond hair was stuck down with sweat.

'Hey,' he said, too upset to make eye contact.

'Hey,' I said, hands on knees, catching my breath.

'Where's Dad?'

'Dunno,' I said. 'I jumped out and he didn't follow me.'

Kevin's eyes widened. 'Did you jump while the car was moving?'

'Kind of, we were pulling away at the lights and I bailed out.'

Kevin nodded and smiled. 'Wow.'

Breathing hard, I smiled too.

Teeth

Kevin and I didn't know this neighbourhood very well. The bendy residential streets twisted and turned more than spaghetti. I knew my way back to the junction. If we followed that main road I'd be able to find the way home. As we approached the spot where I had jumped out, I felt a creepy sensation that Dad was watching us from somewhere, waiting to jump out of his car and shout at us, or worse. I looked left and right and over my shoulder, expecting something. But deeper down I knew Dad wasn't looking for us. He was gone.

There were no pavements so we picked our way along the rocky shale verge beside the main road. Trucks sped by, leaving behind clouds of red dust and grey exhaust fumes. We pulled the necks of our T-shirts up over our noses and settled into a steady marching rhythm, which reminded me of how we used to walk to school together. It took us half an hour to get back to the house and though we didn't say anything, it was the closest I'd ever felt to Kevin. There was something about the way we walked next to each other, close enough to hear each other breathing, close enough to understand what was difficult to say.

A trust existed between us. We were real brothers, not because of our parents but because we wanted to be.

From the top of our street I could hear Ten Bucks barking. I recognised Dad's red Golf parked outside our house, heat shimmering off the bonnet. We opened the front gate and waited, listening at the front door.

'... this is our *home*, Bruce. It's where your sons grew up,' came Mom's voice.

I knelt down and pressed my ear against the varnished wood.

'Why do you have to make a bloody drama out of everything? It's just a house. Bricks and mortar, that's all,' said Dad, 'and I own half of it.'

Kevin whispered, 'What are they fighting about?'

I lifted my finger to my lips. 'Shhhhhh.'

The clomping of Dad's shoes pacing up and down came through the door. Behind that sound was something else, Mom moving in the kitchen. I leaned against the door so hard the wood creaked.

'Why are you doing this?' came Mom's voice. 'You push and you push and you push till you wear me down and you get your own way.'

Dad sighed. 'I'm not pushing you, Grace. I'm being fair. Look, I'll make you a deal. When we sell the house, we'll split the profits sixty-forty. That way you'll have a bigger share to put a down payment on a place with a garden for the boys and I can buy a flat. That's my best offer.'

A chair in the kitchen scraped against the tiles. Mom's bare feet padded closer till she was standing right on the other side of the front door.

'That's your best offer, is it? Well, I have a deal for you.' Mom's voice was quivering. 'We keep the house and in return I won't tell the police how old she is.'

Silence.

How did Mom know? Dad would think I told her. Kevin squeezed in beside me. We both held our breath.

'You're drunk, Grace. Look at you. You're a useless drunk. You've got no idea what you're talking about,' spat Dad. 'How do you live with yourself? What kind of mother raises kids with a bottle in her hand?'

'Her name's Paula,' Mom's tone was deliberate but angry. 'And she's fifteen years old. Fifteen! You son of a bitch!'

Glass smashed inside the house. I flinched my head away from the door.

'Who told you this? Alex?' came Dad's voice.

The tone in Dad's voice reached out and knotted my insides.

'No. Rebecca told me. She came here, with all her bags packed, and told me everything. She said she's going back to Lesotho because she refuses to work in a house full of "bad spirits".'

'And you believed that lying kaffir bitch? You're nuts. Use your brain for a second. How would *Rebecca*, of all people, know anything about Poppy?' Dad's feet shuffled closer. 'That's your problem, Grace, the boys need you but you're too drunk and crazy to look after them.'

'Don't turn this on me,' yelled Mom. 'I'm a *great* mother. But you! You're the one screwing a minor. And as for the boys, where are they?'

'I dropped them off at the shop. They wanted to buy sweets.'

'Don't lie to me, Bruce.'

'So now you're calling me a liar, too? Is it beat-up-Bruce day or something?' said Dad. 'I promise you this, as soon as those divorce papers go through I'm getting half of everything. The house. The savings. Everything! And if you dare try and tell people your little theories about Poppy then I'll expose you as a drunk ... That's right. Oh, don't look at me like that, you know I'm not bluffing. I'll tell the whole world I couldn't stand living with a useless drunk! I'll tell them you're too sick in the head to look after the boys. They'd be better off in foster care or boarding school. *Anywhere* away from *you*! And you know I'll do it. I swear to God, I'll do it.'

Dad's footsteps crunched glass into the tiles. The sound got closer. Kevin and I scrambled to get out of the way but the door bashed open.

'Oh, great!' said Dad, glaring at us crouched in front of the door. 'You're all at it. Snooping around in other people's business.

I thought I brought you up better than that. Especially you, Alex.'

Behind Dad I noticed the maroon liquid and the shards of a broken wineglass scattered across the living-room tiles. Mom was sitting cross-legged on the sofa with tears in her eyes. 'Are you OK, Sonny-o?' she said.

I nodded.

'You see? They're fine,' said Dad to Mom. He turned to us. 'Right, you two, help me pack the car.'

'I don't wanna,' said Kevin.

'Do as I say!' shouted Dad, pointing towards the garage.

We stood frozen by his rage. The trembling in my fingers started again.

'MOVE.'

He herded us out towards the garage and flung the door open as Ten Bucks barked in the background.

'Right. I want all my stuff packed into the back of my car. All those tools, the paint stripper, the pump, those spare car batteries, the tent, the fishing poles, those bathroom tiles, everything.' Dad grabbed the toolbox in one hand and jump leads in the other. 'Don't stand there gawping at me! Move!' he yelled.

I squatted down, lifted an old car battery and waddled to the car. Kevin carried the pump in one hand. When he got to the car he tossed it into the boot and strolled back to the garage for something else.

'Why is that dog barking?' said Dad.

'He always does that,' I answered.

'It's bugging the hell out of me,' said Dad. 'Where is he?'

I pointed. 'Round the back.'

Dad marched behind the house looking for Ten Bucks. I noticed that, while we were away, Mom had completely filled in the pit. All that was left was a big muddy circle on the lawn. I went into the garage and fetched the other battery. As I came out Ten Bucks spun around and growled at me. Trying not to drop the battery, I walked backwards towards the car, keeping both eyes on the dog's mouth.

'He's not barking now, is he?' said Dad, petting Ten Bucks on the head. 'You need to let him get used to the garden, let him mark his territory, then he'll be fine.'

I heaved the battery into the back of the car and went back to the garage for more stuff. I met Kevin halfway. Ten Bucks snarled at him. Kevin pointed Dad's old pool cue at the dog to keep it away.

'Sit, Ten Bucks,' I said, but he didn't budge.

Mom opened the glass sliding door a fraction and called out, 'Who let the dog loose?'

Litchi squirmed past her foot and came bouncing into the garden, wagging her tail. As soon as she saw Ten Bucks she cowered and ran down to the bottom of the garden. Ten Bucks bolted after Litchi. Kevin went after Ten Bucks.

'Kevin,' shouted Dad. 'Get back here and help load the car.'

But he wasn't listening. Kevin chased Ten Bucks, waving the pool cue above his head and screaming, 'Leave her alone!'

Ten Bucks was right behind her like a missile. He nipped Litchi's heels and she tripped, tumbling across the grass. But Ten Bucks was running so fast he overshot her, skidding, clawing the earth, trying to change direction. Litchi jumped to her feet and sprinted, past Kevin to the top of the garden. Now Kevin stood between the two dogs. He held the cue out horizontally with both hands trying to block Ten Bucks from getting by. But the dog was too fast, it dashed right through the flower bed along the side of the house.

Mom slid the door open and stepped out. 'Grab her, Alex, quick!' she said, pointing at Litchi.

I ran with my arms held wide and dived onto the grass trying to get hold of her. I almost had her. My hand touched the fur along her back, her tail slid through my fingers. Litchi yelped with fright and charged up the driveway. I was still lying face down on the grass when Ten Bucks sprinted right by me. One dog after the other, they ran out the gate.

Car tyres screeched. Litchi howled hideously. Metal scrunched against metal. Glass tinkled to the ground.

It all happened in one second.

I jumped to my feet and ran with Mom to the street.

A white car had crashed into the side of Dad's Golf. There was glass all over the street. Hissing sounds came from the engine of the white car. Mom went up and peered into the driver's side window. In the white car was a woman with a perm, sitting behind the wheel, staring out across the bonnet. The weather report was on the radio. '. . . *to be sunny and warm with highs of around thirty-four degrees dropping to eighteen degrees in the evening . . .*'

'Hello. Can you hear me?' said Mom to the woman. 'Don't move. You might be hurt.'

The woman raised her head and looked into the rear-view mirror. Litchi lay in the street, her head slumped at an abnormal angle to the rest of her body. Blood oozed from her nostrils onto the tar, forming a glistening black puddle.

Dad came up behind me. 'No. No. No,' he said, raising both hands to his head. 'I just bought that car six weeks ago!'

The woman opened the door and put her foot out.

'Just stay still,' said Mom.

'It's OK,' said the woman. 'I'm fine, honestly.' She steadied herself and looked over at Litchi's body.

'What the hell have you done to my car?' yelled Dad. He moved round to the front to get a better look at the damage. 'I don't fucking believe this. What were you thinking, you crazy bitch?'

The woman's perm was tight and shaped like a walnut helmet. Her lips were tight too. She glared at Dad for a second, then slammed the door closed. 'Who are you calling a bitch? I was trying to avoid your bloody dogs.'

'So you swerved directly into my brand-new car? Are you insane?'

'Your dogs should be locked up instead of putting people's lives at risk. This accident could have been much worse.'

'How could it have been worse?' said Dad. 'Were you aiming to smash into the front of my house too?'

She stared at Dad, speechless. Mom held up her hands and stepped between them. 'Will everybody just calm down, please.'

Kevin walked right by me and crouched next to Litchi's body. 'Litchi? Are you OK?' he said, stroking her tummy very slowly, but she didn't move, not even a twitch. Ten Bucks loped behind Kevin, sniffing the air. He scratched his missing ear with a hind leg, then sat down on the road, lifted a leg, and began licking his dick.

'Litchi? Puppy?' Kevin's bottom lip began to tremble. 'Please don't die. Please.'

I felt a lump growing in my throat. Tears flowed down his cheeks and I thought he was about to break down and sob. But he bit his lip and lowered his eyebrows. I'd seen him do this just before he fought Darrel at school. He gathered up all his emotions and tied them tightly together, transforming each particular feeling into a single ball of rage.

'Mom,' I said, 'I don't think Kevin's feeling well.'

But she wasn't listening. She had one hand on Dad's chest as he pointed and yelled at the woman with the walnut perm.

Kevin curled his fingers around the pool cue and squeezed it tightly in his fist. He jumped to his feet and charged at Ten Bucks. The pool cue came down hard across Ten Bucks' back. Chasing the dog down the street, Kevin swung the cue wildly, trying to clip the dog's hind legs. The frenzied screams coming from Kevin made Mom, Dad and the walnut woman stop arguing. Ten Bucks tucked in his tail and ran in wide circles, centimetres out of Kevin's reach, frustrating him even more.

'I HATE YOU, I HATE YOU!' Kevin screamed, completely out of control, angrier than I'd ever seen him with Darrel or Dad. He lifted the pool cue high above his head, ready to unleash himself at Ten Bucks. He was going to destroy that dog, break its spine, jab holes in it, mash it into the ground. The dog stopped, crouched, his lips peeled back showing his fangs, the hair on his back raised. He sprang at Kevin, all four paws landing on his chest, toppling him over backwards, and the two of them crumpled to the ground. Kevin screamed, high pitched and terrified, as flashes of yellow teeth snapped at his face. Dreadful, beastly snarling sounds came from Ten Bucks as he bit into Kevin's face again and again. The pool cue clattered to the floor and my brother's arms clutched round the back of the dog's head.

It looked like wrestling.

Like a hug.

Except for the screaming.

Mom sprinted down the street, her bare feet making no sound against the tar, her hands out in front trying to magic away what was happening. Every single movement of her body burned into my brain like a hundred separate photographs strung together.

Ten Bucks shifted off Kevin's chest, round to his neck. The blood on his snout glistened wet. He sank his teeth into the skin between Kevin's neck and shoulder and wrenched his jaw from side to side the way a puppy wrestles a dishcloth. Kevin's fingernails scraped at the tarmac. Ten Bucks tugged backwards in short powerful bursts, dragging Kevin's body. The hungry growling never stopped. My brother's legs kicked aimlessly, his heels dragging on the ground till his shoes popped off. I cupped my hands over my ears and squeezed my head to stop it bursting open. Mom's bare foot kicked Ten Bucks in the ribs but he didn't let go. Falling on him, she clawed her fingers into his mouth, between his fangs, trying to pry Kevin loose. Their growls merged as they fought over Kevin. She pulled his snout back but Ten Bucks' jaws were locked tight. With a vicious scream, Mom rammed her thumb into the dog's eye socket. The jaws opened with a single yelp.

'Kevin? Kettle?' But he wasn't answering. Mom tilted his head to see how bad the wound was. 'Oh, God! No. No. No.' She pressed her hand against his neck.

With my hands still on my head, not sure what to do, I took tiny steps towards Mom. Dad strode up behind me, tutting under his breath. 'I told you not to tie up that dog. I knew this would happen.'

'Bruce!' cried Mom. 'Get the car, quick! Alex, get some towels. Run!'

'Where are your keys?' said Dad. 'We'll take your car.'

'Your car is *right there*, Bruce, just reverse it back here,' said Mom, her fingers sticky with blood. She hooked her free arm behind Kevin's head and pulled him close to her. 'You'll be OK, Kettle,' she said, her voice choking up. 'Be strong. It's OK. Mommy's here.'

Ten Bucks walked in circles trying to rub his eye with a paw.

Dad stood in the middle of the street. He stared at Kevin for a second, then looked back at his red Golf. The white car was still crashed against it and the walnut woman stared at Kevin with both hands cupped over her mouth.

'Look, Grace, we can't take my car. It's just been in an accident. The cops have to examine the crash for the insurance claim.'

Mom stared at Dad as if he was speaking another language, but he carried on, more and more words senselessly pouring out of his mouth. 'Wouldn't it be better if we put him in the back of your car? You don't have leather seats. If any blood gets on those old vinyl seats, it'll wipe right off. I think that's best. Where are your keys? I'll reverse the car out and then you can drive him.'

Kevin was slipping further away; his mouth opened, creating a pink bubble of blood and saliva that popped silently. Mom's stare shifted. It was as if she couldn't see Dad any more. In her mind he had stopped being real. She lifted her head and shouted as loud as she could.

'HELP! Somebody PLEASE help me. HELP! Please, please help me, my son is dying.'

There was so much blood. Too much. More and more flowed out. Spreading around Mom like spilt oil. Spreading everywhere. Dad leaned in closer, shouting at her. 'Where are your bloody keys?' Telling her not to be so stupid, that she was only making things worse. More and more came out. I collapsed to my knees, begging him to stop but more and more came out.

A door slammed. The walnut woman revved the engine and reversed her car, scraping it the length of Dad's Golf.

'What the hell are you doing?' shouted Dad, examining the new damage to his car.

She pulled up next to Mom, jumped out, and opened the back door. She unzipped a sports bag and pulled out a T-shirt and some yellow legwarmers.

'Here, lady,' she said to Mom, 'wrap these round his neck.'

They hurriedly bandaged Kevin's neck. The soaked cloth changed from yellow to brown.

'Press down on the wound to stop the blood, OK? But don't strangle him.'

Mom dragged Kevin onto the back seat of the white car, while the woman lifted his legs. She ran round to the driver's side and closed the door. Not wanting to stay here with Dad, I hopped in the front seat and we sped away, with the front wheel chugging and grinding against the dented panel. Out the back window, I watched Dad poke Litchi's little body with the toe of his boot while Ten Bucks sniffed the blood.

Emergency Exit

The car sped past the security guards at the front gate, swerved to avoid an oncoming ambulance and stopped right in front of the hospital. The walnut woman jumped out and ran into the building, hands out in front of her, shouting, 'Help! Hey! We need help here. Quickly!'

I unclipped my seatbelt, climbed out, and opened the back door. Mom cradled Kevin's head like a baby, pressing the cloth tightly against his neck, her eyes wide, breathing hard in short sobbing bursts. 'It's OK . . . Just hold on, Kettle, please hold on,' she said hysterically, digging her finger into Kevin's mouth and scooping out blood with a wet sucking noise. Her clothes were soaked deep red and clinging to her skin. Kevin's eyes were open, staring straight out, unblinking. One side of his face was covered in gashes. The biggest wound cut straight down, through the middle of his eyebrow, splitting his eyelid and exposing a pink eyeball. The socket was flooded with blood, making his eye float and loll uncontrollably.

I felt like I'd stood up too fast, the inside of my head tilted. I grabbed on to the car to keep my balance.

'Mom. Is he . . . ?'

A big hand landed on my shoulder and pulled me away from the door. 'Excuse me. Let me past.' A man in green doctor's overalls leaned into the car. Behind him were two more people with a trolley and the walnut woman pointing and shouting, '*Maak gou! Dis baie ernstig!*' (Hurry. It's very serious!) They were all talking at the same time, shouting instructions, half in English, half in Afrikaans.

The man in green tried to take hold of Kevin but Mom wouldn't let go, she howled even louder. 'My boy! Don't take my boy!'

More people came running out. One went round the other side of the car and spoke to Mom, while two others eased Kevin out of her grasp and onto the trolley. The doctors immediately put a gas mask over his mouth and pressed a fresh bandage against his neck as they jogged alongside the trolley into the hospital. Mom suddenly jumped out of the car and chased after them, grabbing the side of the trolley. 'I'm still here, Kevin. Mommy's here,' she said, running with them through the main doors.

I watched them disappear. The walnut woman stared at the blood on her arms, on her clothes. Somehow there was no blood on me, not a drop. The car sat idling with all four doors open. She blinked at me and opened her mouth, wanting to say something . . .

'*Haai, wat maak jy?*' shouted a man's voice. (Hey, what are you doing?)

The walnut woman turned to face a driver leaning out of an ambulance.

'Excuse me?' she said.

'You can't park here. Rules is rules, lady. You must go to visitors' parking.' The ambulance driver clicked his tongue, shook his head.

She thought about arguing. I could see the urge to fight rising in her.

'Sorry, lady, rules is rules,' said the ambulance driver again.

She marched round the car, slamming each door shut, then got in and drove away. The ambulance drove by and parked. The driver went inside.

And then it was quiet.

There was only me.

I looked up at the tall multistorey hospital. Above it hung a dark purple evening sky and pale orange clouds, lit by the setting sun. The whole building moved, lurching slowly forward, about to collapse on me. I knew it was an illusion – the clouds were moving not the building – but it felt real, as if the whole hospital was toppling forward. As I stepped back the building seemed to right itself for a moment. At the end of a row of neatly trimmed shrubs an old gardener was loading his tools into a wheelbarrow. His black hands were as rough as old leather gloves. He stopped what he was doing and nodded slowly as if he saw something in me, something that made perfect sense.

I wandered into the hospital. Inside was a huge sign with two words on it, **Emergencies / Noodgevalle.** Under this sign was a reception desk.

'*Kan ek jou help?*' said the nurse at reception. (Can I help you?)

'My brother was bitten by a dog . . . they all came running in here.'

The lines on her forehead creased. 'What was the name?'

'Thorne.'

'Thorn?'

'Yes, Thorne. My name is Alex Thorne. T-h-o-r-n-e. My brother's name is Kevin. Do you know where he is?'

She glanced down at the paperwork on her desk, then turned her back and picked up a phone. The conversation was too low for me to hear what she was saying. She hung up and quickly turned to me with a brave smile.

'Alex, they've taken your brother into theatre, where the doctors are attending to him.'

I knew what this meant but I wasn't sure what I had to do. Would they let me see him? Should I wait outside? The nurse noticed my hesitation. She came out from behind the desk, placed her hand on my shoulder and bent down to look me in the eyes.

'You don't need to worry. Your brother is in very good hands.'

She examined the bruising around my eye from yesterday. 'Are you OK?'

I automatically lifted my hand to the bruising. '*Ja*, I'm fine. It's nothing.'

'Why don't you come through here and wait till we get some news.'

With her hand still on my shoulder, she led me through to a waiting room with black plastic chairs lined up in rows. The chairs were bolted together. Most people sat near the edges because it was too awkward to shuffle towards the middle. The nurse led me to a free seat near the back, behind a woman holding a crying baby. I sat down on a seat, it was higher than expected and only my toes touched the ground.

'Would you like some water?' she said.

'No.'

She smiled professionally. 'Just wait here and as soon as your brother is stable I'll call you, OK?'

'Where's my mom?'

The nurse thought for a second. 'I'm sure she's with your brother. I'll find out. Just wait here,' she said.

The baby in front of me was crying. By the way it howled I knew it was badly hurt. 'Shhhhhhh,' said the mother, rocking her baby and stroking its head, but it didn't help. The wailing went on and on. Every now and then the mother wiped away her own tears. 'Shhhhhhhh.' Near the front was a man who looked very sleepy. A few seats over, a tall, skinny teenager with dark hair sat with his leg up, holding a bloody napkin to his shin. It made me feel queasy looking at his leg and the stains on his jeans. I rubbed my temples. Everyone was suffering. They all needed help, but they all had to wait because Kevin had jumped the queue, because . . . because Kevin was closer to dying than anyone else.

I stood up and thought I might be sick. I leaned my forehead against the drinks machine. The baby never stopped screaming. Round the side of the drinks machine was a small gap. I squeezed in and slid to the floor, my toes against the wall, knees up to my chest and my back against the gently vibrating refrigerator. I leaned forward and buried my face into my hands, pressing hard against my eyes till everything went black, deep dark black. Sitting like this, I felt the nausea settle at the base of my gut. I covered my ears and closed in on myself. The baby's crying disappeared behind the pull and push of my own breathing. My heartbeat pulsed through the swelling of my bruised eye. Each throb fired tingly lights against the backs of my eyelids. Blue, green, purple, red. Blue, green, purple, red. Swirling colours shifted and bled into each other, clinging to a shape, moulding themselves around a mound, a mountain. The floating mountain. The rock peak sailing on a river of mist. I remembered Mom crouching down in front of Kevin and explaining how God put a special camera in our heads, a camera to record all the beautiful things in the world. All we had to do was look at something, really look hard, and say 'click' and it would be with us for ever. I saw us standing together in the freezing cold, clicking each other. I could still see Kevin's face exactly as it was that day, his blond hair blown forward by the breeze. His grin, as he chewed his sandwich, letting bits of bread crust poke out of his cheek. His eyes were blue. Then green. Then purple. Then red.

Kevin's blood-soaked eyeball stared at me, unblinking.

I opened my eyes and took deep breaths. But even as I stared at my knees I couldn't stop the pictures flashing in my head. The green rugby fields were as clear, and Dad's car burning in the veldt. I could see Brandy's river-brown eyes and the earthworm veins in Dad's neck. Charlene's caramel hair and Darrel's waxy pimples, Stripe's tongue and Ten Bucks' ear, the aquamarine sea and the black blood oozing from Litchi's nose. It all swished and swirled together in my head. All the beauty I had tried so carefully to remember was contaminated with horror, which had somehow recorded itself automatically.

Someone touched my shoulder. I sat up straight and blinked at the walnut woman.

'Are you OK?' she said.

Her hands were scrubbed clean and she had washed her face, but there were stains on her blouse and skirt that would never come out.

'Where's your brother?' she said, crouching down next to me.

'The doctors are fixing him,' I said.

'And your mom, where's she?'

'Dunno.'

She rubbed her hands and glanced around the waiting room, finally settling on the coffee machine. She went over, put some change in the slot, and came back with two paper cups of hot chocolate.

'Here. This will make you feel better,' she said.

I sipped from the cup. It was hot and very, very sweet, but it took away that sick feeling. The walnut woman sat on the floor facing me, with her legs straight out in front of her. 'My name's Anita.'

'I'm Alex.'

'Yes, I know. You used to play with my son, Vim.'

I glanced up at her and then looked away. She didn't look like Vim and she didn't sound Afrikaans. She blew the steam away from her cup. 'It's sad that you and Vim don't play together any more. He misses you. You should come and visit?'

'My Dad didn't like us playing together,' I said, but I struggled to remember the exact reasons Dad had given.

She studied me like a chess problem, especially the bruising around my eye. 'Because he's Afrikaans and you're English?' she asked.

I nodded. The shame was so strong I had to turn my head away but she reached over and took my hand.

'No matter what your father says, you boys are always welcome in our home, you understand?'

Inside me something opened. Tears rolled down my face. Anita squeezed my hand, rubbing the back with her thumb. Hot chocolate dribbled across my fingers and I placed the cup down and buried my eyes in the fold of my elbow. I cried till I was completely empty and Anita held my hand the whole time.

The nurse called the woman with the crying baby and they disappeared down the passage. Suddenly the waiting room was very quiet. Humming from the drinks machine was the only sound.

I let go of Anita, wiped my nose and sipped my hot chocolate.

We waited for about an hour, talking about school and movies and different things, but my mind kept drifting to Kevin. What were they doing to Kevin? What would his eye look like with stitches in it? The sound of footsteps, quick direct strides, came from around the corner. I knew that sound. Dad appeared at reception and placed both hands on the desk.

'Is my kid in here? The name's Thorne.'

The nurse recognised the name. 'Yes. Your son is receiving treatment right now, Mr Thorne.'

'Where is he?' said Dad, peering down the corridor at the double doors.

The sleepy man opened his eyes and the skinny teenager stopped biting his nails. Dad was now the centre of everyone's attention but no one dared to stare at him directly.

'You can't go to him at the moment, Mr Thorne, you have to wait.'

But Dad was already walking away, determined to find Kevin. The nurse ran out from behind the desk. 'Mr Thorne. Mr Thorne! You can't go in there. You'll have to wait till your son comes out of theatre.'

For a second Dad's eyes followed the length of the nurse's arm and into the waiting room. She pointed directly at Anita and me sitting on the floor. Dad's focus changed but his temper didn't. As he marched towards us, Anita stood up. It took him a second to recognise her.

'All very cosy, are we?' he said.

Anita put out her hand. 'Mr Thorne, I decided to wait with your son till—'

'I'm glad you're here, lady,' said Dad, refusing to shake her hand. 'The way you drove off, I thought I'd never see you again. You know it's against the law to leave the scene of an accident without exchanging details.'

Anita let her hand drop. 'Excuse me?'

'Don't act like you forgot, like it just *slipped* your mind,' said Dad. He carried on before she could speak. 'Yes, it was very decent of you to rush my son to hospital but also very convenient, wasn't it? You didn't think I'd notice. Well, let me tell you, you've got to be better than that to get one by me.'

Anita closed her mouth. She stared into my face as though she was figuring something out. Her eyes became very sad.

'Hey, lady, are you deaf? I need those insurance details. Have you seen what you did to my car? That's coming out of your pocket, you can count on that,' said Dad, jabbing his finger at her.

She opened her handbag and got out her diary. Using a slim gold pen, she quickly wrote something down. Dad leaned forward to see what she was writing. 'You know, I had to come here in my wife's hatchback. The damage to the Golf is bad, really bad. I wouldn't be surprised if it's a write-off, which puts me in a tight spot. I need that car for important business meetings and stuff.'

Anita put the pen away, tore off the slip of paper and handed it to Dad. 'Those are the details you want and here is my business card.'

'These'd better be right,' said Dad, flicking the paper.

'It's all there,' said Anita.

Dad studied her card. 'So you're a quack.'

Anita tried not to smile. 'Yes, I'm a doctor,' she said, '. . . of law.'

Dad's eyebrows lowered, trying to figure out if she was bluffing. He stepped closer to make it obvious he was bigger than her. 'Well, doc, you'll be hearing from me soon.'

Anita hooked her bag over her shoulder. 'I have absolutely no doubt about that, Mr Thorne,' she said, very politely. She turned to me. 'It was a pleasure to meet you, Alex. Please come and visit, and let me know how your brother is, OK?'

'You can go now,' said Dad.

Without answering, she brushed past Dad who glared at her and continued glaring as she walked past the reception desk and out towards the exit. 'Some people,' he said, shaking his head, 'some fucking people.'

Dad nudged me with his shoe. 'C'mon, Alex. Get up.'

I ignored him.

'Don't make me tell you twice. Stand up.'

I put my head on my knees and wished he would disappear.

Dad sighed. He gripped my wrist and yanked me to my feet. Suddenly I was facing him, my knees felt jittery, the nausea returned. The last time we were this close he had grabbed me by the throat and threatened to end me. My eyes dropped down to the open V-neck of his shirt. One wiry chest hair had worked its way through a buttonhole. He folded his arms tightly across his chest, the fingers of his left hand wrapped themselves around his bicep. There was no longer a pale mark where his wedding ring used to be, only calloused knuckles and black grease ingrained into his fingernails. I shuffled away and flopped onto a plastic chair. Dad checked his watch. He went over to the coffee machine and pretended to put money in the slot, then violently shoved the machine. Everyone in the waiting room jumped in the seats.

'Nurse!' yelled Dad. 'Your machine's buggered!'

The receptionist stood up and two more nurses popped their heads round the corner to see who was shouting.

'Sir, you'll have to keep your voice down,' said the receptionist.

'Don't tell me what to do. You're the one with the broken coffee machine.'

The nurse quickly came over. 'What seems to be the problem, sir?'

'I put money in the machine and it won't give me my coffee.'

'Well, let's take a look at it, shall we?' The nurse peeked into the slot, to see if it was jammed, she checked it was switched on and made sure the nozzle wasn't blocked. Then she took money from her own purse and put it into the machine. 'Let's try this again and see where the problem is. How do you like your coffee?'

'White and sweet, the way I like my women.'

The nurse didn't flinch. She pressed the button and watched the paper cup pop down and the coffee pour in.

'There we go, sir. It seems to have been a glitch, but I'll get the maintenance men to come and have a look at it.'

Dad took his coffee and sat down next to me. I shifted away from him to the next seat over.

'Oh, great! Now you're in the huff,' said Dad. 'I'm the bad guy now, is that it? Somehow this is all *my* fault? I'm a terrible monster, right? So what do you want from me, Alex, huh? A handwritten apology?'

It was a good question. A very good question. What did I really want from him? I couldn't imagine Dad moving back in with us. And he couldn't undo what had happened to Kevin.

He leaned back and sipped his coffee. 'Are you gonna talk to me or just sit there and torture me with your *terrible* silent treatment?' said Dad, with a snort.

'Nothing,' I said, quietly. 'I don't want anything from you.'

But that wasn't quite true. I wanted him to leave us alone. There had to be a way to make him go and never come back. Maybe I could tell him Mom was so upset about Poppy that she had gone crazy and bought herself a gun. For his own safety he shouldn't visit any more. I could make it sound like a secret so it seemed more convincing. Or I might tell him I had photographs of him kissing Poppy and that if he came anywhere near the house I'd give the pictures to the headmaster or even the police. I could do it too. I could lie just as good as Dad. He wouldn't expect me to use his own tricks against him.

Dad shifted his weight and crossed one leg over the other. He scrunched up his empty coffee cup and threw it at the bin. He missed. The paper cup lay on the floor, twisted and used, desperately trying to stretch itself new again. My shoulders got heavier and gradually all my little schemes to get rid of Dad felt silly. Things had become too important and nothing I had learned from Dad was of any help to me now. When the time came I would need to find a far more powerful way to confront him.

'Nurse!' said Dad.

Everyone jumped in their seats.

'How long do I have to wait?'

'Sir, we'll call you as soon as your son is stable. I promise.'

Dad stood up and went to the counter. 'Yeah, well . . . where is his mother? Why does she get to go in? I'm his parent too, you know. I'm that boy's blood!'

The nurse took a deep breath. 'One moment,' she said, and picked up a phone.

As she spoke Dad turned and gave me the thumbs-up, as if we were getting away with something. He waved me over but I stayed seated.

'Alex!' called Dad. 'Come here!'

He would keep shouting if I didn't go. For the sake of everyone in the room, I stood up and walked towards him.

'Alex, when I say come, you'd better move your arse! You got that?'

The nurse put down the phone and said, 'I'll be back in just a minute.' She disappeared into another room behind reception.

I couldn't bear to look at Dad's face any more, it was hard enough standing this close to him. A very old woman pushed her husband along in a wheelchair, her handbag hung from her elbow and she took short little steps towards the exit. I turned away and stared up at the strip lights suspended from the ceiling. The nurse opened the door. 'Mr Thorne, follow me, please.' We went down the hall and turned left, past a man lying on a trolley, past two rooms full of sick-looking people. There were machines and tubes and a curtain rail round each bed. We turned down another corridor, through a set of double doors and around a black man on a ladder checking the smoke alarm. My takkies squeaked on the smooth polished floor. On three different signs I read the word *Casualty*. I whispered it quietly to myself, *Casual-tea*. The nurse never looked back at us and I wondered if I'd be able to find my way back alone. We turned another corner and there, on a row of chairs in a small recess off the corridor, sat Mom. Her clothes were blotched brown with dried blood. She didn't notice us. She held a full cup of tea right in front of her mouth and stared straight ahead without moving a muscle.

'Hello, Mom,' I said. 'Are you all right?'

She drew a deep breath through her nose as if waking up, then blinked at the tea in her hand. 'I'm fine,' she said, looking at me and noticing Dad behind me.

'Where's Kevin?' asked Dad.

Mom put her cup onto a pile of old magazines. 'I don't know. They haven't told me anything.'

'I'll be back in a moment,' said the nurse, holding up her

hand in apology. 'I'll see if I can find out any news on your son's condition.'

Dad stared at her as she walked away, then he sat down next to Mom. 'How long do you think this is going to take?' he said.

Mom stayed silent.

'You see, the thing is, I've got some business to take care of before I start night shift.'

'Why are you telling me this, Bruce?' asked Mom, pinching the bridge of her nose.

'Because that bloody woman smashed into my car and until I can get it fixed, I won't have wheels. So I'm going to have to take your car for a couple of days.'

'And what about us?' asked Mom. 'What about Kevin? How are we going to get him home if you're off somewhere doing God-knows-what in *my* car?'

Dad rolled his eyes. 'For Pete's sake, Grace, why are you doing this to me? Why do you *always* have to make things difficult? You saw my car. If I don't turn up for my shift I could lose my job. You know that. It makes sense that I take your car.'

Mom's mind puzzled over something. 'You've already taken my car, haven't you? That's how you got here. You're not asking to borrow the car. You're telling me you've taken it.'

Dad looked away and sighed.

'But that's how it is, isn't it?' said Mom, her voice getting desperate as if she was about to cry. 'You do whatever you want and to hell with the rest of us. You don't *care* that your son is fighting for his life in there. We're just furniture to you, aren't we? We're just *stuff* you move around to make *your* life more comfortable!'

Dad smirked, shaking his head. 'Calm down, woman, you're getting hysterical. You can get a taxi home.'

Mom jumped to her feet without noticing the nurse who appeared behind her. 'Don't tell me to calm down! I'll yell if I want to! Don't you EVER tell me to calm down!' she shouted, moving right up to Dad's face. 'I'm sick to death of you telling me what to do.'

Dad's smirk stayed where it was. I'd seen him have a hundred different arguments with a hundred different shop managers. Mom didn't intimidate him at all.

'Excuse me,' said the nurse, 'please keep your voices down.'

Mom swung round, ready to attack the nurse, but she stopped herself. A doctor wearing a shower cap and a face mask pulled down under his chin, put out his hand and waited for Mom to take it. Mom's mood changed in an instant. She grabbed the doctor's hand in both of hers. 'How is my son? Is he OK?'

'Your son is stable, Mrs Thorne,' said the doctor, glancing at Dad, 'but his injuries are quite severe. We'll need to keep him in intensive care and monitor his condition closely.'

Mom interlaced her fingers and brought them to her mouth while the doctor spoke.

'Most of the lacerations to his face and neck were superficial and should heal without major scarring. However, there are two areas of concern. The trauma to his right eye caused bleeding and swelling around the socket. This is placing pressure on the optic nerve. We have done what we can, but—'

'What are you saying? Is he blind?' said Dad. 'If my son goes blind, it's because you're not doing your job properly. I'll sue you so fast they'll take every penny in your pocket!'

'Shut up, Bruce!' said Mom.

The doctor kept silent till he was sure everyone was listening, then he spoke. 'I assure you we have done everything in our power to help your son but you need to understand there is a real chance that he will lose the use of his eye for a while, perhaps longer than that.' The doctor turned his head slightly and spoke directly to Mom, without looking at Dad. 'The second issue is more serious. During the attack, there was damage to the oesophagus so we've had to put your son on a ventilator. Also, one of the incisions to the neck punctured the jugular, causing major blood loss.'

The image of Ten Bucks dragging Kevin by the neck came back to me. I could still see his fingers quivering, his fingernails digging into the tar.

'We performed a transfusion and managed to repair the vein but—'

'But he's going to pull through, right?' said Dad.

The doctor didn't agree. 'We will need to monitor his renal output very closely. If anything changes we will inform you immediately. Your son was lucky, Mrs Thorne. If you had got here any later things might have been different.'

There was a moment of silence as each of us replayed what the doctor had just said.

'There's something else I need to ask,' said the doctor. 'The animal which attacked your son, was it a family pet or a stray?'

'It was a pet,' said Dad.

'Then I assume you've had your dog vaccinated against rabies?'

Mom looked at Dad. 'Of course,' said Dad. 'The dog's clean.'

Mom turned to the doctor. 'We have no idea where the dog came from.'

'Has everyone gone deaf?' said Dad, raising his voice. 'I said the dog's clean.'

Mom ignored him and grabbed the doctor's hand. 'Please, do your tests. For the sake of my son.'

The doctor frowned as he analysed Mom's expression, then Dad's. He nodded quietly to himself. I think he understood the situation better than I could have explained it to him.

'We'll do some blood tests,' he said, speaking directly to Mom, 'just to be sure.'

'You'll be wasting your time,' said Dad. 'But, hey, don't listen to me.'

And nobody did. Completely unfazed by Dad's threats and shouting, the doctor scribbled a note and handed it to the nurse. He didn't ignore Dad exactly, he just made him irrelevant. It was amazing. He had a calm certainty which was much more powerful than any of Dad's bluffs. I sensed immediately that I'd found a way to deal with Dad. I could be like this doctor. I'd never be able to force Dad out of my life, I'd never stop him coming to the house or his endless scamming, but I had the power to make him irrelevant.

'Well,' said the doctor, putting his hands behind his back, 'if you would like to see your son, please follow me.'

Like at school, we followed behind him in single file, through a maze of corridors and fire doors till we stopped at a window. Kevin lay on a bed surrounded by boxy grey machines with lots of buttons. His face was mostly covered in bandages. A tube as thick as a hosepipe came out of his mouth. There were wires stuck to his chest and a drip attached to the back of his hand. A nurse came to his bed and held up a syringe. She tapped it twice, then inserted the needle into a valve in the drip and squeezed out the liquid. Mom started to cry, she grabbed my hand and squeezed it hard. It was always tough for Kevin but this didn't seem fair. This was too much. The nurse checked the machine and went away. Kevin just lay there. He looked very small.

Once, long ago, I asked Kevin what he would do if he knew the world was going to end. His answer had always puzzled me.

I put my hand up against the glass and whispered inside my head so no one could hear – no one but Kevin. *It's not the end, Kev. Not yet. Please stay awake, for me and for Mom. Stay awake. I promise you things will get better, just don't go to sleep. Please don't go to sleep.*

Mom's crying got louder. The nurse touched her shoulder. Dad stood, arms folded, shaking his head. 'Stupid little bugger,' he said under his breath.

The doctor spoke to Mom softly. 'We can let you in to see your son, but only for a few minutes.'

Mom nodded, wiping away tears with her wrist.

'However,' said the doctor, 'you'll need to clean the blood off your hands to protect your son from infection.'

Mom stared at the bloodstains on her fingernails and nodded again.

'Nurse Hanna will show you where to wash your hands.'

The nurse took Mom down the passage and round the corner. The doctor turned to me. 'We have gowns for you to wear if you want to go in and see your brother. It's hospital policy.'

'That won't be necessary, doc,' said Dad. 'It doesn't look like Kevin's going anywhere and we've got stuff to do. Right, Alex?'

'I'm staying with Kevin,' I said, staring through the window at the tag around my brother's wrist.

Dad grabbed the back of my neck and shoved me a few metres down the hall. He went back to the doctor and pointed a finger right in his face. 'Fix my kid, OK! No excuses! Or we'll see each other in court and they'll have to close the whole place down.'

'Is that all, Mr Thorne?' said the doctor, flatly.

Dad curled his finger back in on itself and made a fist, staring at the doctor the whole time. I had no idea what Dad was doing, but it didn't matter. I refused to back him up any more. I decided for myself now, and I wanted to be with Kevin.

'I'm staying,' I said, rubbing the back of my neck.

Dad lowered his fist and turned to me. There wasn't going to be a discussion.

'MOVE IT!' he yelled, pointing down the hall. He came up to me, turned me around and marched me down the passage, pinching the back of my neck.

'I've had enough shit from everyone today and I refuse to take it any more,' said Dad, clenching his teeth. We pushed past two black men in orange overalls and turned left, looking for the exit.

'Walk properly, boy, stop dragging your heels.'

'You're hurting me!'

'You don't know what hurt is, but if you keep bitching you'll find out,' said Dad, spitting out his words. 'Here's what's going to happen. We're going home and you *will* help me load the tools into the car and then . . .' He stopped. He looked left and right but didn't recognise anything. We were lost. We went back the way we came, turned the corner, along a narrow passage, through the double doors and left again. '. . . and then, you'll load the tools in the car and . . . how the fuck do you get out of this place?' Dad rushed along the corridor, shoving a hospital porter against the wall. His fingers clamped onto the back of my neck, lifting me up till my toes scuffed the ground. Nurses stood with their backs against the wall, watching us race by.

I tripped and fell to my knees. 'Stop mucking around,' said Dad, yanking me to my feet. 'Where the hell is the exit?' We ran along the corridor through more double doors and were faced with a set of stairs. We doubled back and tried going through a different set of doors.

'You're not allowed to run in here, sir. Calm down,' said a nurse.

'Shut up! Don't tell me what to do!' shouted Dad.

The nurse took a step back. A patient lying on a trolley raised her head to see who was shouting. Dad shoved open a set of double doors almost hitting a group of doctors coming the other way.

'Hey! Slow down,' said one of them.

'SHUT THE FUCK UP!'

They stood, stunned, and we shoved through them as if they weren't there.

'Where's the door? Where's the damn door?' Dad muttered to himself.

His thumb was pressing in behind my ear. 'Let go of me,' I said. 'You're really hurting me.'

Dad brought his mouth right up to my ear. 'SHUT UP.'

As he dragged me around another corner, we came face to face with a cleaning lady. 'How do I get out of here?' shouted Dad.

She stared at us with her mouth open.

'Where's the FUCKING EXIT?'

She ducked with fright and pointed to her left.

We marched off. 'What the hell's wrong with this place?' said Dad. 'Has the whole bloody world gone nuts?' We suddenly stopped. Dad let me go and turned to look at a set of double doors we had just passed. On them was a sign, *EMERGENCY EXIT ONLY*. Dad lifted his leg and kicked the doors wide open. Immediately, an alarm bell rang throughout the whole building.

'What are you doing? You can't go that way!' shouted someone.

Dad grabbed my arm and flung me outside. I scrambled across the parking lot, almost tripping in front of a car. It was night. The whole world had gone dark. The alarm rang and rang. It sounded like the end of break time, the end of school. People came rushing to the door shouting different things.

'Hey, you, did you open these doors?'

'What the hell do you think you're doing?'

'Is there a fire?'

'No, just some crazy guy.'

Dad ignored them all. He pulled the car keys out of his pocket, searching left and right to see where he had parked the car. He walked over to me and grabbed the front of my T-shirt but I batted his hand away. 'I'm staying,' I said, my voice wavering.

'No! You're coming with me.'

'I'm staying, Dad! I don't care what you say!'

'I'm tired of your shit, Alex,' he said, bringing his face right up to mine. 'Now move or I swear to God you'll regret being born.'

I breathed in, straightened my T-shirt and stood absolutely still. Without moving or looking away I showed him a side of myself that I'd always kept hidden, a side that was bigger than him. 'Dad, you're bad for us.'

He raised an eyebrow and laughed a little. I took two steps backwards. 'You're bad for us, and you need to leave us alone.'

The fire alarm filled the air with urgency. Three security guards were coming towards us, homing in on the centre of the trouble. Hospital staff peered out through the open doors, pointing us out to the guards.

'Sir. Are you OK?' called one of the guards. 'Why did you kick open the doors?'

'Stay away from me, kaffir!' said Dad.

The other two guards placed their hands on their guns, their eyes open very wide, while the first one did the talking. 'Please calm down, sir . . . and show me your hands.'

Dad was in no mood to take orders. 'Listen to me, you stupid kaffir, there's no trouble here, all right. You're not the police, so why don't you go and help people park their cars, OK? We're just leaving anyway. Let's go, Alex.'

I took three more backward steps.

Dad followed after me, screaming, 'ALEX! Don't fuck with me!'

The moment Dad raised his voice the guns came out. 'Show me hands! Show me hands!' commanded the guard, rushing past me. As soon as he saw the weapons Dad raised his hands. One hand open, the other wrapped around the car keys. 'Drop it. Drop it now!' shouted the guard. Dad splayed his fingers, letting the keys land on the ground. Two guards rushed him, wrestling his arms behind his back, while the third guard kept his gun pointed right at Dad's chest.

'Let go of me, you stinking fucking monkeys! Get your hands off me!' screamed Dad.

I went over and picked up the car keys.

'Alex, come back here! ALEX!'

I kept stepping away and then I did something Dad told me never to do. I turned my back on the most dangerous person I knew and went inside.

Birthmark

Mom pulled up onto the pavement, behind Dad's brand-new, smashed-up Golf. I wondered what might have happened to Dad, since he hadn't been back to fetch his car yet. Maybe he had lashed out at the security guards and been arrested or maybe he was at work, but it was difficult to picture either scenario properly. It didn't matter to me one way or the other. I got out and watched Mom fumble with her keys as she locked the driver's side door. I turned my face into the breeze. On the street, deep in the grit and tarmac, was the heavy stain where Litchi had died. Further down the street was a bigger, much darker stain like some awful purple birthmark, which I couldn't stop staring at. It stirred up images that hollowed out my stomach, flashes of horror I had been trying to ignore, so I concentrated on the smaller stain, on Litchi. In all the sleepless chaos of the past thirty-six hours I had forgotten about her. I checked up and down the gutter to see if her little corpse had been brushed aside and abandoned. Nothing. Someone must have cleaned it up, one of the neighbours. Perhaps Anita had buried the body. Either way, all that was left of Litchi was a dirty blot.

I held the front gate open for Mom. Our house was still white, the grass still yellow, and the cicada beetles continued to buzz like a headache. But something very important had changed. It was as if we were visiting someone else's house, a place we didn't belong.

Inside, glass and red wine lay scattered across the living-room tiles. I could hardly believe it was still there. It felt as if Mom and Dad's argument had happened years ago, in some other place, about an issue no longer important.

'I don't want to stay long,' said Mom. 'I just want to wash, change and get back to the hospital. We need to be there when Kevin wakes up.' She went into the bathroom and ran some water. Wind rattled the front windows. A few seconds later she came padding across the tiles in her bare feet, with only a white towel wrapped around her. She carried a scrunched-up bundle of blood-stained clothes. Very carefully, on tiptoes, she picked her way between the broken shards of glass, then stuffed her clothes into a grocery bag and dropped the whole lot in the bin.

'Alex, while I'm in the bath, go to Kevin's room and find some clean pyjamas and his comics and . . . um . . .' She closed her black-rimmed eyes and pushed back her fringe. '. . . whatever else you think he needs,' she said, and wandered off into the bathroom.

I stood outside Kevin's room and peered in. I saw his unmade bed, the depression in his pillow and the GI Joes lined up along the window sill. His bedside lamp had been left on. Piles of Super-Hero trading cards lay across his desk, the top corner of each card frayed and bent from counting them so often. The entire room, each insignificant item, had arranged itself around Kevin's existence. And yet there was nothing spooky about it. I stepped onto the carpeted floor and felt no different. His wardrobe was a mess and on the third shelf near the back I found pyjamas, the ones with Spider-Man on the front, his favourite pair. They were freshly washed but smelled of him, the way he smelled at night when we lay together in the dark, whispering. I rolled them up and placed them in his PT bag along with some underpants, two stacks of comics and all his trading cards.

I went through and sat on the sofa waiting for Mom. The house was quieter than the hospital. I closed my eyes and listened to the motor in the fridge click on. Mom pulled out the plug and I heard the water drain from the bathtub. I stood up to get a drink and through the sliding glass doors I spotted Ten Bucks. He sniffed the tyres of Mom's car, lifted his leg and peed on the hubcap.

Mom emerged from the bathroom wearing clean clothes and rubbing her hair with a towel. Wrapping it around her head, she sat down on the edge of the coffee table, picked up the phone and dialled, waiting for an answer.

'Brandy? Hi, it's me.'

A high-pitched 'Hello!' squeaked through the receiver.

'Listen, I have a favour to ask,' said Mom, her voice sounding official. 'There's been some trouble and . . . I know it's a lot to ask, but how soon could you get here?' Mom listened and nodded but remembered Brandy couldn't see her. '*Ja. Ja*, he has,' said Mom, touching her forehead to steady herself, 'and something else has . . . there's more, but I can't talk about it over the phone.'

Mom's eyes focused on nothing as she listened to Brandy. 'Are you sure you don't mind driving through the night? . . . What time do you think you'll arrive? . . . Fine. I'll make sure I'm back at the house for seven. Sorry for calling you like this out of the blue . . . no, I'm coping, honestly, I'm fine . . . OK . . . *ja* . . . *ja* . . . see you tomorrow.'

Mom put the phone down and drew in a deep breath. 'Are you going to get washed, Alex?' she said.

'Do I have to?' I asked.

Mom shrugged, stood up and went to the kitchen. 'Have you packed all of Kevin's things?' she said.

'Some of them. We still need to get his toothbrush.'

Mom took a bottle of white wine from the fridge, opened it and poured herself a glass. 'Brandy is going to be here early tomorrow morning,' she said, more to herself than to me.

'Mom,' I said, nodding towards the window at Ten Bucks. 'Look.'

305

The glass of wine stopped halfway to her mouth. She put it down gently and moved closer to the glass door. She watched him sniff the ground, turn a circle, and lie down on the concrete driveway.

'We'll have to take care of that before we leave,' she said, walking back to the kitchen. She placed both hands on the counter, taking a moment to think, then quickly opened the fridge and hauled out the hindquarter of buck meat. Using the biggest knife in the drawer she started hacking off chunks.

'What are you going to do, Mom?'

'I don't know yet,' she said, sawing quickly through the string of a sinew. 'This would be a lot easier if we owned a gun.'

She placed lump after lump of pink meat to one side till only the bone was left. 'I'll distract him with this while you go and get the car ready,' she said, holding up the bone. Mom shoved the car keys into her pocket and was about to open the door but hesitated. Going back to the kitchen, she grabbed the knife and held it tightly in her fist. 'Stay close to me, Alex,' she said, as she slid open the door.

Ten Bucks raised his head and noticed the bone Mom was waving at him. She threw it as far as she could towards Rebecca's old room. Ten Bucks jumped to his feet and chased after it. He lay on the ground, gnawing at it with his molars.

'Quickly, let's go,' said Mom, pulling my arm.

We opened the garage and lifted off the large grill from the old braai. We carried it between us to the car, holding a corner in each hand. It was covered in black, oily goo that smelled of burned meat. Mom opened the hatchback and we tried to wedge the grill up against the back seat, but it was too big, it wouldn't fit. Eventually, Mom climbed in and began kicking it into place. The corners of the grill tore the ceiling upholstery and scored into the metal roof as each kick bent it into shape. She stopped, brushed her hair away from her face, and gave the grill a strong shake. It was wedged in tight. There was now a barrier between the boot and the back seat, hopefully strong enough to hold Ten Bucks.

Back inside the house I gathered Kevin's stuff and looped Mom's handbag over my shoulder. Mom scooped up a handful of wet venison and tucked the kitchen knife into her back pocket. I locked up the house and the two of us stood watching the dog as he crunched the corner of the bone between his teeth.

'Get into the car and wait for me,' said Mom. She walked towards Ten Bucks and tossed an offcut of raw meat onto the lawn. I jogged up to the car and got in, watching as Mom led Ten Bucks up the drive with a trail of glistening titbits. She picked up the leash and choke chain that Dad had left lying on the ground. I wondered if the dog was clever enough to detect the trap but when Mom threw the last bits of meat into the back of the car he jumped up and stood eating in quick snapping gulps.

'Good dog,' she said, slamming the boot closed.

Mom got in behind the steering wheel and handed me the bundle of dog chains. She performed a three-point turn to avoid driving over the dark unspeakable stains on our street and within minutes we were cruising along the highway. Ten Bucks sat up straight, panting, filling the car with meaty dog breath. Mom opened her window allowing wind to rush through the car as we slipped out of the city, past fields and open veldt, towards Johannesburg. With her pursed lips and fingers wrapped tightly around the steering wheel, Mom concentrated on driving. The last time we had come this way we were going on holiday to Durban. I hung my arm over the back of my seat and watched Ten Bucks through the grill. His blue eye was clear and glassy but his right eye, the green one, was bloodshot, after Mom had rammed her thumb in it pulling him off Kevin. I touched the swelling around my own eye. Ten Bucks stared back at me with a lopsided, disconnected expression. Before he belonged to me, Dad said he had been a witch doctor's dog, full of ju-ju magic, a dog with two souls, capable of taking your sins to hell and your prayers to heaven. I studied one eye, then the other. There were no clues as to which half of him was good and which half bad. Neither colour seemed better or more important. Both eyes were beautiful, in an uneasy sort of way. If Mom planned to get rid of him it seemed a waste to sacrifice such a special dog without even trying to see if the magic worked.

I started with my sins.

I've been a bad brother, I whispered in my mind as I stared into his green, bloodshot eye. *I didn't always protect Kevin when I could have and sometimes I was mean to him. I have also lied, a lot, to Mom, to the police, to Charlene and lots of other people. And I tried really hard to be the man of the house but I failed at that too. I'm very sorry for all that I did. Maybe if I hadn't been such a bad person Kevin wouldn't be in hospital right now. Somehow it feels like my fault. So, when you die, could you please take all that away with you.*

The car slowed down and Mom turned off the highway onto a thin, tarred road full of potholes. There wasn't a lot of time left. I focused on Ten Bucks' blue eye and thought about what I wanted.

Please let Kevin wake up soon. Let the scars on his face heal properly and don't let the doctors remove his eye. Also, please don't let him get teased too much when he goes back to school. He doesn't deserve any of this. Help Mom be happy. I don't like that she drinks all the time and I want to see her smile the way she used to. Look after Rebecca and her family in Lesotho. And also Poppy. I don't really hate her. Keep her and the baby safe from Dad. I know it's impossible to stop Dad from ever coming back to visit but could you keep him busy till Kevin gets better, just till we're strong enough to deal with him again. That's all. I don't want anything for myself. I paused, not knowing how to end, but wanting to make it official. *In Jesus' name. Amen.*

Mom slowed to a stop next to a barely visible dirt track that veered off into the veldt. She shoved the car into first gear and wrestled it along two parallel paths as we bounced on our seats. After about ten minutes we came to a clearing. Mom turned the car around and pulled up the handbrake, but left the engine running. We faced out across the veldt. Currents of air rippled across the yellow grass, moving it like water. Far in the distance the ground swelled into a low hill. Thin white clouds pressed down on the land like a false ceiling, allowing barely enough room to stand up straight. Everywhere was empty.

'What now?' I said.

'We just open the back and let him out,' said Mom. She didn't blink, didn't doubt.

I opened my door and the wind flung it hard against its hinges.

Grabbing the dog's choke chain and leash, I got out and met Mom round the back of the car. She opened the hatchback and moved away, giving Ten Bucks plenty of room. There was no need for the leash as the dog jumped out and cautiously sniffed the ground.

'Close the boot, Alex, so he can't get back in.'

'I know,' I said, slamming it shut.

Mom slowly stepped backwards towards me, brushing aside a strand of hair that had blown into her mouth. Ten Bucks watched us with his head cocked to one side. Mom and I stood side by side between the car and the dog.

'Shoo!' said Mom, waving her hands. '*Voertsek!*'

Ten Bucks moved away a little and stood staring at us, watching for weakness. The tall grass bent and swayed towards him. I snatched a handful of stones and threw one at the ground in front of him. Ten Bucks jumped a little and sniffed the patch where the stone had bounced but he didn't retreat any further. I threw another one which clipped his back leg and he scrambled a few metres down the track.

'Go on. Get!' I shouted. 'You're not my dog any more!'

Ten Bucks dropped his head. Perhaps he knew how deeply he had hurt us, perhaps he was sorry but there was no way back for him now. I didn't feel sorry for him and I didn't feel like a bad person. This had to be done. He couldn't stay with us, not after all the misery he had caused. As I watched him lope off deeper into the veldt, he never looked back, not once, and I doubted his ju-ju magic would really work. Before he disappeared down the curved track, I tried a little magic of my own, the only magic that had ever worked for me. I held up the choke chain and peered through the loop, at the long grass lapping across his back, and whispered, 'Click.'

Mom placed her hand on my shoulder. 'You can get rid of that choke chain, Alex, you won't need it any more.'

I let go of one end of the chain, allowing the noose to slip down, to change its own shape, quickly shrinking tighter and tighter, collapsing in on itself till it finally vanished, leaving an open length of chain swaying gently from my finger.